The Ghouls

Since their beginnings in the days of silent films at the start of this century, horror films have become a widely attended feature of the cinema. Many of the great horror films have been inspired by well-known literary masterpieces, such as *Dr. Jekyll and Mr. Hyde*, *Dracula* and *Frankenstein*. Others have originated from short stories and in *The Ghouls* the author has assembled the very best of these, most of which are out of print although the films which came from them have been reshown time and time again.

A unique anthology about one of the most captivating and enduring literary genres.

The Ghouls

Edited by

PETER HAINING

Introduced by
VINCENT PRICE

With an Afterword by
CHRISTOPHER LEE

W. H. ALLEN
LONDON & NEW YORK
1971

PRINTED AND BOUND IN GREAT BRITAIN BY
THE GARDEN CITY PRESS LIMITED
LETCHWORTH, HERTFORDSHIRE
FOR THE PUBLISHERS
W. H. ALLEN & CO. LTD.
ESSEX STREET, LONDON, WC2R 3JG
ISBN 491 00027 8

CONTENTS

EDITOR'S FOREWORD

"What is horror? Horror is a matter of taste—and I don't mean the blood."

ALFRED HITCHCOCK

EVER since the first moving pictures flickered unsteadily on to a screen in the last days of the nineteenth century, the "horror" or "terror" film has been an integral part of cinema history. No outraged cries of protest (and there have been a good many) or screams of panic from audiences have ever succeeded in substantially denting the popularity of a genre that deals in nightmares, monsters and men of evil purpose. Indeed, its bloodstained progress has survived wars, censorship, banning, any amount of ridicule and even psychological investigation.

Kingsley Amis, the distinguished English novelist and self-professed horror film fan, believes the reason for such enduring popularity lies in the fact that "the appetite for horror is a persistent but not very important strand in the cultural weave of the last couple of centuries, no more connected with an appetite for real horror, real blood, than an interest in the Theatre of Cruelty or the bullfight". Others less analytical may feel more simply that a damn good scare and a laugh afterwards (it can't *really* happen after all!) is just about the best form of relief in a world filled with strife and mistrust.

However we choose to analyse this type of picture (my special contributors, Vincent Price and Christopher Lee, will have more to say on the subject) it is interesting to note how the genre has consistently drawn on literature for its inspiration. Such great classics of terror as *Dr. Jekyll and Mr. Hyde*, *Frankenstein* and *Dracula* have reappeared numerous times over the past seventy years—with ever-increasing popularity—and will doubtless be remade again many times before we all blow ourselves into that great Valhalla of horror beyond the midnight skies.

What to me has been even more interesting than this is the fact that short stories and novellas have played just as significant a part as the full-length novel in the development of the genre—indeed time and time again a new dimension of terror or a more sophisticated style of tension has been brought to the screen after initial conception in a short tale of horror. From my study of this facet of cinema history has grown the collection now in your hands.

In *The Ghouls* I have attempted to bring together not only the best of the short stories, but also those which help illustrate the history of the horror film from its inception in the hands of the French pioneer Méliès through to the present. Many of the original tales have been out of print for decades—despite frequent revivals of the pictures they inspired—and I hope that their reprinting here will prove valuable not only to the student of old films but also to the general reader who enjoys a good late-night thrill. It probably needs to be pointed out for the fastidious reader that some of the finished films—in the good old movie tradition—differed quite extensively from the stories on which they were based, but in very few cases could the inspiration or influence of the written word be denied.

Because of the limitations on its length, the book cannot be as definitive as I would have liked (particularly in covering the period between the two world wars, certainly the "Golden Era" of horror films, or in having to overlook such important directors as Friedrich Wilhelm Murnau and Alfred Hitchcock) but I hope the background notes on the films that are coupled with each story will at least do some justice to all the ghouls so many millions of us have come to know and love. I trust also that the illustrations will help to bridge the gap between the written word and the film.

Finally, I must record my thanks to those who have made compiling this book such a pleasure : Vincent Price and Christopher Lee for their enthusiasm and contributions; my publishers, Sol Stein in America and Jeffrey Simmons in England, for their support given so readily to the project when it was little more than an idea; and the various researchers who have helped in the location of stories and film stills : August Derleth, Paulette Cooper, Laurence James, Richard Davis and Robin James of the Gothique Film Society. The living and the dead are forever in your debt.

PETER HAINING

Birch Green
Essex
May, 1970

INTRODUCTION

by VINCENT PRICE

THERE is perhaps no more personal attachment between audience and actor than the identification of that actor with fear on the part of the audience. I could broaden that statement to include laughter, as these two very human emotions are closely allied in a commodity I sell, entertainment appeal. But the contents of this book deal with those stories that most successfully avoid making an audience laugh, to make them shiver with the kindred delight—fright. Fright makes actor and audience one, just as laughter does. It is something tangible that takes over the audience and makes it one in itself . . . and that is surely one of the, if not the most, important requirements of drama.

This identity the audience feels for the fright-making actor (and the comedian) is a mixed blessing to him, for just to appear in tales of terror can lead to a certain anonymity that can sometimes further starve the actor's too often famished affection for identification. I laugh when I recall the number of times I've been mistakenly asked for Basil Rathbone's or George Sanders' autograph, but it's a hollow laugh, even though I admire both those gentlemen unqualifiedly. When, as has happened many times, people have recalled with squealing delight my Frankenstein or Dracula, I have learned not to fight them off with hurt invectives, but to throw them a simple thank you and make off somewhere so as not to witness the blushing dawn of their confusion when they realize I never played either part, that I'm neither Boris Karloff nor Bela Lugosi. I once made the mistake of arguing with a teenager that I was not the man who was transmuted into a fly in a picture by the same name in which I did appear and ended up in defeat, harbouring the horrid wish that I could turn said teenager into a worm.

What all this facetiousness boils down to is that the actor in thrillers has to admit, perhaps more than other actors are willing to, that the play's the thing, and then just go along for the ride. Happily for most of us, it's a long ride, as audiences seem never to tire of a good scare, and authors, bless them, the best of them, have always been challenged by the thousand different ways this effect can be achieved.

It has been said that Edgar Allan Poe, in his immortal *The Pit And The Pendulum,* captured his readers in all the elements of human fear. He did this without the use of anything "out of this world", but it will have to be admitted that the mind of the hero in this piece was hard put to stay in this world, for Poe threw the book of real and imagined horrors at him, and the only happy ending one can imagine is sanity retained. Yet, going off the deep end is the ultimate terror and in many of these stories insanity is achieved by "the outsiders". The Ghouls are "outsiders" in these cases: *The Beast from 20,000 Fathoms, The Skull, Monster of Terror*. There's no question that these creatures are terrifying, for they represent the unknown which everyone will concede is unthinkable. That the unliving can scare the living daylights out of you is of course the triumph of the undead, as in *Dracula*, but the real terror of Dracula is that he or it is or was a human being just like you and me. The element of "there but for the grace of God" is the key to the success of *Phantom of the Opera, The Fly, Freaks*, and to me those human monsters will always be more fascinating than the Bloblings and Goblins from outer space.

The most fascinating man-monster I have tangled with was the mentally mutilated and visually violated mask maker in *The House Of Wax*. Tragedy in the dramatic theory of Aristotle and other subsequent playwright-philosophers is the highest element of terror, especially if we can identify with that tragedy. If it could happen to Dr. Jekyll, is it not only possible but probable that there is a monster in every man? What made the man who ran the House of Wax a monster was a tragic accident, a fire. It could happen to you, to me. He became Mr. Hyde, but he could still wear a Dr. Jekyll mask of his own making, and the audience was held in suspense because they knew that under that mask of good lay evil, and evil is always a threat, with unthinking evil being the greatest threat of all.

This kind of split personality is the most challenging problem for the actor, and for the audience, too. With *The Beast*, there was no split personality because there was no personality to begin with, and personality is the actor's only problem. With Frankenstein's monster it was different. He was made up of human parts, and there was some humanity left over—so it was with the Golem. These are not monsters as such, for the trace of man that was left with them was their tragedy, it was outweighed by their inhumanity. This imbalance was also what terrified us. So it was, too, with *The Fly*, a man made into a monster; his sadness was that he could not be rescued back into the race fate had taken him away from. Is that not the ultimate fear of every man, that the end of life, Death itself, may be separation from his identity with man?

Enough of my own preferences. All these stories contain elements of Terror, and if I as an actor and reader prefer the human monster to the monster monster, perhaps I can put it down to my belief that what man does to himself, or has done to him by other men, is the most terrifying thing in the world. There may be "more in heaven and earth than is dreamt of in our philosophies", but my nightmares are what can happen to me if my dreams are stifled, if my realities are thwarted, if my fellow man turns out to be inhuman after all.

So wet your lips and lock up tight and read these famous tales of terror and suspense. Masters all are those who wrote them, winners they who bask a moment in their genius and escape the too real horrors of our weary world today. The illustrations are a bonus and show how the super-make-believe of the cinema has tried to bring them visually to life. They illustrate as well sometimes as do the writers what the inner eye can see if allowed to look freely and live in imagination's wonder.

Los Angeles
California

May, 1970

THE DEVIL IN A CONVENT

FRANCIS OSCAR MANN

(Georges Méliès: 1896)

For our first story we turn back to the very beginnings of the cinema at the close of the nineteenth century and the work of the amazing French film pioneer Georges Méliès, whom many regard as the father of the fantasy and horror film. Méliès, previously a stage musician, became fascinated with the newly developing art of cinématographe, *but while other pioneers were experimenting with portraying reality, his vivid imagination and predilection for illusion and the supernatural led him towards the realms of fantasy.*

For his work he built a studio on the outskirts of Paris (the first of its kind in the world) and fitted it with all manner of effects. His first productions, or féeries *(fantasy films), were an immediate success and audiences from all over the capital flocked to see the work of the "Magician of the Screen", as he soon became known. He showed ghosts materializing and dematerializing, eerie underwater scenes and strange occult episodes—all of which were produced with unique and startlingly inventive techniques. Many of his productions were in colour—each frame was painstakingly hand coloured—and lasted from a minute to half an hour.*

Méliès was also one of the first film-makers to appreciate the value of literature as source material and indeed created his masterpiece, A Trip To The Moon *(1902) from* Jules Verne's From Earth to the Moon *and* H. G. Wells's First Men in the Moon. *A lesser known film was* The Devil in a Convent *which Méliès based on a medieval tale retold by Francis Mann. The master himself played the "minstrel" who throws consternation into a convent of nuns, and during the course of the film he introduced a number of strange illusionary sequences and a dramatic climax in which he vanished into thin air! It is a sad postscript on this remarkable man that many of his ideas were shamelessly plagiarized and that ridicule and bankruptcy*

*eventually forced him out of the business to which he had
introduced an entire new genre.*

*

BUCKINGHAM is as pleasant a shire as a man shall see on a seven
days' journey. Neither was it any less pleasant in the days of our Lord
King Edward, the third of that name, he who fought and put the
French to shameful discomfiture at Crecy and Poitiers and at many
another hard-fought field. May God rest his soul, for he now sleeps
in the great church at Westminster.

Buckinghamshire is full of smooth round hills and woodlands of
hawthorn and beech, and it is a famous country for its brooks and
shaded waterways running through the low hay meadows. Upon its
hills feed a thousand sheep, scattered like the remnants of the spring
snow, and it was from these that the merchants made themselves fat
purses, sending the wool into Flanders in exchange for silver crowns.
There were many strong castles there too, and rich abbeys, and the
King's highway ran through it from north to south, upon which
the pilgrims went in crowds to worship at the shrine of the Blessed
Saint Alban. Thereon also rode noble knights and stout men-at-
arms, and these you could follow with the eye by their glistening
armour, as they wound over hill and dale, mile after mile, with
shining spears and shields and fluttering pennons, and anon a
trumpet or two sounding the same keen note as that which rang out
dreadfully on those bloody fields of France. The girls used to come
to the cottage doors or run to hide themselves in the wayside woods
to see them go trampling by; for Buckinghamshire girls love a
soldier above all men. Nor, I warrant you, were jolly friars lacking
in the highways and byways and under the hedges, good men of
religion, comfortable of penance and easy of life, who could tip a
wink to a housewife, and drink and crack a joke with a good man,
going on their several ways with tight paunches, skins full of ale and
a merry salutation for every one. A fat pleasant land was this
Buckinghamshire; always plenty to eat and drink therein, and
pretty girls and lusty fellows; and God knows what more a man can
expect in a world where all is vanity, as the Preacher truly says.

There was a nunnery at Maids Moreton, two miles out from
Buckingham Borough, on the road to Stony Stratford, and the place
was called Maids Moreton because of the nunnery. Very devout
creatures were the nuns, being holy ladies out of families of gentle

blood. They punctually fulfilled to the letter all the commands of the pious founder, just as they were blazoned on the great parchment Regula, which the Lady Mother kept on her reading-desk in her little cell. If ever any of the nuns, by any chance or subtle machination of the Evil One, was guilty of the smallest backsliding from the conduct that beseemed them, they made full and devout confession thereof to the Holy Father who visited them for this purpose. This good man loved swan's meat and galingale, and the charitable nuns never failed to provide of their best for him on his visiting days; and whatsoever penance he laid upon them they performed to the utmost, and with due contrition of heart.

From Matins to Compline they regularly and decently carried out the services of Holy Mother Church. After dinner, one read aloud to them from the Rule, and again after supper there was reading from the life of some notable Saint or Virgin, that thereby they might find example for themselves on their own earthly pilgrimage. For the rest, they tended their herb garden, reared their chickens, which were famous for miles around, and kept strict watch over their haywards and swineherds. If time was when they had nothing more important on hand, they set to and made the prettiest blood bandages imaginable for the Bishop, the Bishop's Chaplain, the Archdeacon, the neighbouring Abbot and other godly men of religion round about, who were forced often to bleed themselves for their health's sake and their eternal salvation, so that these venerable men in process of time came to have by them great chests full of these useful articles. If little tongues wagged now and then as the sisters sat at their sewing in the great hall, who shall blame them, *Eva peccatrice*? Not I; besides, some of them were something stricken in years, and old women are garrulous and hard to be constrained from chattering and gossiping. But being devout women they could have spoken no evil.

One evening after Vespers all these good nuns sat at supper, the Abbess on her high dais and the nuns ranged up and down the hall at the long trestled tables. The Abbess had just said *"Gratias"* and the sisters had sung *"Qui vivit et regnat per omnia saecula saeculorum, Amen"*, when in came the Manciple mysteriously, and, with many deprecating bows and outstretchings of the hands, sidled himself up upon the dais, and, permission having been given him, spoke to the Lady Mother thus :

"Madam, there is a certain pilgrim at the gate who asks refreshment and a night's lodging." It is true he spoke softly, but little pink ears are sharp of hearing, and nuns, from their secluded way of life, love to hear news of the great world.

"Send him away," said the Abbess. "It is not fit that a man should lie within this house."

"Madam, he asks food and a bed of straw lest he should starve of hunger and exhaustion on his way to do penance and worship at the holy shrine of the Blessed Saint Alban."

"What kind of pilgrim is he?"

"Madam, to speak truly, I know not; but he appears of a reverend and gracious aspect, a young man well spoken and well disposed. Madam knows it waxeth late, and the ways are dark and foul."

"I would not have a young man, who is given to pilgrimages and good works, to faint and starve by the wayside. Let him sleep with the haywards."

"But, Madam, he is a young man of goodly appearance and conversation; saving your reverence, I would not wish to ask him to eat and sleep with churls."

"He must sleep without. Let him, however, enter and eat of our poor table."

"Madam, I will strictly enjoin him what you command. He hath with him, however, an instrument of music and would fain cheer you with spiritual songs."

A little shiver of anticipation ran down the benches of the great hall, and the nuns fell to whispering.

"Take care, Sir Manciple, that he be not some light juggler, a singer of vain songs, a mocker. I would not have these quiet halls disturbed by wanton music and unholy words. God forbid." And she crossed herself.

"Madam, I will answer for it."

The Manciple bowed himself from the dais and went down the middle of the hall, his keys rattling at his belt. A little buzz of conversation rose from the sisters and went up to the oak roof-trees, like the singing of bees. The Abbess told her beads.

The hall door opened and in came the pilgrim. God knows what manner of man he was; I cannot tell you. He certainly was lean and lithe like a cat, his eyes danced in his head like the very devil, but his cheeks and jaws were as bare of flesh as any hermit's that lives on roots and ditchwater. His yellow-hosed legs went like the tune of a May game, and he screwed and twisted his scarlet-jerkined body in time with them. In his left hand he held a cithern, on which he twanged with his right, making a cunning noise that titillated the back-bones of those who heard it, and teased every delicate nerve in the body. Such a tune would have tickled the ribs of Death himself. A queer fellow to go pilgrimaging certainly, but why, when they saw him, all the young nuns tittered and the old nuns grinned, until they showed their red gums, it is hard to tell. Even the Lady Mother on the dais smiled, though she tried to frown a moment later.

The pilgrim stepped lightly up to the dais, the infernal devil in his legs making the nuns think of the games the village folk play all night in the churchyard on Saint John's Eve.

"Gracious Mother," he cried, bowing deeply and in comely wise, "allow a poor pilgrim on his way to confess and do penance at the shrine of Saint Alban to take food in your hall, and to rest with the haywards this night, and let me thereof make some small recompense with a few sacred numbers, such as your pious founder would not have disdained to hear."

"Young man," returned the Abbess, "right glad am I to hear that God has moved thy heart to godly works and to go on pilgrimages, and verily I wish it may be to thy soul's health and to the respite of thy pains hereafter. I am right willing that thou shouldst refresh thyself with meat and rest at this holy place."

"Madam, I thank thee from my heart, but as some slight token of gratitude for so large a favour, let me, I pray thee, sing one or two of my divine songs, to the uplifting of these holy Sisters' hearts."

Another burst of chatter, louder than before, from the benches in the hall. One or two of the younger Sisters clapped their plump white hands and cried, "Oh!" The Lady Abbess held up her hand for silence.

"Verily, I should be glad to hear some sweet songs of religion, and I think it would be to the uplifting of these Sisters' hearts. But, young man, take warning against singing any wanton lines of vain imagination, such as the ribalds use on the highways, and the idlers and haunters of taverns. I have heard them in my youth, although my ears tingle to think of them now, and I should think it shame that any such light words should echo among these sacred rafters or disturb the slumber of our pious founder, who now sleeps in Christ. Let me remind you of what saith Saint Jeremie, *Onager solitarius, in desiderio animae suae, attraxit ventum amoris*; the wild ass of the wilderness, in the desire of his heart, snuffeth up the wind of love; whereby that holy man signifies that vain earthly love, which is but

wind and air, and shall avail nothing at all, when this weak, impure
flesh is sloughed away."

"Madam, such songs as I shall sing, I learnt at the mouth of our
holy parish priest, Sir Thomas, a man of all good learning and
purity of heart."

"In that case," said the Abbess, "sing in God's name, but stand at
the end of the hall, for it suits not the dignity of my office a man
should stand so near this dais."

Whereon the pilgrim, making obeisance, went to the end of the
hall, and the eyes of all the nuns danced after his dancing legs, and
their ears hung on the clear, sweet notes he struck out of his cithern
as he walked. He took his place with his back against the great hall
door, in such attitude as men use when they play the cithern. A little
trembling ran through the nuns, and some rose from their seats and
knelt on the benches, leaning over the table, the better to see and
hear him. Their eyes sparkled like dew on meadowsweet on a fair
morning.

Certainly his fingers were bewitched or else the devil was in his
cithern, for such sweet sounds had never been heard in the hall since
the day when it was built and consecrated to the service of the
servants of God. The shrill notes fell like a tinkling rain from a high
roof in mad, fantastic trills and dying falls that brought all one's
soul to one's lips to suck them in. What he sang about, God only
knows; not one of the nuns or even the holy Abbess herself could
have told you, although you had offered her a piece of the True
Cross or a hair of the Blessed Virgin for a single word. But a divine
yearning filled all their hearts; they seemed to hear ten thousand
thousand angels singing in choruses, Alleluia, Alleluia, Alleluia; they
floated up on impalpable clouds of azure and silver, up through the
blissful paradises of the uppermost heaven; their nostrils were filled
with the odours of exquisite spices and herbs and smoke of incense;
their eyes dazzled at splendours and lights and glories; their ears
were full of gorgeous harmonies and all created concords of sweet
sounds; the very fibres of being were loosened within them, as
though their souls would leap forth from their bodies in exquisite
dissolution. The eyes of the younger nuns grew round and large and
tender, and their breath almost died upon their velvet lips. As for
the old nuns, great, salt tears coursed down their withered cheeks
and fell like rain on their gnarled hands. The Abbess sat on her dais
with her lips apart, looking into space, ten thousand thousand miles

away. But no one saw her and she saw no one; every one had forgotten every one else in that delicious intoxication.

Then with a shrill cry, full of human yearnings and desire, the minstrel came to a sudden stop—

> Western wind, when wilt thou blow,
> And the small rain will down rain?
> Christ, if my love were in my arms,
> And I in my bed again.

Silence!—not one of the holy Sisters spoke, but some sighed; some put their hands over their hearts, and one put her hand in her hood, but when she felt her hair shorn close to her scalp, drew it out again sharply, as though she had touched red-hot iron, and cried, "O Jesu."

Sister Peronelle, a toothless old woman, began to speak in a cracked, high voice, quickly and monotonously, as though she spoke in a dream. Her eyes were wet and red, and her thin lips trembled. "God knows," she said, "I loved him; God knows it. But I bid all those who be maids here, to be mindful of the woods. For they are green, they are deep and dark, and it is merry in the springtime with the thick turf below and the good boughs above, all alone with your heart's darling—all alone in the green wood. But God help me, he would not stay any more than snow at Easter. I thought just now that I was back with him in the woods. God keep all those that be maids from the green woods."

The pretty Sister Ursula, who had only just finished her novitiate, was as white as a sheet. Her breath came thickly and quick as though she bore a great burden up hill. A great sigh made her comely shoulders rise and fall. "Blessed Virgin," she cried. "Ah, ye ask too much; I did not know; God help me, I did not know," and her grey eyes filled with sudden tears, and she dropped her head on her arms on the table, and sobbed aloud.

Then cried out Sister Katherine, who looked as old and dead as a twig dropped from a tree of last autumn, and at whom the younger Sisters privily mocked, "It is the wars, the wars, the cursed wars. I have held his head in this lap, I tell you; I have kissed his soul into mine. But now he lies dead, and his pretty limbs all dropped away into earth. Holy Mother, have pity on me. I shall never kiss his sweet lips again or look into his jolly eyes. My heart is broken long since. Holy Mother! Holy Mother!"

"He must come oftener," said a plump Sister of thirty, with a little nose turned up at the end, eyes black as sloes and lips round as a plum. "I go to the orchard day after day, and gather my lap full of apples. He is my darling. Why does he not come? I look for him every time that I gather the ripe apples. He used to come; but that was in the spring, and Our Lady knows that is long ago. Will it not be spring again soon? I have gathered many ripe apples."

Sister Margarita rocked herself to and fro in her seat and crossed her arms on her breast. She was singing quietly to herself.

> "Lulla, lullay, thou tiny little child,
> Lulla, lullay, lullay;
> Suck at my breast that am thereat beguiled,
> Lulla, lullay, lullay."

She moaned to herself, "I have seen the village women go to the well, carrying their babies with them, and they laugh as they go by on the way. Their babies hold them tight round the neck, and their mothers comfort them, saying, 'Hey, hey, my little son; hey, hey, my sweeting'. Christ and the blessed Saints know that I have never felt a baby's little hand in my bosom—and now I shall die without it, for I am old and past the age of bearing children.

> Lulla, lullay, thou tiny little boy,
> Lulla, lullay, lullay;
> To feel thee suck doth soothe my great annoy,
> Lulla, lullay, lullay.

"I have heard them on a May morning, with their pipes and tabors and jolly, jolly music," cried Sister Helen; "I have seen them too, and my heart has gone with them to bring back the white hawthorn from the woods. 'A man and a maid to a hawthorn bough', as it says in the song. They sing outside my window all Saint John's Eve so that I cannot say my prayers for the wild thoughts they put into my brain, as they go dancing up and down in the churchyard; I cannot forget the pretty words they say to each other, 'Sweet love, a kiss'; 'kiss me, my love, nor let me go'; 'As I went through the garden gate'; 'A bonny black knight, a bonny black knight, and what will you give to me? A kiss, and a kiss, and no more than a kiss, under the wild rose tree'. Oh, Mary Mother, have pity on a poor girl's heart, I shall die, if no one love me, I shall die."

"In faith, I am truly sorry, William," said Sister Agnes, who was gaunt and hollow-eyed with long vigils and overfasting, for which the good father had rebuked her time after time, saying that she overtasked the poor weak flesh. "I am truly sorry that I could not wait. But the neighbours made such a clamour, and my father and mother buffeted me too sorely. It is under the oak tree, no more than a foot deep, and covered with the red and brown leaves. It was a pretty sight to see the red blood on its neck, as white as whalebone, and it neither cried nor wept, so I put it down among the leaves, the pretty poppet; and it was like thee, William, it was like thee. I am sorry I did not wait, and now I'm worn and wan for thy sake, this many a long year, and all in vain, for thou never comst. I am an old woman now, and I shall soon be quiet and not complain any more."

Some of the Sisters were sobbing as if their hearts would break; some sat quiet and still, and let the tears fall from their eyes unchecked; some smiled and cried together; some sighed a little and trembled like aspen leaves in a southern wind. The great candles in the hall were burning down to their sockets. One by one they spluttered out. A ghostly, flickering light fell upon the legend over the broad dais, "*Connubium mundum sed virginitas paradisum complet*"—"Marriage replenisheth the World, but virginity Paradise."

"Dong, dong, dong." Suddenly the great bell of the Nunnery began to toll. With a cry the Abbess sprang to her feet; there were tear stains on her white cheeks, and her hand shook as she pointed fiercely to the door.

"Away, false pilgrim," she cried. "Silence, foul blasphemer! *Retro me, Satanas.*" She crossed herself again and again, saying *Pater Noster.*

The nuns screamed and trembled with terror. A little cloud of blue smoke arose from where the minstrel had stood. There was a little tongue of flame, and he had disappeared. It was almost dark in the hall. A few sobs broke the silence. The dying light of a single candle fell on the form of the Lady Mother.

"Tomorrow," she said, "we shall fast and sing *Placebo* and *Dirige* and the *Seven Penitential Psalms*. May the Holy God have mercy upon us for all we have done and said and thought amiss this night. Amen."

THE LUNATICS

EDGAR ALLAN POE

(Edison: 1912 et al)

At the turn of the century, the newly founded Thomas Edison Company in America was quick to see the possibilities of cinematic fantasy as developed by Méliès, and indeed once they had gone into production, soon surpassed the French master—primarily because they could draw on almost limitless resources of finance and talented film producers. They emulated Méliès by drawing on literature and are credited with the very first version of Frankenstein *in 1910.*

*They were also the first to recognize the tremendous cinematic potential of Edgar Allan Poe. It would take an entire volume adequately to cover Poe's contribution to the horror film—certainly more of his work has been adapted for the screen than that of any other single writer. But it was one of his more obscure tales that Edison chose first—*The System of Doctor Tarr and Professor Fether. *He turned it into a part-comedy, part-horror film entitled* Lunatics in Power *which unfortunately failed because it tried too hard to appeal to the two types of audience. If this had been the story's sole appearance on the screen it would not have qualified for inclusion here, but a Frenchman, Maurice Tourneur (and how that should please the "Magician of the Screen", wherever he is!), took the same tale a few years later and transformed it into a horrific and gruesome picture—the title now clipped to* The Lunatics—*which was described by one contemporary American review as "too grim for Sunday showings". Although Poe certainly meant the story to have numerous elements of black comedy, the sinister is very much in evidence, as a reading now will show. . . .*

*

DURING the autumn of 18—, while on a tour through the extreme southern provinces of France, my route led me within a few miles of a certain *Maison de Santé* or private madhouse, about which I had heard much in Paris from my medical friends. As I had never visited a place of the kind, I thought the opportunity too good to be lost;

and so proposed to my travelling companion (a gentleman with whom I had made casual acquaintance a few days before) that we should turn aside for an hour or so and look through the establishment. To this he objected—pleading haste in the first place and in the second, a very usual horror at the sight of a lunatic. He begged me, however, not to let any mere courtesy towards himself interfere with the gratification of my curiosity, and said that he would ride on leisurely so that I might overtake him during the day, or at all events during the next. As he bade me goodbye, I bethought me that there might be some difficulty in obtaining access to the premises and mentioned my fears on this point. He replied that, in fact, unless I had personal knowledge of the superintendent, Monsieur Maillard, or some credential in the way of a letter, a difficulty might be found to exist, as the regulations of these private madhouses were more rigid than the public hospital laws. For himself he added, he had some years since made the acquaintance of Maillard and would so far assist me as to ride up to the door and introduce me, although his feelings on the subject of lunacy would not permit of his entering the house.

I thanked him and turning from the main road we entered a grass-grown by-path, which, in half an hour, nearly lost itself in a dense forest closing the base of a mountain. Through this dank and gloomy wood we rode some two miles, when the *Maison de Santé* came in view. It was a fantastic *château*, much dilapidated and indeed scarcely tenantable through age and neglect. Its aspect inspired me with absolute dread and checking my horse, I half resolved to turn back. I soon, however, grew ashamed of my weakness and proceeded.

As we rode up to the gateway, I perceived it slightly open and the visage of a man peering through. In an instant afterward this man came forth, accosted my companion by name, shook him cordially by the hand and begged him to alight. It was Monsieur Maillard himself. He was a portly, fine-looking gentleman of the old school, with a polished manner and a certain air of gravity, dignity and authority, which was very impressive.

My friend, having presented me, mentioned my desire to inspect the establishment and received Monsieur Maillard's assurance that he would show me all attention, now took leave and I saw him no more.

When he had gone the superintendent ushered me into a small and exceedingly neat parlour, containing, among other indications of refined taste, many books, drawings, pots of flowers and musical instruments. A cheerful fire blazed upon the hearth. At a piano, singing an aria from Bellini, sat a young and very beautiful woman, who, at my entrance, paused in her song and received me with graceful courtesy. Her voice was low and her whole manner subdued. I thought, too, that I perceived the traces of sorrow in her countenance, which was excessively, although to my taste not unpleasingly, pale. She was attired in deep mourning, and excited in my bosom a feeling of mingled respect, interest and admiration.

I had heard, at Paris, that the institution of Monsieur Maillard was managed upon what is vulgarly termed the "system of soothing"—that all punishments were avoided—that even confinement was seldom resorted to—that the patients, while secretly watched, were left much apparent liberty, and that most of them were permitted to roam about the house and grounds in the ordinary apparel of persons in right mind.

Keeping these impressions in view, I was cautious in what I said before the young lady, for I could not be sure that she was sane; and in fact there was a certain restless brilliancy about her eyes which half led me to imagine she was not. I confined my remarks, therefore, to general topics and to such as I thought would not be displeasing or exciting even to a lunatic. She replied in a perfectly rational manner to all that I said, and even her original observations were marked with the soundest good sense; but a long acquaintance with the metaphysics of *mania* had taught me to put no faith in such evidence of sanity, and I continued to practise, throughout the interview, the caution with which I commenced it.

Presently a smart footman in livery brought in a tray with fruit, wine and other refreshments, of which I partook, the lady soon afterwards leaving the room. As she departed I turned my eyes in an inquiring manner towards my host.

"No," he said, "oh, no—a member of my family—my niece, and a most accomplished woman."

"I beg a thousand pardons for the suspicion," I replied, "but of course you will know how to excuse me. The excellent administration of your affairs here is well understood in Paris and I thought it just possible, you know—"

"Yes, yes—say no more—or rather it is myself who should thank you for the commendable prudence you have displayed. We seldom find so much of forethought in young men and, more than once, some unhappy *contretemps* has occurred in consequence of thoughtlessness on the part of our visitors. While my former system was in operation and my patients were permitted the privilege of roaming to and fro at will, they were often aroused to a dangerous frenzy by injudicious persons who called to inspect the house. Hence I was obliged to enforce a rigid system of exclusion, and none obtained access to the premises upon whose discretion I could not rely."

"While your *former* system was in operation!" I said, repeating his words—"do I understand you, then, to say that the 'soothing system' of which I have heard so much is no longer in force?"

"It is now," he replied, "several weeks since we have concluded to renounce it for ever."

"Indeed! you astonish me!"

"We found it, sir," he said with a sigh, "absolutely necessary to return to the old usages. The *danger* of the soothing system was at all times appalling and its advantages have been much overrated. I believe, sir, that in this house it has been given a fair trial, if ever in any. We did everything that rational humanity could suggest. I am sorry that you could not have paid us a visit at an earlier period, that you might have judged for yourself. But I presume you are conversant with the soothing practice—with its details."

"Not altogether. What I have heard has been at third or fourth hand."

"I may state the system then, in general terms, as one in which the patients were *ménagés,* humoured. We contradicted *no* fancies which entered the brains of the mad. On the contrary, we not only indulged but encouraged them; and many of our most permanent cures have been thus effected. There is no argument which so touches the feeble reason of the madman as the *reductio ad absurdum*. We have had men, for example, who fancied themselves chickens. The cure was to insist upon the thing as a fact—to accuse the patient of stupidity in not sufficiently perceiving it to be a fact— thus to refuse him any other diet for a week than that which properly appertains to a chicken. In this manner a little corn and gravel were made to perform wonders."

"But was this species of acquiescence all?"

"By no means. We put much faith in amusements of a simple kind, such as music, dancing, gymnastic exercises generally, cards, certain classes of books and so forth. We affected to treat each individual as if for some ordinary physical disorder, and the word 'lunacy' was never employed. A great point was to set each lunatic to guard the actions of all the others. To repose confidence in the understanding or discretion of a madman is to gain him body and soul. In this way we were enabled to dispense with an expensive body of keepers."

"And you had no punishments of any kind?"

"None."

"And you never confined your patients?"

"Very rarely. Now and then, the malady of some individual growing to a crisis, or taking a sudden turn of fury, we conveyed him to a secret cell, lest his disorder should infect the rest, and there kept him until we could dismiss him to his friends; for with the raging maniac we have nothing to do. He is usually removed to the public hospitals."

"And you have now changed all this—and you think for the better?"

"Decidedly. The system had its disadvantages and even its dangers. It is now, happily, exploded throughout all the *Maisons de Santé* of France."

"I am very much surprised," I said, "at what you tell me; for I made sure that, at this moment, no other method of treatment for mania existed in any portion of the country."

"You are young yet, my friend," replied my host, "but the time will arrive when you will learn to judge for yourself of what is going on in the world, without trusting to the gossip of others. Believe nothing you hear, and only one half that you see. Now, about our *Maisons de Santé*, it is clear that some ignoramus has misled you. After dinner, however, when you have sufficiently recovered from the fatigue of your ride, I will be happy to take you over the house and introduce to you a system which, in my opinion, and in that of every one who has witnessed its operation, is incomparably the most effectual as yet devised."

"Your own?" I inquired—"one of your own invention?"

"I am proud," he replied, "to acknowledge that it is—at least in some measure."

In this manner I conversed with Monsieur Maillard for an hour or two, during which he showed me the gardens and conservatories of the place.

"I cannot let you see my patients," he said, "just at present. To a sensitive mind there is always more or less of the shocking in such exhibitions; and I do not wish to spoil your appetite for dinner. We will dine. I can give you some veal *à la Sainte Ménéhould* with cauliflowers in *velouté* sauce—after that a glass of *Clos Vougeot*—then your nerves will be sufficiently steadied."

At six, dinner was announced and my host conducted me into a large *salle à manger*, where a very numerous company were assembled—twenty-five or thirty in all. They were, apparently, people of rank—certainly of high breeding—although their habiliments, I thought, were extravagantly rich, partaking somewhat too much of the ostentatious finery of the *vieille cour*. I noticed that at least two-thirds of these guests were ladies, and some of the latter were by no means accoutred in what a Parisian would consider good taste at the present day. Many females, for example, whose age could not have been less than seventy, were bedecked with a profusion of jewellery, such as rings, bracelets and ear-rings, and wore their bosoms and arms shamefully bare. I observed, too, that very few of the dresses were well made—or, at least, that very few of them fitted the wearers. In looking about I discovered the interesting girl to whom Monsieur Maillard had presented me in the little parlour; but my surprise was great to see her wearing a hoop and farthingale, with high-heeled shoes, and a dirty cap of Brussels lace, so much too large for her that it gave her face a ridiculously diminutive expression. When I had first seen her she was attired, most becomingly, in deep mourning. There was an air of oddity, in short, about the dress of the whole party, which at first caused me to recur to my original idea of the "soothing system", and to fancy that Monsieur Maillard had been willing to deceive me until after dinner, that I might experience no uncomfortable feelings during the repast at finding myself dining with lunatics; but I remembered having been informed in Paris that the southern provincialists were a peculiarly eccentric people, with a vast number of antiquated notions; and then, too, upon conversing with several members of the company, my apprehensions were immediately and fully dispelled.

The dining-room itself, although perhaps sufficiently comfortable and of good dimensions, had nothing too much of elegance about it. For example, the floor was uncarpeted; in France, however, a carpet is frequently dispensed with. The windows, too, were without curtains; the shutters, being shut, were securely fastened with iron bars, applied diagonally, after the fashion of our ordinary shop-shutters. The apartment, I observed, formed in itself a wing of the *château*, and thus the windows were on three sides of the parallelogram—the door being at the other. There were no less than ten windows in all.

The table was superbly set out. It was loaded with plate and more than loaded with delicacies. The profusion was absolutely barbaric. There were meats enough to have feasted the Anakim. Never in all my life had I witnessed so lavish, so wasteful, an expenditure of the good things of life. There seemed very little taste, however, in the arrangements; and my eyes, accustomed to quiet lights, were sadly offended by the prodigious glare of a multitude of wax candles which, in silver *candelabra*, were deposited upon the table and all about the room, wherever it was possible to find a place. There were several active servants in attendance and upon a large table at the farther end of the apartment were seated seven or eight people with fiddles, fifes, trombones and a drum. These fellows annoyed me very much at intervals during the repast by an infinite variety of noises, which were intended for music and which appeared to afford much entertainment to all present with the exception of myself.

Upon the whole, I could not help thinking that there was much of the *bizarre* about everything I saw—but then the world is made up of all kinds of persons, with all modes of thought and all sorts of conventional customs. I had travelled, too, so much as to be quite an adept in the *nil admirari*; so I took my seat very coolly at the right hand of my host and having an excellent appetite, did justice to the good cheer set before me.

The conversation in the meantime was spirited and general. The ladies, as usual, talked a great deal. I soon found that nearly all the company were well educated and my host was a world of good-humoured anecdote in himself. He seemed quite willing to speak of his position as superintendent of a *Maison de Santé*; and, indeed, the topic of lunacy was, much to my surprise, a favourite one with all present. A great many amusing stories were told having reference to the *whims* of the patients.

"We had a fellow here once," said a fat little gentleman, who sat at my right—"a fellow that fancied himself a teapot; and, by the way, is it not especially singular how often this particular crotchet has entered the brain of the lunatic? There is scarcely an insane asylum in France which cannot supply a human teapot. *Our* gentleman was a Britannia-ware teapot, and was careful to polish himself every morning with buckskin and whiting."

"And then," said a tall man, just opposite, "we had here, not long ago, a person who had taken it into his head that he was a donkey—which, allegorically speaking, you will say, was quite true. He was a troublesome patient and we had much ado to keep him within bounds. For a long time he would eat nothing but thistles, but of this idea we soon cured him by insisting upon his eating nothing else. Then he was perpetually kicking out his heels—so—so—"

"Mr. De Kock! I will thank you to behave yourself!" here interrupted an old lady who sat next to the speaker. "Please keep your feet to yourself! You have spoiled my brocade! Is it necessary, pray, to illustrate a remark in so practical a style? Our friend here can surely comprehend you without all this. Upon my word, you are nearly as great a donkey as the poor unfortunate imagined himself. Your acting is very natural, as I live."

"*Mille pardons! Ma'mselle!*" replied Monsieur De Kock, thus addressed—"a thousand pardons! I had no intention of offending. Ma'mselle Laplace—Monsieur De Kock will do himself the honour of taking wine with you."

Here Monsieur De Kock bowed low, kissed his hand with much ceremony and took wine with Ma'mselle Laplace.

"Allow me, *mon ami*," now said Monsieur Maillard, addressing myself, "allow me to send you a morsel of this veal *à la Ste. Ménéhould*—you will find it particularly fine."

At this instant three sturdy waiters had just succeeded in depositing safely upon the table an enormous dish, or trencher, containing what I suppose to be the "*monstrum, horrendum, informe, ingens, cui lumen ademptum*". A closer scrutiny assured me, however, that it was only a small calf roasted whole and set upon his knees, with an apple in its mouth, as is the English fashion of dressing a hare.

"Thank you, no," I replied. "To say the truth, I am not particularly partial to veal *à la Ste.*—what is it?—for I do not find that it altogether agrees with me. I will change my plate, however, and try some of the rabbit."

There were several side-dishes on the table containing what appeared to be the ordinary French rabbit—a very delicious *morceau*, which I can recommend.

"Pierre," cried the host, "change this gentleman's plate, and give him a side-piece of this rabbit *au-chat*."

"This what?"

"This rabbit *au-chat*."

"Why, thank you—upon second thoughts, no. I will just help myself to some of the ham."

There is no knowing what one eats, thought I to myself, at the tables of these people of the province. I will have none of their rabbit *au-chat*—and, for the matter of that, none of their *cat-au-rabbit* either.

"And then," said a cadaverous-looking personage, near the foot of the table, taking up the thread of the conversation where it had been broken off—"and then, among other oddities, we had a patient once upon a time who very pertinaciously maintained himself to be a Cordova cheese, and went about with a knife in his hand soliciting his friends to try a small slice from the middle of his leg."

"He was a great fool, beyond doubt," interposed someone, "but not to be compared with a certain individual whom we all know, with the exception of this strange gentleman. I mean the man who took himself for a bottle of champagne, and always went off with a pop and a fizz, in this fashion."

Here the speaker, very rudely, as I thought, put his right thumb in his left cheek, withdrew it with a sound resembling the popping of a cork and then, by a dexterous movement of the tongue upon the teeth, created a sharp hissing and fizzing which lasted for several minutes, in imitation of the frothing of champagne. This behaviour, I saw plainly, was not very pleasing to Monsieur Maillard; but that gentleman said nothing and the conversation was resumed by a very lean little man in a big wig.

"And then there was an ignoramus," said he, "who mistook himself for a frog; which, by the way, he resembled in no little degree. I wish you could have seen him, sir,"—here the speaker addressed myself—"it would have done your heart good to see the natural airs that he put on. Sir, if that man was *not* a frog, I can only observe that it is a pity he was not. His croak thus—o-o-o-o-gh—o-o-o-o-gh! was the finest note in the world—B flat; and when he put his elbows upon the table thus—after taking a glass or two of wine—and distended his mouth thus, and rolled up his eyes thus, and winked them with excessive rapidity thus, why then, sir, I take it upon myself to say positively that you would have been lost in admiration of the genius of the man."

"I have no doubt of it," I said.

"And then," said somebody else, "then there was Petit Gaillard, who thought himself a pinch of snuff, and was truly distressed because he could not take himself between his own finger and thumb."

"And then there was Jules Desouliéres, who was a very singular genius indeed, and went mad with the idea that he was a pumpkin. He persecuted the cook to make him up into pies—a thing which the cook indignantly refused to do. For my part I am by no means sure that a pumpkin pie *à la Desouliéres* would not have been very capital eating indeed!"

"You astonish me!" said I, and I looked inquisitively at Monsieur Maillard.

"Ha! ha! ha!" said that gentleman—"he! he! he—hi hi! hi—ho ho! ho!—hu! hu! hu!—very good indeed! You must not be astonished, *mon ami,* our friend here is a wit—a *drôle*—you must not understand him to the letter."

"And then," said some other one of the party, "then there was Bouffon le Grand—another extraordinary personage in his way. He grew deranged through love and fancied himself possessed of two heads. One of these he maintained to be the head of Cicero, the other he imagined a composite one, being Demosthenes from the top of the forehead to the mouth and Lord Brougham from the mouth to the chin. It is not impossible that he was wrong but he would have convinced you of his being in the right, for he was a man of great eloquence. He had an absolute passion for oratory and could not refrain from display. For example, he used to leap upon the dinner-table thus and—and—"

Here a friend, at the side of the speaker, put a hand upon his shoulder and whispered a few words in his ear, upon which he ceased talking with great suddenness and sank back within his chair.

"And then," said the friend who had whispered, "there was Boullard, the tee-totum. I call him the tee-totum because, in fact, he was seized with the droll but not altogether irrational crotchet that he had been converted into a tee-totum. You would have roared with laughter to see him spin. He would turn round upon one heel by the hour, in this manner—so—"

Here the friend whom he had just interrupted by a whisper performed an exactly similar office for himself.

"But then," cried an old lady, at the top of her voice, "your Monsieur Boullard was a madman, and a very silly madman at best, for who, allow me to ask you, ever heard of a human tee-totum? The thing is absurd. Madame Joyeuse was a more sensible person, as you know. She had a crotchet, but it was instinct with common sense and gave pleasure to all who had the honour of her acquaintance. She found, upon mature deliberation, that by some accident she had been turned into a chicken-cock; but, as such, she behaved with propriety. She flapped her wings with prodigious effect—so-so-so—and as for her crow, it was delicious! Cock-a-doodle doo—cock-a-doodle-doo—cock-a-doodle-de-doo-doo-doooo-do-o-o-o-o-o-o-o !"

"Madame Joyeuse, I will thank you to behave yourself!" here interrupted our host, very angrily. "You can either conduct yourself as a lady should do, or you can quit the table forthwith—take your choice."

The lady (whom I was much astonished to hear addressed as Madame Joyeuse, after the description of Madame Joyeuse she had just given) blushed up to the eyebrows and seemed exceedingly abashed at the reproof. She hung down her head and said not a syllable in reply. But another and younger lady resumed the theme. It was my beautiful girl of the little parlour!

"Oh, Madame Joyeuse *was* a fool!" she exclaimed, "but there was really much sound sense, after all, in the opinion of Eugénie Salsafette. She was a very beautiful and painfully modest young lady who thought the ordinary mode of habiliment indecent and wished to dress herself, always, by getting outside instead of inside of her clothes. It is a thing very easily done, after all. You have only to do so— and then so—so—so—and then so—so—so—and then—"

"Mon Dieu! Ma'mselle Salsafette!" here cried a dozen voices at once. "What *are* you about?—forbear!—that is sufficient!—we see, very plainly, how it is done!—hold! hold!" and several persons were already leaping from their seats to withhold Ma'amselle Salsafette from putting herself upon a par with the Medicean Venus, when the point was very effectually and suddenly accomplished by a series of loud screams, or yells, from some portion of the main body of the *château*.

My nerves were very much affected indeed by these yells, but the rest of the company I really pitied. I never saw any set of reasonable people so thoroughly frightened in my life. They all grew as pale as so many corpses and, shrinking within their seats, sat quivering and gibbering with terror and listening for a repetition of the sound. It came again—louder and seemingly nearer—and then a third time *very* loud, and then a fourth time with a vigour evidently diminished. At this apparent dying away of the noise the spirits of the company were immediately regained and all was life and anecdote as before. I now ventured to inquire the cause of the disturbance.

"A mere *bagatelle*," said Monsieur Maillard. "We are used to these things and care really very little about them. The lunatics, every now and then, get up a howl in concert, one starting another, as is sometimes the case with a bevy of dogs at night. It occasionally happens, however, that the *concerto* yells are succeeded by a simultaneous effort at breaking loose, when, of course, some little danger is to be apprehended."

"And how many have you in charge?"

"At present we have not more than ten altogether."

"Principally females, I presume?"

"Oh, no—every one of them men, and stout fellows, too, I can tell you."

"Indeed! I have always understood that the majority of lunatics were of the gentler sex."

"It is generally so, but not always. Some time ago there were about twenty-seven patients here and of that number no less than eighteen were women, but lately matters have changed very much, as you see."

"Yes—have changed very much, as you see," here interrupted the gentlemen who had broken the shins of Ma'mselle Laplace.

"Yes—have changed very much, as you see!" chimed in the whole company at once.

"Hold your tongues, every one of you!" said my host, in a great rage. Whereupon the whole company maintained a dead silence for nearly a minute. As for one lady she obeyed Monsieur Maillard to the letter and thrusting out her tongue, which was an excessively long one, held it very resignedly, with both hands, until the end of the entertainment.

"And this gentlewoman," said I to Monsieur Maillard, bending over and addressing him in a whisper—"this good lady who has just spoken, and who gives us the cock-a-doodle-de-doo—she, I presume, is harmless—quite harmless, eh?"

"Harmless!" ejaculated he, in unfeigned surprise, "Why—why, what *can* you mean?"

"Only slightly touched?" said I, touching my head. "I take it for granted that she is not particularly—not dangerously affected, eh?"

"*Mon Dieu!*" what *is* it you imagine? This lady, my particular old friend, Madame Joyeuse, is as absolutely sane as myself. She has her little eccentricities to be sure—but then, you know, all old women—all *very* old women are more or less eccentric!"

"To be sure," said I—"to be sure—and then the rest of these ladies and gentlemen—"

"Are my friends and keepers," interrupted Monsieur Maillard, drawing himself up with *hauteur*—"my very good friends and assistants."

"What! all of them?" I asked—"the women and all?"

"Assuredly," he said—"we could not do at all without the women, they are the best lunatic nurses in the world; they have a way of their own, you know; their bright eyes have a marvellous effect— something like the fascination of the snake, you know."

"To be sure," said I—"to be sure! They behave a little odd, eh? —they are a little *queer*, eh?—don't you think so?"

"Odd!—queer!—why, do you *really* think so? We are not very prudish, to be sure, here in the South—do pretty much as we please —enjoy life, and all that sort of thing, you know—"

"To be sure," said I, "to be sure."

"And then, perhaps, this *Clos de Vougeot* is a little heady, you know—a little *strong*—you understand, eh?"

"To be sure," said I, "to be sure. By-the-by, monsieur, did I understand you to say that the system you have adopted, in place of the celebrated soothing system, was one of very rigorous severity?"

"By no means. Our confinement is necessarily close, but the treatment—the medical treatment, I mean—is rather agreeable to the patients than otherwise."

"And the new system is one of your own invention?"

"Not altogether. Some portions of it are referable to Doctor Tarr, of whom you have necessarily heard; and again there are modifications in my plan which I am happy to acknowledge as belong of right to the celebrated Fether, with whom, if I mistake not, you have the honour of an intimate acquaintance."

"I am quite ashamed to confess," I replied, "that I have never even heard the name of either gentleman before."

"Good Heavens!" ejaculated my host, drawing back his chair abruptly and uplifting his hands. "I surely do not hear you aright! You did not intend to say, eh? that you had never *heard* either of the learned Doctor Tarr or of the celebrated Professor Fether?"

"I am forced to acknowledge my ignorance," I replied, "but the truth should be held inviolate above all things. Nevertheless I feel humbled to the dust not to be acquainted with the works of these, no doubt, extraordinary men. I will seek out their writings forthwith and peruse them with deliberate care. Monsieur Maillard, you have really—I must confess it—you have *really*—made me ashamed of myself!"

And this was the fact.

"Say no more, my good young friend," he said kindly, pressing my hand—"join me now in a glass of Sauterne."

We drank. The company followed our example, without stint. They chatted—they jested—they laughed—they perpetrated a thousand absurdities—the fiddles shrieked—the drum row-de-dowed— the trombones bellowed like so many brazen bulls of Phalaris—and the whole scene, growing gradually worse and worse as the wines gained the ascendancy, became at length a sort of Pandemonium *in petto*. In the meantime, Monsieur Maillard and myself, with some bottles of Sauterne and Clos Vougeot between us, continued our conversation at the top of the voice. A word spoken in an ordinary key stood no more chance of being heard than the voice of a fish from the bottom of Niagara Falls.

"And, sir," said I, screaming in his ear, "you mentioned something before dinner about the danger incurred in the old system of soothing. How is that?"

"Yes," he replied, "there was occasionally very great danger indeed. There is no accounting for the caprices of madmen and, in my opinion, as well as in that of Dr. Tarr and Professor Fether, it is *never* safe to permit them to run at large unattended. A lunatic may be 'soothed', as it is called, for a time, but in the end he is very apt to become obstreperous. His cunning, too, is proverbial and great. If he has a project in view he conceals his design with a marvellous wisdom, and the dexterity with which he counterfeits sanity presents to the metaphysician one of the most singular problems in the study of mind. When a madman appears *thoroughly* sane, indeed, it is high time to put him in a straitjacket."

"But the *danger*, my dear sir, of which you were speaking—in your own experience—during your control of this house—have you had practical reason to think liberty hazardous in the case of a lunatic?"

"Here?—in my own experience?—why, I may say yes. For example, no *very* long while ago a singular circumstance occurred in this very house. The 'soothing system', you know, was then in operation and the patients were at large. They behaved remarkably well—especially so—any one of sense might have known that some devilish scheme was brewing from that particular fact, that the fellows behaved so *remarkably* well. And, sure enough, one fine morning the keepers found themselves pinioned hand and foot and thrown into the cells, where they were attended, as if *they* were the lunatics, by the lunatics themselves, who had usurped the offices of the keepers."

"You don't tell me so! I never heard of anything so absurd in my life!"

"Fact—it all came to pass by means of a stupid fellow—a lunatic —who by some means had taken it into his head that he had invented a better system of government than any ever heard of before —of lunatic government, I mean. He wished to give his invention a trial, I suppose, and so he persuaded the rest of the patients to join him in a conspiracy for the overthrow of the reigning powers."

"And he really succeeded?"

"No doubt of it. The keepers and kept were soon made to exchange places. Not that exactly either, for the madmen had been free, but the keepers were shut up in cells forthwith and treated, I am sorry to say, in a very cavalier manner."

"But I presume a counter-revolution was soon effected. This condition of things could not have long existed. The country people in the neighbourhood—visitors coming to see the establishment— would have given the alarm."

"There you are out. The head rebel was too cunning for that. He admitted no visitors at all—with the exception, one day, of a very stupid-looking young gentleman of whom he had no reason to be afraid. He let him in to see the place—just by way of variety —to have a little fun with him. As soon as he had gammoned him sufficiently, he let him out and sent him about his business."

"And *how* long, then, did the madmen reign?"

"Oh, a very long time, indeed—a month certainly—how much longer I can't precisely say. In the meantime, the lunatics had a jolly season of it—that you may swear. They doffed their own shabby clothes and made free with the family wardrobe and jewels. The cellars of the *château* were well stocked with wine; and these madmen are just the devils that know how to drink it. They lived well, I can tell you."

"And the treatment—what was the particular species of treatment which the leader of the rebels put into operation?"

"Why, as for that, a madman is not necessarily a fool, as I have already observed; and it is my honest opinion that his treatment was a much better treatment than that which it superseded. It was a very capital system indeed—a simple—neat—no trouble at all, in fact it was delicious—it was—"

Here my host's observations were cut short by another series of yells, of the same character as those which had previously disconcerted us. This time, however, they seemed to proceed from persons rapidly approaching.

"Gracious heavens!" I ejaculated—"the lunatics have most undoubtedly broken loose."

"I very much fear it is so," replied Monsieur Maillard, now becoming excessively pale. He had scarcely finished the sentence before loud shouts and imprecations were heard beneath the windows; and immediately afterwards it became evident that some persons outside were endeavouring to gain entrance into the room. The door was beaten with what appeared to be a sledge-hammer and the shutters were wrenched and shaken with prodigious violence.

A scene of the most terrible confusion ensued. Monsieur Maillard, to my excessive astonishment, threw himself under the sideboard. I had expected more resolution at his hands. The members of the orchestra, who for the last fifteen minutes had been seemingly too much intoxicated to do duty, now sprang all at once to their feet and to their instruments and, scrambling upon their table, broke out with one accord into "Yankee Doodle", which they performed, if not exactly in tune at least with an energy superhuman, during the whole of the uproar.

Meantime, upon the main dining-table, among the bottles and glasses, leaped the gentleman who with such difficulty had been restrained from leaping there before. As soon as he fairly settled himself he commenced an oration, which no doubt was a very capital one if it could only have been heard. At the same moment, the man with the tee-totum predilections set himself to spinning around the apartment with immense energy, and with arms outstretched at right angles with his body, so that he had all the air of a tee-totum in fact and knocked everybody down that happened to get in his way. And now, too, hearing an incredible popping and fizzing of champagne, I discovered at length that it proceeded from the person who performed the bottle of that delicate drink during dinner. And then, again, the frog-man croaked away as if the salvation of his soul depended upon every note that he uttered. And in the midst of all this, the continuous braying of a donkey arose over all. As for my old friend Madame Joyeuse, I really could have wept for the poor lady, she appeared so terribly perplexed. All she did, however, was to stand up in a corner by the fireplace and sing out incessantly, at the top of her voice, "Cock-a-doodle-de-dooooooh!"

And now came the climax—the catastrophe of the drama. As no resistance beyond whooping and yelling and cock-a-doodleing was offered to the encroachments of the party without, the ten windows were very speedily and almost simultaneously broken in. But I shall never forget the emotions of wonder and horror with which I gazed when, leaping through these windows and down among us *pêle-mêle*, fighting, stamping, scratching and howling, there rushed a perfect army of what I took to be chimpanzees, orang-outangs or big black baboons of the Cape of Good Hope.

I received a terrible beating, after which I rolled under a sofa and lay still. After lying there some fifteen minutes, however, during which time I listened with all my ears to what was going on in the room, I came to some satisfactory *dénouement* of this tragedy. Monsieur Maillard, it appeared, in giving me the account of the lunatic who had excited his fellows to rebellion, had been merely relating his own exploits. This gentleman had, indeed, some two or three years before been the superintendent of the establishment, but grew crazy himself and so became a patient. This fact was unknown to the travelling companion who introduced me. The keepers, ten in number, having been suddenly overpowered, were first well tarred, then carefully feathered and then shut up in underground cells. They had been so imprisoned for more than a month, during which period Monsieur Maillard had generously allowed them not only the tar and feathers (which constituted his "system"), but some bread and abundance of water. The latter was pumped on them daily. At length, one escaping through a sewer gave freedom to all the rest.

The "soothing system", with important modifications, has been resumed at the *château*; yet I cannot help agreeing with Monsieur Maillard that his own "treatment" was a very capital one of its kind. As he justly observed, it was "simple, neat and gave no trouble at all—not the least".

I have only to add that although I have searched every library in Europe for the works of Doctor *Tarr* and Professor *Fether*, I have, up to the present day, utterly failed in my endeavours at procuring an edition.

PURITAN PASSIONS

NATHANIEL HAWTHORNE

(Film Guild-Hodkinson: 1923)

Film makers on both sides of the Atlantic were soon drawing on literature for their raw material, and in America the booming Broadway stage was also able to provide excellent contributions to the horror film genre in the twenties and thirties (The Bat *and* The Cat and the Canary *are two examples*).

One of the successes of the twenties was The Scarecrow *by Percy MacKay, a story of witchcraft set in Salem and based on an almost unknown piece by Nathaniel Hawthorne called* Feathertop. *In the tale an old woman brings a scarecrow to life and sends it off to court the daughter of a local dignitary—with the most surprising and unexpected results.*

The film, based on both the original story and the stage play, was directed by the talented Frank Tuttle and sardonically depicted much of the fanaticism which surrounded witchcraft in the seventeenth century. It had an eerie, netherworld quality—heightened by the lack of sound or music—and today still retains the power to send a shiver up the spine of even the most hardened horror fan.

*

"DICKON," cried Mother Rigby, "a coal for my pipe!"

The pipe was in the old dame's mouth when she said these words. She had thrust it there after filling it with tobacco, but without stooping to light it at the hearth, where indeed there was no appearance of a fire having been kindled that morning. Forthwith, however, as soon as the order was given, there was an intense red glow out of the bowl of the pipe, and a whiff of smoke from Mother Rigby's lips. Whence the coal came, and how brought thither by an invisible hand, I have never been able to discover.

"Good!" quoth Mother Rigby, with a nod of her head. "Thank ye, Dickon! And now for making this scarecrow. Be within call, Dickon, in case I need you again."

The good woman had risen thus early (for as yet it was scarcely sunrise) in order to set about making a scarecrow which she intended to put in the middle of her corn-patch. It was now the latter week of May, and the crows and blackbirds had already discovered the little green, rolled-up leaf of the Indian corn just peeping out of the soil. She was determined, therefore, to contrive as life-like a scarecrow as ever was seen, and to finish it immediately from top to toe, so that it should begin its sentinel's duty that very morning. Now Mother Rigby (as everybody must have heard) was one of the most cunning and potent witches in New England, and might, with very little trouble, have made a scarecrow ugly enough to frighten the minister himself. But on this occasion, as she had awakened in an uncommonly pleasant humour, and was further dulcified by her pipe of tobacco, she resolved to produce something fine, beautiful, and splendid, rather than hideous and horrible.

"I don't want to set up a hobgoblin in my own corn-patch, and almost at my own doorstep," said Mother Rigby to herself, puffing out a whiff of smoke; "I could do it if I pleased, but I'm tired of doing marvellous things, and so I'll keep within the bounds of everyday business, just for variety's sake. Besides, there is no use in scaring the little children for a mile roundabout, though 'tis true I'm a witch."

It was settled therefore in her own mind, that the scarecrow should represent a fine gentleman of the period, so far as the materials at hand would allow. Perhaps it may be as well to enumerate the chief of the articles that went to the composition of this figure.

The most important item of all, probably, although it made so little show, was a certain broomstick, on which Mother Rigby had taken many an airy gallop at midnight, and which now served the scarecrow by way of a spinal column, or, as the unlearned phrase it, a backbone. One of its arms was a disabled flail which used to be wielded by Goodman Rigby, before his spouse worried him out of this troublesome world; the other, if I mistake not, was composed of the pudding stick and a broken rung of a chair, tied loosely together at the elbow. As for its legs, the right one was a hoe-handle, and the left an undistinguished and miscellaneous stick from the woodpile. Its lungs, stomach, and other affairs of that kind were nothing better than a meal-bag stuffed with straw. Thus we have made out the skeleton and entire corporeity of the scarecrow, with the exception of its head; and this was admirably supplied by a somewhat withered and shrivelled pumpkin, in which Mother Rigby cut two holes for the eyes, and a slit for the mouth, leaving a bluish-coloured knob in the middle to pass for a nose. It was really quite a respectable face.

"I've seen worse ones on human shoulders, at any rate," said

Mother Rigby. "And many a fine gentleman has a pumpkin-head, as well as my scarecrow."

But the clothes in this case were to be the making of the man. So the good old woman took down from a peg an ancient plum-coloured coat of London make and with relics of embroidery on its seams, cuffs, pocket-flaps, and buttonholes, but lamentably worn and faded, patched at the elbows, tattered at the skirts, and thread-bare all over. On the left breast was a round hole, whence either a star of nobility had been rent away, or else the hot heart of some former wearer had scorched it through and through. The neighbours said that this rich garment belonged to the Black Man's wardrobe, and that he kept it at Mother Rigby's cottage for the convenience of slipping it on whenever he wished to make a grand appearance at the governor's table.

To match the coat there was a velvet waistcoat of very ample size and formerly embroidered with foliage that had been as brightly golden as the maple-leaves in October, but which had now quite van-ished out of the substance of the velvet. Next came a pair of scarlet breeches once worn by the French governor of Louisbourg, and the knees of which had touched the lower step of the throne of Louis le Grand. The Frenchman had given these smallclothes to an Indian pow-wow, who parted with them to the old witch for a gill of strong waters, at one of their dances in the forest. Furthermore, Mother Rigby produced a pair of silk stockings and put them on the figure's legs, where they showed as unsubstantial as a dream with the wooden reality of the two sticks making itself miserably apparent through the holes. Lastly, she put her dead husband's wig on the bare scalp of the pumpkin, and surmounted the whole with a dusty three-cornered hat, in which was stuck the longest tail-feather of a rooster.

Then the old dame stood the figure up in a corner of her cottage and chuckled to behold its yellow semblance of a visage, with its nobby little nose thrust into the air. It had a strangely self-satisfied aspect, and seemed to say, "Come look at me!"

"And you are well worth looking at, that's a fact!" quoth Mother Rigby, in admiration at her own handiwork. "I've made many a puppet since I've been a witch; but methinks this is the finest of them all. 'Tis almost too good for a scarecrow. And, by the by, I'll just fill a fresh pipe of tobacco, and then take him out to the corn-patch."

While filling her pipe, the old woman continued to gaze with almost motherly affection at the figure in the corner. To say the truth, whether it were chance, or skill, or downright witchcraft, there was something wonderfully human in this ridiculous shape, bedizened with its tattered finery; and as for the countenance, it appeared to shrivel its yellow surface into a grin—a funny kind of expression betwixt scorn and merriment—as if it understood itself to be a jest at mankind. The more Mother Rigby looked the better she was pleased.

"Dickon," cried she, sharply, "another coal for my pipe!"

Hardly had she spoken, when, just as before, there was a red-glowing coal on the top of the tobacco. She drew in a long whiff and puffed it forth again into the bar of morning sunshine which struggled through the one dusty pane of her cottage window. Mother Rigby always liked to flavour her pipe with a coal of fire from the particular chimney-corner whence this had been brought. But where the chimney-corner might be, or who brought the coal from it—further than that invisible messenger seemed to respond to the name of Dickon—I cannot tell.

"That puppet yonder," thought Mother Rigby, still with her eyes fixed on the scarecrow, "is too good a piece of work to stand all summer in a corn-patch, frightening away the crows and black-birds. He's capable of better things. Why, I've danced with a worse one, when partners happened to be scarce, at our witch-meetings in the forest! What if I should let him take his chance among the other men of straw and empty fellows who go bustling about the world?"

The old witch took three or four more whiffs at her pipe and smiled.

"He'll meet plenty of his brethren at every street-corner!" continued she. "Well, I didn't mean to dabble in witchcraft today, further than the lighting of my pipe; but a witch I am, and a witch I'm likely to be, and there's no use in trying to shirk it. I'll make a man of my scarecrow, were it only for the joke's sake!"

While muttering these words, Mother Rigby took the pipe from her own mouth and thrust it into the crevice which represented the same feature in the pumpkin visage of the scarecrow.

"Puff, darling, puff!" said she. "Puff away, my fine fellow! Your life depends on it!"

This was a strange exhortation, undoubtedly, to be addressed to a mere thing of sticks, straw, and old clothes, with nothing better than a shrivelled pumpkin for a head; as we know to have been the scarecrow's case. Nevertheless, as we must carefully hold in remembrance, Mother Rigby was a witch of singular power and dexterity; and keeping this fact duly before our minds, we shall see nothing beyond credibility in the remarkable incidents of our story. Indeed, the great difficulty will be at once got over if we can only bring ourselves to believe that as soon as the old dame bade him puff, there came a whiff of smoke from the scarecrow's mouth. It was the very feeblest of whiffs, to be sure; but it was followed by another and another, each more decided than the preceding one.

"Puff away, my pet; puff away, my pretty one!" Mother Rigby kept repeating, with her pleasant smile. "It is the breath of life to ye; and that you may take my word for."

Beyond all question the pipe was bewitched. There must have been a spell either in the tobacco or in the fiercely glowing coal that so mysteriously burned on top of it, or in the pungently aromatic smoke which exhaled from the kindled weed. The figure, after a few doubtful attempts, at length blew forth a volley of smoke extending all the way from the obscure corner into the bar of sunshine. There it eddied and melted away among the motes of dust. It seemed a convulsive effort; for the two or three next whiffs were fainter, although the coal still glowed and threw a gleam over the scarecrow's visage. The old witch clapped her skinny hands together, and smiled encouragingly upon her handiwork. She saw that the charm worked well. The shrivelled, yellow face, which heretofore had been no face at all, had already a thin, fantastic haze, as it were, of human likeness, shifting to and fro across it; sometimes vanishing entirely, but growing more perceptible than ever with the next whiff from the pipe. The whole figure, in like manner, assumed a show of life. If we must needs pry closely into the matter, it may be doubted whether there was any real change, after all, in the sordid, worn-out, worthless and ill-jointed substance of the scarecrow; but merely a spectral illusion, and a cunning effect of light and shade so coloured and contrived as to delude the eyes of most men. The miracles of witchcraft seem always to have had a very shallow subtlety; and, at least, if the above explanation do not hit the truth of the process, I can suggest no better.

"Well puffed, my pretty lad!" still cried old Mother Rigby. "Come, another good stout whiff, and let it be with might and main. Puff for thy life, I tell thee! Puff out of the very bottom of thy heart; if any heart thou hast, or any bottom to it! Well done, again! Thou didst suck in that mouthful as if for the pure love of it."

And then the witch beckoned to the scarecrow, throwing so much magnetic potency into her gesture that it seemed as if it must inevitably be obeyed.

"Why lurkest thou in the corner, lazy one?" said she. "Step forth! Thou hast the world before thee!"

In obedience to Mother Rigby's word, and extending its arms as if to reach her outstretched hand, the figure made a step forward—a kind of hitch and jerk, however, rather than a step—then tottered and almost lost its balance. What could the witch expect? It was nothing after all, but a scarecrow stuck upon two sticks. But the strong-willed old beldam scowled and beckoned, and flung the energy of her purpose so forcibly at this poor combination of rotten wood and musty straw and ragged garments, that it was compelled to show itself a man, in spite of the reality of things.

So it stepped into the bar of sunshine. There it stood—poor devil of a contrivance that it was!—with only the thinnest vesture of human similitude about it, through which was evident the stiff, rickety, incongruous, faded, tattered, good-for-nothing patchwork of its substance, ready to sink in a heap on the floor, as conscious of its own unworthiness to be erect. Shall I confess the truth? At its present point of vivification, the scarecrow reminds me of some of the lukewarm and abortive characters, composed of heterogeneous materials, used for the thousandth time, and never worth using, with which romance writers (and myself, no doubt, among the rest) have so overpeopled the world of fiction.

But the fierce old hag began to get angry and show a glimpse of her diabolic nature (like a snake's head peeping with a hiss out of her bosom) at this pusillanimous behaviour of the thing which she had taken the trouble to put together.

"Puff away, wretch!" cried she, wrathfully. "Puff, puff, puff, thou thing of straw and emptiness! thou rag or two! thou meal-bag! thou pumpkin-head! thou nothing! Where shall I find a name vile enough to call thee by? Puff, I say, and suck in thy fantastic life along with the smoke; else I snatch the pipe from thy mouth and hurl thee where that red coal came from."

Thus threatened, the unhappy scarecrow had nothing for it but to puff away for dear life. As need was, therefore, it applied itself lustily to the pipe and sent forth such abundant volleys of tobacco smoke that the small cottage-kitchen became all vaporous. The one sunbeam struggled mistily through, and could but imperfectly define the image of the cracked and dusty window-pane on the opposite wall. Mother Rigby, meanwhile, with one brown arm akimbo and the other stretched towards the figure, loomed grimly amid the obscurity with such port and expression as when she was wont to heave a ponderous nightmare on her victims and stand at the bedside to enjoy their agony. In fear and trembling did this poor scarecrow puff. But its efforts, it must be acknowledged, served an excellent purpose; for, with each successive whiff, the figure lost more and more of its dizzy and perplexing tenuity and seemed to take denser substance. Its very garments, moreover, partook of the magical change, and shone with the gloss of novelty and glistened with the skilfully embroidered gold that had long been rent away. And, half revealed among a smoke, a yellow visage bent its lustreless eyes on Mother Rigby.

At last the old witch clenched her fist and shook it at the figure. Not that she was positively angry, but merely acting on the principle —perhaps untrue, or not the only truth, though as high a one as Mother Rigby could be expected to attain—that feeble and torpid natures, being incapable of better inspiration, must be stirred up by fear. But here was the crisis. Should she fail in what she now sought to effect, it was her ruthless purpose to scatter the miserable simulacrum into its original elements.

"Thou hast a man's aspect," said she, sternly. "Have also the echo and mockery of a voice! I bid thee speak!"

The scarecrow gasped, struggled, and at length emitted a murmur, which was so incorporated with its smoky breath that you could scarcely tell whether it were indeed a voice or only a whiff of tobacco. Some narrators of this legend held the opinion that Mother Rigby's conjurations, and the fierceness of her will, had compelled a familiar spirit into the figure, and that the voice was his.

"Mother," mumbled the poor stifled voice, "be not so awful with me! I would fain speak; but being without wits, what can I say?"

"Thou canst speak, darling, canst thou?" cried Mother Rigby, relaxing her grim countenance into a smile. "And what shalt thou say, quotha! Say, indeed! Art thou of the brotherhood of the empty skull, and demandest of me what thou shalt say? Thou shalt say a thousand things, and saying them a thousand times over, thou shalt still have said nothing! Be not afraid, I tell thee! When thou comest into the world (whither I purpose sending thee forth-with), thou shalt not lack the wherewithal to talk. Talk! Why, thou shalt babble like a mill-stream, if thou wilt. Thou hast brains enough for that, I trow!"

"At your service, mother," responded the figure.

"And that was well said, my pretty one," answered Mother Rigby. "Then thou spakest like thyself, and meant nothing. Thou shalt have a hundred such set phrases, and five hundred to the boot of them. And now, darling, I have taken so much pains with thee, and thou art so beautiful, that, by my troth, I love thee better than any witch's puppet in the world; and I've made them of all sorts—clay, wax, straw, sticks, night-fog, morning-mist, sea-foam, and chimney-smoke. But thou art the very best. So give heed to what I say."

"Yes, kind mother," said the figure, "with all my heart!"

"With all thy heart!" cried the old witch, setting her hands to her sides and laughing loudly. "Thou hast such a pretty way of speaking. With all thy heart! And thou didst put thy hand to the left side of thy waistcoat, as if thou really hadst one!"

So now, in high good humour with this fantastic contrivance of hers, Mother Rigby told the scarecrow that it must go and play its part in the great world, where not one man in a hundred, she affirmed, was gifted with more real substance than itself. And, that he might hold up his head with the best of them, she endowed him, on the spot, with an unreckonable amount of wealth. It con-sisted partly of a gold mine in Eldorado, and of ten thousand shares in a broken bubble, and of half a million acres of vineyard at the North Pole, and of a castle in the air, and a château in Spain, together with all the rents and income therefrom accruing. She further made over to him the cargo of a certain ship, laden with salt of Cadiz, which she herself, by her necromantic arts, had caused to founder, ten years before, in the deepest part of mid-ocean. If the salt were not dissolved, and could be brought to market, it would fetch a pretty penny among the fishermen. That he might not lack ready money, she gave him a copper farthing of Birmingham manufacture, being all the coin she had about her, and likewise a great deal of brass, which she applied to his forehead, thus making it yellower than ever.

"With that brass alone," quoth Mother Rigby, "thou canst pay thy way all over the earth. Kiss me, pretty darling! I have done my best for thee."

Furthermore, that the adventurer might lack no possible advantage towards a fair start in life, this excellent old dame gave him a token by which he was to introduce himself to a certain magistrate, member of the council, merchant, and elder of the church (the four capacities constituting but one man), who stood at the head of society in the neighbouring metropolis. The token was neither more nor less than a single word which Mother Rigby whispered to the scarecrow, and which the scarecrow was to whisper to the merchant.

"Gouty as the old fellow is, he'll run thy errands for thee, when once thou hast given him that word in his ear," said the old witch. "Mother Rigby knows the worshipful Justice Gookin, and the worshipful Justice knows Mother Rigby!"

Here the witch thrust her wrinkled face close to the puppet's, chuckling irrepressibly, and fidgeting all through her system, with delight at the idea which she meant to communicate.

"The worshipful Master Gookin," whispered she, "hath a comely maiden to his daughter. And hark ye, my pet! Thou hast a fair outside, and a pretty wit enough of thine own. Yea, a pretty wit enough! Thou wilt think better of it when thou hast seen more of other people's wits. Now, with thy outside and thy inside, thou art the very man to win a young girl's heart. Never doubt it! I tell thee it shall be so. Put but a bold face on the matter, sigh, smile, flourish thy hat, thrust forth thy leg like a dancing-master, put thy right hand to the left side of thy waistcoat, and pretty Polly Gookin is thine own!"

All this while the new creature had been sucking in and exhaling the vapoury fragrance of his pipe, and seemed now to continue the occupation as much for the enjoyment it afforded as because it was an essential condition of his existence. It was wonderful to see how exceedingly like a human being it behaved. Its eyes (for it appeared to possess a pair) were bent on Mother Rigby, and at suitable junctures it nodded or shook its head. Neither did it lack words proper for the occasion : "Really! Indeed! Pray tell me! Is it possible! Upon my word! By no means! Oh! Ah! Hem!" and other such weighty utterances as imply attention, inquiry, acquiescence, or dissent on the part of the auditor. Even had you stood by and seen the scarecrow made, you could scarcely have resisted the conviction that it perfectly understood the cunning counsels which the old witch poured into its counterfeit of an ear. The more earnestly it applied its lips to the pipe the more distinctly was its human likeness stamped among visible realities, the more sagacious grew its expression, the more life-like its gestures and movements, and the more intelligibly audible its voice. Its garments, too, glistened so much the brighter with an illusionary magnificence. The very pipe, in which burned the spell of all this wonder-work, ceased to appear as a smoke-blackened earthen stump, and became a meerschaum, with painted bowl and amber mouthpiece.

It might be apprehended, however, that as the life of the illusion seemed identical with the vapour of the pipe, it would terminate simultaneously with the reduction of the tobacco to ashes. But the beldam foresaw the difficulty.

"Hold thou the pipe, my precious one," said she, "while I fill it for thee again."

It was sorrowful to behold how the fine gentleman began to fade back into a scarecrow while Mother Rigby shook the ashes out of the pipe and proceeded to replenish it from her tobacco-box.

"Dickon," cried she, in her high, sharp tone, "another coal for this pipe!"

No sooner said than the intensely red speck of fire was glowing within the pipe bowl; and the scarecrow, without waiting for the witch's bidding, applied the tube to his lips and drew in a few short, convulsive whiffs, which soon, however, became regular and equable.

"Now, mine own heart's darling," quoth Mother Rigby, "whatever may happen to thee, thou must stick to thy pipe. Thy life is in it; and that, at least, thou knowest well, if thou knowest nought besides. Stick to thy pipe, I say! Smoke, puff, blow thy cloud; and tell the people, if any question be made, that it is for thy health, and that so the physician orders thee to do. And, sweet one, when thou shalt find thy pipe getting low, go apart into some corner and (first filling thyself with smoke) cry sharply, 'Dickon, a fresh pipe of tobacco!' and 'Dickon, another coal for my pipe!' and have it into thy pretty mouth as speedily as may be. Else, instead of a gallant gentleman in a gold-laced coat, thou wilt be but a jumble of sticks and tattered clothes, and a bag of straw, and a withered pumpkin! Now depart, my treasure, and good luck go with thee!"

"Never fear, mother!" said the figure, in a stout voice, and sending forth a courageous whiff of smoke. "I will thrive, if an honest man and a gentleman may!"

"Oh, thou wilt be the death of me!" cried the old witch, convulsed with laughter. "That was well said. If an honest man and a gentleman may! Thou playest thy part to perfection. Get along with thee for a smart fellow; and I will wager on thy head, as a man of pith and substance, with a brain, and what they call a heart, and all else that a man should have, against any other thing on two legs. I hold myself a better witch than yesterday, for thy sake. Did not I make thee? And I defy any witch in New England to make such another! Here; take my staff along with thee!"

The staff, though it was but a plain oaken stick, immediately took the aspect of a gold-headed cane.

"That gold head has as much sense in it as thine own," said Mother Rigby, "and it will guide thee straight to worshipful Master Gookin's door. Get thee gone, my treasure; and if any ask thy name, it is Feathertop. For thou hast a feather in thy hat, and I have thrust a handful of feathers into the hollow of thy head, and thy wig, too, is of the fashion they call Feathertop—so be Feathertop thy name!"

And, issuing from the cottage, Feathertop strode manfully towards town. Mother Rigby stood at the threshold, well pleased to see how the sunbeams glistened on him, as if all his magnificence were real, and how diligently and lovingly he smoked his pipe, and how handsomely he walked, in spite of a little stiffness of his legs. She watched him until out of sight, and threw a witch benediction after her darling, when a turn of the road snatched him from her view.

Betimes in the forenoon, when the principal street of the neighbouring town was just at its acme of life and bustle, a stranger of very distinguished figure was seen on the sidewalk. His port as well as his garments betokened nothing short of nobility. He wore a richly embroidered plum-coloured coat, a waistcoat of costly velvet magnificently adorned with golden foliage, a pair of splendid scarlet breeches, and the finest and glossiest of white silk stockings. His head was covered with a peruke, so daintily powdered and adjusted that it would have been sacrilege to disorder it with a hat; which therefore (and it was a gold-laced hat, set off with a snowy feather) he carried beneath his arm. On the breast of his coat glistened a star. He managed his gold-headed cane with an airy grace peculiar to the fine gentlemen of the period; and, to give the highest possible finish to his equipment, he had lace ruffles at his wrist, of a most ethereal delicacy, sufficiently avouching how idle and aristocratic must be the hands which they half concealed.

It was a remarkable point in the accoutrement of this brilliant personage, that he held in his left hand a fantastic kind of a pipe, with an exquisitely painted bowl and an amber mouthpiece. This he applied to his lips as often as every five or six paces, and inhaled a deep whiff of smoke, which, after being retained a moment in his lungs, might be seen to eddy gracefully from his mouth and nostrils.

As may well be supposed, the street was all astir to find out the stranger's name.

"It is some great nobleman, beyond question," said one of the townspeople. "Do you see the star at his breast?"

"Nay; it is too bright to be seen," said another. "Yes; he must needs be a nobleman, as you say. But by what conveyance, think you, can his lordship have voyaged or travelled hither? There has been no vessel from the old country for a month past; and if he have arrived overland from the southward, pray where are his attendants and equipage?"

"He needs no equipage to set off his rank," remarked a third. "If he came among us in rags, nobility would shine through a hole in his elbow. I never saw such dignity of aspect. He has the old Norman blood in his veins, I warrant him."

"I rather take him to be a Dutchman, or one of your high Germans," said another citizen. "The men of those countries have always the pipe at their mouths."

"And so has a Turk," answered his companion. "But, in my judgment, this stranger hath been bred at the French court, and hath there learned politeness and grace of manner, which none understand so well as the nobility of France. That's gait, now! A vulgar spectator might deem it stiff—he might call it a hitch and jerk, but, to my eyes, it hath an unspeakable majesty, and must have been acquired by constant observation of the deportment of the Grand Monarque. The stranger's character and office are evident enough. He is a French ambassador, come to treat with our rulers about the cession of Canada."

"More probably a Spaniard," said another, "and hence his yellow complexion; or, most likely, he is from the Havana, or from some port on the Spanish main, and comes to make investigation about the piracies which our governor is thought to connive at. Those settlers in Peru and Mexico have skins as yellow as the gold which they dig out of their mines."

"Yellow or not," cried a lady, "he is a beautiful man"—so tall, so slender! such a fine, noble face, with so well-shaped a nose, and all that delicacy of expression about the mouth! And, bless me, how bright his star is! It positively shoots out flames!"

"So do your eyes, fair lady," said the stranger, with a bow and a flourish of his pipe; for he was just passing at the instant. "Upon my honour, they have quite dazzled me."

"Was ever so original and exquisite a compliment?" murmured the lady, in an ecstasy of delight.

Amid the general admiration excited by the stranger's appearance, there were only two dissenting voices. One was that of an impertinent cur, which after snuffing at the heels of the glittering figure, put its tail between its legs and skulked into its master's back yard, vociferating an execrable howl. The other dissentient was a young child, who squalled at the fullest stretch of his lungs, and babbled some unintelligible nonsense about a pumpkin.

Feathertop, meanwhile, pursued his way along the street. Except for the few complimentary words to the lady, and now and then a slight inclination of the head in requital of the profound reverences of the bystanders, he seemed wholly absorbed in his pipe. There needed no other proof of his rank and consequence than the perfect equanimity with which he comported himself, while the curiosity and admiration of the town swelled almost into clamour around him. With a crowd gathering behind his footsteps, he finally reached the mansion-house of the worshipful Justice Gookin, entered the gate, ascended the steps of the front door, and knocked. In the interim, before his summons was answered, the stranger was observed to shake the ashes out of his pipe.

"What did he say in that sharp voice?" inquired one of the spectators.

"Nay, I know not," answered his friend. "But the sun dazzles my eyes strangely. How dim and faded his lordship looks all of a sudden! Bless my wits, what is the matter with me?"

"The wonder is," said the other, "that his pipe, which was out only an instant ago, should be all alight again, and with the reddest coal I ever saw. There is something mysterious about this stranger. What a whiff of smoke was that! Dim and faded did you call him? Why, as he turns about, the star on his breast is all ablaze."

"It is, indeed," said his companions; "and it will go near to dazzle pretty Polly Gookin, whom I see peeping at it out of the chamber-window."

The door being now opened, Feathertop turned to the crowd, made a stately bend of his body like a great man acknowledging the reverence of the meaner sort, and vanished into the house. There was a mysterious kind of a smile, if it might not better be called a grin or grimace, upon his visage; but of all the throng that beheld him not an individual appears to have possessed insight enough to detect the illusive character of the stranger except a little child and a cur dog.

Our legend here loses somewhat of its continuity, and, passing over the preliminary explanations between Feathertop and the merchant, goes in quest of the pretty Polly Gookin. She was a damsel of a soft, round figure, with light hair and blue eyes, and a fair, rosy face, which seemed neither very shrewd nor very simple. This young lady had caught a glimpse of the glistening stranger while standing at the threshold, and had forthwith put on a laced cap, a string of beads, her finest kerchief, and her stiffest damask petticoat, in preparation for the interview. Hurrying from her chamber to the parlour, she had ever since been viewing herself in the large looking-glass and practising pretty airs—now a smile, now a ceremonious dignity of aspect, and now a softer smile than the former, kissing her hand likewise, tossing her head, and managing her fan; while within the mirror an unsubstantial little maid repeated every gesture and did all the foolish things that Polly did, but without making her ashamed of them. In short, it was the fault of pretty Polly's ability rather than her will if she failed to be as complete an artifice as the illustrious Feathertop himself; and, when she thus tampered with her own simplicity, the witch's phantom might well hope to win her.

No sooner did Polly hear her father's gouty footsteps approaching the parlour door, accompanied with the stiff clatter of Feathertop's high-heeled shoes, than she seated herself bolt-upright and inno-cently began warbling a song.

"Polly! daughter Polly!" cried the old merchant. "Come hither, child."

Master Gookin's aspect, as he opened the door, was doubtful and troubled.

"This gentleman," continued he, presenting the stranger, "is the

Chevalier Feathertop—nay, I beg his pardon, my Lord Feathertop
—who hath brought me a token of remembrance from an ancient
friend of mine. Pay your duty to his lordship, child, and honour him
as his quality deserves."

After these few words of introduction, the worshipful magistrate
immediately quitted the room. But, even in that brief moment, had
the fair Polly glanced aside at her father instead of devoting herself
wholly to the brilliant guest, she might have taken warning of some
mischief nigh at hand. The old man was nervous, fidgety, and very
pale. Purposing a smile of courtesy, he had deformed his face with
a sort of galvanic grin, which, when Feathertop's back was turned,
he exchanged for a scowl, at the same time shaking his fist and
stamping his gouty foot—an incivility which brought his retribution
along with it.

The truth appears to have been, that Mother Rigby's word of
introduction, whatever it might be, had operated far more on the
rich merchant's fears than on his good-will. Moreover, being a man
of wonderfully acute observation, he had noticed that the painted
figures on the bowl of Feathertop's pipe were in motion. Looking
more closely, he became convinced that these figures were a party
of little demons, each duly provided with horns and a tail, and
dancing hand in hand, with gestures of diabolical merriment, round
the circumference of the pipe-bowl. As if to confirm his suspicions,
while Master Gookin ushered his guest along a dusky passage from
his private room to the parlour, the star on Feathertop's breast had
scintillated actual flames, and threw a flickering gleam upon the
wall, the ceiling, and the floor.

With such sinister prognostics manifesting themselves on all hands,
it is not to be marvelled at that the merchant should have felt that
he was committing his daughter to a very questionable acquaintance.
He cursed, in his secret soul, the insinuating elegance of Feathertop's manners, as this brilliant personage bowed, smiled, put his
hand on his heart, inhaled a long whiff from his pipe, and enriched
the atmosphere with the smoky vapour of a fragrant and visible
sigh. Gladly would poor Master Gookin have thrust his dangerous
guest into the street; but there was a constraint and terror within
him. This respectable old gentleman, we fear, at an earlier period
of life, had given some pledge or other to the evil principle, and
perhaps was now to redeem it by the sacrifice of his daughter.

It so happened that the parlour door was partly of glass, shaded
by a silken curtain, the folds of which hung a little awry. So strong

was the merchant's interest in witnessing what was to ensue between the fair Polly and the gallant Feathertop, that after quitting the room he could by no means refrain from peeping through the crevice of the curtain.

But there was nothing very miraculous to be seen; nothing—except the trifles previously noticed—to confirm the idea of a supernatural peril environing the pretty Polly. The stranger, it is true, was evidently a thorough and practised man of the world, systematic and self-possessed, and therefore the sort of a person to whom a parent ought not to confide a simple young girl, without due watchfulness for the result.

The worthy magistrate, who had been conversant with all degrees and qualities of mankind, could not but perceive every motion and gesture of the distinguished Feathertop came in its proper place; nothing had been left rude or native in him; a well-digested conventionalism had incorporated itself thoroughly with his substance and transformed him into a work of art. Perhaps it was this peculiarity that invested him with a species of ghastliness and awe. It is the effect of anything completely and consummately artificial, in human shape, that the person impresses us as an unreality and as having hardly pith enough to cast a shadow upon the floor. As regarded Feathertop, all this resulted in a wild, extravagant, and fantastical impression, as if his life and being were akin to the smoke that curled upward from his pipe.

But pretty Polly Gookin felt not thus. The pair were now promenading the room; Feathertop with his dainty stride and no less dainty grimace; the girl with a native maidenly grace, just touched, not spoiled, by a slightly affected manner, which seemed caught from the perfect artifice of her companion. The longer the interview continued, the more charmed was pretty Polly, until, within the first quarter of an hour (as the old magistrate noted by his watch), she was evidently beginning to be in love. Nor need it have been witchcraft that subdued her in such a hurry; the poor child's heart, it may be, was so very fervent that it melted her with its own warmth as reflected from the hollow semblance of a lover. No matter what Feathertop said, his words found depth and reverberation in her ear; no matter what he did, his action was heroic to her eye. And by this time it is to be supposed there was a blush on Polly's cheek, a tender smile about her mouth, and a liquid softness in her glance; while the star kept coruscating on Feathertop's breast, and the little demons careered with more frantic merriment than ever about the circumference of his pipe-bowl. O pretty Polly Gookin, why should these imps rejoice so madly that a silly maiden's heart was about to be given to a shadow! Is it so unusual a misfortune, so rare a triumph?

By and by Feathertop paused, and throwing himself into an imposing attitude, seemed to summon the fair girl to survey his figure and resist him longer if she could. His star, his embroidery, his buckles, glowed at that instant with unutterable splendour; the picturesque hues of his attire took a richer depth of colouring; there was a gleam and polish over his whole presence betokening the perfect witchery of well-ordered manners. The maiden raised her eyes and suffered them to linger upon her companion with a bashful and admiring gaze. Then, as if desirous of judging what value her own simple comeliness might have side by side with so much brilliancy, she cast a glance towards the full-length looking-glass in front of which they happened to be standing. It was one of the truest plates in the world, and incapable of flattery. No sooner did the images therein reflected meet Polly's eye than she shrieked, shrank from the stranger's side, gazed at him for a moment in the wildest dismay, and sank insensible upon the floor. Feathertop likewise had looked towards the mirror, and there beheld, not the glittering mockery of his outside show, but a picture of the sordid patchwork of his real composition, stripped of all witchcraft.

The wretched simulacrum! We almost pity him. He threw up his arms with an expression of despair that went further than any of his previous manifestations towards vindicating his claims to be reckoned human : for perchance the only time since this so often empty and deceptive life of mortals began its course, an illusion had seen and fully recognized itself.

Mother Rigby was seated by her kitchen hearth in the twilight of this eventful day, and had just shaken the ashes out of a new pipe, when she heard a hurried tramp along the road. Yet it did not seem so much the tramp of human footsteps as the clatter of sticks or the rattling of dry bones.

"Ha!" thought the old witch, "what step is that? Whose skeleton is out of its grave now, I wonder?"

A figure burst headlong into the cottage door. It was Feathertop!

His pipe was still alight; the star still flamed upon his breast; the embroidery still glowed upon his garments; nor had he lost, in any degree or manner that could be estimated, the aspect that assimilated him with our mortal brotherhood. But yet, in some indescribable way (as is the case with all that has deluded us when once found out), the poor reality was felt beneath the cunning artifice.

"What has gone wrong?" demanded the witch. "Did yonder sniffling hypocrite thrust my darling from his door? The villain! I'll set twenty fiends to torment him till he offer thee his daughter on his bended knees!"

"No, mother," said Feathertop, despondingly; "it was not that."

"Did the girl scorn my precious one?" asked Mother Rigby, her fierce eyes glowing like two coals of Tophet. "I'll cover her face with pimples! Her nose shall be as red as the coal in thy pipe! Her front teeth shall drop out! In a week hence she shall not be worth thy having!"

"Let her alone, mother," answered poor Feathertop; "the girl was half won; and methinks a kiss from her sweet lips might have made me altogether human. But," he added, after a brief pause and then a howl of self-contempt, "I've seen myself, mother! I've seen myself for the wretched, ragged, empty thing I am! I'll exist no longer!"

Snatching the pipe from his mouth, he flung it with all his might against the chimney, and at the same instant sank upon the floor a medley of straw and tattered garments, with some sticks protruding from the heap and a shrivelled pumpkin in the midst. The eyeholes were now lustreless; but the rudely carved gap, that just before had been a mouth, still seemed to twist itself into a despairing grin, and was so far human.

"Poor fellow!" quoth Mother Rigby, with a rueful glance at the relics of her ill-fated contrivance. "My poor, dear, pretty Feathertop! There are thousands upon thousands of coxcombs and charlatans in the world, made up of just such a jumble of worn-out, forgotten and good-for-nothing trash as he was! Yet they live in fair repute, and never see themselves for what they are. And why should my poor puppet be the only one to know himself and perish for it?"

While thus muttering, the witch had filled a fresh pipe of tobacco, and held the stem between her fingers, as doubtful whether to thrust it into her own mouth or Feathertop's.

"Poor Feathertop!" she continued. "I could easily give him another chance and send him forth again tomorrow. But no; his feelings are too tender, his sensibilities too deep. He seems to have too much heart to bustle for his own advantage in such an empty and heartless world. Well! well! I'll make a scarecrow of him after all. 'Tis an innocent and a useful vocation, and will suit my darling well; and if each of his human brethren had as fit a one, 'twould be the better for mankind; and as for this pipe of tobacco, I need it more than he."

So saying Mother Rigby put the stem between her lips. "Dickon!" cried she, in her high, sharp tone, "another coal for my pipe!"

PHANTOM OF THE OPERA

GASTON LEROUX

(*Universal: 1925* et al)

Phantom of the Opera *was unquestionably the finest horror film made during the silent era. Although it has since been remade twice with all the benefits (some would say) of sound and Technicolor, the quality of the original and the truly brilliant acting of Lon Chaney (the first great international horror star after the German Werner Krauss in* The Cabinet of Dr. Caligari *filmed in 1919) make it stand out as a landmark in the history of the cinema, not merely of the horror film genre.*

The near-perfection of Chaney's performance as the disfigured dweller in the Paris Opera House was achieved through much hardship and personal suffering. To twist his face into a horrible death mask he used pieces of wire to distend his eyes and expose his gums; indeed rumours were prevalent at the time of the shooting that the star looked so hideous that it was doubtful whether the finished picture would ever be shown. But it was shown, although it suffered a little because of certain disagreements between actor and director, and it proved to be a masterpiece.

The picture was based on a very popular tale by the Frenchman, Gaston Leroux, which was first published in Paris in 1908. Much admired at the time, it has since, inexplicably, remained out of print for many years. Since the original story is stylistically somewhat pedestrian and long-winded, this special abridgement has been prepared which remains not only faithful to the original, but also emphasises the drama of the film—a film which in my opinion well merits the claim made for it by Carlos Clarens in his book, An Illustrated History of the Horror Film, *that "Consciously or not, the influence of the* Phantom of the Opera *has been felt in most horror efforts ever since."*

*

IT was the evening on which Messieurs Debienne and Poligny, the managers of the Opera, were giving a farewell gala performance to mark their retirement. Suddenly, the dressing room of La Sorelli, one of the principal dancers, was invaded by half a dozen young ladies of the ballet who rushed in amid great confusion, shrieking with terror. Sorelli looked around angrily as little Jammes—the girl with the tiptilted nose and rose-red cheeks—exclaimed in a trembling voice, "It's the ghost!"

Sorelli shuddered when she heard the girl speak of the ghost—for she was superstitious about ghosts in general and the Opera ghost in particular. At once she asked for details, "Have you seen him?"

"As plainly as I see you now!" moaned little Jammes, dropping into a chair.

Thereupon another girl added, "If that's the ghost, he's very ugly!"

"Oh, yes!" cried the chorus of ballet girls.

And they all began to talk at once. The ghost had suddenly appeared to them clad in dress-clothes, in the passage, without their knowing where he came from. He seemed to have loomed through the wall.

"Pooh!" said one of the girls who had more or less kept her head. "You see the ghost everywhere!"

And it was true. For several months there had been nothing discussed at the Opera but this ghost in dress-clothes who stalked about the building like a shadow, who spoke to nobody and who vanished as soon as he was seen. All the girls pretended to have met this supernatural being more or less often, yet who had actually seen him? You meet so many men in dress-clothes at the Opera who are not ghosts. But this dress-suit had a peculiarity of its own—it clothed a skeleton. At least, so the ballet girls said. And it had a death's-head.

The truth is that this was the description given by Joseph Buquet, the chief scene-shifter, who really had seen the ghost. He had run up against him on the little staircase by the footlights which leads straight down to the cellars. He had seen him for a second—for the ghost had fled—and to any one who cared to listen to him he told this story :

"He is extraordinarily thin and his dress-coat hangs on a skeleton frame. His eyes are so deep set that you can hardly see the pupils. All you see is two big black holes, as in a dead man's skull. His skin, which is stretched across his bones like a drumhead, is a dirty yellow. He has hardly any nose to speak of and the only hair he has is three or four long dark locks on his forehead and behind the ears."

Sensible men, hearing the story, began by saying that Joseph Buquet had been the victim of a joke played by one of his assistants. And then there came an incident so curious and so inexplicable that the very shrewdest people began to feel uneasy.

A fireman named Pampin, who had gone to make a round of inspection in the cellars, suddenly reappeared on the stage, pale and trembling. He had seen a head of fire without a body coming towards him. After that, could anyone be sure ... ?

"It's the ghost!" cried little Jammes again and then, flinging herself terrified into the furthest corner of the wall, she whispered : "Listen !"

Everybody seemed to hear a rustling outside the door like light silk gliding along the panel. Then it stopped.

Sorelli tried to show more pluck than the others. She went up to the door and, in a quavering voice, asked : "Who's there?"

But nobody answered. Then, feeling all eyes upon her, she made an effort to look courageous, and said very loudly : "Is there anyone behind the door?"

No reply. She flung the door open and looked into the passage. A gas flame cast a red and sinister light into the surrounding darkness, but the passage was empty.

Sorelli shut the door and turned to the girls, "Come children," she said, "pull yourselves together ! I daresay no one has ever seen the ghost."

"Yes, yes, we saw him just now !" the girls cried. "He had his death's-head and his dress-coat, just the same as when Joseph Buquet saw him !"

"Joseph Buquet would do better to hold his tongue."

"That's Ma's opinion," said Meg, lowering her voice, "Ma says the ghost doesn't like being talked about."

"And why does your mother say so?"

"Because ... because ... nothing ..."

This reticence exasperated the curiosity of the young ladies, who crowded round Meg, begging her to explain herself.

"I swore not to tell !" gasped Meg.

But they left her no peace and promised to keep the secret, until

Meg, burning to say all she knew, began, with her eyes fixed on the door :

"Well, it's because of the private box..."

"What private box?"

"The ghost's box! It's Box 5, you know, the box on the grand tier, next to the left-hand stage-box."

"Oh, nonsense!"

"I tell you it is... Ma has charge of it. But you swear you won't say a word?"

"Of course, of course!"

"Well, that's the ghost's box ... No one has had it for over a month, except the ghost, and orders have been given at the box-office that it must never be sold."

"And does the ghost really come there?"

"Yes."

"Then somebody does come?"

"Why, no!... The ghost comes, but there is nobody there."

"Giry, child, what are you saying!"

Thereupon little Giry began to cry :

"I ought to have held my tongue. If Ma ever got to know!... But it's true enough, Joseph Buquet had no business to talk of things that don't concern him... it will bring him bad luck... Ma was saying so last night."

There was a sound of heavy and hurried footsteps in the passage, and a breathless voice cried :

"Cecile! Cecile! Are you there?"

Sorelli opened the door. Thereupon a corpulent lady burst into the dressing-room and dropped groaning into a vacant armchair.

"How awful!" she said. "Joseph Buquet is dead! He was found hanging in the third-floor cellar!"

"It's the ghost!" blurted little Giry.

All around her, her panic-stricken companions repeated, under their breaths :

"Yes, it must be the ghost!"

The horrid news soon spread all over the Opera, for Joseph Buquet was very popular. The dressing-rooms emptied and the little ballet-girls made for the foyer through the ill-lit passages. On the first landing, Sorelli ran against the Comte de Chagny, who was coming upstairs. The count seemed greatly excited :

"I was just coming to you," he said, taking off his hat. "Oh, Sorelli, what an evening! And Christine Daae : what a triumph!"

They all rushed on to the foyer of the ballet, which was already full of people. The Comte de Chagny was right : no gala performance had ever equalled this. All the great composers of the day had conducted their own works in turn. Faure and Krauss had sung; and on that evening the young soprano Christine Daae had revealed her true self for the first time to the astonished and enthusiastic audience. She began by singing a few passages from *Romeo and Juliet* and those who heard her said that her voice in these passages was seraphic, but this was nothing to the superhuman notes that she gave forth in the prison scene and the final trio in Faust, which she sang in the place of La Carlotta, who was ill. No one had ever heard or seen anything like it.

Christine Daae revealed a new Margarita that night, a Margarita of a splendour and radiance hitherto unsuspected. The whole house went mad, rising to its feet, shouting, cheering and clapping, while Christine sobbed and fainted in the arms of her fellow singers and had to be carried to her dressing-room. Till then, Christine Daae had played a good Siebel to Carlotta's rather too splendidly massive Margarita. And it had needed Carlotta's incomprehensible and inexcusable absence from this gala night for little Christine, at a moment's notice, to show all that she could do in a part of the programme reserved for the Spanish diva. Now what the subscribers wanted to know was, why had Debienne and Poligny applied to Daae, when Carlotta was taken ill? Did they know of her hidden genius? And why had she kept it hidden? Oddly enough, she was not known to have a voice instructor at that moment. The whole thing was a mystery.

The Comte de Chagny, standing up in his box, listened to all this frenzy and took part in it by applauding loudly. Philippe Georges Marie Comte de Chagny was just forty-one years of age. He was a great aristocrat and a good-looking man, exquisitely polite to the women and a little haughty to the men, who did not always forgive him his social successes. He had an excellent heart and an irreproachable conscience. On the death of old Count Philibert, he had become the head of one of the oldest and most distinguished families in France, whose arms dated back to the fourteenth century.

His brother Raoul was born twenty years after him, and at the time of the old count's death Raoul was twelve years old. Philippe busied himself actively with the youngster's education. He was admirably assisted in this work, first by his sisters and afterwards by an old aunt, the widow of a naval officer, who lived at Brest and gave young Raoul a taste for the sea. The lad entered the Borda training-ship, finished his course with honours and sailed around the world.

He remained shy and innocent. As a matter of fact, petted as he was by his two sisters and his old aunt, he had retained from this purely feminine education manners that were almost candid, stamped with a charm which nothing had yet been able to spoil. He was now a little over twenty-one and looked eighteen with his fair hair and blue eyes.

Philippe spoiled Raoul and took advantage of the young man's leave of absence to show him Paris, with all its luxurious and artistic delights. He took him with him wherever he went, even introducing him to the foyer of the ballet, where the count was said to be "on terms" with Sorelli. He often came to spend an hour or two after dinner in the company of the dancer who, though not very witty, had the finest eyes that ever were seen.

Still, Philippe would perhaps not have taken his brother behind the scenes of the Opera if Raoul had not been the first to ask him, repeatedly renewing his request with a gentle obstinacy which the count remembered at a later date.

On that evening, Phillipe, after applauding Christine Daae, turned to Raoul and saw that he was quite pale. "Let's go," said Raoul in a trembling voice.

"Where do you want to go?" asked the count, astonished at his brother's sudden excitement.

"Let's go and see her. She never sang like that before."

The count gave his brother a curious, smiling glance and looked quite pleased. He understood now why Raoul was absent-minded when spoken to and why he always tried to turn every conversation to the Opera.

Postponing his usual visit to Sorelli for a few minutes, the count followed his brother down the passage that led to Christine Daae's dressing-room and saw that it was full of people. The girl had not yet come to and the theatre doctor had just arrived at the moment when Raoul entered on his heels. So, Christine received first aid from the one, while opening her eyes in the arms of the other. The count and many more crowded in the doorway.

"Don't you think, doctor, that these gentlemen had better clear the room?" asked Raoul coolly.

"You're quite right," said the doctor.

And he sent every one away, except Raoul and the maid, who looked at Raoul with undisguised astonishment. She had never seen him before and yet dared not question him. The doctor, for his part, imagined that the young man was acting as he did because he had every right to do so.

Meanwhile, Christine Daae gave a deep sigh. She turned her head, saw Raoul and started. "Monsieur," she said, in a whisper, "who are you?"

"Mademoiselle," replied the young man, kneeling before her and pressing a fervent kiss on the diva's hand, "I rescued your scarf from the sea many years ago."

Christine looked at the doctor, then at the maid, and all three began to laugh.

Raoul turned very red and stood up. "Mademoiselle," he said, "since you are pleased not to recognize me, I should like to say something to you in private, something very important."

"I think you should go," said the doctor, with his most pleasant smile. "Leave me to attend to Mademoiselle."

"Thank you, doctor. I should like to be alone. Please go away, all of you. Leave me. I feel very restless this evening."

The doctor tried to protest, but, seeing the girl's evident agitation, though that the best remedy was not to thwart her. And he went away, saying to Raoul outside :

"She is not herself tonight. She is usually such a gentle girl."

Then he said goodnight and Raoul was left alone. The whole of this part of the theatre was now deserted, as he waited in silent solitude, hiding himself in the shadow of a doorway.

Finally the dressing-room door opened and the maid came out by herself, carrying bundles. He stopped her and asked her how her mistress was. The woman laughed and said that she was quite well, but that he must not disturb her for she wished to be left alone. With that she went away. A single idea crossed Raoul's mind—of course, Christine wished to be left alone for him! Had he not told her that he wanted to speak to her privately?

Hardly breathing, he went up to the dressing-room, and, with his ear to the door, prepared to knock. Suddenly he heard a man's voice in the dressing-room, saying in a curiously masterful tone, "Christine, you must love me!"

And Christine's voice, infinitely sad and trembling, replied, "How can you talk like that, when I sing only for you!"

The man's voice spoke again, "Are you very tired?"

"Tonight I gave you my soul and I am exhausted!"

"Your soul is a beautiful thing, child," replied the man's voice gravely, "and I thank you. No emperor ever received so fair a gift. Even the angels wept tonight."

Raoul heard nothing after that. He leaned against the door, hating himself for what he had just heard. Nevertheless, he did not go away, but returned to his dark corner, determined to wait for the man to leave the room. He knew that he loved Christine with all his heart. Now he wanted to know his rival. To his great astonishment, the door opened and Christine Daae came out alone, wrapped in furs, with her face hidden in a lace veil. She closed the door behind her, but did not lock it. She passed him. He did not even follow her, for his eyes were fixed on the door, which remained firmly closed.

When the passage was once more deserted, he crossed it, opened the door of the dressing-room, went in and shut the door. He found himself in absolute darkness. The gas had been turned out. Raoul heard only the sound of his own breathing. He struck a match and its flame lit the room. There was no one there. Raoul searched the wardrobe, opened the cupboards and felt the walls but found no one at all.

During this time the farewell ceremony was taking place to mark the retirement of Monsieur Debienne and Monsieur Poligny. Everybody remarked that the retiring managers looked cheerful and they were already beaming lavishly upon Sorelli, who had begun to recite her speech, when all of a sudden little Jammes cried out, "The Opera ghost!"

Everyone turned in the direction where she was pointing, among the crowd of dandies, to a face so pale and horrible that they were convinced it was a joke. Everybody laughed and pushed his neighbour and wanted to offer the Opera ghost a drink but he was gone as suddenly as he had appeared.

The first few days which the new managers spent at the Opera were given over to the delight of finding themselves at the head of so magnificent an enterprise and they had forgotten all about that curious story of the ghost, when an incident occurred which proved to them that the joke—if joke it were—was not over. Monsieur Firmin Richard reached his office that morning at eleven o'clock. His secretary, Monsieur Remy, showed him half a dozen letters which he had not opened because they were marked "private". One of the letters at once attracted Richard's attention, not only because the envelope was addressed in red ink, but because he seemed to have seen the writing before. He soon remembered that it was the red handwriting which had appeared so curiously in the lease. He recognized the clumsy, childish hand. He opened the letter and read :

Cher Monsieur,
I am sorry to have to trouble you at a time when you must be so very busy renewing important engagements, signing fresh contracts and generally displaying your excellent taste. I know what you have done for Carlotta, Sorelli and little Jammes, not to mention others whose admirable qualities of talent or genius you have suspected.
Of course, when I use these words, I do not mean to apply them to La Carlotta, who sings like a cockroach, nor to La Sorelli, who owes her success mainly to the coach-builders; not to little Jammes, who dances like a calf in a field. And I am not speaking of Christine Daae either, though her genius is certain, whereas your jealousy prevents her from creating any important part.
All the same, I should like to hear Christine Daae this evening in the part of Siebel—as that of Margarita has been withheld from her since her triumph of the other night—and I must ask you not to dispose of my box today nor on the following days. For I cannot end this letter without telling you how disagreeably surprised I have been of late, on arriving at the Opera, to hear that my box had been sold at the box office by your orders.
I did not protest, first because I dislike scandal and, secondly

because I thought that your predecessors, Messieurs Debienne and Poligny, who were always charming to me, had neglected before leaving to mention my little privileges. I have now received a reply to my letter from these gentlemen asking for an explanation which proves that you know all about my clause in the lease and consequently that you are treating me with outrageous contempt. If you wish to live in peace, you must not begin by taking away my private box.

Your most humble and obedient servant,

The Phantom of the Opera

Monsieur Firmin Richard had hardly finished reading this letter, when Monsieur Armand Moncharmin entered carrying another exactly the same. They looked at each other and burst out laughing.

"They are keeping up the joke," said Moncharmin.

"I am not in the mood to allow myself to be humbugged much longer," said his partner.

"It's harmless enough," Moncharmin observed. "They just want a box for tonight."

Monsieur Firmin Richard told his secretary to give Box 5 on the grand tier to Messieurs Debienne and Poligny, provided it was not sold. It was not. It was sent round to them. Debienne lived at the corner of the rue Scribe and the boulevard des Capucines, Poligny in the Rue Auber. The Ghost's two letters had been posted at the boulevard des Capucines post office, as Moncharmin remarked after examining the envelopes.

"You see!" said Richard.

They shrugged their shoulders and regretted that two men of that age should amuse themselves with such childish tricks.

Next morning, the managers received a card of thanks from the ghost.

Cher Monsieur,

Thank you for a charming evening. Daae exquisite. Choruses want waking up. Will write you soon for the 240,000 francs, or 233,424 fr. 70c., to be correct. Messieurs Debienne and Poligny have sent me the 6575 fr. 30c. representing the first ten days of my allowance for the current year. Their privileges finished on the evening of the 10th inst.

With regards,

The Phantom

On the other hand, there was a letter from Messieurs Debienne and Poligny.

Gentlemen,

We are much obliged for your kind thought of us, but you will easily understand that the prospect of again hearing Faust, pleasant though it may be to ex-managers of the Opera, cannot make us forget that we have no right to occupy Box 5 on the grand tier, which is the exclusive property of him of whom we spoke to you when we went through the lease with you last. See Clause 63, final paragraph.

"Oh, these fellows are beginning to annoy me!" exclaimed Firmin Richard, snatching up the letter.

Finally, the managers decided to look into the matter of Box 5 for themselves.

Christine Daae, owing to a series of intrigues to which I will return later, did not immediately continue her triumph at the Opera. After the famous gala night, she sang once for the Duchess de Durich but this was the last occasion on which she was heard in society. She refused, without plausible excuse, to appear at a charity concert to which she had promised her assistance. She acted throughout as though she were no longer the mistress of her own destiny and as though she dreaded a fresh triumph.

She showed herself nowhere and the Vicomte de Chagny tried in vain to meet her. He wrote to her, asking leave to call upon her, but had given up all hope of receiving a reply, when, one morning, she sent him the following note :

I have not forgotten the little boy who went into the sea to rescue my scarf. I feel that I must write to you today, as I am going to Perros. Tomorrow is the anniversary of the death of my father, whom you knew and who was very fond of you. He is buried there in the graveyard of the little church, at the bottom of the hill where we used to play as children and where later we said goodbye for the last time.

Raoul, ecstatic at the thought of seeing her again, immediately took the night train to Perros. The nearer he drew to her, the more fondly he remembered the story of the little Swedish singer ...

Christine Daae's father was a natural musician, and there was not a fiddler in all of Scandinavia who played as well as he did. His reputation was widespread and when his wife died the father—who cared only for his daughter and his music—sold his patch of ground and went to Upsala in search of fame and fortune. He found nothing but poverty.

He returned to the country, wandering from fair to fair, while Christine, who never left his side, sang to his playing. One day, a Professor Valerius heard them at Limby Fair and took them to Gothenburg. He believed that the daughter had the makings of a great artist. He provided for her education and she made rapid progress, charming everyone with her beauty and grace.

When Valerius and his wife went to settle in France they took Daae and Christine with them. Madame Valerius treated Christine as a daughter, but Daae began to pine away with home-sickness.

One day Christine was walking by the sea singing to herself in her usual fashion when the wind blew her scarf far out on the waves. Just then she heard a voice nearby say :

"Don't worry, I'll go and fetch your scarf."

She turned and saw a little boy running into the sea. The next minute he was back and both boy and scarf were soaked through. Christine laughed and kissed the little boy, who was none other than the Vicomte Raoul de Chagny, staying at Lannion with his aunt.

That was the beginning of their friendship and during the season they saw each other almost every day. At the aunt's request, and seconded by Professor Valerius, Daae consented to give the young viscount some violin lessons. In this way, Raoul learned to love the same airs that had charmed Christine's childhood. Then autumn came and parted Raoul and Christine.

Christine tried not to think of him and devoted herself wholly to her art. She made wonderful progress and those who heard her prophesied that she would be the greatest singer in the world. But then her father died very suddenly, and with this loss she seemed also to lose her genius. She retained just enough to enter the Conservatoire, where she did not distinguish herself, attending the classes without enthusiasm and taking a prize only to please old Madame Valerius.

The first time that Raoul saw Christine at the Opera, he was charmed by the girl's beauty and by the sweet images of the past which it evoked, but at the same time he was puzzled by her sadness.

She seemed to have lost touch with things. He tried to attract her attention. More than once, he walked after her to the door of her box, but she did not see him. She appeared, for that matter, to see nobody. She was all indifference. Raoul suffered, for she was very beautiful, while he was shy and dared not confess his love, even to himself. And then came the revelation of that gala performance, when her angel's voice conquered his heart.

And then there was that man's voice behind the door—"You must love me!"—and no one in the room.

Why did she laugh when he reminded her of the incident of the scarf. Why did she not recognize him? And why had she now written to him?

Raoul reached Perros at last. He walked into the smoky parlour of the hotel and Christine stood smiling before him.

"You have come," she said. "I felt that I should find you here when I came back from Mass. Someone told me so at church."

"Who?" asked Raoul, taking her little hand in his.

"Why, my poor dead father!"

There was silence and then Raoul asked:

"Did your father tell you that I love you, Christine, and that I cannot live without you?"

Christine blushed to the eyes and turned away her head. In a trembling voice, she said, "I did not send for you to tell me such things as that."

"You sent for me, Christine; you knew that your letter would not leave me indifferent and that I would hasten to Perros. How can you have thought that, if you did not think I loved you?"

"I thought you would remember your games here, as children, in which my father so often joined. I really don't know what I thought. Perhaps I was wrong to write to you. This anniversary and your sudden appearance in my room at the Opera the other evening reminded me of the time long past and made me write to you."

There was something in Christine's attitude that struck Raoul as not quite natural. He did not feel any hostility in her, far from it. The sad tenderness shining in her eyes told him that. But why was this tenderness so sad? That was what he wished to know and what was irritating him.

"But why do you think I came to you, if not out of love?" continued Raoul, unburdening his heart to her, "When you saw me in your dressing-room, was that the first time you noticed me, Christine?"

She was incapable of lying. "No," she said, "I had often seen you in your brother's box. And also on the stage."

"I thought so!" said Raoul, "but then why, when you saw me in your room, at your feet, why did you answer me as though you did not know me?

"You don't answer!" he said angrily and unhappily. "Well, I will answer for you. It was because there was someone else in the room, Christine, someone to whom you said, 'I sing only for you! Tonight, I gave you my soul...' "

Christine seized Raoul's arm:

"Then you were listening behind the door?"

"Yes, because I love you ... And I heard everything."

"You heard what?"

"He said to you, 'Christine, you must love me!' "

At these words a deathly pallor spread over Christine's face, "Go on!" she commanded. "Go on! Tell me all you heard!"

At an utter loss to understand, Raoul answered:

"I heard him reply, when you said that you had given him your soul, 'Your soul is a beautiful thing, child, and I thank you. No emperor ever received so fair a gift. The angels wept tonight.' "

Christine gave a cry of grief and pain. Raoul was terror-stricken and tried to take her in his arms, but she escaped and fled in great disorder.

Raoul returned to the inn, feeling weary and very sad. He was told that Christine had gone to her bedroom, saying that she would not be down to dinner. Raoul dined alone, went to his room and tried to read, went to bed and tried to sleep. There was no sound in the next room.

The hours passed slowly. It was about half past eleven when he distinctly heard someone moving, with a light, stealthy step, in the room next to his. Without troubling for a reason, Raoul dressed, taking care not to make a sound, and waited. His heart gave a bound when he heard Christine's door turn slowly on its hinges. Softly opening the door, he saw Christine in the moonlight slip along the passage. She went down the stairs and he leant over the the banister above her. Suddenly, he heard two voices in rapid conversation. He caught one sentence.

"Don't lose the key."

It was the landlady's voice. The door facing the sea was opened and locked again. Then all was still.

Raoul ran back to his room and threw open the window. He could just make out Christine's white form on the deserted quay.

The first floor of the Setting Sun was at no great height and a tree growing against the wall enabled Raoul to climb down, unknown to the landlady. The good woman's amazement, therefore, was great when the young man was brought back to her the next morning half-frozen and more dead than alive. When she learnt that he had been found stretched at full length on the steps of the high altar of the little church she ran at once to tell Christine, who hurried down and did her best to revive him. He soon opened his eyes and was not long in recovering when he saw his friend's charming face bent over him.

A few weeks later, when the tragedy at the Opera necessitated the intervention of the public prosecutor, Monsieur Mifroid, the commissaire of police, examined the Vicomte de Chagny touching the events of the night at Perros. I quote the questions and answers as given in the official report (pp. 150 *et seq*):

Q. Did Mademoiselle Daae not see you come down from your room by the curious road which you selected?

R. No, Monsieur, although when walking behind her I took no pains to deaden the sound of my footsteps. In fact I was anxious that she should turn round and see me. But she seemed not to hear me and acted exactly as though I were not there. She quietly left the quay and then suddenly turned quickly up the road. The church clock had struck a quarter to twelve and I thought that this must have made her hurry, for she began almost to run and continued at this pace till she came to the churchyard.

Q. Was the gate open?

R. Yes, Monsieur, and this surprised me, but it did not seem to surprise Mademoiselle Daae.

Q. Was there no one in the churchyard?

R. I did not see anyone and if there had been I must have seen him. The moon was shining on the snow and made the night quite light.

Q. Are you superstitious?

R. No, Monsieur, I am a practising Catholic.

Q. In what condition of mind were you?

R. Very sane, I assure you. Mademoiselle Daae's curious action in going out at that hour had worried me at first, but as soon as I saw her go to the churchyard I thought that she meant to fulfil some pious duty on her father's grave. She knelt down by the grave and began to pray. At that moment, it struck midnight. At the last stroke, I saw her lift her eyes to the sky and stretch out her arms as though in ecstasy. I was wondering what the reason could be, when I myself raised my head and everything within me seemed drawn towards the Unseen, which was playing the most perfect music. Christine and I knew that music; we had heard it as children. But it had never been executed with such divine art, not even by her father. I remembered the story that Christine had told me about her Angel of Music. Her father used to say that when he died he would send his Angel of Music to protect her. If Christine's angel had existed, he could not have played more beautifully that night. When the music stopped, I seemed to hear a noise from the heap of bones—it was as though they were laughing, and I could not help shuddering.

Q. Did it not occur to you that the musician might be hiding behind that very heap of bones?

R. It was the one thought that did occur to me, Monsieur, so much so that I omitted to follow Mademoiselle Daae when she stood up and walked slowly to the gate. She was so much absorbed just then that I am not surprised that she did not see me.

Q. Then what happened, that you were found in the morning lying half-dead on the steps of the high altar?

R. First a skull rolled to my feet, then another and suddenly I saw a shadow glide along the sacristy wall. I ran up. The shadow had already pushed open the door and entered the church. But I was quicker than the shadow and caught hold of a corner of its cloak. At that moment we were just in front of the high altar and the moonlight fell straight upon us through the stained-glass windows of the apse. As I did not let go of the cloak, the shadow turned round and I saw a terrible death's head which stared at me with a pair of scorching eyes. I felt as if I were face to face with Satan and in the presence of this unearthly apparition my heart gave way, my courage failed me... and I remember nothing more until I recovered consciousness at the Setting Sun...

The next Saturday morning, on reaching their office, the joint managers found a letter from O.G., which said :

My Dear Sirs,

So is it to be war between us? If you still care for peace, here is my ultimatum. It consists of the four following conditions:

1. You must give me back my private box and I shall expect to have it at my free disposal from this day forward.

2. The part of Margarita shall be sung tonight by Christine Daae. Never mind about Carlotta: she will be ill.

3. I absolutely insist upon the good and loyal services of Madame Giry, my box-keeper.

4. Let me know by a letter handed to Madame Giry, who will see that it reaches me, that you accept, as did your predecessors, the terms of the lease relating to my monthly allowance. I will inform you later how you are to pay it to me.

If you refuse, you will give Faust tonight in a house with a curse upon it.

Take my advice and be warned in time.

The Phantom

That night the first act passed without incident.

When Christine entered the stage, she raised her head and saw the Vicomte de Chagny in his box. From that moment, her voice seemed less sure, less crystal clear than usual.

"What a queer girl she is!" said one of Carlotta's friends. "The other day she was divine and today she can't sing a note!"

In the beginning of the third act Carlotta made her entrance and, certain of herself and her success, she flung herself into her part without the least modesty or restraint. She was applauded all the more and her duet with Faust seemed about to bring her a new success, when suddenly a terrible thing happened.

Just as she sang, "Oh, how strange! Like a spell does the evening bind me!" Carlotta's voice fell and, "Co-ack!" She croaked like a toad!

There was consternation on Carlotta's face and on the faces of all the audience. The uproar in the house was indescribable. If the thing had happened to anyone but Carlotta, she would have been hooted. But everyone knew how perfect her voice was, and there was no display of anger, but only horror and dismay.

Meanwhile, in Box 5, Moncharmin and Richard had turned very pale. Leaning over the ledge of their box, they stared at Carlotta

as though they did not recognize her. The ghost had told them it
would come! The house had a curse upon it! Richard was calling
to Carlotta, in a smothered voice, "Well, go on!"

Bravely she started afresh on the fatal line at the end of which
the toad had appeared.

An awful silence succeeded the uproar. Again Carlotta's voice
filled the house.

"I feel without alarm... Co-ack!" The toad also had started
afresh.

The house broke into a wild tumult. The two managers collapsed
in their chairs and dared not even turn round. They had not the
strength, for the ghost was chuckling behind their backs. They
distinctly heard his mouthless voice saying in their ears:

"Tonight her singing will bring the chandelier down!"

They raised their eyes to the ceiling and cried out in horror. The
chandelier, the immense mass of the chandelier was slipping down,
coming towards them, at the call of that fiendish voice. Released
from its hook, it plunged from the ceiling and came smashing into
the middle of the stalls amid a thousand shouts of terror and a wild
rush for the doors.

The papers of the day state that there were numbers wounded and
one killed. The chandelier had crashed down upon the head of a
wretched woman who had come to the Opera for the first time in
her life, the woman whom Monsieur Richard had appointed to
succeed Madame Giry, the ghost's box-keeper.

That tragic evening was a bad one for all concerned. Carlotta
fell ill. As for Christine Daae, she disappeared after the performance
and was not seen for a fortnight.

Raoul was grief-stricken and told his brother everything that had
occurred. The count consoled him, without asking for explanations,
and suggested taking him out to dinner. Overcome as he was with
despair, Raoul would probably have refused any invitation that
evening if the count had not, as an inducement, told him that the
lady of his thoughts had been seen the night before with a man in
the Bois. At first, the viscount refused to believe it, but he was
given such exact details that he ceased protesting. She had been
seen, it appeared, driving in a brougham, with the window down.
There was a full moon shining, and she was recognized beyond a
doubt. As for her companion, only his shadowy outline was seen,

leaning back in the darkness. The carriage was going at a walking pace down a lonely drive behind the grandstand at Longchamp.

Raoul dressed in frantic haste, prepared to forget his distress in flinging himself, as people say, into "the vortex of pleasure". Alas, he was but a dull guest and, leaving his brother early, found himself by ten o'clock in the evening in a cab behind the Longchamp race-course.

It was freezing hard. The road lay deserted and very bright under the moonlight. He told the driver to wait for him at the corner of an avenue and, hiding as best he could stood stamping his feet to keep warm. He had remained like this for half an hour or so when a carriage turned into the road and came quietly in his direction, at a walking pace.

As it approached, he saw that a woman was leaning her head from the window. And suddenly the moon shed a pale gleam over her features.

"Christine!"

The sacred name of his love had sprung from his heart, but the next minute he would have given anything to withdraw it, for his call threw Christine into confusion. The window was raised and the carriage dashed past him before he could leap in front of the horses' heads. In a moment the brougham was no more than a black spot on the white road . . .

When his valet brought his letters the next morning he found Raoul sitting on his bed. He had not undressed and at the sight of his face the servant feared that some disaster had occurred. Raoul snatched the letters from the man's hands. He recognized Christine's paper and handwriting.

My dear,

Go to the masked ball at the Opera on the night after to-morrow. At twelve o'clock, be in the little room behind the chimney-piece of the big room. Stand near the door that leads to the Rotunda. Don't mention this appointment to a living soul. Wear a white domino and see that you are well masked. If you love me, do not let yourself be recognized.

Christine

The hour of the appointment came at last. With his face in a mask trimmed with long, thick lace, looking very foolish in his white wrap, the viscount thought himself most ridiculous. Men of the world do not go to the Opera ball in fancy dress. It was laughable. One thought, however, consoled the viscount : he would certainly never be recognized.

This ball was an exceptional affair, given some little time before Shrovetide, and it was expected to be much gayer, noisier and more Bohemian than the ordinary masked ball. Numbers of artists had arranged to go, accompanied by a whole cohort of models and pupils, and by midnight they were creating a tremendous din. Raoul arrived at five minutes to twelve, but did not linger to look at the motley dresses displayed all the way up the marble staircase, replied to no one and shook off the bold familiarity of a number of couples who had already become a trifle too gay. Crossing the big room and escaping from a mad whirl of dancers in which he was momentarily caught, he at last entered the room mentioned in Christine's letter. He found it crammed, for this small space was the point where all those who were going to supper in the Rotunda converged with those who were returning and here the fun waxed fast and furious.

Raoul leant against a door post and waited. He did not wait long. A black domino passed and made him a sign with her hand. He understood that it was she and followed her.

"Is that you, Christine?" he asked, between his teeth.

The black domino turned round promptly and raised her finger to her lips, no doubt to warn him not to mention her name again. Raoul continued to follow her in silence.

The black domino turned back from time to time to see if he was still following.

As Raoul once more passed through the great room, this time in the wake of his guide, he could not help noticing a group crowding round a person whose disguise, eccentric air and cadaverous appearance were causing a sensation. It was a man dressed all in scarlet, with a huge hat and feathers on the top of a wonderful death's-head. From his shoulders hung an immense red velvet cloak which trailed along the floor like a king's train; and on this cloak was embroidered, in gold letters, which everyone read and repeated aloud :

"Touch me not! I am Red Death!"

Then one, greatly daring, did try to touch him ... but a skeleton hand shot out of a crimson sleeve and violently seized the rash one's wrist and he, feeling the knuckle-bone clutch of Death, uttered a cry of pain and terror. When Red Death released him at last, he ran away like a madman, pursued by the jeers of the bystanders. It was at this moment that Raoul passed in front of the funereal masquerader, who had just happened to turn in his direction. And he nearly exclaimed : "The death's-head of Perros-Guirec!"

He had recognized him! He wanted to dart forward, forgetting Christine, but the black domino, who also seemed a prey to some strange excitement, caught him by the arm and dragged him from the room, far from the mad crowd through which Red Death was stalking.

The black domino kept on looking back and on two occasions apparently saw something that startled her, for she hurried her pace and Raoul's as though they were being pursued.

They went up two floors. Here the stairs and corridors were almost deserted. The black domino opened the door of a private box and beckoned Raoul to follow her. Then Christine, whom he now knew by the sound of her voice, closed the door behind them and warned him in a whisper to remain at the back of the box and on no account to show himself. Raoul took off his mask. Christine kept on hers. And when Raoul was about to ask her to remove it, he was surprised to see her put her ear to the partition and listen eagerly for a sound outside. Then she opened the door ajar, looked out into the corridor and in a low voice said, "He must have gone up higher."

Suddenly she exclaimed : "He is coming down again!"

She tried to close the door, but Raoul prevented her, for he had seen, on the top step of the staircase that led to the floor above, a red foot, followed by another . . . and slowly, majestically, the whole scarlet dress of Red Death met his eyes. And he once more saw the death's-head of Perros-Guirec :

"It's he!" he exclaimed. "This time he shall not escape me!"

But Christine had slammed the door at the moment when Raoul was on the point of rushing out. He tried to push her aside.

"Who do you mean?" she asked, in a changed voice. "Who shall not escape you?"

Raoul tried to overcome the girl's resistance by force, but she repelled him with a strength which he would not have suspected in her. He understood, or thought he understood, and at once lost his temper.

"Who?" he repeated, angrily. "Why, he, the man who hides

behind that hideous mask of death! The evil genius of the churchyard at Perros! Red Death! In a word, Madame, your friend ...
your Angel of Music! But I shall snatch off his mask, as I shall
snatch off my own, and this time we shall look each other in the
face, with no veil and no lies between us; and I shall know whom
you love and who loves you!"

He burst into a mad laugh, while Christine gave a disconsolate
moan behind her velvet mask. With a tragic gesture, she flung herself against the door : "In the name of our love, Raoul, you shall
not pass!"

He stopped. What had she said?... In the name of their love?
Never before had she confessed that she loved him. And yet she
had had opportunities enough! She wished to give the Red Death
time to escape. And in accents of childish hatred he cried, "You
lie, Madame, for you do not love me and you have never loved
me. What a poor fellow I must be to let you mock and flout me as
you have done. Why did you give me every reason for hope at
Perros?... for honest hope, Madame, for I am an honest man and
I believed you to be an honest woman, when your only intention
was to deceive me. You have taken a shameful advantage of the
candid affection of your benefactress herself, who continues to
believe in your sincerity, while you go about the Opera ball with
Red Death!... I despise you!"

And he burst into tears. She allowed him to insult her. She
thought of but one thing, to prevent him from leaving the box.

"You will beg my pardon one day for all those ugly words, Raoul,
and I shall forgive you!"

He shook his head.

"No, no, you have driven me mad! When I think that I had
only one object in life—to give my name to an Opera wench!"

"Raoul!... How can you?"

"I shall die of shame!"

"No, dear, live!" said Christine, in a grave and breaking voice.
"And ... goodbye. Goodbye, Raoul!"

The boy stepped towards her, risking one more sarcasm.

"Oh, but you must let me come and applaud you from time to
time."

"I shall never sing again, Raoul."

"Really?" he replied, still more sarcastically. "So he is taking you
off the stage, I congratulate you! But shall we meet in the Bois, one
of these evenings?"

"Not in the Bois nor anywhere, Raoul, you shall not see me again."

"May one at least ask to what darkness you are returning? For what hell are you leaving, mysterious lady . . . or for what paradise?"

"I came to tell you, dear, but I cannot tell you now . . . you would not believe me. You have lost faith in me, Raoul. It is finished!"

She spoke in such a despairing voice that the young man began to feel remorse for his cruelty.

"But can't you tell me what all this means?" he cried. "You are free, explain yourself, Christine, I beg of you!"

Christine simply took off her mask and said, "My dear, it is a tragedy!"

Raoul now saw her face and could not restrain an exclamation of surprise and terror. The fresh complexion of former days was gone. A mortal pallor covered those features which he had known so charming and so gentle, and sorrow had traced dark and unspeakably sad shadows under her eyes.

"My dearest!" he moaned, holding out his arms. "You promised to forgive me . . ."

"Perhaps. Some day, perhaps," she said, resuming her mask; and she went away, forbidding him, with a gesture, to follow her.

He tried to disobey her but she turned round and repeated her gesture of farewell with such authority that he dared not move a step.

He watched her till she was out of sight. Then he also went down among the crowd with an aching heart.

His footsteps took him to that room where he had first known suffering. He tapped at the door. There was no answer. He entered, as he had that night when he looked everywhere for the man's voice. The room was empty. A gas jet was burning, turned down low. He saw some letter paper on a little desk. He thought of writing to Christine, but he heard steps in the passage. He only just had time to hide in the inner room, which was separated from the dressing-room by a curtain.

Christine entered, took off her mask with a weary gesture and flung it on the table. She sighed and let her pretty head fall into her two hands. What was she thinking of? Of Raoul? No, for Raoul heard her murmur, "Poor Erik!"

What had this Erik to do with Christine's sighs and why was she pitying Erik when Raoul was so unhappy?

Christine began to write, deliberately and calmly, filling two, three, four sheets. Suddenly she raised her head and hid the sheets in her bodice. She seemed to be listening. Raoul also listened. Whence came that strange sound, that distant rhythm? A faint singing seemed to issue from the walls. The song became plainer ... now the words were distinguishable. He heard a voice, a very beautiful, very soft, very captivating voice which came nearer and nearer. It came through the wall and now it was in the room, in front of Christine. Christine rose and addressed the voice, as though speaking to someone beside her.

"Here I am, Erik," she said. "I am ready. But you are late."

Raoul, peeping from behind the curtain, could not believe his eyes, for they showed him nothing. Christine's face lit up. A smile of happiness appeared upon her bloodless lips, a smile like that of sick people when they receive the first hope of recovery.

The voice was singing the Wedding Night Song from *Romeo and Juliet*. Raoul saw Christine stretch out her arms to the voice as she had done, in the churchyard at Perros, to the invisible violin playing the Resurrection of Lazarus. And nothing could describe the passion with which the voice sang, "Fate links thee to me for ever and a day!"

The strains went through Raoul's heart. He managed to draw back the curtain that hid him and walked to where Christine stood. She herself was moving to the back of the room, the whole wall of which was occupied by a great mirror that reflected her image, but not his, for he was just behind and entirely concealed by her.

Christine walked towards her image in the glass and the image came towards her. The two Christines—the real one and the re-flection—touched and Raoul put out his arms to clasp the two in one embrace. But all of a sudden in a dazzle of light that sent him staggering, Raoul was suddenly flung back, an icy blast swept across his face and he saw not two but four, eight, twenty Christines spinning round him, laughing at him and fleeing so swiftly that he could not touch one of them. At last, everything stood still again and he saw himself in the glass. But Christine had disappeared.

The day after Christine had vanished before his eyes Raoul called to see Madame Valerius. He came upon a charming picture. Christine herself was seated by the old lady's bedside, and the latter was sitting up against her pillows, knitting. The pink and white had

returned to the young girl's cheeks. The dark rings round her eyes
had disappeared. If a veil of melancholy had not lingered over those
adorable features, the last trace of the weird drama in whose toils
that mysterious child was struggling, he could have believed that
Christine was not its heroine at all.

She rose, without showing any emotion, and offered him her
hand. But Raoul's stupefaction was so great that he stood there
dumbfounded, without saying a word.

"Well, Monsieur de Chagny," exclaimed Madame Valerius, "don't
you know our Christine? Her good fairy has sent her back to us!"

"Mama!" the girl broke in promptly, "you know there is no
such thing as the Angel of Music! I promised to explain everything to you one of these days and I hope to do so, but you promised
me, until that day, to be silent and to ask me no more questions
ever!"

"Provided that you promised never to leave me again. But have
you promised that, Christine?"

"Mama, all this cannot interest Monsieur de Chagny."

"On the contrary, Mademoiselle," said the young man, in a
voice which he tried to make firm and brave, but which still
trembled. "Anything that concerns you interests me to an extent
which perhaps you will one day understand. I do not deny that my
surprise equals my pleasure at finding you with your mother and
that, after what happened between us yesterday, I hardly expected
to see you here so soon. And I have been your friend too long not to
be alarmed, with Madame Valerius, at a disastrous adventure which
will remain dangerous until we have unravelled its threads and
which will certainly end by making you its victim, Christine."

"What does this mean?" cried Madame Valerius. "Is Christine in
danger?"

"Yes, Madame," said Raoul, "there is a terrible mystery around
us, which concerns you and Christine."

"Don't believe him, Mama, don't believe him," Christine
implored.

"Then tell me that you will never leave me again," begged her
mother.

Christine was silent and Raoul said, "That is what you must
promise, Christine."

"That is a promise which I refuse to make!" said the young girl,
haughtily. "I am mistress of my own actions, Monsieur de Chagny,
you have no right to control them and I will beg you to desist

henceforth. As to what I have done during the last fortnight, there is only one man in the world who has the right to demand an account of me—my husband! Well, I have no husband and I mean never to marry!"

She threw out her hands to emphasize her words and Raoul turned pale, not only because of the words which he had heard, but because he had caught sight of a plain gold ring on Christine's finger.

"You have no husband and yet you wear a wedding ring!"

He tried to seize her hand, but she swiftly drew it back.

"That's a present!" she said, blushing once more and vainly striving to hide her embarrassment.

"Christine! As you have no husband, that ring can only have been given by one who hopes to make you his wife! Why deceive us further? That ring is a promise and that promise has been accepted!"

"That's what I said!" exclaimed the old lady.

"And what did she answer, Madame?"

"What I chose," said Christine, driven to exasperation. "Don't you think, Monsieur, that this cross-examination has lasted long enough? As far as I am concerned . . ."

Raoul was afraid to let her finish her speech. He interrupted her.

"I beg your pardon for speaking as I did, Mademoiselle. But allow me to tell you what I have seen or what I thought I saw, for, to tell you the truth, I have sometimes been inclined to doubt the evidence of my eyes."

"Well, what did you see, sir, or think you saw?"

"I saw your ecstasy at the sound of the voice, Christine, the voice that came through the wall and that is what makes me so afraid for you. I believe you are under a very dangerous spell."

Raoul spoke with so much love and despair in his voice that Christine could not keep back a sob. She took his hands and looked at him with all the pure affection of which she was capable.

"Raoul," she pleaded urgently, "forget that voice. You must never try to fathom the mystery."

"Is it so very terrible?"

"There is no more awful mystery on this earth. Swear to me that you will make no attempt to find out," she insisted. "Swear to me that you will never come to my dressing-room again, unless I send for you."

"Then you promise to send for me sometimes, Christine?"

"I promise."

"When?"

"Tomorrow."

"Then I swear to do as you ask."

He kissed her hands and went away, cursing Erik and resolving to be patient.

The next day he saw her at the Opera. She was still wearing the plain gold ring. She was gentle and kind to him. She talked to him of the plans which he was forming, of his future, of his career.

He told her that the date of his next voyage had been put forward and that he would leave France in three weeks, or a month at latest. She suggested, almost gaily, that he must look upon the voyage with delight, as a stage towards his coming fame. And when he replied that fame without love was no attraction in his eyes, she treated him as a child whose sorrows were but short-lived.

She no longer smiled or jested. She seemed to be thinking of some new thing that had entered her mind for the first time. Her eyes were all aglow with it.

"What are you thinking of, Christine?"

"I am thinking that we shall not see each other again."

"And does that make you so radiant?"

"And that, in a month, we shall have to say goodbye for ever."

"Unless, Christine, we pledge our faith and wait for each other for ever."

She put her hand on his mouth.

"Hush, Raoul! You know there is no question of that. And we shall never be married, that is understood. But, if we cannot be married, we can be engaged! No one will know but ourselves, Raoul. We can be engaged, dear, for a month. In a month, you will go away and I can be happy at the thought of that month all my life long!"

She was enchanted with her inspiration and Raoul jumped at the idea. He bowed to Christine and said :

"Mademoiselle, I have the honour to ask for your hand."

"Why, you have both of them already, my dear betrothed! Oh, Raoul, how happy we shall be! We must play at being engaged from morning till night."

It was the most wonderful game in the world and they enjoyed it like the children they were. They played at hearts as other children might play at ball; only, as it was really their two hearts that they flung to and fro, they had to be very, very careful to catch them, each time, without hurting them.

Christine returned to the Opera in triumph. She renewed her extraordinary success of the gala performance. Since the "toad" incident Carlotta had not been able to appear on the stage. The terror of a fresh "co-ack" filled her heart and deprived her of all her power of singing and the theatre that had witnessed her incomprehensible disgrace had become odious to her. She contrived to cancel her contract. Christine was offered the vacant place for the time being.

The viscount, who was of course present, was the only one to suffer on hearing the thousand echoes of this fresh triumph, for Christine still wore her plain gold ring. A distant voice whispered in his ear, "She is wearing the ring again tonight and you did not give it to her. She gave her soul again tonight and did not give it to you. If she will not tell you what she has been doing these last two days, you must go and ask Erik!"

He ran behind the scenes and placed himself in her way.

"I will remove you from his power, Christine, I swear it. And you shall not think of him any more."

"Is it possible?"

She allowed herself the doubt—the encouragement—and she drew the young man up to the topmost floor of the theatre; far, far from the trapdoors.

"I shall hide you in some unknown corner of the world, where he cannot come to look for you. You will be safe, and then I shall go away, as you have sworn never to marry."

Christine seized Raoul's hands and squeezed them rapturously. But, suddenly alarmed, she turned away her head :

"Higher!" was all she said. "Higher still!"

And she dragged him up towards the topmost floor of the building.

He had difficulty in following her. They were soon under the roof, in the maze of timberwork. They slipped through the buttresses and the rafters; they ran from beam to beam as they might have run from tree to tree in a forest.

And, despite the care which she took to look behind her at every moment, she failed to see a shadow which followed her like her own shadow, which stopped when she stopped, which started again when she did and made no more noise than a well-conducted shadow should. They reached the roof and the shadow had followed behind them, clinging to every step. They little suspected its presence when they at last sat down, trustingly, under the mighty protection of Apollo, who, with a sweep of his bronze arm, lifted his huge lyre to the heart of a crimson sky.

Christine said, "Soon we shall go farther and faster than the clouds, to the end of the world and then you will leave me, Raoul. But if, when the moment comes for you to take me away, I refuse to go with you, you must carry me off by force!"

"Are you afraid that you will change your mind, Christine?"

"I don't know," she said, shaking her head. "He is a demon!" And she shivered and nestled in Raoul's arms with a moan. "I am afraid now of going back to live with him... in the ground!"

"But what compels you to go back, Christine?" he asked frantically.

"If I do not go back to him, terrible misfortunes may happen! But I can't do it, I know one ought to be sorry for people who live underground but he is too horrible! I have only a day left and, if I do not go, he will drag me down with him, and go on his knees before me. He will tell me that he loves me! And he will cry! Oh, those tears, Raoul, I cannot bear to see those tears flow again!"

She wrung her hands in anguish, while Raoul pressed her to his heart.

"No, no, you shall never again hear him tell you that he loves you, or see his tears! We must leave at once, Christine!"

And he tried to drag her away then and there. But she stopped him.

"No, no," she said, shaking her head sadly. "Not now! It would be too cruel. Let him hear me sing tomorrow evening, and then we will go away. You must come and fetch me in my dressing-room at midnight exactly. He will be waiting for me by the lake. You must take me away, Raoul, even if I refuse, for I feel that, if I go back this time, I shall perhaps never return..."

And she gave a sigh which seemed to be echoed by another sigh behind her.

"Did you hear that?"

"No," said Raoul, "I heard nothing..."

"It is too terrible," she said, "to be always trembling like this! And yet we run no danger here. We are at home, in the sky, in the open air, in the light. The sun is flaming and night-birds cannot bear to look at the sun. I have never seen him by daylight. It must be awful! Oh, the first time I saw him I thought I would die.

"I heard his voice for three months without seeing him. The first time, I thought as you did that the angelic voice was singing in another room. I went out and looked everywhere, but I could not find the voice outside my room, though it went on steadily inside. And it not only sang, but it spoke to me and answered my questions, like a real man's voice. I had never forgotten the Angel of Music whom my poor father had promised to send to me as soon as he was dead. I really think that Mama was a little bit to blame. I told her about it, and she at once said, 'It must be the Angel; at any rate you can do no harm by asking him.' I did so, and the man's voice replied that yes, it was the Angel's voice, the voice which I was expecting and which my father had promised me.

"From that time onward, the voice and I became great friends. It asked if it could give me lessons every day. You have no idea, though you have heard the voice, of what those lessons were like.

"We were accompanied by a music which I had never heard before. It was behind the wall and wonderfully accurate. The voice seemed to understand mine exactly.

"One day it said, 'Wait and see; we shall conquer Paris!' And I waited and lived on in a sort of ecstatic dream. It was then that I saw you for the first time, one evening, in the audience. I was so glad to see you again that I never thought of concealing my delight when I reached my dressing-room. Unfortunately the voice was there before me and soon noticed that something had happened. It asked what was the matter and I saw no reason for keeping our story secret or concealing the place which you filled in my heart. Then the voice was silent. I called to it, but it did not reply; I begged and entreated, but in vain. I was terrified lest it had gone for good. I wish to heaven it had, dearest! That night, I went home feeling desperate. I told Mama who said, 'Why, of course, the voice is jealous!' "

Christine stopped and laid her head on Raoul's shoulder. They sat like that for a moment, in silence, and they did not see a few steps away from them, the creeping shadow of two great black wings, a shadow that came along the roof, so near that it could have stifled them with one gesture.

"The next day," continued Christine with a sigh, "I went back to my dressing-room and the voice was there. It told me plainly that if I must bestow my heart on earth, there was nothing for it to do but to go back to Heaven. And it said this with such an accent of human sorrow that I ought then and there to have suspected and begun to believe that I was the victim of my deluded senses. But my faith in the voice, with which the memory of my father was so closely mingled, remained undisturbed. I feared nothing so much as that I might never hear it again. I had thought about my love for you and realized how useless it was. Whatever happened, your position in society forbade me to contemplate the possibility of ever marrying you, and I swore to the voice that you were no more to me than a brother, nor ever would be, and that my heart was incapable of any earthly love. And that, dear, was why I refused to recognize or see you, when I met you on the stage or in the passages.

"I don't know how it was that Carlotta did not come to the theatre that night nor why I was called upon to sing in her stead, but I sang with a rapture I had never felt before and I felt for a moment as if my soul were leaving my body. Then I felt myself fainting. I closed my eyes and when I opened them you were by my side. But the voice was there also, Raoul! It said that, if I did not love you, I would not avoid you, but treat you like any other friend. At last I said to the voice, 'That will do! I am going to Perros tomorrow, to pray on my father's grave, and I shall ask Monsieur Raoul de Chagny to go with me.' 'Do as you please, replied the voice, 'but I shall be at Perros too, for I am wherever you are, Christine.' "

"But why did you not get rid of the nightmare, once you knew the truth about him?" Raoul begged her.

"Know the truth, Raoul? But I was not caught in the nightmare until the day when I learned the truth! Do you remember the terrible evening when the chandelier crashed to the floor of the opera house? The voice had told me that it would be at the performance and I was really afraid for it, just as if it had been an ordinary person. I thought that if it was safe it would be sure to be in my dressing-room, so I went there immediately. Suddenly I heard a long, beautiful wail and recognized it to be the music which you and I heard at Perros. Then the voice began to sing, 'Come! And believe me! Who so believes in me shall never die!' I cannot tell you the effect which that music had upon me. It seemed to command me, personally, to come to it and I followed. There was a mirror in front of me and suddenly I was outside the room without knowing how!

"I was in a dark passage and I saw a faint red glimmer in a distant angle of the wall. I cried out. My voice was the only sound, for the

singing and the violin had stopped. And then I felt a hand on mine
—or rather a stone-cold, bony thing that seized my wrist and did not
let go. I struggled for a little while and then gave up. I was dragged
towards the little red light and then I saw that I was in the hands of
a man wrapped in a large cloak and wearing a mask that hid his
whole face. I made one last effort; I opened my mouth to scream
but a hand closed it, a hand that smelt of death. Then I fainted.
When I opened my eyes, we were still surrounded by darkness. We
were on the edge of a lake whose leaden waters stretched into the
darkness. The red light lit up the bank and I saw a little boat fastened
to an iron ring on the wharf. The man lifted me into the boat, jumped
in and seized the oars. He rowed with a quick, powerful stroke and
his eyes, under the mask, never left me. We slipped across the noiseless water in the red light. Then we were in the dark again as we
touched the shore. And I was once more taken up in the man's arms.
I cried aloud. Then there was a dazzling light and I found myself
in the middle of a drawing-room which seemed to be decorated with
nothing but flowers, cut flowers, magnificent and stupid at the same
time, because of the silk ribbons that tied them into baskets. They
were much too elegant, like those which I used to find in my dressing-
room after a first night. And, in the midst of all these flowers, stood
the black shape of the man in the mask, who said, 'Don't be afraid,
Christine, you are in no danger.' It was the voice! I rushed at the
mask and tried to snatch it away, so as to see the face of the voice.
But it backed away and said, 'You are in no danger, so long as you
do not touch the mask.' Taking me gently by the wrists, he forced
me into a chair, then went down on his knees before me. I felt that
this was some terrible, eccentric person who had mysteriously succeeded in taking up his abode there, under the cellars of the Opera
House. And the voice which was on its knees before me was a man!
I began to cry. The man, still kneeling, must have understood the
cause of my tears, for he said, 'It is true, Christine! I am not an
angel, nor a genius, nor a ghost ... I am Erik!' "

Christine's narrative was again interrupted. An echo behind them
seemed to repeat the word after her:

"Erik!"

They both turned round and saw that night had fallen. Raoul
made a movement as though to rise, but Christine pulled him
back, "Don't go," she said. "I want you to know everything here!"

"But why here, Christine?"

"Because we are safe here."

"But Christine! Something tells me that we are wrong to wait till tomorrow evening and that we ought to fly at once."

"I tell you that, if he does not hear me sing tomorrow, it will cause him infinite pain."

"Does he love you so much?"

"He would commit murder for me."

"Then why, when you were able to run away, did you go back to him?"

"Because I had to. And you will understand that when I tell you how I left him."

"Oh, I hate him!" cried Raoul. "And you, Christine, tell me, do you hate him too?"

"No," said Christine, simply. "He fills me with horror, but I do not hate him. How can I hate him, Raoul? Think of Erik at my feet, in the house on the lake, underground. He lays at my feet an immense and tragic love. He has imprisoned me with him underground, for love! But he respects me. And, when I stood up, Raoul, and told him that I could only despise him if he did not give me my liberty, he offered it. Then he sang to me. And I listened and stayed! That night, we did not exchange another word. He sang me to sleep.

"When I woke up I was alone, lying on a sofa in a simply-furnished little bedroom. I soon discovered that I was a prisoner. I saw on the chest of drawers a note in red ink which said, 'My dear Christine, you do not need to be afraid. You have no better, no more respectful, friend in the world than myself. You are at home here.' I felt sure that I had fallen into the hands of a madman. I ran round the room, looking for a way of escape, but could not find one. I was completely alone in the silence when I heard three taps against the wall. Erik walked in through a door which I had not noticed and which he left open. His arms were full of boxes and parcels and he arranged them on the bed while I shouted at him and called upon him to take off his mask if it covered the face of an honest man. He replied 'You shall never see Erik's face.' Then he said that he loved me, but that he would never tell me so except when I gave him leave and that the rest of the time would be spent in music. 'What do you mean by the rest of time?' I asked. 'Five days,' he replied. I asked him if I should then be free and he said, 'You will be free, Christine, for, when those five days are past, you will have learned not to fear me and then you will come back to see your poor Erik!'

"He said he would like to show me over his flat, and he opened a door before me. 'This is my room, if you care to see it. It is rather curious.' I felt as if I were entering a mortuary chamber. The walls were all hung with black. In the middle of the room was a canopy, hung with red brocade curtains, and under the canopy an open coffin. 'That is where I sleep,' said Erik. 'One has to get used to everything in life, even to eternity.' The sight upset me so much that I turned away my head.

"Then I saw the keyboard of an organ which filled one whole side of the wall. On the desk was a music-book covered with red notes. I asked leave to look at it, and, on the first page, read, *Don Juan Triumphant*. 'Yes,' he said, 'I compose sometimes. I began that work twenty years ago. When I have finished, I shall take it away with me in that coffin and never wake up again.' 'You must work at it as seldom as you can,' I said. He replied, 'I sometimes work at it for fourteen days and nights together, during which I live on music only, and then I rest for years at a time.' 'Will you play me something out of your *Don Juan Triumphant*?' I asked, thinking to please him. 'You must never ask me that,' he said, in a gloomy voice. 'I will play you Mozart if you like, but my Don Juan burns, Christine. You see, there is some music so terrible that it consumes all who approach it. Fortunately you have not come to that music yet, for you would lose all your pretty colouring and nobody would know you when you returned to Paris. Let us sing something operatic!' He spoke these last words as though he were flinging an insult at me.

"We at once began the duet in Othello, and I sang Desdemona with a despair, a terror, which I had never displayed before. As for him, his voice thundered forth his vengeful soul at every note. Love, jealousy, hatred burst out around us in harrowing cries. Erik was Othello himself. Suddenly, I wanted desperately to see beneath the mask. I wanted to know the face of the voice and, with a movement which I was utterly unable to control, my fingers swiftly tore away the mask. Oh, horror, horror, horror!

"If I live to be a hundred, I shall never forget the superhuman cry of grief and rage which he uttered when the terrible sight appeared before my eyes. Raoul, you have seen death's-heads, when they have been dried and withered by the years and perhaps you saw his death's-head at Perros. And then you saw the Red Death at the masked ball. But all those death's-heads were motionless. Imagine, the terror of the Red Death's mask suddenly coming to

life in the mighty fury of a demon. I fell back against the wall and
he came to me, grinding his teeth hideously, and, as I fell upon my
knees, he hissed mad, incoherent words and curses at me. Leaning
over me, he cried, 'Look! Do you want to see? See! Feast your
eyes, and your soul on my cursed ugliness! Look at Erik's face!
Are you satisfied? I'm a good-looking fellow, eh? When a woman
has seen me she belongs to me. She loves me for ever! I am a kind
of Don Juan, you know!' And, drawing himself up to his full
height, with his hands on his hips, wagging the hideous thing that
was his head on his shoulders, he roared, 'Look at me! *I am Don
Juan triumphant!*' And when I turned away my head and begged
for mercy, he drew my head back to him, brutally, twisting his
dead fingers into my hair."

"Enough! Enough!" cried Raoul. "I will kill him. In heaven's
name, Christine, tell me where he is! I must kill him!"

"Oh, Raoul, listen, listen! He dragged me by my hair and then . . .
and then . . . Oh, it is too horrible!"

"Well, what? Out with it!" exclaimed Raoul, fiercely.

"Then he hissed at me, 'Ah, I frighten you, do I? Perhaps you
think that I have another mask, eh, and that this head is a mask?
Well,' he roared, 'tear it off as you did the other! I insist! Give me
your hands!' And he seized my hands and dug them into his awful
face. He tore his flesh with my nails, his terrible dead flesh! 'Know,'
he shouted, 'that it is a corpse that loves you and adores you and
will never, never leave you! Look, I am not laughing now, I am
crying, crying for you, Christine, who have torn off my mask and
who therefore can never leave me again! As long as you thought
I was handsome you could have come back, I know you would have
come back . . . but now that you know my hideousness, you would
run away for good. So I must keep you here! Oh, mad Christine,
who wanted to see me!' He had let go of me at last and was sobbing dreadfully. Then he disappeared into his room, closed the
door and left me alone again.

"Presently I heard the sound of the organ, and what he played
was utterly different from what had charmed me up to then. His
Don Juan Triumphant (for I was sure that he had rushed to his
masterpiece to forget the horror of the moment) seemed to me at
first one long, agonizing, magnificent sob. But, little by little, I
began to feel that it expressed every emotion, every suffering of
which mankind is capable. It intoxicated me and I opened the
door that separated us. Erik rose, as I entered, but dared not turn

in my direction. 'Erik,' I cried 'show me your face without fear! I swear that you are the most unhappy and sublime of men, and, if ever again I tremble when I see your face it will be because I am thinking of the splendour of your genius!'

"Then Erik turned round, for he believed me. He fell at my feet with words of love in his dead mouth. What more can I tell you, dear? This went on for a fortnight, a fortnight during which I lied to him. My lies were as hideous as the monster who inspired them but they were the price of my liberty. Gradually, I gave him such confidence that he ventured to take me walking on the banks of the lake and to row me in the boat. Towards the end of my captivity, he let me out through the gates that close the underground passages in the rue Scribe. Here a carriage awaited us and took us to the Bois. The night when we met you was nearly fatal to me, for he is terribly jealous of you and I had to tell him that you were soon going away. At last, after a fortnight during which I was filled with pity, enthusiasm, despair and horror by turns, he believed me when I told him I would come back."

"And you went back, Christine," groaned Raoul.

"Yes, dear, and I must tell you that it was not his frightful threats when setting me free that helped me to keep my word, but his terrible unhappiness which bound me to him more than I realized when I left him. Poor Erik!"

"Christine," said Raoul, rising, "you tell me that you love me, but you were free for only a few hours when you returned to Erik. Remember the masked ball!"

"Yes, but remember also that those few hours I spent with you Raoul, were dangerous for both, of us."

"I doubted your love for me during those hours."

"Do you doubt it still, Raoul? Then know that each of my visits to Erik increased my horror of him, for each time I saw him it seemed to drive him mad with love! And I am so frightened, so frightened!"

"You are frightened, but do you love me? If Erik were good-looking, would you love me, Christine?"

She rose in her turn, threw her two trembling arms round the young man's neck and said, "Oh, my dearest Raoul, if I did not love you, I would not give you my lips! Take them, for the first time and the last."

They heard a low moan which seemed to come from far away and then rose in volume until the night was suddenly rent asunder with Erik's rage. They fled, but before they disappeared they saw high above them astride Apollo's great statue the outline of a huge night-bird that stared at them with its eyes blazing forth sparks of fire.

Raoul and Christine ran and ran, not stopping until they came to the eighth floor.

There was no performance at the Opera that night and the passages were empty. Suddenly a strange man appeared before them. "No, not this way!" he said urgently.

He pointed to another passage by which they were to reach the wings. Raoul wanted to stop and ask for an explanation. But the form, clad in a long frock-coat and a pointed cap, said, "Quick! Run quickly!"

Christine was already dragging Raoul away.

"But who is he? Who is that man?" he asked.

Christine replied, "It's the Persian."

"What's he doing here?"

"I don't know. He is always in the Opera."

"You are making me run away, for the first time in my life, when I should have stayed. If that really was Erik we saw I ought to have nailed him to Apollo's lyre!"

"You are getting like me now," Christine warned, "seeing him everywhere! What we took for his blazing eyes was probably a couple of stars shining through the strings of the lyre."

And with that she left him abruptly.

Raoul spent the next day in his preparations for their flight together. At nine o'clock that evening a carriage with the curtains drawn took its place in the rank on the Rotunda side. In front of it were three broughams, belonging respectively to Carlotta, who had suddenly returned to Paris, to Sorelli and, at the head of the rank, to the Comte Philippe de Chagny. No one left the barouche. The coachman remained on his box. And the three other coachmen remained on theirs.

A shadow in a long black coat moved along the pavement between the Rotunda and the carriages, examined the barouche carefully, went up to the horses and the coachman and then went away without saying a word.

They were giving Faust, as it happened, to a splendid house. Christine Daae unfortunately met with a rather cold reception, as the audience found it difficult to accept a debutante in such a difficult part. The singer felt that the house was against her and was confused by their attitude.

As a result she lost her self-assurance. She trembled. She felt on the verge of breakdown. In the front of the house, people remembered the catastrophe that had befallen Carlotta at the end of that act and the historic "co-ack" which had momentarily interrupted her career in Paris.

Just then, Carlotta made a sensational entrance in a box facing the stage. Poor Christine raised her eyes and recognized her rival. She thought she saw a sneer on her lips, and that saved her. She forgot everything in order to triumph once more. From that moment, the prima donna sang with all her heart and soul. She tried to surpass all that she had done up to that time and she succeeded.

But at the moment which was to have been her greatest triumph, when she sang with her angel's voice, "My spirit longs with thee to rest," the stage was suddenly plunged into darkness. It happened so quickly that the spectators hardly had time to realize what was going on, for when the lights immediately came on again Christine Daae was no longer there!

Raoul's first thought after Christine's fantastic disappearance was to accuse Erik. He no longer doubted the almost supernatural powers of the man in this domain of the Opera where he had set up his empire. Raoul rushed through the Opera house in a mad fit of love and despair.

"Where are you going so fast, Monsieur de Chagny?" asked a voice behind him.

Raoul turned and recognized the Persian of the night before. He stopped short.

"It's you!" he cried, in a feverish voice. "You know Erik's secrets. Who are you?"

"You know who I am. I am the Persian. I hope, Monsieur de Chagny, that you have not betrayed Erik's secret?"

"And why should I hesitate to betray that monster, sir?" Raoul rejoined haughtily, trying to shake off the stranger.

"I hope that you said nothing about Erik, sir, because Erik's secret is also Christine Daae's and to talk about one is to talk about the other."

"Sir," said Raoul, becoming more and more impatient, "you

seem to know about many things that interest me, but I have no time to listen to you!"

"Once more," the man interrupted, "where are you going so fast?"

"Can you not guess? To Christine Daae's assistance."

"Then, sir, stay here, for Christine Daae is here!"

"How do you know?"

"I was at the performance and I know that no one in the world but Erik could contrive an abduction like that! Oh," he said, with a deep sigh, "I recognized the monster's touch!"

"Sir," said Raoul, "I do not know what your intentions are, but can you do anything to help me find her?"

"I think so, Monsieur de Chagny; that is why I spoke to you."

And the Persian led him down passages which Raoul had never seen before, even with Christine. They arrived at Christine's dressing-room and the Persian went straight to the very thin partition that separated the dressing-room from the room next to it. He listened and then coughed loudly.

There was a sound of someone moving in the next room, and a few seconds later there was a tap at the door.

"Come in," said the Persian.

A man entered, dressed in the same manner as the Persian. He took a case from under his coat, put it on the dressing-table, bowed and went to the door.

"Did no one see you come in, Darius?"

"No, master."

"Let no one see you go out."

The servant glanced down the passage and swiftly disappeared. The Persian opened the case. It contained a pair of long pistols.

"When Christine Daae was carried off, I sent word to my servant to bring me these pistols," he explained. "I have had them a long time and they can be relied upon."

"Do you mean to fight a duel?" asked the young man.

"It will certainly be a duel which we shall have to fight," said the other, examining the priming of his pistols, and handing him one.

"But I do not understand why you are risking your life," said Raoul. "You must certainly hate Erik!"

"No, Monsieur," replied the Persian, sadly, "I do not hate him. If I hated him, he would long ago have ceased to do harm."

"Has he done you harm?"

"I have forgiven him the harm which he has done me."

"I do not understand you. You treat him as a monster, you speak of his crimes, and yet I find in you the same inexplicable pity that I saw in Christine!"

The Persian did not reply. He fetched a stool and set it against the wall facing the great mirror that filled the whole of the partition opposite. Then he climbed on the stool and seemed to be looking for something.

"Ah," he said, after a long search, "I have it!" He pressed against a corner in the pattern of the paper. Then he turned round and jumped off the stool. "In half a minute," he said, "we shall be on his road!"

And, crossing the whole length of the dressing-room, he felt the great mirror. "No, it is not yielding yet," he muttered. Bearing against the mirror after a short silence he said, "It takes some time to release the counterbalance, when you press on the spring from the inside of the room. It is different when you are behind the wall and can act directly on the counterbalance. Then the mirror turns at once."

"It's not turning!" said Raoul, impatiently.

"Oh, wait! You have time enough to be impatient, sir. The mechanism has obviously become rusty, or else the spring isn't working—unless it is something else," added the Persian anxiously.

"What?"

"He may simply have cut the cord of the counterbalance and blocked the whole apparatus."

"Why should he? He does not know that we are coming this way!"

"I daresay he suspects it, for he knows that I understand the system."

"It's not turning! And Christine, sir, Christine?"

The Persian said coldly: "We shall do all that it is humanly possible to do. But he may stop us at the first step. He commands the walls, the doors and the trapdoors. In my country, he was known by a name which means 'the trapdoor lover'."

"But why do these walls obey him alone? He did not build them!"

"Yes, sir, that is just what he did do."

Raoul looked at him in amazement, but the Persian made a sign for him to be silent and pointed to the glass. There was a sort of shivering reflection, then all became stationary again.

"You see, sir, that it is not turning," Raoul said. "Let us take another road."

"Tonight, there is no other," declared the Persian in a sad voice. "Now look out! And be ready to fire!"

He raised his pistol opposite the glass. Raoul imitated his movement. With his free arm, the Persian drew the young man to his chest and the mirror turned in a blinding daze of cross-lights, hurling them from the full light into the deepest darkness.

"Hold your hand high, ready to fire!" repeated Raoul's companion quickly.

The wall behind them closed again and the two men stood motionless for a moment, holding their breaths.

At last the Persian made a movement, and Raoul heard him drop to his knees and feel for something in the dark. He stood up and Raoul saw that he had a lantern. The little red disc turned in every direction and Raoul observed that the floor, the walls and the ceiling were all made out of planking. This was Erik's secret route to reach Christine's dressing-room. It had been contrived at the time of the Paris Commune, to allow the gaolers to move their prisoners straight to the dungeons constructed for them in the cellars.

The Persian went on his knees again and put his lantern on the ground. He seemed to be working at the floor. Suddenly he turned off his light. Then Raoul heard a faint click and saw a very pale luminous square in the floor of the passage. It was as though he had opened a window.

"Follow me," the Persian commanded, "and do all that I do."

Raoul turned to the opening and saw his guide, who was still on his knees, then hang by his hands from the rim, with his pistol between his teeth, and slide into the cellar below. Raoul went on his knees also and hung from the trap with both hands.

"Let go!" said a voice.

He dropped into the arms of the Persian and found he was in the cellars.

The cellars of the Opera are enormous and five in number. Following the Persian, Raoul wondered what he would have done without him in that extraordinary labyrinth. They eventually arrived in the huge cellars directly below the stage. The Persian touched a partition-wall and said, "If I am not mistaken, this wall belongs to the house on the lake."

Raoul flung himself against the wall and listened eagerly. But he heard nothing, nothing except distant steps sounding on the floor of the upper portions of the theatre.

The Persian darkened his lantern again. "We shall try another way of getting in."

And he led him back to the little staircase by which they had descended.

They went up, stopping at each step, until they reached the third cellar. Here the Persain motioned to Raoul to go down on his knees and in this way they crawled to the end wall. The Persian pressed against the wall; then a stone gave way, leaving a narrow hole in the wall.

He stopped almost at once. Raoul heard him say in a whisper, "We shall have to drop a few yards, without making a noise. Take off your boots."

He crawled a little farther on his knees, then turned right round and, facing Raoul, said : "I am going to hang by my hands from the edge of the stone and let myself drop into his house. You must do exactly the same. Do not be afraid. I will catch you in my arms."

Raoul soon heard a dull thud as the Persian jumped down and then dropped in his turn.

"Hush!" whispered the Persian.

And they stood motionless, listening.

The Persian stooped and picked up something, a sort of cord, which he examined for a second and flung away with horror.

"The Punjab lasso!"

"What is it?" asked Raoul.

The Persian shivered : "It might very well be the rope which Joseph Buquet was hanged with, the rope which they spent such a long time looking for!"

And, suddenly seized with a fresh anxiety, he moved his lantern over the walls. Then they saw a curious thing; the trunk of a tree, which seemed to be still quite alive, and the branches of that tree running right up the walls and disappearing into the ceiling.

Because of the light's smallness, it was difficult at first to make out what it looked like. They saw a corner of a branch, a leaf, then another leaf and next to it, nothing at all but a ray of light that seemed to make its own reflection. Raoul passed his hand over that reflection, "The wall is a looking-glass!" he said excitedly.

"Yes, a looking-glass!" gasped the Persian. Passing the hand that held the pistol over his moist forehead, he said, "We have dropped into the torture-chamber!"

What the Persian knew of this torture-chamber and what happened to his companion and himself shall be told in his own words, as set down in a manuscript which he left behind him and which I reproduce as I found it.

THE PERSIAN'S NARRATIVE

It was the first time that I had ever been to the house on the lake. I had often begged Erik to open its mysterious doors to me. He always refused. Watch him as I might, the darkness was always too impenetrable to allow me to see how he worked the door in the wall on the lake. One day, when I thought I was alone, I stepped into the boat and rowed towards that part of the wall through which I had seen Erik disappear. It was then that I heard the siren who guarded the approach and whose charm was very nearly fatal to me.

I had no sooner left the bank than the silence was disturbed by a sort of whispered singing that hovered all around me. It rose softly from the waters of the lake, following me, moving with me, and it was so soft that it did not even alarm me. On the contrary, in my longing to approach the source of that sweet and enticing harmony, I leaned out of my little boat for I believed that the singing came from the water itself. By this time I was in the middle of the lake. The voice—for it was now distinctly a voice—was beside me, in the water.

I leant farther and farther over the side, and suddenly two monstrous arms seized me by the neck, dragging me down to the depths. I should certainly have been lost, if I had not had time to give a cry by which Erik knew me. For it was he in the water and, instead of drowning me, as was certainly his first intention, he swam with me and laid me gently on the bank.

"How imprudent you are!" he said as he stood before me, dripping with water. "Why do you try to enter my house? I did not invite you. I don't want you there, nor anybody! Did you save my life only to make it unbearable to me? However great the service rendered, Erik will perhaps end by forgetting it, and you know that nothing can restrain Erik, not even Erik himself."

I spoke to him severely. "You nearly killed me!" I said. "And your trick may have been fatal to others! You know what you promised me, Erik? No more murders!"

"Have I really committed murders?" he asked, putting on his most amiable air.

"Wretched man!" I cried. "Have you forgotten Mazenderan?"

"Yes," he replied, in a sadder tone, "I prefer to forget it."

"All that belongs to the past," I declared, "but there is the present, because if I had wished there would have been none at all for you. Remember that, Erik; I saved your life!"

And I took advantage of the turn in the conversation to speak to him of something that had long been on my mind.

"Erik," I asked, "Erik, swear that..."

"Swear what?" he retorted. "You know I never keep my oaths. Oaths are made to catch fools with."

"The chandelier, Erik."

"What about the chandelier?"

"You know what I mean."

"Oh," he sniggered, "I don't mind telling you about *that*. It wasn't I! The chandelier was very old and worn."

When Erik laughed he was more terrible than ever. He jumped into the boat, laughing so horribly that I could not help trembling. "Very old and worn, my dear Daroga!* And now, Daroga, take my advice and go dry yourself, or you'll catch cold. And whatever you do, don't try to enter my house. I should be sorry to have to dedicate my Requiem Mass to you!"

So, still chuckling, he pushed off from shore and soon disappeared in the darkness of the lake.

From that day, I gave up all thought of penetrating into his house by way of the lake. That entrance was obviously too well guarded, especially since he had learnt that I knew about it. But I felt that there must be another entrance, for I had often seen Erik disappear in the third cellar, though I could not imagine how.

By watching his movements, I soon discovered the curious relationship which existed between the monster and Christine Daae. Hiding in her room, I listened to wonderful musical displays that evidently sent Christine into such ecstasy, but I was puzzled at how Erik's voice—which was as loud as thunder or as soft as an angel's voice—could have made her forget his ugliness. I understood, however, when I learned that Christine had never seen him! I went to the dressing-room and, remembering the lessons he had once given me, I had no difficulty in discovering the trick that

* *Editor's note: Daroga* is Persian for chief of police.

made the wall with the mirror swing round, and thus I ascertained the means by which he made his voice carry to Christine. In this way also I discovered the road that led to the well and the dungeon —the Communards' dungeon—and also the trapdoor that enabled Erik to go straight to the cellars below the stage.

I discovered that Christine was a prisoner in the house on the lake. Without hesitation, I resolved to return to the shore, notwithstanding the certain danger. For twenty-four hours, I lay watching for the monster to appear. I was beginning to think that he had gone through the other door, in the third cellar when I heard a slight splash in the dark. I saw the two yellow eyes shining like candles and soon the boat touched shore. Erik jumped out and walked up to me. His anger was terrible to see. "Yes, you must learn," he said, "once and for all. I tell you that with your recklessness I shall soon be discovered, and if I am you will be in trouble! I won't be answerable for anything that happens to you."

"It's not Erik that I'm after!" I replied.

"Who then?"

"You know as well as I do, it's Christine Daae."

He was furious, "I have every right to see her in my house. I am loved for my own sake."

"That's not true," I said. "You have carried her off and are keeping her locked up."

"Christine Daae shall leave as she pleases and come back again! She will come back because she loves me for myself!"

I said, "I shall believe you if I see Christine Daae come out of the house on the lake and go back to it of her own accord."

"And you won't meddle any more in my affairs?"

"No."

"Very well, you shall see her tonight. Come to the masked ball. Christine and I will go and then you can hide in her room where you will see her come back to me by the underground passage."

I was greatly interested in the relationship between Erik and Christine Daae, not from any morbid curiosity, but because of the terrible thought that Erik was capable of anything if he discovered that he was not loved for himself alone. I continued my investigations in the Opera house and soon discovered the truth of the matter. He filled Christine's mind, through the terror with which he inspired her, but the child's heart belonged wholly to the Vicomte Raoul de Chagny. While they played about like an innocent engaged couple, they little suspected that I was watching over their safety. I was prepared to go to any lengths; to kill the monster, if necessary, and explain to the police afterwards. But Erik did not show himself, and I felt none the more comfortable for that.

On the day of the abduction of Christine Daae, I did not come to the theatre until rather late in the evening. Her abduction in the Prison Act, which naturally surprised everybody, found me prepared. It was quite certain that she had been spirited away by Erik, that prince of conjurors. The chances were in my favour that Erik, at that moment, was thinking only of his captive. This was the moment to enter his house through the third cellar, and I resolved to take with me the Vicomte de Chagny, who accepted with a confidence that touched me profoundly. He is a brave fellow, and he knew hardly anything about his adversary, which was all the better.

I knew Erik too well to feel at all comfortable when I jumped into his house, for I knew what he had done in a certain palace at Mazenderan. He soon turned it into a house of the very devil, and with his trapdoors the monster was responsible for endless tragedies of all kinds. He hit upon astonishing inventions. Of these, the most curious, horrible and dangerous was the so-called torture-chamber. My alarm, therefore, was great when I saw that the room into which Monsieur le Vicomte de Chagny and I had dropped was an exact copy of the torture-chamber of Mazenderan! At our feet, I found the Punjab lasso which I had been dreading all the evening. I was convinced that this rope had already been used for Joseph Buquet who like myself, must have caught Erik one evening working the stone in the third cellar. He probably tried it in his turn and fell into the torture-chamber. I could well imagine Erik dragging the body, in order to get rid of it, to the scene from the Roi de Lahore and hanging it there as an example, or to increase the superstitious terror that would help him in guarding the approaches to his lair.

We were then, in the middle of a small hexagonal room, the sides of which were covered with mirrors from floor to ceiling. Suddenly, we heard noises on our left. It sounded at first like a door opening and shutting in the next room, and then we heard a dull moan. I clutched Monsieur de Chagny's arm when we distinctly heard these words, "You must make your choice! The wedding mass or the requiem mass!"

I recognized the voice of the monster.

There followed another moan, then complete silence.

I was sure by now that the monster was unaware of our presence in his house, for otherwise he would certainly have kept silent. Besides, I was certain that if he had known of our presence the tortures would have begun at once.

The important thing was not to let him know, and I dreaded that the Vicomte de Chagny, who wanted to rush through the walls to Christine Daae, would give us away.

"The requiem mass is not at all gay," Erik's voice resumed, "whereas the wedding mass is magnificent! I can't go on living like this, like a mole under the ground! *Don Juan Triumphant* is finished. Now I want to live like a normal man and have a wife like everybody else. You will be the happiest of women, you know. And we will sing, all by ourselves, until we swoon away with delight. You are crying! You are afraid of me! And yet I am not really wicked. Love me and you shall see! All I wanted was to be loved for myself. If you loved me, I should be as gentle as a lamb, and you could do anything with me that you pleased."

Soon the moans grew louder and longer. Monsieur de Chagny and I recognized that this terrible lamentation came from Erik himself. Three times over, Erik fiercely bewailed his fate. "You don't love me! You don't love me! You don't love me!" And then, more gently, "Why do you cry? You know it hurts to see you cry!"

A silence.

Suddenly, the silence in the next room was disturbed by the ringing of a bell. There was a bound on the other side of the wall and Erik's voice of thunder, "Somebody ringing! Come in!" A sinister chuckle: "Who has come bothering me now? Wait for me here. I am going to tell the siren to open the door."

We heard his steps move away, a door close. I had no time to think of the fresh horror that he was preparing. My only thought was that Christine was alone behind the wall!

The Vicomte de Chagny was already calling to her, "Christine! Christine!"

At last, a faint voice reached us: "I am dreaming!" it said.

"Christine, it is Raoul!"

A silence.

"But answer me, Christine! In heaven's name, if you are alone, answer me!"

Then Christine's voice whispered Raoul's name.

"Yes!" he cried, "Yes! It is I! It is not a dream! Christine, trust me! We are here to save you, but be careful! When you hear the monster, warn us!"

Trembling lest Erik should discover where Raoul was hidden, she told us in a few hurried words that Erik had gone quite mad with love and that he had decided to kill everybody and himself if she did not consent to become his wife. He had given her till eleven o'clock the next evening for reflection. If the answer was still no, he had repeated, "everybody will be dead and buried."

"Can you tell us where Erik is?" I asked.

She replied that he must have left the house.

"Could you make sure?"

"No, I am fastened. I cannot stir a limb."

When we heard this, Monsieur de Chagny and I were dumb-founded. Our safety, the safety of all the three of us depended on the girl's freedom of movement.

"There are only two doors in my room," she said, "one which Erik uses and another which he has never opened because he says it is the door to the torture-chamber."

"Christine, that is where we are!"

"You are in the torture-chamber?"

"Yes, but we cannot see the door."

"Oh, if I could only drag myself so far! I would knock at the door and that would tell you where it is."

"Is it a door with a lock to it?" I asked.

"Yes, and I know where the key is," she said, in a voice that seemed exhausted by the effort she had made. "But I am fastened so tight. Oh, the wretch!"

"Where is the key?" I asked.

"In the next room, near the organ, with another little bronze key. Oh, Raoul! Fly! Everything is mysterious and terrible here and Erik will soon have gone quite mad and you are in the torture chamber. Go back the way you came."

"Christine," said the young man, "we will go from here together or die together."

"Mademoiselle," I declared, "the monster bound you and he shall unbind you. You have only to play the necessary part. Remember that he loves you."

"Alas!" we heard. "Am I likely to forget it!"

"Remember it and smile on him, entreat him, tell him that your bonds hurt you."

But Christine Daae said, "Hush! I hear something in the wall on the lake. It is he. Go away. Go away!"

Heavy steps dragged slowly behind the wall, then came a

tremendous sigh, followed by a cry of pain from Christine, and we heard Erik's voice :

"Why did you cry out, Christine?"

"Because I am in pain, Erik."

"I thought I had frightened you."

"Erik, unloose my bonds. Am I not your prisoner?"

"You will try to kill yourself again."

"You have given me till eleven o'clock tomorrow evening, Erik."

The foosteps dragged along the floor once more.

"After all, since we are to die together and since I am just as eager to die as you are, yes, I have had enough of this life, you know . . . Wait, don't move, I will release you . . . you have only one word to say, 'No!' And it will be finished. There, turn round —you're free now. Oh, Christine, look at your poor dear wrists. Tell me, have I hurt them? That alone deserves death."

Then the voice asked angrily, "What have you done with my bag? So it was to take my bag that you asked me to release you!"

"Listen to me, Erik," sighed the girl. "As it is settled that we are to live together, what difference can it make to you?"

"You know there are only two keys in it," said the monster. "What do you want to do?"

"I want to look at this room which I have never seen and which you have always kept hidden from me."

"Give me the key, will you, you inquisitive little thing!"

And he chuckled, while Christine gave a cry of pain. Erik had evidently recovered the bag from her.

At that moment, the viscomte could not help himself any longer and cried out with rage.

"What's that?" said the monster. "Did you hear that, Christine?"

"No, no!" replied the poor girl. "I heard nothing!"

"I thought I heard a cry."

"A cry! Are you going mad, Erik? Whom do you expect to cry out in this house? I cried out, because you hurt me!"

"I don't like the way you said that. You're trembling. You're lying! There was a cry. There is someone in the torture-chamber! Ah, I understand now!"

"There is no one there, Erik!"

"I understand."

"No one!"

"The man you want to marry, perhaps!"

"I don't want to marry anybody, you know I don't."

Another nasty chuckle. "Well, it won't take long to find out Christine, my love, we need not open the door to see what is hap-pening in the torture-chamber. Would you like to see? If there is someone, you will see the invisible window light up at the top of the wall, near the ceiling. We have only to draw back the black curtain and put out the light in here. There, that's it. Let's put out the light! You're not afraid of the dark, when you're with your little husband!"

Then we heard Christine's cry of anguish.

"No! I'm frightened! I tell you, I'm afraid of the dark! I don't care about that room now!"

And that which I feared above all things was set in motion. The room was suddenly flooded with light. The Vicomte de Chagny was so much taken by surprise that he staggered where he stood. And the angry voice roared :

"I told you there was someone! Do you see the window now? The lighted window up there? The man behind the wall can't see it! But you shall go up the folding steps. That is what they are there for! You have often asked me to tell you and now you know! They are there to see the torture-chamber! Go and look through the little window, dear!"

I do not know if the viscount heard the girl's swooning voice, for he was too much absorbed by the astounding spectacle that he now saw before him. As for me, I had seen that sight too often, through the little window at Mazenderan.

We heard the steps being dragged against the wall.

"Up with you! No? Then I will go up myself, dear!"

"No, let me go!"

At that moment, we distinctly heard these words above our heads :

"There is no one there, dear!"

"No one? Are you sure there is no one?"

"Why, of course not . . . No one!"

"Well, that's all right! What's the matter, Christine? You're not going to faint, are you, considering there is no one there? Here come down. That's it! Pull yourself together. How do you like the view from the little window?"

"Oh, very much!"

"There, that's right! You're better now, aren't you? And what a funny house it is, isn't it?"

"It's very handsome! Did you make it? You're a great artist, Erik."

"Yes, a great artist, in my own line."

"But tell me, Erik, why did you call that room the torture-chamber?"

"Oh, it's very simple. First of all, what did you see?"

"I saw a forest."

"And what is in a forest?"

"Trees."

"And you saw branches! And what is in the branches?" asked the terrible voice. "There's a gibbet! That is why I call my forest the torture-chamber!"

Christine was distraught. "Put the light out in the little window!" she entreated him, "Erik, do put out the light!"

For she saw that this light, which appeared so suddenly and of which the monster had spoken in so threatening a voice, must mean something terrible. One thing must have pacified her for a moment, and that was seeing the two of us behind the wall in the midst of that dazzling light, alive and well.

But then she cried out again, "What does this mean? The wall is quite hot! The wall is burning!"

And the monster replied, "It is because of the forest next door."

"Well, what has that got to do with it?"

"Why, didn't you see that it was an African forest?"

And the monster laughed so loudly and hideously that we could no longer distinguish Christine's cries. The Vicomte de Chagny shouted and banged against the wall like a madman, I could not restrain him. But we heard nothing except the monster's laughter. Then there was the sound of a body falling on the floor and being dragged along, a door slammed and then another—nothing more save the scorching silence of the torture-chamber!

There was only one possible outlet—that opening into the room where Erik and Christine Daae were. But, though this outlet looked like just an ordinary door on their side, it was absolutely invisible to us. When I was quite sure that there was no hope for us from Christine Daae's side, I resolved to set to work without delay.

But I had first to calm Monsieur de Chagny, who was already walking about like a madman, uttering incoherent cries. The snatches of conversation which he had caught between Christine and the monster had driven him mad with despair; add to that the shock of the magic forest and the scorching heat which was beginning to make the perspiration stream down his temples and you will have no difficulty in understanding his state of mind. He shouted Christine's name, brandished his pistol, and rushed against the glass walls in his endeavours to break through them. The torture was beginning to work its spell upon a brain unprepared to resist it.

I did my best to induce the poor viscount to listen to reason. I made him touch the mirrors and the iron tree and the branches and explained to him logically all the luminous imagery which surrounded us.

"We are in a room, a little room; that is what you must keep saying to yourself. And we shall leave the room as soon as we have found the door."

Forgetting the forest, I tackled a glass panel and began to finger it in every direction, hunting for the spot which I must press in order to turn the door. The spring might lay hidden under a mere speck on the glass no larger than a pea. I hunted and hunted, feeling as high as my hands could reach.

While groping over the successive panels with the greatest care, I endeavoured not to lose a minute, for I was feeling more and more overcome with the heat and we were literally roasting in that blazing forest.

I had been working like this for half an hour and had finished three panels when, as ill-luck would have it, I heard a muttered exclamation from the viscount and turned round.

"I am stifling," he said. "All these mirrors are sending out an infernal heat! Do you think you will find that spring soon, because if you are much longer about it we shall be roasted alive!"

I returned to my panel, after giving him a word of encouragement, but I had made the mistake of taking a few steps while speaking, and in the maze of reflections I was no longer able to make sure of the panel! I had to begin all over again at random: feeling, fumbling, groping.

Now the fever laid hold of me in turn, for I found nothing, absolutely nothing. In the next room, all was silence. We were utterly lost in the forest, without an outlet, a compass, a guide or anything. Oh, I knew what awaited us if I did not find the spring! But, look as I might, I found nothing but branches, beautiful branches that stood straight up before me or spread gracefully over my head, but they gave no shade.

At last, I saw Monsieur de Chagny raise himself up and point to a spot on the horizon. He had discovered an oasis!

Yes, far in the distance was an oasis, an oasis with limpid water! No, it was the mirage; I recognized it at once—the worst of all Erik's tricks! No one had ever been able to fight against it. I did my utmost to keep my head and not hope for water, because I knew that if a man hoped for water there was only one thing for him to do—hang himself on the iron tree!

"Don't look!" I cried to Monsieur de Chagny, "It's the mirage! Don't believe in water! It's another trick of the mirrors!"

Then he flatly told me that I was mad to imagine that all the water flowing over there, among those countless, splendid trees, was not real water! The forest was real! And it was no use trying to take him in. And he dragged himself along repeating over and over again, "Water! Water!"

And his mouth was open, as though he were drinking. And my mouth was open too as though I were drinking . . .

Lastly—and this was the most pitiless torture of all—we heard the rain and it was not raining! Ah, you should have seen us putting out our tongues and dragging ourselves towards the rippling river bank! When we reached the mirror, Monsieur de Chagny licked it and I also licked the glass.

It was burning hot!

Then we rolled on the floor crying with despair. Monsieur de Chagny put the one pistol that was still loaded to his temple, and I stared at the Punjab lasso at the foot of the iron tree.

Then, as I stared at it, I saw a thing which made me start so violently that I seized my friend by the arm and dragged myself on my knees towards what I had seen.

I had discovered, near the Punjab lasso, in a groove in the floor, a black-headed nail which I recognized. At last I had found the spring!

I felt the nail and, as we watched in amazement, it yielded to my pressure.

The mechanism released a trapdoor in the floor. Cool air rushed up through the black hole below. We stooped down with our faces in the cool shade and we drank in the coolness.

I thrust my arm into the darkness and came upon a stone, then another—a dark staircase leading into the cellar. The viscount wanted to fling himself down the hole but, fearing a new trick of the monster's, I stopped him, turned on my dark lantern and went down first.

The staircase was a winding one. We soon reached the bottom. Our eyes were beginning to be accustomed to the dark, to distinguish shapes around us. Then we saw circular shapes. We were in Erik's cellar. It was here that he must keep his wine and perhaps his drinking water. We went down on our knees and started scratching at the seal with a small knife which I carried. Monsieur de Chagny put his two hands together underneath it and, with a last effort, I burst the seal.

"What's this?" cried the viscount. "This isn't water!"

The viscount put his two full hands close to my lantern. I stooped to look and, at the same moment, flung away my lantern with such violence that it broke and went out, leaving us in utter darkness.

What I had seen in his hands was gunpowder! The discovery flung us into a state of alarm that made us forget all our past and present sufferings. We now knew what the monster meant when he said to Christine Daae, "If your answer is no, everybody will be dead or buried!"

Yes, buried under the ruins of the Paris Opera House!

The monster had given her until eleven o'clock in the evening. He had chosen his time well. There would be many people up there in the theatre, and we would all be blown up in the middle of the performance if Christine Daae said no!

And what else could she say but no? She did not know that her decision would decide the fate of hundreds of people.

We dragged ourselves through the darkness, feeling our way to the stone steps. At last, I found the staircase, but suddenly I stopped on the first step, for a terrible thought had come into my mind—what was the time?

Eleven o'clock tomorrow evening might be now, might be this very moment! Who could tell us the time? We seemed to have been imprisoned in that hell for days and days, for years, since the beginning of the world. Perhaps we should be blown up then and there! Ah, a sound! A crack!

"Did you hear that? There, in the corner—good heavens! Like a sound of machinery. Again! Oh, for a light! Perhaps it's the machinery which will blow everything up!"

Monsieur de Chagny and I began to yell like madmen. Fear

spurred us on. We rushed up the treads of the staircase, stumbling as we went. We found the trapdoor still open, but it was now as dark in the room of mirrors as in the cellar we had just left. We dragged ourselves along the floor of the torture-chamber, the floor between us and the gunpower room. What was the time? We argued, we tried to calculate the time which we had spent there, but we were incapable of reasoning. If only we could see the face of a watch! Mine had stopped, but Monsieur de Chagny's was still going. He told me that he had wound it up before dressing for the Opera. We had not a match upon us, so he broke the glass of his watch and felt the two hands. Judging by the space between the hands, he thought it might be just eleven o'clock.

Suddenly I thought I heard footsteps in the next room. Someone tapped against the wall, and Christine's voice cried out, "Raoul! Raoul!"

We all began to talk at once, on either side of the wall. Christine sobbed, and told us that the monster had been terrible and had done nothing but rave, waiting for her to give him the "yes" which she refused. She had promised him that "yes", if he would take her to the torture-chamber, but he had been obstinate and at last, after many hours of that hell, he had gone out, leaving her alone to reflect for the last time.

"Hours and hours? What is the time now? What is the time, Christine?"

"It is eleven o'clock! Eleven o'clock, in all but five minutes! He told me so before he went. He is quite mad. He said, 'Five minutes! I leave you alone!' And he gave me the little bronze key that opens the two ebony caskets on the mantelpiece. Then he said, 'In one of the caskets you will find a scorpion, in the other, a grasshopper. They will say yes or no for you. If you turn the scorpion I shall understand, when I come back, that you have said yes. The grasshopper will mean no.' And he laughed like a demon. I did nothing but beg and entreat him to give me the key of the torture-chamber, promising to be his wife if he granted me this request. But he told me that there was no further need for that key and that he was going to throw it into the lake! And he laughed again and left me."

There was a pause.

"Christine," I cried, "where are you?"

"By the scorpion."

"Don't touch it!"

I had the idea that the monster had perhaps deceived the girl once more. Perhaps it was the scorpion that would blow everything up. After all, why wasn't he there? The five minutes were long past and he was not back. Perhaps he had taken shelter and was waiting for the explosion! Why had he not returned? He could not really expect Christine ever to consent to becoming his voluntary prey!

"Don't touch the scorpion!" I repeated.

"Here he comes!" cried Christine. "I hear him! Here he is!"

We heard his steps approaching the Louis-Philippe room. He came up to Christine, but did not speak. Then I raised my voice, "Erik! It is I! Do you know me?"

With extraordinary calmness he at once replied, "So you are not dead in there? Well then, keep quiet!"

I tried to speak, but he said coldly, "Not a word, Daroga, or I shall blow everything up." And he added, "The honour rests with Mademoiselle. Mademoiselle has not touched the scorpion nor the grasshopper. If you turn the grasshopper, Mademoiselle, we shall all be blown up. There is enough gunpowder under our feet to blow up half of Paris. If you turn the scorpion all that powder will be flooded by the lake. Now, to celebrate our wedding, you shall make a very handsome present to a few hundred Parisians who are at this moment applauding a poor masterpiece of Meyerbeer's. You shall make them a present of their lives. For with your own fair hands you shall turn the scorpion and merrily, merrily, we shall be married!"

A pause, and then:

"If, in two minutes, Mademoiselle, you have not turned the scorpion, I shall turn the grasshopper, and the grasshopper, I assure you, will hop high!"

There was a terrible silence again. The Vicomte de Chagny, realizing that there was nothing left to do but pray, went down on his knees and prayed.

At last, we heard Erik's voice.

"The two minutes are gone. Goodbye, Mademoiselle! Hop, grasshopper!"

"Erik!" cried Christine, "do you swear to me, monster, do you swear to me that the scorpion is the one to turn?"

"Yes, to hop at our wedding."

"Ah, you see! You said, to hop!"

"At our wedding, ingenuous child! The scorpion opens the ball. But that will do! You won't have the scorpion? Then I turn the grasshopper!"

"Erik!"

"Enough!"

I was crying out in concert with Christine. Monsieur de Chagny was still on his knees, praying.

"Erik! I have turned the scorpion!"

Oh, the second which we waited to find ourselves blown to fragments, amid the roar of the explosion!

It came softly at first, then louder, then very loud ...

But it was not the hiss of fire. It was more like the hiss of water. And now it became a gurgling sound.

We rushed to the trapdoor. All our thirst, which had vanished when the terror came, now returned with the sound of the water.

The water rose in the cellar, above the powder barrels and we went down to it with parched throats. The water spread over the floor of the room. If this went on the whole house on the lake would be swamped. Surely there was water enough now! Erik must stop it now!

"Erik! Erik! That is water enough for the gunpowder! Turn it off! Turn off the scorpion!"

But Erik did not reply. We heard nothing but the water rising, now half-way up to our waists!

"Christine!" cried Monsieur de Chagny. "Christine! The water is up to our knees!"

But Christine did not reply. We heard nothing but the water rising.

There was no one in the next room, no one to turn the tap, no one to turn the scorpion! We were alone, left to drown!

By this time we had lost our foothold and were carried away by the water, which dashed us against the dark mirrors, then thrust us back again. Our voices, raised above the roar of the whirlpool, shouted in vain for help. Our arms became entangled as we tried to swim, we choked, we struggled in the dark water. Already we could hardly breathe above the water, as the air was escaping through some hole or other in the ceiling.

I lost my strength, I tried in vain to lay hold of the glass walls! We whirled round again! We began to sink! One last effort! A last cry:

"Erik ! . . . Christine ! . . ."

Then I lost consciousness entirely.

That is the end of the story which the Persian left behind.

Notwithstanding the horrors of a situation which seemed to abandon them to their deaths, Monsieur de Chagny and his companion were saved by the sublime devotion of Christine Daae. I had the rest of the story from the lips of the Daroga himself.

When I went to see him, he was still living in his little flat in the Rue de Rivoli, opposite the Tuileries. He was very ill and it took all my persuasion as an historian pledged to tell the truth to persuade him to live the incredible tragedy over again for my benefit. His poor face looked very worn, but his mind was quite clear and he told me his story with perfect lucidity.

It seems that when he opened his eyes the Daroga found himself lying on a bed. Monsieur de Chagny was asleep on a sofa beside the wardrobe. An angel and a devil were watching over them.

After the fantastic deceptions and illusions of the torture-chamber, the normality of that quiet little room seemed invented for the express purpose of once more puzzling the mind of the mortal rash enough to stray into that house of living nightmare. And the masked figure seemed all the more formidable in this old-fashioned setting. It bent down over the Persian and said in his ear :

"Are you better, Daroga?"

Christine Daae did not say a word; she moved about noiselessly, like a sister of charity who had taken a vow of silence. She brought a cup of cordial, or of hot tea, he did not remember which. The man in the mask took it from her hands and gave it to the Persian. Monsieur de Chagny was still sleeping.

Erik poured a drop of rum into the Daroga's cup and, pointing to the vicomte, said, "He came to himself long before we knew if you were still alive. He is quite well and sleeping."

Erik left the room for a moment and the Persian raised himself on his elbow, looked around and saw Christine sitting by the fireside. He called to her, but he was still very weak and fell back on his pillow. She came to him, laid her hand on his forehead and went away again. And the Persian remembered that, as she went, she did not so much as glance at Monsieur de Chagny, who was sleeping peacefully, and she sat down again in her chair by the chimney-corner.

Erik returned with some little bottles which he placed on the mantelpiece. And, again in a whisper so as not to wake Monsieur de Chagny, he said to the Persian, after feeling his pulse. "You are now saved, both of you. And soon I shall take you up to the surface of the earth again, to please my wife."

Thereupon he rose, without further explanation, and disappeared once more.

The Persian now looked at Christine's quiet profile under the lamp. She was reading a tiny book with gilt edges. Very gently, he called her again but Christine was rapt in her book and did not hear him.

Erik returned, mixed the Daroga a draught and advised him not to speak to "his wife" again nor to anyone, because it might be very dangerous to everybody.

Eventually, the Persian fell asleep, like Monsieur de Chagny, and did not wake until he was in his own room, nursed by his faithful servant, who told him that, on the night before, he had been found propped against the door of his flat, where he had been brought by a stranger who rang the bell before going away.

As soon as the Daroga recovered his strength and his wits, he sent to Count Philippe's house to enquire after the vicomte's health. The answer was that the young man had not been seen and that Count Philippe was dead. His body was found on the bank of the Opera lake, on the Rue Scribe side. The Persian remembered the requiem mass which he had heard from behind the wall of the torture-chamber and had no doubt regarding the crime and the criminal. Knowing Erik as he did, he easily reconstructed the tragedy. Thinking that his brother had run away with Christine Daae, Philippe must have dashed in pursuit of him along the Brussels road, where he knew that everything was prepared for the elopement. Failing to find the pair, he hurried back to the Opera. He remembered Raoul's strange confidence about his fantastic rival and learned that the vicomte had made every effort to enter the cellars of the theatre and that he had disappeared, leaving his hat in the prima donna's dressing-room beside an empty pistol-case. And the count, who no longer entertained any doubt of his brother's madness, in his turn darted into that infernal underground maze. This was enough, in the Persian's eyes, to explain the discovery of the Comte de Chagny's corpse on the shore of the lake, where the siren—Erik's siren—kept watch.

The Persian did not hesitate. He decided to inform the police.

However, the case was in the hands of an unimaginative examining magistrate called Faure, who took down the Daroga's testimony and proceeded to treat him as a madman.

Despairing of ever obtaining a hearing, the Persian sat down to write. As the police did not want his evidence, he thought perhaps the press would be glad of it. He had just written the last line of the narrative which I have quoted in the preceding pages, when his servant announced the visit of a stranger who refused his name, who would not show his face and who declared simply that he did not intend to leave the place until he had spoken to the Daroga.

The Persian guessed at once who his singular visitor was and ordered him to be shown in. It was Erik.

He looked extremely weak and leant against the wall, as though afraid of falling. Taking off his hat, he revealed a forehead white as wax. The rest of his face was hidden by the mask.

The Persian rose to his feet as Erik entered.

"Murderer of Count Philippe, what have you done with Monsieur de Chagny and Christine Daae?"

Erik staggered under this direct attack, dragged himself to a chair and heaved a deep sigh. Then, speaking in short phrases and gasping for breath between the words, he said, "Daroga, don't talk to me ... about Count Philippe. He was dead ... by the time ... I left my house ... he was dead when ... the siren sang. It was an accident, a very sad accident. He fell very awkwardly ... into the lake!"

"You lie!" shouted the Persian.

Erik bowed his head and said :

"I have not come here ... to talk about Count Philippe ... but to tell you that ... I am going to die."

"Where are Raoul de Chagny and Christine Daae?"

"I am going to die."

"Raoul de Chagny and Christine Daae?"

"Daroga ... I am dying of love. I loved her so! And I love her still, Daroga. If you knew how beautiful she was ... when she let me kiss her ... alive. It was the first time, Daroga, the first time I ever kissed a woman. I kissed her alive, and she looked as beautiful as if she had been dead!"

The Persian shook Erik by the arm.

"Will you tell me if she is alive or dead?"

"Why do you shake me like that?" asked Erik, making an effort to control himself. "I tell you I am going to die ... Yes, I kissed her alive."

"And now she is dead?"

"I tell you I kissed her just like that, on her forehead, and she did not draw back her forehead from my lips! Oh, she is a good girl! As to her being dead, I don't think so, but it has nothing to do with me. No, no she is not dead! And no one shall touch a hair of her head! She is a good honest girl and she saved your life, Daroga, at a moment when I would not have given twopence for your Persian skin. After all, who cared about you? But she had turned the scorpion and she had, through her own free will, become engaged to me!

"When you were drowning Christine came to me and swore that she would be my living wife! She said she would not kill herself. It was a bargain. A minute later, all the water was back in the lake, and I had a hard job carrying you, Daroga. Upon my honour, I thought you were dead! It was understood that I would take you both up to the surface of the earth."

"But what have you done with the Vicomte de Chagny?" interrupted the Persian.

"Ah, you see, Daroga, I couldn't carry him up like that at once. He was a hostage. But I could not keep him in the house on the lake either, because of Christine. So, I locked him up comfortably in the Communard's dungeon, which is in the most remote and deserted part of the Opera below the fifth cellar, where no one ever comes and no one ever hears you. Then I went back to Christine. She was waiting for me."

Erik rose solemnly. Then he continued, but as he spoke he trembled with emotion. "Yes, she was waiting for me . . . a real, living bride. And, when I came forward, more timid than a little child, she did not run away. I even believe, Daroga, that she put out her forehead a little . . . oh, not much . . . just a little, like a living bride. And . . . and . . . I kissed her! And she did not die! Oh, how good it is, Daroga, to kiss a person! You can't tell, you can't! My mother, Daroga, my poor, unhappy mother would never . . . let me kiss her. She used to run away! Nor any other woman . . . ever, ever! Ah, you can understand, my happiness was so great, I fell at her feet, crying . . . and I kissed her feet, her little feet, crying. You're crying too, Daroga . . . and she too . . . the angel cried!"

Erik sobbed aloud and the Persian himself could not restrain his tears.

"Yes, Daroga, I felt her tears on my forehead. They mingled with the tears in my eyes . . . they flowed between my lips. Listen, Daroga, listen to what I did. I tore off my mask so as not to lose one of her tears and she did not run away! And she did not die! She was alive, she wept with me. Ah, I have tasted all the happiness the world can offer!"

And Erik fell into a chair, gasping for breath, "Ah, I am not going to die yet. Presently I shall, but let me tell you! While I was at her feet, I heard her say, 'Poor, unhappy Erik!' And she took my hand! I had become no more than a poor dog ready to die for her. I held out a ring, a plain gold ring which I had given her, which she had lost, and I had found again. I slipped it into her little hand and said, 'There! Take it for you, and him! It is my wedding present, to you both—a present from your poor, unhappy Erik. I know you love him, so don't cry any more!' Then she asked me, in a very soft voice, what I meant.

"I made her understand that I was ready to die for her and that she should marry the young man when she pleased, because she had wept with me and mingled her tears with mine!"

Erik's emotion was so great that he had to tell the Persian not to look at him, for he was choking and must take off his mask. The Daroga went to the window and opened it. His heart was full of pity, but he took care to keep his eyes fixed on the trees in the Tuileries gardens, lest he should see the monster's face.

"I went and released the young man," Erik continued, "and told him to come with me to Christine. They embraced before me in the Louis-Philippe room. Christine had my ring. I made her swear to come back one night when I was dead and bury me in the greatest secrecy with the gold ring, which she was to wear until that moment. I told her where she would find my body and what to do with it. Then Christine kissed me for the first time herself, here on the forehead—don't look, Daroga!

"They went off together. Christine had stopped crying. I alone cried . . . alone. Daroga, if Christine keeps her promise, she will come back soon!"

Erik stopped. The Persian asked him no questions. He believed every word of what Erik had just told him.

The monster put on his mask once again and collected his strength to leave. He told the Daroga that, when he felt his end to be close at hand, he would send him—in gratitude for the kindness which the Persian had once shown him—the things which he held most dear; all Christine Daae's letters to Raoul which she had left with Erik, together with a few objects belonging to her—a pair of gloves, a shoe-buckle and two pocket-handkerchiefs. Erik told him that the young people had resolved to go and look for a priest in some lonely spot where they could hide their happiness. Lastly, Erik relied on the Persian, as soon as he received the promised relics and papers, to inform the young couple of his death and to put a notice in the *Epoque*.

That was all. The Persian saw Erik to the door of his flat and the servant helped him down to the street. A carriage was waiting for him. Erik stepped in, and the Persian, who had gone back to the window, heard him say to the driver :

"To the Opera."

With that the carriage drove off into the night.

Three weeks later, the *Epoque* published this announcement :

Erik is dead.

THE MAGICIAN

SOMERSET MAUGHAM

(*Metro-Goldwyn-Mayer: 1926*)

The history of the horror film is sadly dotted with examples of "lost" films—pictures which were made and then for some reason disappeared or were destroyed. Probably the most famous of these is The Magician, *which was produced in 1926 by Rex Ingram, creator of such distinguished films as* The Four Horsemen of the Apocalypse *and* Scaramouche.

The film of The Magician *was based on the work of the same name by Somerset Maugham, which dealt in a thinly disguised fictional form with the activities of the notorious Black Magician Aleister Crowley, who performed ritual magic and animal sacrifice, indulged in drug taking and sex orgies and lived a life devoted to the premise of "evil for evil's sake". In Maugham's story,* Oliver Haddo—*as Crowley is called—has "magical powers of extraordinary character" and frequently conducts "the blasphemous ceremonies of the Black Mass". He is also said to be "attempting to create human beings" (shades of Frankenstein, no less).*

Ingram had read the story shortly after its publication in 1908 and nurtured it in his mind for a film which he made in France in 1925–26. So much of the plot rang true for Ingram (Crowley was still active at this time and often made newspaper headlines) that he was able to bring a vivid realism to the finished picture, introducing some fine episodes of Satanism and necromancy. However these very elements caused the critics, almost to a man, to condemn the film as tasteless and vulgar. In a matter of a few years the three existing prints had disappeared and Ingram's career was on the decline.

Reports of the picture which still exist (plus a pathetic handful of stills) indicate that a high point of the film was the mesmeric sequence in which Haddo introduces a young girl to the "delights" of devil worship through hypnotism. It is this same dramatic episode from the story which is reproduced here, vividly demonstrating just what a loss Ingram's "missing" film is to the cinema....

*

IT was a fine Paris afternoon and Margaret decided on a walk. As she set out across the courtyard she suddenly started nervously, for there before her was the mysterious man of whom she had heard so much, the man who was reputed to dabble in the Black Arts and who, at this very moment in time, was supposedly engaged in the search for some still more terrible secret. Yes, it was indeed the magician Oliver Haddo who passed slowly by. He did not seem to see her. Suddenly he stopped, put his hand to his heart, and fell heavily to the ground. The *concierge,* the only person at hand, ran forward with a cry. She knelt down and, looking round with terror, caught sight of Margaret.

"*Oh, mademoiselle, venez vite,*" she cried.

Margaret was obliged to go. Her heart beat horribly. She looked down at Oliver, and he seemed to be dead. She forgot that she loathed him. Instinctively she knelt down by his side and loosened his collar. He opened his eyes. An expression of terrible anguish came into his face.

"For the love of God, take me in for one moment," he sobbed. "I shall die in the street."

Her heart was moved towards him. He could not go into the poky den, evil-smelling and airless, of the *concierge.* But with her help Margaret raised him to his feet, and together they brought him to the studio. He sank painfully into a chair.

"Shall I fetch you some water?" asked Margaret.

"Can you get a pastille out of my pocket?"

He swallowed a white tabloid, which she took out of a case attached to his watch-chain.

"I'm very sorry to cause you this trouble," he gasped. "I suffer from a disease of the heart and sometimes I am very near death."

"I'm glad that I was able to help you," she said.

He seemed able to breathe more easily. She left him to himself for a while, so that he might regain his strength. She took up a book and began to read. Presently, without moving his chair, he spoke.

"You must hate me for intruding on you."

His voice was stronger, and her pity waned as he seemed to recover. She answered with freezing indifference.

"I couldn't do any less for you than I did. I would have brought a dog into my room if it seemed hurt."

"I see that you wish me to go."

He got up and moved towards the door, but he staggered and

with a groan tumbled to his knees. Margaret sprang forward to help him. She reproached herself bitterly for those scornful words. The man had barely escaped death, and she was merciless.

"Oh, please stay as long as you like," she cried. "I'm sorry, I didn't mean to hurt you."

He dragged himself with difficulty back to the chair, and she, conscience-stricken, stood over him helplessly. She poured out a glass of water, but he motioned it away as though he would not be beholden to her even for that.

"Is there nothing I can do for you at all?" she exclaimed, painfully.

"Nothing, except allow me to sit in this chair," he gasped.

"I hope you'll remain as long as you choose."

He did not reply. She sat down again and pretended to read. In a little while he began to speak. His voice reached her as if from a long way off.

"You think me a charlatan because I aim at things that are unknown to you. You won't try to understand. You won't give me any credit for striving with all my soul to a very great end."

She made no reply, and for a time there was silence. His voice was different now and curiously seductive.

"You look upon me with disgust and scorn. You almost persuaded yourself to let me die in the street rather than stretch out to me a helping hand. And if you hadn't been merciful then, almost against your will, I should have died."

"It can make no difference to you how I regard you," she whispered.

She did not know why his soft, low tones mysteriously wrung her heartstrings. Her pulse began to beat more quickly.

"It makes all the difference in the world. It is horrible to think of your contempt. I feel your goodness and your purity. I can hardly bear my own unworthiness. You turn your eyes away from me as though I were unclean."

She turned her chair a little and looked at him. She was astonished at the change in his appearance. His hideous obesity seemed no longer repellant, for his eyes wore a new expression; they were incredibly tender now and they were moist with tears. His mouth was tortured by a passionate distress. Margaret had never seen so much unhappiness on a man's face and an overwhelming remorse seized her.

"I don't want to be unkind to you," she said.

"I will go. That is how I can best repay you for what you have done."

The words were so bitter, so humiliated, that the colour rose to her cheeks.

"I ask you to stay. But let us talk of other things."

For a moment he kept silence. He seemed no longer to see Margaret, and she watched him thoughtfully. His eyes rested on a print of *La Gioconda* which hung on the wall. Suddenly he began to speak. He recited the honeyed words with which Walter Pater expressed his admiration for that consummate picture.

Hers is the head upon which all the ends of the world are come, and the eyelids are a little weary. It is a beauty wrought out from within upon the flesh, the deposit, little cell by cell, of strange thoughts and fantastic reveries and exquisite passions. Set it for a moment beside one of those white Greek goddesses or beautiful women of antiquity, and how would they be troubled by this beauty, into which the soul with all its maladies has passed. All the thoughts and experience of the worlds have etched and moulded there, in that which they have of power to refine and make expressive the outward form, the animalism of Greece, the lust of Rome, the mysticism of the Middle Ages, with its spiritual ambition and imaginative loves, the return of the pagan world, the sins of the Borgias.

His voice, poignant and musical, blended with the suave music of the words so that Margaret felt she had never before known their divine significance. She was intoxicated with their beauty. She wished him to continue, but had not the strength to speak. As if he guessed her thought, he went on, and now his voice had a richness in it as of an organ heard afar off. It was like an overwhelming fragrance and she could hardly bear it.

She is older than the rocks among which she sits; like the vampire, she has been dead many times, and learned the secrets of the grave; and has been a diver in deep seas, and keeps their fallen day about her; and trafficked for strange evils with Eastern merchants; and, as Leda, was the mother of Helen of Troy, and, as Saint Anne, the mother of Mary; and all this has been to her but as the sound of lyres and flutes, and lives only in the delicacy with which it has moulded the changing lineaments, and tinged the eyelids and the hands.

Oliver Haddo began then to speak of Leonardo da Vinci, mingling with his own fantasies the perfect words of that essay which, so wonderful was his memory, he seemed almost to know by heart. He found exotic fancies in the likeness between Saint John the Baptist, with his soft flesh and waving hair, and Bacchus, with his ambiguous smile. Seen through his eyes, the seashore in the Saint Anne had the airless lethargy of some damasked chapel in a Spanish nunnery, and over the landscapes brooded a wan spirit of evil that was very troubling. He loved the mysterious pictures in which the painter has sought to express something beyond the limits of painting, something of unsatisfied desire and of longing for unhuman passions. Oliver Haddo found this quality in unlikely places and his words gave a new meaning to paintings that Margaret had passed thoughtlessly by. There was the portrait of a statuary by Bronziho in the Long Gallery of the Louvre. The features were rather large, the face rather broad. The expression was sombre, almost surly in the repose of the painted canvas, and the eyes were brown, almond-shaped like those of an Oriental; the red lips were exquisitely modelled and the sensuality was curiously disturbing; the dark, chestnut hair, cut short, curled over the head with an infinite grace. The skin was like ivory softened with a delicate carmine. There was in that beautiful countenance more than beauty, for what most fascinated the observer was a supreme and disdainful indifference to the passion of others. It was a vicious face, except that beauty could never be quite vicious; it was a cruel face, except that indolence could never be quite cruel. It was a face that haunted you and yet your admiration was alloyed with an unreasoning terror. The hands were nervous and adroit, with long, fashioning fingers; and you felt that at their touch the clay almost moulded itself into gracious forms. With Haddo's subtle words the character of that man rose before her, cruel yet indifferent, indolent and passionate, cold yet sensual; unnatural secrets dwelt in his mind, and mysterious crimes, and a lust for the knowledge that was arcane. Oliver Haddo was attracted by all that was unusual, deformed and monstrous, by the pictures that represented the hideousness of man or that reminded you of his mortality. He summoned before Margaret the whole array of Ribera's ghoulish dwarfs, with their cunning smile, the insane light of their eyes, and their malice : he dwelt with a horrible fascination upon their malformations, the humped backs, the club feet, the hydrocephalic heads. He described the picture by Valdes Leal in a certain place at Seville, which represents a priest at the altar; and the altar is sumptuous with gilt and florid carving. He wears a magnificent cope and a surplice of exquisite lace, but he wears them as though their weight was more than he could bear; and in the meagre trembling hands, and in the white, ashen face, in the dark hollowness of the eyes, there is a bodily corruption that is terrifying. He seems to hold together with difficulty the bonds of the flesh, but with no eager yearning of the soul to burst its prison, only with despair; it is as if the Lord Almighty had forsaken him and the high heavens were empty of their solace. All the beauty of life appears forgotten, and there is nothing in the world but decay. A ghastly putrefaction has attacked already the living man; the worms of the grave, the piteous horror of mortality, and the darkness before him, offer naught but fear. Beyond, dark night is seen and a turbulent sea, the dark night of the soul of which the mystics write, and the troublous sea of life whereon there is no refuge for the weary and the sick at heart.

Then, as if in pursuance of a definite plan, he analysed with a searching, vehement intensity the curious talent of the modern Frenchman, Gustave Moreau. Margaret had lately visited the Luxembourg and his pictures were fresh in her memory. She had found in them little save a decorative arrangement marred by faulty drawing; but Oliver Haddo gave them at once a new, esoteric import. Those effects as of a Florentine jewel, the clustered colours like emeralds and rubies, like sapphires deeper than the sea, the atmosphere of scented chambers, the mystic persons who seem ever about secret, religious rites, combined in his cunning phrases to create, as it were, a pattern on her soul of morbid and mysterious intricacy. Those pictures were filled with a strange sense of sin, and the mind that contemplated them was burdened with the decadence of Rome and with the passionate vice of the Renaissance; and it was tortured, too, by all the introspections of this later day.

Margaret listened, rather breathlessly, with the excitement of an explorer before whom is spread out the plain of an undiscovered continent. The painters she knew spoke of their art technically, and this imaginative appreciation was new to her. She was horribly fascinated by the personality that imbued these elaborate sentences. Haddo's eyes were fixed upon hers and she responded to his words like a delicate instrument made for recording the beatings of the heart. She felt an extraordinary languor. At last he stopped. Margaret neither moved nor spoke. She might have been under some spell. It seemed to her that she had no power in her limbs.

"I want to do something for you in return for what you have done for me," he said.

He stood up and went to the piano.

"Sit in this chair," he said.

She did not dream of disobeying. He began to play. Margaret was hardly surprised that he played marvellously. Yet it was almost incredible that those fat, large hands should have such a tenderness of touch. His fingers caressed the notes with a peculiar suavity and he drew out of the piano effects which she had scarcely thought possible. He seemed to put into the notes a troubling, ambiguous passion and the instrument had the tremulous emotion of a human being. It was very strange and rather terrifying. She was vaguely familiar with the music to which she listened; but there was in it, under his fingers, an exotic savour that made it harmonious with all that he had said that afternoon. His memory was indeed astonishing. He had an infinite tact to know the feeling that occupied Margaret's heart, and what he chose seemed to be exactly that which at the moment she imperatively needed. Then he began to play things she did not know. It was music of the like of which she had never heard, barbaric, with a plaintive weirdness that brought to her fancy the moonlit nights of desert places, with palm-trees mute in the windless air, and tawny distances. She seemed to know tortuous narrow streets, white houses of silence with strange moon-shadows and the glow of yellow light within, and the tinkling of uncouth instruments, and the acrid scents of Eastern perfumes. It was like a procession passing through her mind of persons who were not human, yet existed mysteriously, with a life of vampires. Mona Lisa and Saint John the Baptist, Bacchus and the mother of Mary, went with enigmatic motions. But the daughter of Herodias raised her hands as though, engaged for ever in a mystic rite, to invoke outlandish gods. Her face was very pale and her dark eyes were sleepless; the jewels of her girdle gleamed with sombre fires and her dress was of colours that have long been lost. The smile, in which was all the sorrow of the world and all its wickedness, beheld the wan head of the Saint, and with a voice that was cold with the coldness of death she murmured the words of the poet:

I am amorous of thy body, Iokanaan! Thy body is white like the lilies of a field that the mower hath never mowed. Thy body is white like the snows that lie on the mountains of Judaea, and come down into the valleys. The roses in the garden of the Queen of Arabia are not so white as thy body. Neither the roses in the garden of the Queen of Arabia, the garden of spices of the Queen of Arabia, nor the feet of the dawn when they light on the leaves, nor the breast of the moon when she lies on the breast of the sea.... There is nothing in the world so white as thy body. Suffer me to touch thy body.

Oliver Haddo ceased to play. Neither of them stirred. At last Margaret sought by an effort to regain her self-control.

"I shall begin to think that you really are a magician," she said, lightly.

"I could show you strange things if you cared to see them," he answered, again raising his eyes to hers.

"I don't think you will ever get me to believe in occult philosophy," she laughed.

"Yet it reigned in Persia with the magi, it endowed India with wonderful traditions, it civilized Greece to the sounds of Orpheus' lyre."

He stood before Margaret, towering over her in his huge bulk, and there was a singular fascination in his gaze. It seemed that he spoke only to conceal from her that he was putting forth now all the power that was in him.

"It concealed the first principles of science in the calculations of Pythagoras. It established empires by its oracles, and at its voice tyrants grew pale upon their thrones. It governed the minds of some by curiosity and others it ruled by fear."

His voice grew very low and it was so seductive that Margaret's brain reeled. The sound of it was overpowering, like too sweet a fragrance.

"I tell you that for this art nothing is impossible. It commands the elements and knows the language of the stars and directs the planets in their courses. The moon at its bidding falls blood red from the sky. The dead rise up and form into ominous words the night wind that moans through their skulls. Heaven and Hell are in its province; and all forms, lovely and hideous; and love and hate. With Circe's wand it can change men into beasts of the field and to them it can give a monstrous humanity. Life and death are in the right hand and in the left of him who knows its secrets. It confers wealth by the transmutation of metals and immortality by its quintessence."

Margaret could not hear what he said. A gradual lethargy seized her under his baleful glance and she had not even the strength to wish to free herself. She seemed bound to him already by hidden chains.

"If you have powers show them," she whispered, hardly conscious that she spoke.

Suddenly he released the enormous tension with which he held her. Like a man who had exerted all his strength to some end, the victory won, he loosened his muscles, with a faint sigh of exhaustion. Margaret did not speak, but she knew that something horrible was about to happen. Her heart beat like a prisoned bird, with helpless flutterings, but it seemed too late now to draw back. Her words by a mystic influence had settled something beyond possibility of recall.

On the stove was a small bowl of polished brass in which water was kept in order to give a certain moisture to the air. Oliver Haddo put his hand in his pocket and drew out a little silver box. He tapped it, with a smile, as a man taps a snuff-box, and opened it. He took an infinitesimal quantity of a blue powder that it contained and threw it on the water in the brass bowl. Immediately a bright flame sprang up and Margaret gave a cry of alarm. Oliver looked at her quickly and motioned her to remain still. She saw that the water was on fire. It was burning as brilliantly, as hotly as if it were common gas, and it burned with the same dry hoarse roar. Suddenly it was extinguished. She leaned forward and saw that the bowl was empty.

The water had been utterly consumed, as though it were straw, and not a drop remained. She passed her hand absently across her forehead.

"But water cannot burn," she muttered to herself.

It seemed that Haddo knew what she thought, for he smiled strangely.

"Do you know that nothing more destructive can be invented than this blue powder, and I have enough to burn up all the water in Paris? Who dreamt that water might be burnt like chaff?"

He paused, seeming to forget her presence. He looked thoughtfully at the little silver box.

"But it can be made only in trivial quantities, at enormous expense and with exceeding labour; it is so volatile that you cannot keep it for three days. I have sometimes thought that with a little ingenuity I might make it more stable, I might so modify it that, like radium, it lost no strength as it burned; and then I should possess the greatest secret that has ever been in the mind of man. For there would be no end of it. It would continue to burn while there was a drop of water on the earth and the whole world would be consumed. But it would be a frightful thing to have in one's hands; for once it were cast upon the waters, the doom of all that existed would be sealed beyond repeal."

He took a long breath and his eyes glittered with a devilish ardour. His voice was hoarse with overwhelming emotion.

"Sometimes I am haunted by the wild desire to have seen that great and final scene when the irrevocable flames poured down the river, hurrying along the streams of the earth, searching out the moisture in all growing things, tearing it even from the eternal rocks; when the flames poured down like the rushing of the wind and all that lived fled from before them till they came to the sea, and the sea itself was consumed in vehement fire."

Margaret shuddered, but she did not think the man was mad. She had ceased to judge him. He took one more particle of that atrocious powder and put it in the bowl. Again he thrust his hand in his pocket and brought out a handful of some crumbling substance that might have been dried leaves, leaves of different sorts, broken and powdery. There was a trace of moisture in them still, for a low flame sprang up immediately at the bottom of the dish and a thick vapour filled the room. It had a singular and pungent odour that Margaret did not know. It was difficult to breathe and she coughed. She wanted to beg Oliver to stop but could not. He took the bowl in his hands and brought it to her.

"Look," he commanded.

She bent forward and at the bottom saw a blue fire, of a peculiar solidity, as though it consisted of molten metal. It was not still, but writhed strangely, like serpents of fire tortured by their own unearthly ardour.

"Breathe very deeply."

She did as he told her. A sudden trembling came over her and darkness fell across her eyes. She tried to cry out but could utter no sound. Her brain reeled. It seemed to her that Haddo bade her cover her face. She gasped for breath and it was as if the earth spun under her feet. She appeared to travel at an immeasurable speed. She made a slight movement and Haddo told her not to look round. An immense terror seized her. She did not know whither she was borne and still they went quickly, quickly; and the hurricane itself would have lagged behind them. At last their motion ceased and Oliver was holding her arm.

"Don't be afraid," he said. "Open your eyes and stand up."

The night had fallen, but it was not the comfortable night that soothes the troubled minds of mortal men; it was a night that agitated the soul mysteriously so that each nerve in the body tingled. There was a lurid darkness which displayed them and yet distorted the objects that surrounded them. No moon shone in the sky but small stars appeared to dance on the heather, vague night-fires like spirits of the damned. They stood in a vast and troubled waste, with huge stony boulders and leafless trees, rugged and gnarled like tortured souls in pain. It was as if there had been a devastating storm and the country reposed after the flood of rain and the tempestuous wind and the lightning. All things about them appeared dumbly to suffer, like a man racked by torments who has not the strength even to realize that his agony has ceased. Margaret heard the flight of monstrous birds and they seemed to whisper strange things on their passage. Oliver took her hand. He led her steadily to a crossroad, and she did not know if they walked amid rocks or tombs.

She heard the sound of a trumpet and from all parts, strangely appearing where before was nothing, a turbulent assembly surged about her. That vast empty space was suddenly filled by shadowy forms, and they swept along like the waves of the sea, crowding upon one another's heels. And it seemed that all the mighty dead appeared before her; and she saw grim tyrants, and painted courtesans, and Roman emperors in their purple, and sultans of the East. All those fierce evil women of olden time passed by her side, and now it was Mona Lisa and now the subtle daughter of Herodias. And Jezebel looked out upon her from beneath her painted brows, and Cleopatra turned away a wan, lewd face; and she saw the insatiable mouth and the wanton eyes of Messalina, and Faustine was haggard with the eternal fires of lust. She saw cardinals in their scarlet and warriors in their steel, gay gentlemen in periwigs and ladies in powder and patch. And on a sudden, like leaves by the wind, all these were driven before the silent throngs of the oppressed; and they were innumerable as the sands of the sea. Their thin faces were earthy with want and cavernous from disease, and their eyes were dull with despair. They passed in their tattered motley, some in the fantastic rags of the beggars of Albrecht Dürer and some in the grey cerecloths of Le Nain; many wore the blouses and the caps of the rabble in France, and many the dingy, smoke-grimed weeds of English poor. And they surged onward like a rioutous crowd in narrow streets flying in terror before the mounted troops. It seemed as though all the world were gathered there in strange confusion.

Then all again was void and Margaret's gaze was riveted upon a great, ruined tree that stood in that waste place, alone, in ghastly desolation; and though a dead thing it seemed to suffer a more than human pain. The lightning had torn it asunder but the wind of centuries had sought in vain to drag up its roots. The tortured branches, bare of any twig, were like a Titan's arms, convulsed with intolerable anguish. And in a moment she grew sick with fear, for a change came into the tree and the tremulousness of life was in it; the rough bark was changed into brutish flesh and the twisted branches into human arms. It became a monstrous, goat-legged thing, more vast than the creatures of nightmare. She saw the horns and the long beard, the great hairy legs with their hoofs, and the man's rapacious hands. The face was horrible with lust and cruelty, and yet it was divine. It was Pan, playing on his pipes, and the lecherous eyes caressed her with a hideous tenderness. But even while she looked, as the mist of early day, rising, discloses a fair country, the animal part of that ghoulish creature seemed to fall away and she saw a lovely youth, titanic but sublime, leaning against a massive rock. He was more beautiful than the Adam of Michel-angelo who wakes into life at the call of the Almighty; and, like him freshly created, he had the adorable languor of one who feels still in his limbs the soft rain on the loose brown earth. Naked and full of majesty he lay, the outcast son of the morning; and she dared not look upon his face, for she knew it was impossible to bear the undying pain that darkened it with ruthless shadows. Impelled by a great curiosity, she sought to come nearer, but the vast figure seemed strangely to dissolve into a cloud; and immediately she felt herself again surrounded by a hurrying throng. Then came all the legendary monsters and foul beasts of a madman's fancy; in the darkness she saw enormous toads, with paws pressed to their flanks, and huge limping scarabs, shelled creatures the like of which she had never seen, and noisome brutes with horny scales and round crabs' eyes, uncouth primeval things, and winged serpents, and creeping animals begotten of the slime. She heard shrill cries and peals of laughter and the terrifying rattle of men at the point of death. Haggard women, dishevelled and lewd, carried wine; and when they spilt it there were stains like the stains of blood. And it seemed to Margaret that a fire burned in her veins and her soul fled from her body; but a new soul came in its place and suddenly she knew all that was obscene. She took part in some festival of hideous lust and the wickedness of the world was patent to her eyes. She saw things so vile that she screamed in terror, and she heard Oliver laugh in derision by her side. It was a scene of indescribable horror and she put her hands to her eyes so that she might not see.

She felt Oliver Haddo take her hands. She would not let him drag them away. Then she heard him speak.

"You need not be afraid."

His voice was quite natural once more and she realized with a start that she was sitting quietly in the studio. She looked around her with frightened eyes. Everything was exactly as it had been. The early night of autumn was fallen and the only light in the room came from the fire. There was still that vague, acrid scent of the substance which Haddo had burned.

'Shall I light the candles?" he said.

He struck a match and lit those which were on the piano. They threw a singular light. Then Margaret suddenly remembered all that she had seen and she remembered that Haddo had stood by her side. Shame seized her, intolerable shame so that the colour, rising to her cheeks, seemed actually to burn them. She hid her face in her hands and burst into tears.

"Go away," she said. "For God's sake, go."

He looked at her for a moment and a smile came to his lips He knew another victim was in his power.

FREAKS

TOD ROBBINS

(Metro-Goldwyn-Mayer: 1932)

The director who probably played the most important role in the early days of horror-film making in Hollywood was Tod Browning, a former circus man who was almost morbidly obsessed with the macabre, the unusual and the off-beat. In his pictures he demanded the most incredible and painful disguises for his monsters and quite possibly introduced more genuine stomach-turning horror per yard of film than any other director before or since. Browning was responsible for directing Lon Chaney in some of his most tortuous and brilliant sequences and also created the first really outstanding version of Dracula with Bela Lugosi in 1931.

But all his achievements pale in comparison with Freaks, which so stunned some of the preview audience that several women ran screaming from the cinema, and the major distributors refused to handle it. The film was based on a story called Spurs by a moderately successful English fantasy writer, Tod Robbins, and dealt gruesomely with the revenge of a circus midget and his friends on his normal size wife and her acrobat lover. The tale had been mentioned to Browning by a midget he had used in a previous horror film, and he determined to bring it to the screen—with real freaks.

Despite strong opposition to the project at M.G.M., Browning went ahead, employing his camera with incredible dexterity to make the abnormal seem normal and the ugly beautiful. The outcome was probably predictable: rejected as too gruesome, the picture initiated the decline in Browning's career as a film maker and was not shown in many countries for a great many years (in Britain it was on the banned list until 1963 and is even now only shown with caution). It may well be true to say that Freaks is the most horrific film ever made.

*

I

JACQUES COURBÉ was a romanticist. He measured only twenty-eight inches from the soles of his diminutive feet to the crown of his head; but there were times, as he rode into the arena on his gallant charger, St. Eustache, when he felt himself a doughty knight of old about to do battle for his lady.

What matter that St. Eustache was not a gallant charger except in his master's imagination—not even a pony, indeed, but a large dog of a nondescript breed, with the long snout and upstanding ears of a wolf? What matter that Monsieur Courbé's entrance was invariably greeted with shouts of derisive laughter and bombardments of banana skins and orange peel? What matter that he had no lady and that his daring deeds were severely curtailed to a mimicry of the bareback riders who preceded him? What mattered all these things to the tiny man who lived in dreams and who resolutely closed his shoe-button eyes to the drab realities of life?

The dwarf had no friends among the other freaks in Copo's Circus. They considered him ill-tempered and egotistical, and he loathed them for their acceptance of things as they were. Imagination was the armour that protected him from the curious glances of a cruel, gaping world, from the stinging lash of ridicule, from the bombardments of banana skins and orange peel. Without it, he must have shrivelled up and died. But these others? Ah, they had no armour except their own thick hides! The door that opened on the kingdom of imagination was closed and locked to them; and although they did not wish to open this door, although they did not miss what lay beyond it, they resented and mistrusted anyone who possessed the key.

Now it came about, after many humiliating performances in the arena, made palatable only by dreams, that love entered the circus tent and beckoned commandingly to Monsieur Jacques Courbé. In an instant the dwarf was engulfed in a sea of wild, tumultuous passion.

Mademoiselle Jeanne Marie was a daring bareback rider. It made Monsieur Jacques Courbé's tiny heart stand still to see her that first night of her appearance in the arena, performing brilliantly on the broad back of her aged mare, Sappho. A tall, blonde woman of the amazon type, she had round eyes of baby blue which held no spark of her avaricious peasant's soul, carmine lips and cheeks, large white teeth which flashed continually in a smile, and hands which, when doubled up, were nearly the size of the dwarf's head.

Her partner in the act was Simon Lafleur, the Romeo of the circus tent—a swarthy, Herculean young man with bold black eyes and hair that glistened with grease like the back of Solon, the trained seal.

From the first performance Monsieur Jacques Courbé loved Mademoiselle Jeanne Marie. All his tiny body was shaken with longing for her. Her buxom charms, so generously revealed in tights and spangles, made him flush and cast down his eyes. The familiarities allowed to Simon Lafleur, the bodily acrobatic contacts of the two performers, made the dwarf's blood boil. Mounted on St. Eustache, awaiting his turn at the entrance, he would grind his teeth in impotent rage to see Simon circling round and round the ring, standing proudly on the back of Sappho and holding Mademoiselle Jeanne Marie in an ecstatic embrace, while she kicked one shapely bespangled leg skyward.

"Ah, the dog!" Monsieur Jacques Courbé would mutter. "Some day I shall teach this hulking stable-boy his place! *Ma foi,* I will clip his ears for him!"

St. Eustache did not share his master's admiration for Mademoiselle Jeanne Marie. From the first he evinced his hearty detestation for her by low growls and a ferocious display of long, sharp fangs. It was little consolation for the dwarf to know that St. Eustache showed still more marked signs of rage when Simon Lafleur approached him. It pained Monsieur Jacques Courbé to think that his gallant charger, his sole companion, his bedfellow, should not also love and admire the splendid giantess who each night risked life and limb before the awed populace. Often, when they were alone together, he would chide St. Eustache on his churlishness.

"Ah, you devil of a dog!" the dwarf would cry. "Why must you always growl and show your ugly teeth when the lovely Jeanne Marie condescends to notice you? Have you no feelings under your tough hide? Cur, she is an angel and you snarl at her! Do you not remember how I found you, a starving puppy in a Paris gutter? And now you must threaten the hand of my princess! So this is your gratitude, great hairy pig!"

Monsieur Jacques Courbé had one living relative—not a dwarf, like himself, but a fine figure of a man, a prosperous farmer living just outside the town of Roubaix. The elder Courbé had never married and so one day, when he was found dead from heart failure, his tiny nephew—for whom, it must be confessed, the farmer had always felt an instinctive aversion—fell heir to a comfortable property. When the tidings were brought to him, the dwarf threw both arms about the shaggy neck of St. Eustache and cried out:

"Ah, now we can retire, marry and settle down, old friend! I am worth many times my weight in gold!"

That evening, as Mademoiselle Jeanne Marie was changing her gaudy costume after the performance, a light tap sounded on the door.

"Enter!" she called, believing it to be Simon Lafleur, who had promised to take her that evening to the Sign of the Wild Boar for a glass of wine to wash the sawdust out of her throat. "Enter, *mon chéri*!"

The door swung slowly open and in stepped Monsieur Jacques Courbé, very proud and upright, in the silks and laces of a courtier, with a tiny gold-hilted sword swinging at his hip. Up he came, his shoe-button eyes all a-glitter to see the more than partially revealed charms of his robust lady. Up he came to within a yard of where she sat, and down on one knee he went and pressed his lips to her red-slippered foot.

"Oh, most beautiful and daring lady," he cried, in a voice as shrill as a pin scratching on a window-pane, "will you not take mercy on the unfortunate Jacques Courbé? He is hungry for your smiles, he is starving for your lips! All night long he tosses on his couch and dreams of Jeanne Marie!"

"What play-acting is this, my brave little fellow?" she asked, bending down with the smile of an ogress. "Has Simon Lafleur sent you to tease me?"

"May the black plague have Simon!" the dwarf cried, his eyes seeming to flash blue sparks. "I am not play-acting. It is only too true that I love you, mademoiselle, that I wish to make you my lady. And now that I have a fortune, now that—" He broke off suddenly and his face resembled a withered apple. "What is this, mademoiselle?" he said, in the low, droning tone of a hornet about to sting. "Do you laugh at my love? I warn you, mademoiselle— do not laugh at Jacques Courbé!"

Mademoiselle Jeanne Marie's large, florid face had turned purple from suppressed merriment. Her lips twitched at the corners. It was all she could do not to burst out into a roar of laughter.

Why, the ridiculous little manikin was serious in his love-making! This pocket-sized edition of a courtier was proposing marriage to her! He, this splinter of a fellow, wished to make her his wife! Why, she could carry him about on her shoulder like a trained marmoset!

What a joke this was—what a colossal, corset-creaking joke! Wait till she told Simon Lafleur! She could fairly see him throw back his sleek head, open his mouth to its widest dimensions and shake with silent laughter. But *she* must not laugh—not now. First she must listen to everything the dwarf had to say, draw all the sweetness out of this bonbon of humour before she crushed it under the heel of ridicule.

"I am not laughing," she managed to say. "You have taken me by surprise. I never thought, I never even guessed—"

"That is well, mademoiselle," the dwarf broke in. "I do not tolerate laughter. In the arena I am paid to make laughter, but these others pay to laugh at *me*. I always make people pay to laugh at me!"

"But do I understand you aright, Monsieur Courbé? Are you proposing an honourable marriage?"

The dwarf rested his hand on his heart and bowed. "Yes. mademoiselle, an honourable marriage, and the wherewithal to keep the wolf from the door. A week ago my uncle died and left me a large estate. We shall have a servant to wait on our wants, a horse and carriage, food and wine of the best, and leisure to amuse ourselves. And you? Why, you will be a fine lady! I will clothe that beautiful big body of yours with silks and laces! You will be as happy, mademoiselle, as a cherry tree in June!"

The dark blood slowly receded from Mademoiselle Jeanne Marie's full cheeks, her lips no longer twitched at the corners, her eyes had narrowed slightly. She had been a bareback rider for years and she was weary of it. The life of the circus tent had lost its tinsel. She loved the dashing Simon Lafleur, but she knew well enough that this Romeo in tights would never espouse a dowerless girl.

The dwarf's words had woven themselves into a rich mental tapestry. She saw herself a proud lady, ruling over a country estate, and later welcoming Simon Lafleur with all the luxuries that were so near his heart. Simon would be overjoyed to marry into a country estate. These pygmies were a puny lot. They died young! She would do nothing to hasten the end of Jacques Courbé. No, she would be kindness itself to the poor little fellow, but, on the other hand, she would not lose her beauty mourning for him.

"Nothing that you wish shall be withheld from you as long as you love me, mademoiselle," the dwarf continued. "Your answer?"

Mademoiselle Jeanne Marie bent forward and, with a single movement of her powerful arms, raised Monsieur Jacques Courbé and placed him on her knee. For an ecstatic instant she held him thus, as if he were a large French doll, with his tiny sword cocked coquettishly out behind. Then she planted on his cheek a huge kiss that covered his entire face from chin to brow.

"I am yours!" she murmured, pressing him to her ample bosom. "From the first I loved you, Monsieur Jacques Courbé!"

2

The wedding of Mademoiselle Jeanne Marie was celebrated in the town of Roubaix, where Copo's Circus had taken up its temporary quarters. Following the ceremony, a feast was served in one of the tents, which was attended by a whole galaxy of celebrities.

The bridegroom, his dark little face flushed with happiness and wine, sat at the head of the board. His chin was just above the table-cloth, so that his head looked like a large orange that had rolled off the fruit-dish. Immediately beneath his dangling feet, St. Eustache, who had more than once evinced by deep growls his disapproval of the proceedings, now worried a bone with quick, sly glances from time to time at the plump legs of his new mistress. Papa Copo was on the dwarf's right, his large round face as red and benevolent as a harvest moon. Next him sat Griffo, the giraffe boy, who was covered with spots, and whose neck was so long that he looked down on all the rest, including Monsieur Hercule Hippo, the giant. The rest of the company included Mademoiselle Lupa, who had sharp white teeth of an incredible length, and who growled when she tried to talk; the tiresome Monsieur Jejongle, who insisted on juggling fruit, plates and knives, although the whole company was heartily sick of his tricks; Madame Samson, with her trained baby boa constrictors coiled about her neck and peeping out timidly, one above each ear; Simon Lafleur and a score of others.

The bareback rider had laughed silently and almost continually ever since Jeanne Marie had told him of her engagement. Now he sat next to her in his crimson tights. His black hair was brushed back from his forehead and so glistened with grease that it reflected the lights overhead, like a burnished helmet. From time to time he tossed off a brimming goblet of Burgundy, nudged the bride in the ribs with his elbow and threw back his sleek head in another silent outburst of laughter.

"And you are sure that you will not forget me, Simon?" she

whispered. "It may be some time before I can get the little ape's money."

"Forget you, Jeanne?" he muttered. "By all the dancing devils in champagne, never! I will wait as patiently as Job till you have fed that mouse some poisoned cheese. But what will you do with him in the meantime, Jeanne? You must allow him no liberties. I grind my teeth to think of you in his arms!"

The bride smiled and regarded her diminutive husband with an appraising glance. What an atom of a man! And yet life might linger in his bones for a long time to come. Monsieur Jacques Courbé had allowed himself only one glass of wine and yet he was far gone in intoxication. His tiny face was suffused with blood and he stared at Simon Lafleur belligerently. Did he suspect the truth?

"Your husband is flushed with wine!" the bareback rider whispered. "*Ma foi, madame,* later he may knock you about! Possibly he is a dangerous fellow in his cups. Should he maltreat you, Jeanne, do not forget that you have a protector in Simon Lafleur."

"You clown!" Jeanne Marie rolled her large eyes roguishly and laid her hand for an instant on the bareback rider's knee. "Simon, I could crack his skull between my finger and thumb, like this hickory nut!" She paused to illustrate her example, and then added reflectively : "And, perhaps, I shall do that very thing, if he attempts any familiarities. Ugh! The little ape turns my stomach!"

By now the wedding guests were beginning to show the effects of their potations. This was especially marked in the case of Monsieur Jacque's associates in the side-show.

Griffo, the giraffe boy, had closed his large brown eyes and was swaying his small head languidly above the assembly, while a slightly supercilious expression drew his lips down at the corners. Monsieur Hercule Hippo, swollen out by his libations to even more colossal proportions, was repeating over and over : "I tell you I am not like other men. When I walk, the earth trembles!" Mademoiselle Lupa, her hairy upper lip lifted above her long white teeth, was gnawing at a bone, growling unintelligible phrases to herself and shooting savage, suspicious glances at her companions. Monsieur Jejongle's hands had grown unsteady and, as he insisted on juggling the knives and plates of each new course, broken bits of crockery littered the floor. Madame Samson, uncoiling her necklace of baby boa constrictors, was feeding them lumps of sugar soaked in rum. Monsieur Jacques Courbé had finished his second glass of wine and was surveying the whispering Simon Lafleur through narrowed eyes.

There can be no genial companionship among great egotists who have drunk too much. Each one of these human oddities thought that he or she alone was responsible for the crowds that daily gathered at Copo's Circus; so now, heated with the good Burgundy, they were not slow in asserting themselves. Their separate egos rattled angrily together, like so many pebbles in a bag. Here was gunpowder which needed only a spark.

"I am a big—a very big man!" Monsieur Hercule Hippo said sleepily. "Women love me. The pretty little creatures leave their pygmy husbands, so that they may come and stare at Hercule Hippo of Copo's Circus. Ha, and when they return home, they laugh at other men always! 'You may kiss me again when you grow up', they tell their sweethearts."

"Fat bullock, here is one woman who has no love for you!" cried Mademoiselle Lupa, glaring sidewise at the giant over her bone. "That great carcass of yours is only so much food gone to waste. You have cheated the butcher, my friend. Fool, women do not come to see *you*! As well might they stare at the cattle being led through the street. Ah, no, they come from far and near to see one of their own sex who is not a cat!"

"Quite right," cried Papa Copo in a conciliatory tone, smiling and rubbing his hands together. "Not a cat, mademoiselle, but a wolf. Ah, you have a sense of humour! How droll!"

"I *have* a sense of humour," Mademoiselle Lupa agreed, returning to her bone, "and also sharp teeth. Let the erring hand not stray too near!"

"You, Monsieur Hippo and Mademoiselle Lupa, are both wrong," said a voice which seemed to come from the roof. "Surely it is none other than me whom the people come to stare at!"

All raised their eyes to the supercilious face of Griffo, the giraffe boy, which swayed slowly from side to side on its long, pipe-stem neck. It was he who had spoken, although his eyes were still closed.

"Of all the colossal impudence!" cried the matronly Madame Samson. "As if my little dears had nothing to say on the subject!" She picked up the two baby boa constrictors, which lay in drunken slumber on her lap, and shook them like whips at the wedding guests. "Papa Copo knows only too well that it is on account of these little charmers, Mark Antony and Cleopatra, that the side-show is so well attended!"

The circus owner, thus directly appealed to, frowned in perplexity. He felt himself in a quandary. These freaks of his were difficult to handle. Why had he been fool enough to come to Monsieur Jacques Courbé's wedding feast? Whatever he said would be used against him.

As Papa Copo hesitated, his round, red face wreathed in ingratiating smiles, the long deferred spark suddenly alighted in the powder. It all came about on account of the carelessness of Monsieur Jejongle, who had become engrossed in the conversation and wished to put in a word for himself. Absent-mindedly juggling two heavy plates and a spoon, he said in a petulant tone : "You all appear to forget *me* !"

Scarcely were the words out of his mouth when one of the heavy plates descended with a crash on the thick skull of Monsieur Hippo, and Monsieur Jejongle was instantly remembered. Indeed, he was more than remembered, for the giant, already irritated to the boiling-point by Mademoiselle Lupa's insults, at this new affront struck out savagely past her and knocked the juggler head-over-heels under the table.

Mademoiselle Lupa, always quick-tempered and especially so when her attention was focused on a juicy chicken bone, evidently considered her dinner companion's conduct far from decorous and promptly inserted her sharp teeth in the offending hand that had administered the blow. Monsieur Hippo, squealing from rage and pain like a wounded elephant, bounded to his feet, overturning the table.

Pandemonium followed. Every freak's hands, teeth, feet, were turned against the others. Above the shouts, screams, growls and hisses of the combat, Papa Copo's voice could be heard bellowing for peace :

"Ah, my children, my children ! This is no way to behave ! Calm yourselves, I pray you ! Mademoiselle Lupa, remember that you are a lady as well as a wolf !"

There is no doubt that Monsieur Jacques Courbé would have suffered most in this undignified fracas had it not been for St. Eustache, who had stationed himself over his tiny master and who now drove off all would-be assailants. As it was, Griffo, the unfortunate giraffe boy, was the most defenceless and therefore became the victim. His small, round head swayed back and forth to blows like a punching bag. He was bitten by Mademoiselle Lupa, buffeted by Monsieur Hippo, kicked by Monsieur Jejongle, clawed by Madame Samson, and nearly strangled by both the baby boa constrictors, which had wound themselves about his neck like hangmen's nooses. Undoubtedly he would have fallen a victim to circumstances had it not been for Simon Lafleur, the bride and half a dozen of her acrobatic friends, whom Papa Copo had implored to restore peace. Roaring with laughter, they sprang forward and tore the combatants apart.

Monsieur Jacques Courbé was found sitting grimly under a fold of the tablecloth. He held a broken bottle of wine in one hand. The dwarf was very drunk and in a towering rage. As Simon Lafleur approached with one of his silent laughs, Monsieur Jacques Courbé hurled the bottle at his head.

"Ah, the little wasp!" the bareback rider cried, picking up the dwarf by his waistband. "Here is your fine husband, Jeanne! Take him away before he does me some mischief. *Parbleu,* he is a blood-thirsty fellow in his cups!"

The bride approached, her blonde face crimson from wine and laughter. Now that she was safely married to a country estate she took no more pains to conceal her true feelings.

"Oh, *la, la*!" she cried, seizing the struggling dwarf and holding him forcibly on her shoulder. "What a temper the little ape has! Well, we shall spank it out of him before long!"

"Let me down!" Monsieur Jacques Courbé screamed in a par-oxysm of fury. "You will regret this, madame! Let me down, I say!"

But the stalwart bride shook her head. "No, no, my little one!" she laughed. "You cannot escape your wife so easily! What, you would fly from my arms before the honeymoon!"

"Let me down!" he cried again. "Can't you see that they are laughing at me?"

"And why should they not laugh, my little ape? Let them laugh, if they will, but I will not put you down. No, I will carry you thus, perched on my shoulder, to the farm. It will set a pre-cedent which brides of the future may find a certain difficulty in following!"

"But the farm is quite a distance from here, my Jeanne," said Simon Lafleur. "You are as strong as an ox and he is only a marmo-set, still, I will wager a bottle of Burgundy that you set him down by the roadside."

"Done, Simon!" the bride cried, with a flash of her strong white teeth. "You shall lose your wager, for I swear that I could carry my little ape from one end of France to the other!"

Monsieur Jacques Courbé no longer struggled. He now sat bolt upright on his bride's broad shoulder. From the flaming peaks of blind passion he had fallen into an abyss of cold fury. His love was dead, but some quite alien emotion was rearing an evil head from its ashes.

"So, madame, you could carry me from one end of France to the other!" he droned in a monotonous undertone. "From one end of France to the other! I will remember that always, madame!"

"Come!" cried the bride suddenly. "I am off. Do you and the others, Simon, follow to see me win my wager."

They all trooped out of the tent. A full moon rode the heavens and showed the road, lying as white and straight through the meadows as the parting in Simon Lafleur's black, oily hair. The bride, still holding the diminutive bridegroom on her shoulder, burst out into song as she strode forward. The wedding guests followed. Some walked none too steadily. Griffo, the giraffe boy, staggered pitifully on his long, thin legs. Papa Copo alone remained behind.

"What a strange world!" he muttered, standing in the tent door and following them with his round blue eyes. "Ah, these children of mine are difficult at times—very difficult!"

3

A year had rolled by since the marriage of Mademoiselle Jeanne Marie and Monsieur Jacques Courbé. Copo's Circus had once more taken up its quarters in the town of Roubaix. For more than a week the country people for miles around had flocked to the side-show to get a peep at Griffo, the giraffe boy; Monsieur Hercule Hippo, the giant; Mademoiselle Lupa, the wolf lady; Madame Samson, with her baby boa constrictors; and Monsieur Jejongle, the famous juggler. Each was still firmly convinced that he or she alone was responsible for the popularity of the circus.

Simon Lafleur sat in his lodgings at the Sign of the Wild Boar. He wore nothing but red tights. His powerful torso, stripped to the waist, glistened with oil. He was kneading his biceps tenderly with some strong-smelling fluid.

Suddenly there came the sound of heavy, laborious footsteps on the stairs. Simon Lafleur looked up. His rather gloomy expression lifted, giving place to the brilliant smile that had won for him the hearts of so many lady acrobats.

"Ah, this is Marcelle!" he told himself. "Or perhaps it is Rose, the English girl; or, yet again, little Francesca, although she walks more lightly. Well, no matter—whoever it is, I will welcome her!"

But now the lagging, heavy footfalls were in the hall and, a moment later, they came to a halt outside the door. There was a timid knock.

Simon Lafleur's brilliant smile broadened. "Perhaps some new admirer who needs encouragement," he told himself. But aloud he said : "Enter, mademoiselle!"

The door swung slowly open and revealed the visitor. She was a tall, gaunt woman dressed like a peasant. The wind had blown her hair into her eyes. Now she raised a large, toil-worn hand, brushed it back across her forehead and looked long and attentively at the bareback rider.

"You do not remember me?" she said at length.

Two lines of perplexity appeared above Simon Lafleur's Roman nose; he slowly shook his head. He, who had known so many women in his time, was now at a loss. Was it a fair question to ask a man who was no longer a boy and who had lived? Women change so in a brief time! Now this bag of bones might at one time have appeared desirable to him.

Parbleu! Fate was a conjurer! She waved her wand and beautiful women were transformed into hags, jewels into pebbles, silks and laces into hempen cords. The brave fellow who danced tonight at the prince's ball might tomorrow dance more lightly on the gallows tree. The thing was to live and die with a full belly. To digest all that one could—that was life!

"You do not remember me?" she said again.

Simon Lafleur once more shook his sleek, black head. "I have a poor memory for faces, madame," he said politely. "It is my misfortune, when there are such beautiful faces."

"Ah, but you should have remembered, Simon!" the woman cried, a sob rising up in her throat. "We were very close together, you and I. Do you not remember Jeanne Marie?"

"Jeanne Marie!" the bareback rider cried. "Jeanne Marie, who married a marmoset and a country estate? Don't tell me, madame, that you—"

He broke off and stared at her, open-mouthed. His sharp black eyes wandered from the wisps of wet, straggling hair down her gaunt person till they rested at last on her thick cowhide boots, encrusted with layer on layer of mud from the countryside.

"It is impossible!" he said at last.

"It is indeed Jeanne Marie," the woman answered, "or what is left of her. Ah, Simon, what a life he has led me! I have been merely a beast of burden! There are no ignominies which he has not made me suffer!"

"To whom do you refer?" Simon Lafleur demanded. "Surely you cannot mean that pocket edition husband of yours—that dwarf, Jacques Courbé?"

"Ah, but I do, Simon! Alas, he has broken me!"

"He—that toothpick of a man?" the bareback rider cried, with one of his silent laughs. "Why, it is impossible! As you once said yourself, Jeanne, you could crack his skull between finger and thumb like a hickory nut!"

"So I thought once. Ah, but I did not know him then, Simon! Because he was small, I thought I could do with him as I liked. It seemed to me that I was marrying a manikin. 'I will play Punch and Judy with this little fellow,' I said to myself. Simon, you may imagine my surprise when he began playing Punch and Judy with me!"

"But I do not understand, Jeanne. Surely at any time you could have slapped him into obedience!"

"Perhaps," she assented wearily, "had it not been for St. Eustache. From the first that wolf dog of his hated me. If I so much as answered his master back, he would show his teeth. Once, at the beginning, when I raised my hand to cuff Jacques Courbé, he sprang at my throat and would have torn me limb from limb had not the dwarf called him off. I was a strong woman, but even then I was no match for a wolf!"

"There was poison, was there not?" Simon Lafleur suggested.

"Ah, yes, I, too, thought of poison, but it was of no avail. St. Eustache would eat nothing that I gave him and the dwarf forced me to taste first of all food that was placed before him and his dog. Unless I myself wished to die, there was no way of poisoning either of them."

"My poor girl!" the bareback rider said, pityingly. "I begin to understand, but sit down and tell me everything. This is a revelation to me, after seeing you stalking homeward so triumphantly with your bridegroom on your shoulder. You must begin at the beginning."

"It was just because I carried him thus on my shoulder that I have had to suffer so cruelly," she said, seating herself on the only other chair the room afforded. "He has never forgiven me the insult which he says I put upon him. Do you remember how I boasted that I could carry him from one end of France to the other?"

"I remember. Well, Jeanne?"

"Well, Simon, the little demon has figured out the exact distance in leagues. Each morning, rain or shine, we sally out of the house—he on my back, the wolf dog at my heels—and I tramp along the dusty roads till my knees tremble beneath me from fatigue. If I so much as slacken my pace, if I falter, he goads me with his cruel little golden spurs, while, at the same time, St. Eustache nips my ankles. When we return home, he strikes so many leagues off a score which he says is the number of leagues from one end of France to the other. Not half that distance has been covered and I am no longer a strong woman, Simon. Look at these shoes!"

She held up one of her feet for his inspection. The sole of the cowhide boot had been worn through; Simon Lafleur caught a glimpse of bruised flesh caked with the mire of the highway.

"This is the third pair that I have had," she continued hoarsely. "Now he tells me that the price of shoe leather is too high, that I shall have to finish my pilgrimage barefooted."

"But why do you put up with all this, Jeanne?" Simon Lafleur asked angrily. "You, who have a carriage and a servant, should not walk at all!"

"At first there was a carriage and a servant," she said, wiping the tears from her eyes with the back of her hand, "but they did not last a week. He sent the servant about his business and sold the carriage at a near-by fair. Now there is no one but me to wait on him and his dog."

"But the neighbours?" Simon Lafleur persisted. "Surely you could appeal to them?"

"We have no near neighbours, the farm is quite isolated. I would have run away many months ago if I could have escaped unnoticed, but they keep a continual watch on me. Once I tried, but I hadn't travelled more than a league before the wolf dog was snapping at my ankles. He drove me back to the farm and the following day I was compelled to carry the little fiend till I fell from sheer exhaustion."

"But tonight you got away?"

"Yes," she said, with a quick, frightened glance at the door. "Tonight I slipped out while they were both sleeping and came here to you. I knew that you would protect me, Simon, because of what we have been to each other. Get Papa Copo to take me back in the circus and I will work my fingers to the bone! Save me, Simon!"

Jeanne Marie could no longer suppress her sobs. They rose in her throat, choking her, making her incapable of further speech.

"Calm yourself, Jeanne," Simon Lafleur said soothingly. "I will do what I can for you. I shall have a talk with Papa Copo tomorrow. Of course, you are no longer the same woman that you were a year ago. You have aged since then, but perhaps our good Papa Copo could find you something to do."

He broke off and eyed her intently. She had stiffened in the chair, her face, even under its coat of grime, had gone a sickly white.

"What troubles you, Jeanne?" he asked a trifle breathlessly.

"Hush!" she said, with a finger to her lips. "Listen!"

Simon Lafleur could hear nothing but the tapping of the rain on the roof and the sighing of the wind through the trees. An unusual silence seemed to pervade the Sign of the Wild Boar.

"Now don't you hear it?" she cried with an inarticulate gasp. "Simon, it is in the house—it is on the stairs!"

At last the bareback rider's less sensitive ears caught the sound his companion had heard a full minute before. It was a steady *pit-pat, pit-pat,* on the stairs, hard to dissociate from the drip of the rain from the eaves, but each instant it came nearer, grew more distinct.

"Oh, save me, Simon, save me!" Jeanne Marie cried, throwing herself at his feet and clasping him about the knees. "Save me! It is St. Eustache!"

"Nonsense, woman!" the bareback rider said angrily, but nevertheless he rose. "There are other dogs in the world. On the second landing there is a blind fellow who owns a dog. Perhaps it is he you hear."

"No, no—it is St. Eustache's step! My God, if you had lived with him a year, you would know it, too! Close the door and lock it!"

"That I will not," Simon Lafleur said contemptuously. "Do you think I am frightened so easily? If it is the wolf dog, so much the worse for him. He will not be the first cur I have choked to death with these two hands!"

Pit-pat, pit-pat—it was on the second landing. *Pit-pat, pit-pat*—now it was in the corridor, and coming fast. *Pit-pat*—all at once it stopped.

There was a moment's breathless silence and then into the room trotted St. Eustache. Monsieur Jacques Courbé sat astride the dog's broad back, as he had so often done in the circus ring. He held a tiny drawn sword, his shoe-button eyes seemed to reflect its steely glitter.

The dwarf brought the dog to a halt in the middle of the room and took in, at a single glance, the prostrate figure of Jeanne Marie. St. Eustache, too, seemed to take silent note of it. The stiff hair on his back rose up, he showed his long white fangs hungrily and his eyes glowed like two live coals.

"So I find you *thus*, madame!" Monsieur Jacques Courbé said at last. "It is fortunate that I have a charger here who can scent out my enemies as well as hunt them down in the open. Without him, I might have had some difficulty in discovering you. Well, the little game is up. I find you with your lover!"

"Simon Lafleur is not my lover!" she sobbed. "I have not seen him once since I married you until tonight! I swear it!"

"Once is enough," the dwarf said grimly. "The impudent stable-boy must be chastised!"

"Oh, spare him!" Jeanne Marie implored. "Do not harm him, I beg of you! It is not his fault that I came! I—"

But at this point Simon Lafleur drowned her out in a roar of laughter.

"Ho, ho!" he roared, putting his hands on his hips. "You would chastise me, eh? *Nom d'un chien!* Don't try your circus tricks on *me*! Why, hop-o-my thumb, you who ride on a dog's back like a flea, out of this room before I squash you! Begone, melt, fade away!" He paused, expanded his barrel-like chest, puffed out his cheeks and blew a great breath at the dwarf. "Blow away, insect," he bellowed, "lest I put my heel on you!"

Monsieur Jacques Courbé was unmoved by this torrent of abuse. He sat very upright on St. Eustache's back, his tiny sword resting on his tiny shoulder.

"Are you done?" he said at last, when the bareback rider had run dry of invectives. "Very well, monsieur! Prepare to receive cavalry!" He paused for an instant, then added in a high, clear voice : "Get him, St. Eustache!"

The dog crouched and, at almost the same moment, sprang at Simon Lafleur. The bareback rider had no time to avoid him and his tiny rider. Almost instantaneously the three of them had come to death grips. It was a gory business.

Simon Lafleur, strong man as he was, was bowled over by the

wolf dog's unexpected leap. St. Eustache's clashing jaws closed on his right arm and crushed it to the bone. A moment later the dwarf, still clinging to his dog's back, thrust the point of his tiny sword into the body of the prostrate bareback rider.

Simon Lafleur struggled valiantly, but to no purpose. Now he felt the fetid breath of the dog fanning his neck and the wasp-like sting of the dwarf's blade, which this time found a mortal spot. A convulsive tremor shook him and he rolled over on his back. The circus Romeo was dead.

Monsieur Jacques Courbé cleansed his sword on a kerchief of lace, dismounted and approached Jeanne Marie. She was still crouching on the floor, her eyes closed, her head held tightly between both hands. The dwarf touched her imperiously on the broad shoulder which had so often carried him.

"Madame," he said, "we now can return home. You must be more careful hereafter. *Ma foi,* it is an ungentlemanly business cutting the throats of stable-boys!"

She rose to her feet, like a large trained animal at the word of command.

"You wish to be carried?" she said between livid lips.

"Ah, that is true, madame," he murmured. "I was forgetting our little wager. Ah, yes! Well, you are to be congratulated, madame—you have covered nearly half the distance."

"Nearly half the distance," she repeated in a lifeless voice.

"Yes, madame," Monsieur Jacques Courbé continued. "I fancy that you will be quite a docile wife by the time you have done." He paused and then added reflectively : "It is truly remarkable how speedily one can ride the devil out of a woman—with spurs!"

Papa Copo had been spending a convivial evening at the Sign of the Wild Boar. As he stepped out into the street he saw three familiar figures preceding him—a tall woman, a tiny man and a large dog with upstanding ears. The woman carried the man on her shoulder, the dog trotted at her heels.

The circus owner came to a halt and stared after them. His round eyes were full of childish astonishment.

"Can it be?" he murmured. "Yes, it is! Three old friends! And so Jeanne Marie still carries him! Ah, but she should not poke fun at Monsieur Jacques Courbé! He is so sensitive; but, alas, they are the kind that are always henpecked!"

MOST DANGEROUS GAME

RICHARD CONNELL

(RKO-Radio: 1932 et al)

Not all the early horror films relied entirely on monsters and things that go bump in the night for their effect. Indeed, as the genre grew more sophisticated, adventurous producers and directors started looking even further afield for subjects that terrorized by implication or frightened by tension. A distinguished example of this type of production is Most Dangerous Game, *made in 1932 and based on the story of the same title which had won its American author, Richard Connell, the O'Henry Memorial Award in 1924.*

The plot concerns a sadistic Russian general who lures unsuspecting people on to the Caribbean island where he lives, and then gives them a chance to run for freedom—pursuing them as human prey with his bloodhounds. The camera-work in the film is particularly outstanding during the main chase sequence, when the human quarry (here, differing from the story, a man and a woman) slowly begin to turn the tables on their pursuer, skilfully using the general's own methods of hunting to bring about his downfall. The picture expertly develops terror and tension as it progresses, allowing the audience little respite, and reflects great credit on the directing team of Ernest B. Schoedsack and Irving Pichel.

In his definitive study, Le Surréalisme au Cinema, *Ado Kyrou describes* Most Dangerous Game *as "the perfect example of the good sadistic film ... a masterpiece of surrealist cinema". (The story has also been refilmed twice, in 1945 as* A Game of Death, *directed by Robert Wise, and in 1956 as* Run For the Sun, *with Trevor Howard and Richard Widmark.)*

*

THERE was no sound in the night as Rainsford sat there but the muffled throb of the engine that drove the yacht swiftly through the darkness, and the swish and ripple of the wash of the propeller. Rainsford, reclining in a steamer chair, indolently puffed on his favourite briar. "It's so dark," he thought, "that I could sleep without closing my eyes; the night would be my eyelids—"

An abrupt sound startled him. Off to the right he heard it and his ears, expert in such matters, could not be mistaken. Again he heard the sound, and again. Somewhere, off in the blackness, someone had fired a gun three times. Rainsford sprang up and moved quickly to the rail, mystified. He strained his eyes in the direction from which the reports had come, but it was like trying to see through a blanket. He leaped upon the rail and balanced himself there, to get greater elevation; his pipe, striking a rope, was knocked from his mouth. He lunged for it; a short, hoarse cry came from his lips as he realized he had reached too far and had lost his balance. The cry was pinched off short as the blood-warm waters of the Caribbean Sea closed over his head.

He struggled up to the surface and tried to cry out, but the wash from the speeding yacht slapped him in the face and the salt water in his open mouth made him gag and strangle. Desperately he struck out with strong strokes after the receding lights of the yacht, but he stopped before he had swum fifty feet. A certain coolheadedness had come to him; it was not the first time he had been in a tight place. There was a chance that his cries could be heard by someone aboard the yacht, but that chance was slender and grew more slender as the yacht raced on. He wrestled himself out of his clothes and shouted with all his power. The lights of the yacht became faint and ever-vanishing fireflies; then they were blotted out entirely by the night.

Rainsford remembered the shots. They had come from the right, and doggedly he swam in that direction, swimming with slow, deliberate strokes, conserving his strength. For a seemingly endless time he fought the sea. He began to count his strokes; he could do possibly a hundred more, he thought, and then—

Rainsford heard a sound. It came out of the darkness, a high, screaming sound, the sound of an animal in an extremity of anguish and terror. He did not recognize the animal that made the sound, he did not try to; with fresh vitality he swam towards the sound. He heard it again, then it was cut short by another noise, crisp, staccato.

"Pistol shot," muttered Rainsford, swimming on.

Ten minutes of determined effort brought another sound to his ears—the most welcome he had ever heard—the muttering and growling of the sea breaking on a rocky shore. He was almost on the rocks before he saw them; on a night less calm he would have been shattered against them. With his remaining strength he dragged himself from the swirling waters. Gasping, his hands raw, he reached a flat place at the top. Dense jungle came down to the very edge of the cliffs. What perils that tangle of trees and underbrush might hold for him did not concern Rainsford just then. All he knew was that he was safe from his enemy, the sea, and that utter weariness was on him. He flung himself down at the jungle edge and tumbled headlong into the deepest sleep of his life.

When he opened his eyes he knew from the position of the sun that it was late in the afternoon. Sleep had given him new vigour; a sharp hunger was picking at him. He looked about him, almost cheerfully.

"Where there are pistol shouts there are men. Where there are men there is food," he thought. But what kind of men, he wondered, in so forbidding a place? An unbroken front of snarled and ragged jungle fringed the shore.

He saw no sign of a trail through the closely knit web of weeds and trees; it was easier to go along the shore and Rainsford floundered along by the water. Not far from where he had landed, he stopped. Some wounded thing, by the evidence a large animal, had thrashed about in the underbrush; the jungle weeds were crushed down and the moss was lacerated; one patch of weeds was stained crimson. A small, glittering object not far away caught Rainsford's eye and he picked it up. It was an empty cartridge.

"A twenty-two," he remarked. "That's odd. It must have been a fairly large animal, too. The hunter had his nerve with him to tackle it with a light gun. It's clear that the brute put up a fight."

He examined the ground closely and found what he had hoped to find—the print of hunting boots. They pointed along the cliff in the direction he had been going. Eagerly he hurried along, now slipping on a rotten log or a loose stone, but making headway; night was beginning to settle down on the island.

Bleak darkness was blacking out the sea and jungle when Rainsford sighted the lights. He came upon them as he turned a crook in the coastline, and his first thought was that he had come upon a village, for there were many lights. But as he forged his way along he saw to his astonishment that all the lights were in one enormous building—a lofty structure with pointed towers plunging upwards into the gloom. His eyes made out the shadowy outlines of a palatial château; it was set on a high bluff and on three sides of it cliffs dived down to where the sea licked greedy lips in the shadows.

"Mirage," thought Rainsford. But it was no mirage, he found, when he opened the tall spiked iron gate. The stone steps were real enough, the massive door with a leering gargoyle for a knocker was real enough, yet about it all hung an air of unreality. He lifted the knocker and it creaked up stiffly as if it had never before been used. He let it fall and it startled him with its booming loudness. He thought he heard steps within, the door remained closed. Again Rainsford lifted the heavy knocker and let it fall. The door opened then, opened as suddenly as if it were on a spring, and Rainsford stood blinking in the river of glaring gold light that poured out. The first thing his eyes discerned was the largest man Rainsford had ever seen—a gigantic creature, solidly made and black-bearded to the waist. In his hand the man held a long-barrelled revolver and he was pointing it straight at Rainsford's heart. Out of the snarl of beard two small eyes regarded Rainsford.

"Don't be alarmed," said Rainsford, with a smile which he hoped was disarming. "I'm no robber. I fell off a yacht. My name is Sanger Rainsford of New York City."

The menacing look in the eyes did not change. The revolver pointed as rigidly as if the giant were a statue. He gave no sign that he understood Rainsford's words, or that he had even heard them. He was dressed in uniform, a black uniform trimmed with grey astrakhan.

"I'm Sanger Rainsford of New York," Rainsford began again. "I fell off a yacht. I am hungry."

The man's only answer was to raise with his thumb the hammer of his revolver. Then Rainsford saw the man's free hand go to his forehead in a military salute and he saw him click his heels together and stand at attention. Another man was coming down the broad marble steps, an erect, slender man in evening clothes. He advanced to Rainsford and held out his hand. In a cultivated voice marked by a slight accent that gave it added precision and deliberateness, he said : "It is a very great pleasure and honour to welcome Mr. Sanger Rainsford, the celebrated hunter, to my home. I've read your book about hunting snow leopards in Tibet, you see," explained the man. "I am General Zaroff."

Rainsford's first impression was that the man was singularly handsome; his second was that there was an original, almost bizarre quality about the general's face. He was a tall man past middle age, for his hair was a vivid white, but his thick eyebrows and pointed military moustache were as black as the night from which Rainsford had come. His eyes, too, were black and very bright. He had high cheekbones, a sharp-cut nose, a spare, dark face, the face of a man used to giving orders, the face of an aristocrat. Turning to the giant in uniform, the general made a sign. The giant put away his pistol, saluted, withdrew.

"Ivan is an incredibly strong fellow," remarked the general, "but he has the misfortune to be deaf and dumb. A simple fellow, but, I'm afraid, like all his race, a bit of a savage."

"Is he Russian?"

"He is a Cossack," said the general, and his smile showed red lips and pointed teeth. "So am I."

"Come," he said, "we shouldn't be chatting here. We can talk later. Now you want clothes, food, rest. You shall have them. This is a most restful spot. Follow Ivan, if you please, Mr. Rainsford. I was about to have my dinner when you came. I'll wait for you. You'll find that my clothes will fit you, I think."

It was to a huge beam-ceiling bedroom with a canopied bed big enough for six men that Rainsford followed the silent giant. Ivan laid out an evening suit and Rainsford, as he put it on, noticed that it came from a London tailor who ordinarily cut and sewed for none below the rank of duke.

The dining room to which Ivan conducted him was in many ways remarkable. It suggested a baronial hall of feudal times with its oaken panels, its high ceiling, its vast refectory table where two score men could sit down to eat. About the hall were the mounted heads of many animals—lions, tigers, elephants, moose, bears; larger or more perfect specimens Rainsford had never seen. The table appointments were of the finest—the linen, the crystal, the silver, the china.

Half apologetically General Zaroff said : "We do our best to preserve the amenities of civilization here. Please forgive any lapses. We are well off the beaten track, you know."

The general seemed a most thoughtful and affable host, a true cosmopolite. But whenever he looked up from his plate Rainsford found the general studying him, appraising him narrowly.

"Perhaps," said General Zaroff, "you were surprised that I recognized your name. You see, I read all books on hunting published in English, French, and Russian. I have but one passion in my life, Mr. Rainsford, and it is the hunt."

"You have some wonderful heads here," said Rainsford. "That Cape buffalo is the largest I ever saw. I've always thought that the Cape buffalo is the most dangerous of all big game."

For a moment the general did not reply; he was smiling his curious red-lipped smile. Then he said slowly : "No. You are wrong, sir. The Cape buffalo is not the most dangerous big game." He sipped his wine. "Here in my preserve on this island," he said, in the same slow tone, "I hunt more dangerous game."

Rainsford expressed his surprise. "Is there big game on this island?"

"Oh, it isn't here naturally, of course, I have to stock the island."

"What have you imported, General?" Rainsford asked. "Tigers?"

The general smiled. "No," he said. "Hunting tigers ceased to interest me some years ago. No thrill left in tigers, no real danger. I live for danger, Mr. Rainsford. We will have some capital hunting, you and I. I shall be most glad to have your society."

"But what game—" began Rainsford.

"I'll tell you," said the general. "You will be amused, I know. I think I may say, in all modesty, that I have done a rare thing. I have invented a new sensation."

The general continued : "God makes some men poets. Some He makes kings, some beggars. Me He made a hunter. My hand was made for the trigger, my father said. When I was only five years old he gave me a little gun, especially made in Moscow for me, to shoot sparrows with. I killed my first bear when I was ten. My whole life has been one prolonged hunt. I went into the army and for a time commanded a division of Cossack cavalry, but my real interest was always the hunt. I have hunted every kind of game in every land. It would be impossible for me to tell you how many animals I have killed.

"After the debacle in Russia I left the country; for it was imprudent for an officer of the Tsar to stay there. Luckily, I had invested heavily in American securities, so I shall never have to open a tea room in Monte Carlo or drive a taxi in Paris. Naturally, I continued to hunt—grizzlies in your Rockies, crocodiles in the Ganges, rhinoceroses in East Africa. I went to the Amazon to hunt jaguars, for I had heard that they were unusually cunning. They weren't." The Cossack sighed. "They were no match at all for a hunter with his wits about him, and a high-powered rifle. I was bitterly disappointed. I was lying in my tent with a splitting headache one night when a terrible thought pushed its way into my mind. Hunting was beginning to bore me! And hunting, remember, had been my life. I asked myself why the hunt no longer fascinated me. You are much younger than I am, Mr. Rainsford, and have not hunted as much, but you perhaps can guess the answer."

"What was it?"

"Simply this : hunting had ceased to be what you call 'a sporting proposition'. It had become too easy. I always got my quarry. Always. There is no greater bore than perfection."

The general lit a fresh cigarette. "No animal had a chance with me any more. That is no boast, it is a mathematical certainty. The animal had nothing but his legs and his instinct. Instinct is no match for reason. When I thought of this it was a tragic moment for me, I tell you."

Rainsford leaned across the table, absorbed in what his host was saying.

"It came to me as an inspiration what I must do," the general went on.

"And that was?"

The general smiled the quiet smile of one who has faced an obstacle and surmounted it with success. "I had to invent a new animal to hunt," he said.

"A new animal? You're joking."

"Not at all," said the general. "I never joke about hunting. I bought this island, built this house, and here I do my hunting. The island is perfect for my purposes—there are jungles with a maze of trails in them, hills, swamps—"

"But the animal, General Zaroff?"

"Oh," said the general, "it supplies me with the most exciting hunting in the world. Every day I hunt, and I never grow bored now, for I have a quarry with which I can match my wits."

Rainsford's bewilderment showed in his face.

"I wanted the ideal animal to hunt," explained the general. "So I said : 'What are the attributes of an ideal quarry?' And the answer was, of course : 'It must have courage, cunning and, above all, it must be able to reason.' "

"But no animal can reason," objected Rainsford.

"My dear fellow," said the general, "there is one that can."

"But you can't mean—" gasped Rainsford.

"And why not?"

"I can't believe you are serious, General Zaroff. This is a grisly joke."

"Why should I not be serious? I am speaking of hunting."

"Hunting? Good God, General Zaroff, what you speak of is murder."

The general laughed. He regarded Rainsford quizzically. "I refuse to believe that so modern a man harbours romantic ideas about the value of human life. Surely your experiences in the war—"

"Did not make me condone cold-blooded murder," finished Rainsford, stiffly.

Laughter shook the general. "How extraordinary droll you are!" he said. "One does not expect nowadays to find a young man of the educated class, even in America, with such a naïve and, if I may say so, mid-Victorian point of view. It's like finding a snuff-box in a limousine. I'll wager you'll forget your notions when you go hunting with me. You've a genuine new thrill in store for you, Mr. Rainsford."

"Thank you, I'm a hunter, not a murderer."

"Dear me," said the general, quite unruffled, "again that unpleasant word. But I think I can show you that your scruples are quite ill-founded."

"Yes?"

"Life is for the strong, to be lived by the strong, and if needs be, taken by the strong. The weak of the world were put here to give the strong pleasure. I am strong. Why should I not use my gift? If I wish to hunt, why should I not? I hunt the scum of the earth—sailors from tramp ships—lascars, blacks, Chinese, whites, mongrels—a thoroughbred horse or hound is worth more than a score of them."

"But where do you get them?"

"This island is called Ship Trap," he answered. "Sometimes an angry god of the high seas sends them to me. Sometimes, when Providence is not so kind, I help Providence a bit. Come to the window with me.

"Watch! Out there!" exclaimed the general, pointing into the night. As the general pressed a button, far out to sea Rainsford saw the flash of lights.

The general chuckled. "They indicate a channel," he said, "where there's none : giant rocks with razor edges crouch like a sea monster with wide-open paws. They can crush a ship as easily as I crush this nut." He dropped a walnut on the hardwood floor and brought his heel grinding down on it. "Oh, yes," he said, casually, as if in answer to a question, "I have electricity. We try to be civilized here."

"Civilized? And you shoot down men?"

A trace of anger was in the general's black eyes, but it was there for but a second, and he said, in his most pleasant manner : "Dear me, what a righteous young man you are ! That would be barbarous. I treat these visitors with every consideration. They get plenty of good food and exercise. They get into splendid physical condition. You shall see for yourself tomorrow."

"What do you mean?"

"We'll visit my training school," smiled the general. "It's in the cellar. I have about a dozen pupils down there now. They're from the Spanish bark *Sanlucar* that had the bad luck to go on the rocks out there. A very inferior lot, I regret to say. Poor specimens and more accustomed to the deck than to the jungle."

He raised his hand, and Ivan brought thick Turkish coffee. Rainsford, with an effort, held his tongue in check.

"It's a game, you see," pursued the general, blandly. "I suggest to one of them that we go hunting. I give him a supply of food and an excellent hunting knife. I give him three hours' start. I am to follow, armed only with a pistol of the smallest calibre and range. If my quarry eludes me for three whole days, he wins the game. If I find him"—the general smiled—"he loses."

"Suppose he refuses to be hunted?"

"Oh," said the general, "I give him his option, of course. If he does not wish to hunt, I turn him over to Ivan. Ivan once had the honour of serving as official knouter to the Great White Tsar, and he has his own ideas of sport. Invariably, Mr. Rainsford, invariably they choose the hunt."

"And if they win?"

The smile on the general's face widened. "To date I have not lost," he said. Then he added, hastily, "I don't wish you to think me a braggart, Mr. Rainsford. Many of them afford only the most elementary sort of problem. Occasionally I strike a tartar. One almost did win. I eventually had to use the dogs."

The general steered Rainsford to a window. The lights from the windows sent a flickering illumination that made grotesque patterns on the courtyard below and Rainsford could see moving about there a dozen or so huge black shapes; as they turned towards him, their eyes glittered greenly.

"A rather good lot, I think," observed the general. "They are let out at seven every night. If anyone should try to get into my house —or out of it—something extremely regrettable would occur to him." He hummed a snatch of song.

"And now," said the general, "I want to show you my new collection of heads. Will you come with me to the library?"

"I hope," said Rainsford, "that you will excuse me tonight, General. I'm really not feeling at all well."

"Ah, indeed?" the general inquired, solicitously. "Well, I suppose that's only natural, after your long swim. Tomorrow, you'll feel like a new man, I'll wager. Then we'll hunt, eh? I've one rather promising prospect—"

Rainsford was hurrying from the room.

"Sorry you can't go with me tonight," called the general. "I expect rather fair sport—a big, strong black. He looks resourceful— Well, good night, Mr. Rainsford, I hope you have a good night's rest."

The bed was good and the pyjamas of the softest silk, and he was tired in every fibre of his being, but nevertheless Rainsford could not quiet his brain with the opiate of sleep. He lay, eyes wide open. Once he thought he heard stealthy steps in the corridor outside his room. He sought to throw open the door, it would not open. He went to the window and looked out. His room was high up in one of the towers. The lights of the château were out now and it was dark and silent, but there was a fragment of sallow moon and by its light he could see, dimly, the courtyard; there, weaving in and out in the pattern of shadow, were black, noiseless forms; the hounds heard him at the window and looked up expectantly, with their green eyes. Rainsford went back to the bed and lay down. He had achieved a doze when, just as morning began to come, he heard, far off in the jungle, the faint report of a pistol.

General Zaroff did not appear until luncheon. He was dressed faultlessly in the tweeds of a country squire. He was solicitous about the state of Rainsford's health.

"As for me," sighed the general, "I do not feel so well. I am worried, Mr. Rainsford. Last night I detected traces of my old complaint. The hunting was not good last night. The fellow lost his head. He made a straight trail that offered no problems at all. That's the trouble with these sailors, they have dull brains to begin with and they do not know how to get about in the woods. It's most annoying."

"General," said Rainsford, firmly, "I wish to leave this island at once."

The general raised his thickets of eyebrows, he seemed hurt. "But, my dear fellow," the general protested, "you've only just come. You've had no hunting—"

"I wish to go today," said Rainsford. He saw the dead black eyes of the general on him, studying him. General Zaroff's face suddenly brightened.

"Tonight," said the general, "we will hunt—you and I."

Rainsford shook his head. "No, General," he said, "I will not hunt."

The general shrugged his shoulders. "As you wish, my friend," he said. "The choice rests entirely with you. But may I not venture to suggest that you will find my idea of sport more diverting than Ivan's?"

"You don't mean—" cried Rainsford.

"My dear fellow," said the general, "have I not told you I always mean what I say about hunting? This is really an inspiration. I drink to a foeman worthy of my steel—at last."

The general raised his glass, but Rainsford sat staring at him.

"You'll find this game worth playing," the general said, enthusiastically. "Your brain against mine. Your woodcraft against mine. Your strength and stamina against mine. And the stake is not without value, eh?"

"And if I win—" began Rainsford huskily.

"I'll cheerfully acknowledge myself defeated if I do not find you by midnight of the third day," said General Zaroff. "My sloop will place you on the mainland near a town. I will give you my word as a gentleman and a sportsman. Of course, you, in turn, must agree to say nothing of your visit here."

"I'll agree to nothing of the kind," said Rainsford.

"Oh," said the general, "in that case—but why discuss that now?" Then a business-like air animated him. "Ivan," he said to Rainsford, "will supply you with hunting clothes, food, a knife. I suggest you wear moccasins, they leave a poorer trail. I suggest, too, that you avoid the big swamp in the southeast corner of the island. We called it Death Swamp. There's quicksand there. One foolish fellow tried it. The deplorable part of it was that Lazarus followed him. I loved Lazarus, he was the finest hound in my pack. Well, I must beg you to excuse me now. I always take a siesta after lunch. You'll hardly have time for a nap, I fear. You'll want to start, no doubt. I shall not follow till dusk. Hunting at night is

so much more exciting than by day, don't you think? *Au revoir,*
Mr. Rainsford, *au revoir.*"

General Zaroff, with a deep, courtly bow, strolled from the room.
From another door came Ivan. Under one arm he carried khaki
hunting clothes, a haversack of food, a leather sheath containing a
long-bladed hunting knife; his right hand rested on a cocked
revolver thrust in the crimson sash about his waist.

Rainsford had fought his way through the bush for two hours.
"I must keep my nerve. I must keep my nerve," he said, through
tight teeth.

He had not been entirely clear-headed when the château gates
snapped shut behind him. His whole idea at first was to put distance
between himself and General Zaroff, and to this end he had plunged
along, spurred on by panic. Now he had got a grip on himself, had
stopped and was taking stock of himself and the situation.

He saw that straight flight was futile, inevitably it would bring
him face to face with the sea. "I'll give him a trail to follow," muttered Rainsford, and he struck off from the rude path he had been
following into the trackless wilderness.

He executed a series of intricate loops, he doubled on his trail
again and again, recalling all the lore of the fox hunt, and all the
dodges of the fox. Night found him leg-weary, with hands and face
lashed by the branches, on a thickly wooded ridge. A big tree with
a thick trunk and outspread branches was near by, and taking care
to leave not the slightest mark he climbed up into the crotch, and
stretching out on one of the broad limbs, after a fashion, rested.
Rest brought him new confidence and almost a feeling of security.
Even so zealous a hunter as General Zaroff could not trace him
there, he told himself; only the devil himself could follow that
complicated trail through the jungle after dark.

Towards morning, when a dingy grey was varnishing the sky, the
cry of some startled bird focused Rainsford's attention. Something
was coming by the same winding way Rainsford had come. He
flattened himself down on the limb and through a screen of leaves
almost as thick as tapestry he watched. The thing that was approaching was a man.

It was General Zaroff. He made his way along with his eyes fixed
in utmost concentration on the ground before him. He paused
almost beneath the tree, dropped to his knees and studied the

ground. Rainsford's impulse was to hurl himself down like a panther, but he saw that the general's right hand held something metallic— a small automatic pistol.

The hunter shook his head several times, as if he were puzzled. Then he straightened up and took from his case one of his black cigarettes; its pungent smoke floated up to Rainsford's nostrils.

Rainsford held his breath. The general's eyes had left the ground and were travelling inch by inch up the tree. Rainsford froze there, every muscle tensed for a spring. But the sharp eyes of the hunter stopped before they reached the limb where Rainsford lay; a smile spread over his face. Very deliberately he blew a smoke ring into the air, then he turned his back on the tree and walked carelessly away, back along the trail he had come. Swish of the underbrush against his hunting boots grew fainter and fainter.

The pent-up air burst hotly from Rainsford's lungs. His first thought made him feel sick and numb. The general could follow a trail through the woods at night, he could follow an extremely difficult trail; only by the merest chance had the Cossack failed to see his quarry.

Rainsford's second thought was even more terrible. Why had the general smiled? Why had he turned back? Rainsford did not want to believe what his reason told him was true. The general was playing with him! The general was saving him for another day's sport! The Cossack was the cat; he was the mouse. Then it was that Rainsford knew the full meaning of terror.

"I will not lose my nerve. I will not."

He slid down from the tree and struck off again into the woods. His face was set and he forced the machinery of his mind to function. Three hundred yards from his hiding place he stopped where a huge dead tree leaned precariously on a smaller, living one. Throwing off his sack of food Rainsford took his knife from its sheath and began to work with all his energy.

The job was finished at last and he threw himself down behind a fallen log a hundred feet away. He did not have to wait long. The cat was coming again to play with the mouse.

Following the trail with the sureness of a bloodhound came General Zaroff. Nothing escaped those searching black eyes, no crushed blade of grass, no bent twig, no mark, no matter how faint, in the moss. So intent was the Cossack on his stalking that he was upon the thing Rainsford had made before he saw it. His foot touched the protruding bough that was the trigger. Even as he touched it, the general sensed his danger and leaped back with the agility of an ape. But he was not quite quick enough; the dead tree struck the general a glancing blow on the shoulder as it fell; he staggered, but he did not fall; or did he drop his revolver. He stood there, rubbing his injured shoulder, and Rainsford, with fear again gripping his heart, heard the general's mocking laugh ring through the jungle.

"Rainsford," called the general, "if you are within sound of my voice, as I suppose you are, let me congratulate you. Not many men know how to make a Malay man-catcher. Luckily for me, I too have hunted in Malacca. You are proving of interest, Mr. Rainsford. I am going now to have my wound dressed; it's only a slight one. But I shall be back. I shall be back."

When the general, nursing his bruised shoulder, had gone, Rainsford took up flight again. It was flight now, a desperate, hopeless flight. Dusk came, then darkness, and still he pressed on. The ground grew softer under his moccasins, the vegetation grew ranker, denser, insects bit him savagely. Then, as he stepped forwards, his foot sank into the ooze. He tried to wrench it back, but the muck sucked viciously at his foot. With a violent effort he tore his foot loose. He knew where he was now. Death Swamp and its quicksand. The softness of the earth gave him an idea. He stepped back from the quicksand a dozen feet or so and began to dig. The pit grew deeper; when it was above his shoulders he climbed out and from some hard saplings cut stakes and sharpened them to a fine point. These stakes he planted in the bottom of the pit with the points sticking up. With flying fingers he wove a rough carpet of weeds and branches and with it he covered the mouth of the pit. Then, wet with sweat and aching with tiredness, he crouched behind the stump of a lightning-charred tree.

He knew his pursuer was coming, he heard the padding sound of feet on the soft earth, and the night breeze brought him the perfume of the general's cigarette. Rainsford, crouching there, lived a year in a minute. Then he felt an impulse to cry aloud with joy, for he heard the sharp crackle of the breaking branches as the cover of the pit gave way; he heard the sharp scream of pain as the pointed stakes found their mark. He leaped up from his place of concealment. Then he cowered back. Three feet from the pit a man was standing, with an electric torch in his hand.

"You've done well, Rainsford," the voice of the general called. "Your Burmese tiger pit has claimed one of my best dogs. Again you score. I think, Mr. Rainsford, I'll see what you can do against my whole pack. I'm going home for a rest now. Thank you for a most amusing evening."

At daybreak Rainsford, lying near the swamp, was awakened by a sound that made him know that he had new things to learn about fear. It was the baying of a pack of hounds. For a moment he stood there, thinking. An idea that held a wild chance came to him, and tightening his belt he headed away from the swamp.

The baying of the hounds drew nearer, then still nearer, nearer, ever nearer. On a ridge Rainsford climbed a tree. Down a water-course, not a quarter of a mile away, he could see the bush moving. Straining his eyes, he saw the lean figure of General Zaroff; just ahead of him, Rainsford made out another figure whose wide shoulders surged through the tall jungle weeds; it was the giant Ivan, holding the pack in leash.

They would be on him any minute now. His mind worked frantically. He thought of a native trick he had learned in Uganda. He slid down the tree. He caught hold of a springy young sapling and to it he fastened his hunting knife, with the blade pointing down the trail; with a bit of wild grapevine he tied back the sapling. Then he ran for his life. The hounds raised their voices as they hit the fresh scent.

He had to stop to get his breath. The baying of the hounds stopped abruptly and Rainsford's heart stopped, too. They must have reached the knife.

He shinned excitedly up a tree and looked back, but the hope in his brain died, for he saw in the shallow valley that General Zaroff was still on his feet. Ivan was not. The knife, driven by the recoil of the springing tree, had not wholly failed.

Rainsford had hardly tumbled to the ground when the pack took up the cry again.

"Nerve, nerve, nerve!" he panted, as he dashed along. A blue gap showed between the trees dead ahead. Rainsford forced himself on towards that gap. It was the shore of the sea. Across a cove he could see the gloomy grey stone of the château. Twenty feet below him the sea rumbled and hissed. Rainsford hesitated. He heard the hounds. Then he leaped far out into the sea....

When the general and his pack reached the place by the sea, the

Cossack stopped. For some minutes he stood regarding the blue-green expanse of water. He shrugged his shoulders. Then he sat down, took a drink of brandy from a silver flask and hummed a bit from *Madame Butterfly*.

General Zaroff had an exceedingly good dinner in his great panelled dining hall that evening. Two slight annoyances kept him from perfect enjoyment. One was the thought that it would be difficult to replace Ivan, the other was that his quarry had escaped him. In his library he read, to soothe himself, from the works of Marcus Aurelius. At ten he went up to his bedroom. He was deliciously tired, he said to himself, as he locked himself in. There was a little moonlight, so before turning on his light he went to the window and looked down at the courtyard. He could see the great hounds and called : "Better luck another time", to them. Then he switched on the light.

A man who had been hiding in the curtains of the bed was standing there.

"Rainsford !" cried the general. "How in God's name did you get here?"

"Swam," said Rainsford. "I found it quicker than walking through the jungle."

The general sucked in his breath and smiled. "I congratulate you," he said. "You have won the game."

Rainsford did not smile. "I am still a beast at bay," he said, in a low, hoarse voice. "Get ready, General Zaroff."

The general made one of his deepest bows. "I see," he said. "Splendid ! One of us is to furnish a repast for the hounds. The other will sleep in this very excellent bed. On guard, Rainsford. . . ."

He had never slept in a better bed, Rainsford decided.

DRACULA'S DAUGHTER

BRAM STOKER

(*Universal: 1936*)

It is interesting to see how, throughout the history of the horror film, the various successful monsters have spawned offspring in succeeding generations. Frankenstein has seen his prodigy create monster after monster with the same success—or lack of it, whichever way you care to look at the results—for the past seventy years. Robert Louis Stevenson's Dr. Jekyll and his alter ego Mr. Hyde were also discovered early by the film makers (the first time in 1908 by Selig Polyscope), and have been revived thirteen times in various guises since then.

Equally productive has been Bram Stoker's night prowler, Count Dracula, who has served the industry no less than seven times—and doubtless has inspired many other vampire pictures. With one exception, though, all the sequels were the creations of new authors and script writers and owed nothing except the basic characters to the great originals. The one exception is Dracula's Daughter. *This film, made by Lambert Hillyer, was based on a short story by Stoker entitled* Dracula's Guest, *which the author had originally intended as part of* Dracula. *He was forced to withdraw it from the main body of the story when the publishers asked him to cut the book to make it financially viable. A virtually unknown actress, Gloria Holden, was selected by Hillyer for the leading part and turned in a performance which helped the picture rise above the status of just another sequel to a famous "first".*

Dracula's Daughter *has an originality and power which few other Dracula remakes until the advent of Christopher Lee have been able to match.*

*

WHEN we started for our drive the sun was shining brightly on Munich and the air was full of the joyousness of early summer. Just as we were about to depart, Herr Delbrück (the *maître d'hôtel* of the Quatre Saisons, where I was staying) came down, bareheaded, to the carriage and, after wishing me a pleasant drive, said to the

coachman, still holding his hand on the handle of the carriage
door : "Remember you are back by nightfall. The sky looks bright
but there is a shiver in the north wind that says there may be a
sudden storm. But I am sure you will not be late." Here he smiled
and added, "for you know what night it is".

Johann answered with an emphatic, "*Ja, mein Herr*", and, touching his hat, drove off quickly. When we had cleared the town, I
said, after signalling to him to stop : "Tell me, Johann, what is
tonight?"

He crossed himself as he answered laconically : "Walpurgisnacht."
Then he took out his watch, a great, old-fashioned German silver
thing as big as a turnip, and looked at it, with his eyebrows gathered
together and a little impatient shrug of his shoulders. I realized that
this was his way of respectfully protesting against the unnecessary
delay and sank back in the carriage, merely motioning him to
proceed. He started off rapidly, as if to make up for lost time. Every
now and then the horses seemed to throw up their heads and
sniffed the air suspiciously. On such occasions I often looked round
in alarm. The road was pretty bleak, for we were traversing a sort
of high, wind-swept plateau. As we drove, I saw a road that looked
but little used and which seemed to dip through a little, winding
valley. It looked so inviting that, even at the risk of offending him, I
called Johann to stop—and when he had pulled up I told him I
would like to drive down that road. He made all sorts of excuses
and frequently crossed himself as he spoke. This somewhat piqued
my curiosity so I asked him various questions. He answered fenc-
ingly and repeatedly looked at his watch in protest. Finally I said :
"Well, Johann, I want to go down this road. I shall not ask you to
come unless you like; but tell me why you do not like to go, that
is all I ask." For answer he seemed to throw himself off the box, so
quickly did he reach the ground. Then he stretched out his hands
appealingly to me and implored me not to go. There was just
enough of English mixed with the German for me to understand
the drift of his talk. He seemed always just about to tell me something—the very idea of which evidently frightened him, but each
time he pulled himself up, saying, as he crossed himself : "Walpurgisnacht !"

I tried to argue with him, but it was difficult to argue with a
man when I did not know his language. The advantage certainly
rested with him, for although he began to speak in English, of a
very crude and broken kind, he always got excited and broke into

his native tongue—and every time he did so he looked at his watch. Then the horses became restless and sniffed the air. At this he grew very pale and, looking around in a frightened way, he suddenly jumped forward, took them by the bridles and led them on some twenty feet. I followed and asked why he had done this. For answer he crossed himself, pointed to the spot we had left and drew his carriage in the direction of the other road, indicating a cross, and said, first in German, then in English: "Buried him—him what killed themselves."

I remembered the old custom of burying suicides at cross-roads: "Ah! I see, a suicide. How interesting!" But for the life of me I could not make out why the horses were frightened.

Whilst we were talking we heard a sort of sound between a yelp and a bark. It was far away, but the horses got very restless and it took Johann all his time to quiet them. He was pale and said, "It sounds like a wolf—but yet there are no wolves here now."

"No?" I said, questioning him; "isn't it long since the wolves were so near the city?"

"Long, long," he answered, "in the spring and summer, but with the snow the wolves have been here not so long."

Whilst he was petting the horses and trying to quiet them, dark clouds drifted rapidly across the sky. The sunshine passed away and a breath of cold wind seemed to drift past us. It was only a breath, however, and more in the nature of a warning than a fact, for the sun came out brightly again. Johann looked under his lifted hand at the horizon and said: "The storm of snow, he comes before long time." Then he looked at his watch again and, straightway, holding his reins firmly—for the horses were still pawing the ground restlessly and shaking their heads—he climbed to his box as though the time had come for proceeding on our journey.

I felt a little obstinate and did not at once get into the carriage. "Tell me," I said, "about this place where the road leads," and I pointed down.

Again he crossed himself and mumbled a prayer before he answered, "It is unholy."

"What is unholy?" I enquired.

"The village."

"Then there is a village?"

"No, no. No one lives there hundreds of years." My curiosity was piqued, "But you said there was a village."

"There was."

"Where is it now?"

Whereupon he burst out into a long story in German and English, so mixed up that I could not quite understand exactly what he said, but roughly I gathered that long ago, hundreds of years, men had died there and been buried in their graves; and sounds were heard under the clay and when the graves were opened, men and women were found rosy with life, and their mouths red with blood. And so, in haste to save their lives (aye, and their souls!—and here he crossed himself) those who were left fled away to other places, where the living lived and the dead were dead and not—not something. He was evidently afraid to speak the last words. As he proceeded with his narration he grew more and more excited. It seemed as if his imagination had got hold of him and he ended in a perfect paroxysm of fear—white-faced, perspiring, trembling and looking round him, as if expecting that some dreadful presence would manifest itself there in the bright sunshine on the open plain. Finally, in an agony of desperation, he cried: "Walpurgisnacht!" and pointed to the carriage for me to get in. All my English blood rose at this and, standing back, I said: "You are afraid, Johann—you are afraid. Go home, I shall return alone; the walk will do me good." The carriage door was open. I took from the seat my oak walking-stick—which I always carry on my holiday excursions—and closed the door, pointing back to Munich, and said, "Go home, Johann—Walpurgisnacht doesn't concern Englishmen."

The horses were now more restive than ever and Johann was trying to hold them in, while excitedly imploring me not to do anything so foolish. I pitied the poor fellow, he was deeply in earnest, but all the same I could not help laughing. His English was quite gone now. In his anxiety he had forgotten that his only means of making me understand was to talk my language, so he jabbered away in his native German. It began to be a little tedious. After giving the direction, "Home!" I turned to go down the cross-road into the valley.

With a despairing gesture, Johann turned his horses towards Munich. I leaned on my stick and looked after him. He went slowly along the road for a while: then there came over the crest of the hill a man tall and thin. I could see so much in the distance. When he drew near the horses, they began to jump and kick about, then to scream with terror. Johann could not hold them in; they bolted down the road, running away madly. I watched them out of sight. then looked for the stranger, but I found that he, too, was gone.

With a light heart I turned down the side road through the deepening valley to which Johann had objected. There was not the slightest reason, that I could see, for his objection, and I daresay I tramped for a couple of hours without thinking of time or distance, and certainly without seeing a person or a house. So far as the place was concerned it was desolation itself. But I did not notice this particularly till, on turning a bend in the road, I came upon a scattered fringe of wood; then I recognized that I had been impressed unconsciously by the desolation of the region through which I had passed.

I sat down to rest myself and began to look around. It struck me that it was considerably colder than it had been at the commencement of my walk—a sort of sighing sound seemed to be around me, with, now and then, high overhead, a sort of muffled roar. Looking upwards I noticed that great thick clouds were drifting rapidly across the sky from north to south at a great height. There were signs of coming storm in some lofty stratum of the air. I was a little chilly and, thinking that it was the sitting still after the exercise of walking, I resumed my journey.

The ground I passed over was now much more picturesque. There were no striking objects that the eye might single out, but in all there was a charm of beauty. I took little heed of time and it was only when the deepening twilight forced itself upon me that I began to think of how I should find my way home. The brightness of the day had gone. The air was cold and the drifting of clouds high overhead was more marked. They were accompanied by a sort of far-away rushing sound, through which seemed to come at intervals that mysterious cry which the driver had said came from a wolf. For a while I hesitated. I had said I would see the deserted village, so on I went and presently came on a wide stretch of open country, shut in by hills all around. Their sides were covered with trees which spread down to the plain, dotting, in clumps, the gentler slopes and hollows which showed here and there. I followed with my eye the winding of the road and saw that it curved close to one of the densest of these clumps and was lost behind it.

As I looked there came a cold shiver in the air and the snow began to fall. I thought of the miles and miles of bleak country I had passed and then hurried on to seek the shelter of the wood in front. Darker and darker grew the sky and faster and heavier fell the snow, till the earth before and around me was a glistening white carpet, the farther edge of which was lost in misty vagueness. The road was here but crude and when on the level its boundaries were not so marked, as when it passed through the cuttings; and in a little while I found that I must have strayed from it, for I missed underfoot the hard surface and my feet sank deeper in the grass and moss. Then the wind grew strong and blew with ever increasing force, till I was fain to run before it. The air became icy cold and in spite of my exercise I began to suffer. The snow was now falling so thickly and whirling around me in such rapid eddies that I could hardly keep my eyes open. Every now and then the heavens were torn asunder by vivid lightning, and in the flashes I could see ahead of me a great mass of trees, chiefly yew and cypress, all heavily coated with snow.

I was soon amongst the shelter of the trees, and there, in comparative silence, I could hear the rush of the wind high overhead. Presently the blackness of the storm had become merged in the darkness of the night. By and by the storm seemed to be passing away : it now only came in fierce puffs or blasts. At such moments the weird sound of the wolf appeared to be echoed by many similar sounds around me.

Now and again, through the black mass of drifting cloud, came a straggling ray of moonlight, which lit up the expanse and showed me that I was at the edge of a dense mass of cypress and yew trees. As the snow had ceased to fall, I walked out from the shelter and began to investigate more closely. It appeared to me that, amongst so many old foundations as I had passed, there might be still standing a house in which, though in ruins, I could find some sort of shelter for a while. As I skirted the edge of the copse I found that a low wall encircled it, and following this I presently found an opening. Here the cypresses formed an alley leading up to a square mass of some kind of building. Just as I caught sight of this, however, the drifting clouds obscured the moon and I passed up the path in darkness. The wind must have grown colder, for I felt myself shiver as I walked; but there was hope of shelter and I groped my way blindly on.

I stopped, for there was a sudden stillness. The storm had passed and, perhaps in sympathy with nature's silence, my heart seemed to cease to beat. But this was only momentarily, for suddenly the moonlight broke through the clouds, showing me that I was in a graveyard and that the square object before me was a great massive tomb of marble, as white as the snow that lay on and all around it. With the moonlight there came a fierce sigh of the storm, which appeared to resume its course with a long, low howl, as of many dogs or wolves. I was awed and shocked and felt the cold percept-ibly grow upon me till it seemed to grip me by the heart. Then, while the flood of moonlight still fell on the marble tomb, the storm gave further evidence of renewing, as though it was returning on its track. Impelled by some sort of fascination I approached the sepulchre to see what it was and why such a thing stood alone in such a place. I walked around it and read, over the Doric door, in German :

COUNTESS DOLINGEN OF GRATZ

IN STYRIA

SOUGHT AND FOUND DEATH

1801

On the top of the tomb, seemingly driven through the solid marble—for the structure was composed of a few vast blocks of stone—was a great iron spike or stake. On going to the back I saw, graven in great Russian letters :

THE DEAD TRAVEL FAST.

There was something so weird and uncanny about the whole thing that it gave me a turn and made me feel quite faint. I began to wish, for the first time, that I had taken Johann's advice. Here a thought struck me, which came under almost mysterious circum-stances and with a terrible shock. This was Walpurgis Night!

Walpurgis Night, when, according to the belief of millions of people, the devil was abroad—when the graves were opened and the dead came forth and walked. When evil things of earth and air and water held revel. This very place the driver had specially shunned. This was the depopulated village of centuries ago. This was where the suicide lay; and this was the place where I was alone—un-manned, shivering with cold in a shroud of snow with a wild storm gathering again upon me! It took all my philosophy, all the religion I had been taught, all my courage, not to collapse in a paroxysm of fright.

And now a perfect tornado burst upon me. The ground shook as though thousands of horses thundered across it, and this time the storm bore on its icy wings, not snow, but great hailstones which drove with such violence that they might have come from the thongs of Balearic slingers—hailstones that beat down leaf and branch and made the shelter of the cypresses of no more avail than though their stems were standing corn. At the first I had rushed to the nearest tree, but I was soon fain to leave it and seek the only spot that seemed to afford refuge, the deep Doric doorway of the marble tomb. There, crouching against the massive bronze door, I gained a certain amount of protection from the beating of the hailstones, for now they only drove against me as they ricocheted from the ground and the side of the marble.

As I leaned against the door it moved slightly and opened inwards. The shelter of even a tomb was welcome in that pitiless tempest and I was about to enter it when there came a flash of forked lightning that lit up the whole expanse of the heavens. In the instant, as I am a living man, I saw, as my eyes were turned into the darkness of the tomb, a beautiful woman with rounded cheeks and red lips, seemingly sleeping on a bier. As the thunder broke overhead I was grasped as by the hand of a giant and hurled out into the storm. The whole thing was so sudden that, before I could realize the shock, moral as well as physical, I found the hailstones beating me down. At the same time I had a strange, dominating feeling that I was not alone. I looked towards the tomb. Just then there came another blinding flash, which seemed to strike the iron stake that surmounted the tomb and to pour through to the earth, blasting and crumbling the marble, as in a burst of flame. The dead woman rose for a moment of agony, while she was lapped in the flame, and her bitter scream of pain was drowned in the thundercrash. The last thing I heard was this mingling of dreadful sound, as again I was seized in the giant-grasp and dragged away, while the hailstones beat on me, and the air around seemed reverberant with the howling of wolves. The last sight that I remembered was a vague, white, moving mass, as if all the graves around me had sent out the phantoms of their sheeted-dead, and that they were closing in on me through the white cloudiness of the driving hail.

Gradually there came a sort of vague beginning of consciousness, then a sense of weariness that was dreadful. For a time I remembered nothing, but slowly my senses returned. My feet seemed positively racked with pain, yet I could not move them. They seemed to be numbed. There was an icy feeling at the back of my neck and all down my spine, and my ears, like my feet, were dead, yet in torment; but there was in my breast a sense of warmth which was,

by comparison, delicious. It was as a nightmare—a physical nightmare, if one may use such an expression—for some heavy weight on
my chest made it difficult for me to breathe.

This period of semi-lethargy seemed to remain a long time, and
as it faded away I must have slept or swooned. Then came a sort
of loathing, like the first stage of sea-sickness, and a wild desire to be
free from something—I knew not what. A vast stillness enveloped
me, as though all the world were asleep or dead—only broken by
the low panting as of some animal close to me. I felt a warm rasping
at my throat, then came a consciousness of the awful truth, which
chilled me to the heart and sent the blood surging up through my
brain. Some great animal was lying on me and now licking my
throat. I feared to stir, for some instinct of prudence bade me lie
still, but the brute seemed to realize that there was now some change
in me, for it raised its head. Through my eyelashes I saw above
me the two great flaming eyes of a gigantic wolf. Its sharp white
teeth gleamed in the gaping red mouth and I could feel its hot
breath fierce and acrid upon me.

For another spell of time I remembered no more. Then I became
conscious of a low growl, followed by a yelp, renewed again and
again. Then, seemingly very far away, I heard a "Holloa! holloa!"
as of many voices calling in unison. Cautiously I raised my head and
looked in the direction whence the sound came, but the cemetery
blocked my view. The wolf still continued to yelp in a strange way
and a red glare began to move round the grove of cypresses, as
though following the sound. As the voices drew closer, the wolf
yelped faster and louder. I feared to make either sound or motion.
Nearer came the red glow, over the white pall which stretched into
the darkness around me. Then all at once from beyond the trees
there came at a trot a troop of horsemen bearing torches. The wolf
rose from my breast and made for the cemetery. I saw one of the
horsemen (soldiers, by their caps and their long military cloaks)
raise his carbine and take aim. A companion knocked up his arm,
and I heard the ball whizz over my head. He had evidently taken
my body for that of the wolf. Another sighted the animal as it slunk
away and a shot followed. Then, at a gallop, the troop rode forward—some towards me, others following the wolf as it disappeared
amongst the snow-clad cypresses.

As they drew nearer I tried to move, but was powerless, although
I could see and hear all that went on around me. Two or three of
the soldiers jumped from their horses and knelt beside me. One of

them raised my head and placed his hand over my heart. "Good news, comrades!" he cried. "His heart still beats!"

Then some brandy was poured down my throat; it put vigour into me and I was able to open my eyes fully and look around. Lights and shadows were moving among the trees and I heard men call to one another. They drew together, uttering frightened exclamations, and the lights flashed as the others came pouring out of the cemetery pell-mell, like men possessed. When the farther ones came close to us, those who were around me asked them eagerly: "Well, have you found him?"

The reply rang out hurriedly: "No! no! Come away quick—quick! This is no place to stay, and on this of all nights!"

"What was it?" was the question, asked in all manner of keys. The answer came variously and all indefinitely as though the men were moved by some common impulse to speak, yet were restrained by some common fear from giving their thoughts.

"It—it—indeed!" gibbered one, whose wits had plainly given out for the moment.

"A wolf—and yet not a wolf!" another put in shudderingly.

"No use trying for him without the sacred bullet," a third remarked in a more ordinary manner.

"Serve us right for coming out on this night! Truly we have earned our thousand marks!" were the ejaculations of a fourth.

"There was blood on the broken marble," another said after a pause—"the lightning never brought that there. And for him—is he safe? Look at his throat! See, comrades, the wolf has been lying on him and keeping his blood warm."

The officer looked at my throat and replied: 'He is all right, the skin is not pierced. What does it all mean? We should never have found him but for the yelping of the wolf."

"What became of it?" asked the man who was holding up my head and who seemed the least panic stricken of the party, for his hands were steady and without tremor. On his sleeve was the chevron of a petty officer.

"It went to its home," answered the man, whose long face was pallid and who actually shook with terror as he glanced around him fearfully. "There are graves enough there in which it may lie. Come, comrades—come quickly! Let us leave this cursed spot."

The officer raised me to a sitting posture, as he uttered a word of command, then several men placed me upon a horse. He sprang to the saddle behind me, took me in his arms, gave the word to advance and, turning our faces away from the cypresses, we rode away in swift, military order.

As yet my tongue refused its office and I was perforce silent. I must have fallen asleep, for the next thing I remembered was finding myself standing up, supported by a soldier on each side of me. It was almost broad daylight and to the north a red streak of sunlight was reflected, like a path of blood, over the waste of snow. The officer was telling the men to say nothing of what they had seen, except that they found an English stranger, guarded by a large dog.

"Dog! that was no dog," cut in the man who had exhibited such fear. "I think I know a wolf when I see one."

The young officer answered calmly : "I said a dog."

"Dog!" reiterated the other ironically. It was evident that his courage was rising with the sun and, pointing to me, he said, "Look at his throat. Is that the work of a dog, master?"

Instinctively I raised my hand to my throat, and as I touched it I cried out in pain. The men crowded round to look, some stooping down from their saddles, and again there came the calm voice of the young officer : "A dog, as I said. If aught else were said we should only be laughed at."

I was then mounted behind a trooper and we rode on into the suburbs of Munich. Here we came across a stray carriage, into which I was lifted, and it was driven off to the Quatre Saisons—the young officer accompanying me, whilst a trooper followed with his horse and the others rode off to their barracks.

When we arrived, Herr Delbrück rushed so quickly down the steps to meet me that it was apparent he had been watching within. Taking me by both hands he solicitously led me in. The officer saluted me and was turning to withdraw when I recognized his purpose, and insisted that he should come to my rooms. Over a glass of wine I warmly thanked him and his brave comrades for saving me. He replied simply that he was more than glad and that Herr Delbrück had at the first taken steps to make all the searching party pleased; at which ambiguous utterance the *maître d'hôtel* smiled, while the officer pleaded duty and withdrew.

"But Herr Delbrück," I enquired, "how and why was it that the soldiers searched for me?"

He shrugged his shoulders, as if in depreciation of his own deed, as he replied : "I was so fortunate as to obtain leave from the commander of the regiment in which I served, to ask for volunteers."

"But how did you know I was lost?" I asked.

"The driver came hither with the remains of his carriage, which had been upset when the horses ran away."

"But surely you would not send a search-party of soldiers merely on this account?"

"Oh, no!" he answered, "but even before the coachman arrived I had this telegram from the Boyar whose guest you are," and he took from his pocket a telegram which he handed to me, and I read :

Bistritz

Be careful of my guest—his safety is most precious to me. Should aught happen to him, or if he be missed, spare nothing to find him and ensure his safety. He is English and therefore adventurous. There are often dangers from snow and wolves and night. Lose not a moment if you suspect harm to him. I answer your zeal with my fortune—*Dracula*.

As I held the telegram in my hand the room seemed to whirl around me, and if the attentive *maître d'hôtel* had not caught me I think I should have fallen. There was something so strange in all this, something so weird and impossible to imagine, that there grew on me a sense of my being in some way the sport of opposite forces —the mere vague idea of which seemed in a way to paralyze me. I was certainly under some form of mysterious protection. From a distant country had come, in the very nick of time, a message that took me out of the danger of the snow-sleep and the jaws of the wolf.

ALL THAT MONEY CAN BUY

STEPHEN VINCENT BENÉT

(RKO-Radio: 1941)

*The advent of the Second World War had no adverse effect
on the popularity of the horror films—whatever one might
have expected. Indeed, if anything, their stock went up among
audiences. Producers did not demonstrate a great deal of inventiveness or ingenuity during this period, however (which
is perhaps not surprising when one remembers the restrictions
under which they were forced to operate), and most tended
to fall back on the tried and tested styles of horror like the
good old-fashioned monsters and traffic with evil forces.*

*For a number of years tales of deals with the Devil had
become increasingly popular, allowing as they did free reign
for the director to create all manner of horrendous demons to
be conjured up on lonely moors amidst smoke, lightning and
general terror all round.*

*In 1941 a unique picture of this type appeared—one of the
gems of the war years—*All That Money Can Buy. *The film,
apart from its intrinsic strength, is also notable for a superb
performance by Walter Huston (father of director John
Huston) as a homely, cigar-smoking Devil devoid of all the
usual hellish trappings. The director, William Dieterle (himself an accomplished horror actor), remained faithful to the
story on which the picture was based, Stephen Vincent Benét's*
The Devil and Daniel Webster, *and invested it with both black
humour and a clever insight into the power of superstition.*
All That Money Can Buy *provided wartime audiences throughout the free world with outstanding entertainment.*

*

IT'S a story they tell in the border country, where Massachusetts
joins Vermont and New Hampshire.

Yes, Dan'l Webster's dead—or, at least, they buried him. But
every time there's a thunderstorm around Marshfield, they say you
can hear his rolling voice in the hollows of the sky. And they say
that if you go to his grave and speak loud and clear, "Dan'l

Webster—Dan'l Webster!" the ground'll begin to shiver and the
trees begin to shake. And after a while you'll hear a deep
voice saying, "Neighbour, how stands the Union?" Then you better
answer the Union stands as she stood, rock-bottomed and copper-
sheathed, one and indivisible, or he's liable to rear right out of the
ground. At least, that's what I was told when I was a youngster.

You see, for a while, he was the biggest man in the country. He
never got to be President, but he was the biggest man. There were
thousands that trusted in him right next to God Almighty, and
they told stories about him and all the things that belonged to him
that were like the stories of patriarchs and such. They said, when
he stood up to speak, stars and stripes came right out in the sky,
and once he spoke against a river and made it sink into the ground.
They said, when he walked the woods with his fishing rod, Killall,
the trout would jump out of the streams right into his pockets, for
they knew it was no use putting up a fight against him; and, when
he argued a case, he could turn on the harps of the blessed and the
shaking of the earth underground. That was the kind of man he
was, and his big farm up at Marshfield was suitable to him. The
chickens he raised were all white meat down through the drum-
sticks, the cows were tended like children, and the big ram he called
Goliath had horns with a curl like a morning-glory vine and could
butt through an iron door. But Dan'l wasn't one of your gentleman
farmers; he knew all the ways of the land, and he'd be up by
candlelight to see that the chores got done. A man with a mouth
like a mastiff, a brow like a mountain and eyes like burning anthracite—that was Dan'l Webster in his prime. And the biggest case he
argued never got written down in the books, for he argued it against
the devil, nip and tuck and no holds barred. And this is the way I
used to hear it told.

There was a man named Jabez Stone, lived at Cross Corners,
New Hampshire. He wasn't a bad man to start with, but he was an
unlucky man. If he planted corn, he got borers; if he planted
potatoes, he got blight. He had good-enough land, but it didn't
prosper him; he had a decent wife and children, but the more
children he had, the less there was to feed them. If stones cropped
up in his neighbour's field, boulders boiled up in his; if he had a
horse with the spavins, he'd trade it for one with the staggers and
give something extra. There's some folks bound to be like that,
apparently. But one day Jabez Stone got sick of the whole business.

He'd been ploughing that morning and he'd just broke the

ploughshare on a rock that he could have sworn hadn't been there yesterday. And, as he stood looking at the ploughshare, the off horse began to cough—that ropy kind of cough that means sickness and horse doctors. There were two children down with the measles, his wife was ailing, and he had a whitlow on his thumb. It was about the last straw for Jabez Stone. "I vow," he said, and he looked around him kind of desperate, "I vow it's enough to make a man want to sell his soul to the devil! And I would, too, for two cents!"

Then he felt a kind of queerness come over him at having said what he'd said; though, naturally, being a New Hampshireman, he wouldn't take it back. But, all the same, when it got to be evening and, as far as he could see, no notice had been taken, he felt relieved in his mind, for he was a religious man. But notice is always taken, sooner or later, just like the Good Book says. And, sure enough, next day, about suppertime, a soft-spoken, dark-dressed stranger drove up in a handsome buggy and asked for Jabez Stone.

Well, Jabez told his family it was a lawyer, come to see him about a legacy. But he knew who it was. He didn't like the looks of the stranger, nor the way he smiled with his teeth. They were white teeth, and plentiful—some say they were filed to a point, but I wouldn't vouch for that. And he didn't like it when the dog took one look at the stranger and ran away howling, with his tail between his legs. But having passed the word, more or less, he stuck to it, and they went out behind the barn and made their bargain. Jabez Stone had to prick his finger to sign, and the stranger lent him a silver pin. The wound healed clean, but it left a little white scar.

After that, all of a sudden, things began to pick up and prosper for Jabez Stone. His cows got fat and his horses sleek, his crops were the envy of the neighbourhood, and lightning might strike all over the valley, but it wouldn't strike his barn. Pretty soon he was one of the prosperous people of the county; they asked him to stand for selectman, and he stood for it; there began to be talk of running him for state senate. All in all, you might say the Stone family was as happy and contented as cats in a dairy. And so they were, except for Jabez Stone.

He'd been contented enough for the first few years. It's a great thing when bad luck turns; it drives most other things out of your head. True, every now and then, especially in rainy weather, the little white scar on his finger would give him a twinge. And once a

year, punctual as clockwork, the stranger with the handsome buggy
would come driving by. But the sixth year the stranger lighted,
and, after that, his peace was over for Jabez Stone.

The stranger came up through the lower field, switching his boots
with a cane—they were handsome black boots, but Jabez Stone
never liked the look of them, particularly the toes. And, after he'd
passed the time of day, he said, "Well, Mr. Stone, you're a hummer!
It's a very pretty property you've got here, Mr. Stone."

"Well, some might favour it and others might not," said Jabez
Stone, for he was a New Hampshireman.

"Oh, no need to decry your industry!" said the stranger, very
easy, showing his teeth in a smile. "After all, we know what's been
done, and it's been according to contract and specifications. So
when—ahem—the mortgage falls due next year, you shouldn't
have any regrets."

"Speaking of that mortgage, mister," said Jabez Stone, and he
looked around for help to the earth and the sky, "I'm beginning to
have one or two doubts about it."

"Doubts?" said the stranger not quite so pleasantly.

"Why, yes," said Jabez Stone. "This being the U.S.A. and me
always having been a religious man." He cleared his throat and got
bolder. "Yes, sir," he said, "I'm beginning to have considerable
doubts as to that mortgage holding in court."

"There's courts and courts," said the stranger, clicking his teeth.
"Still, we might as well have a look at the original document." And
he hauled out a big black pocketbook, full of papers. "Sherwin,
Slater, Stevens, Stone," he muttered.

" 'I, Jabez Stone, for a term of seven years—' Oh, it's quite in
order, I think."

But Jabez Stone wasn't listening, for he saw something else flutter
out of the black pocketbook. It was something that looked like a
moth, but it wasn't a moth. And as Jabez Stone stared at it, it
seemed to speak to him in a small sort of piping voice, terrible
small and thin, but terrible human. "Neighbour Stone!" it squeaked.
"Neighbour Stone! Help me! For God's sake, help me!"

But before Jabez Stone could stir hand or foot, the stranger
whipped out a big bandanna handkerchief, caught the creature in
it, just like a butterfly, and started tying up the ends of the
bandanna.

"Sorry for the interruption," he said. "As I was saying—"

But Jabez Stone was shaking all over like a scared horse.

"That's Miser Steven's voice!" he said in a croak. "And you've got him in your handkerchief!"

The stranger looked a little embarrassed.

"Yes, I really should have transferred him to the collecting box," he said with a simper, "but there were some rather unusual specimens there and I don't want them crowded. Well, well, these little contretemps will occur."

"I don't know what you mean by contertan," said Jabez Stone, "but that was Miser Steven's voice! And he ain't dead! You can't tell me he is! He was just as spry and mean as a woodchuck Tuesday!"

"In the midst of life..." said the stranger, kind of pious. "Listen!" Then a bell began to toll in the valley and Jabez Stone listened, with the sweat running down his face. For he knew it was tolled for Miser Stevens and that he was dead.

"These long-standing accounts," said the stranger with a sigh; "one really hates to close them. But business is business."

He still had the bandanna in his hand, and Jabez Stone felt sick as he saw the cloth struggle and flutter.

"Are they all as small as that?" he asked hoarsely.

"Small?" said the stranger. "Oh, I see what you mean. Why, they vary." He measured Jabez Stone with his eyes, and his teeth showed. "Don't worry, Mr. Stone," he said. "You'll go with a very good grade. I wouldn't trust you outside the collecting box. Now, a man like Dan'l Webster, of course—well, we'd have to build a special box for him, and even at that, I imagine the wing spread would astonish you. He'd certainly be a prize. I wish we could see our way clear to him. But, in your case, as I was saying—"

"Put that handkerchief away!" said Jabez Stone, and he began to beg and to pray. But the best he could get at the end was a three years' extension, with conditions.

But till you make a bargain like that, you've got no idea of how fast four years can run. By the last months of those years Jabez Stone's known all over the state and there's talk of running him for governor—and it's dust and ashes in his mouth. For every day, when he gets up, he thinks, "There's one more night gone," and every night, when he lies down, he thinks of the black pocketbook and the soul of Miser Stevens, and it makes him sick at heart. Till, finally, he can't bear it any longer, and, in the last days of the last year, he hitches up his horse and drives off to seek Dan'l Webster. For Dan'l was born in New Hampshire, only a few miles from

Cross Corners, and it's well known that he has a particular soft spot for old neighbours.

It was early in the morning when he got to Marshfield, but Dan'l was up already, talking Latin to the farm hands and wrestling with the ram, Goliath, and trying out a new trotter and working up speeches to make against John C. Calhoun. But when he heard a New Hampshireman had come to see him, he dropped everything else he was doing, for that was Dan'l's way. He gave Jabez Stone a breakfast that five men couldn't eat, went into the living history of every man and woman in Cross Corners, and finally asked him how he could serve him.

Jabez Stone allowed that it was a kind of mortgage case.

"Well, I haven't pleaded a mortgage case in a long time, and I don't generally plead now, except before the Supreme Court," said Dan'l, "but if I can, I'll help you."

"Then I've got hope for the first time in ten years," said Jabez Stone and told him the details.

Dan'l walked up and down as he listened, hands behind his back, now and then asking a question, now and then plunging his eyes at the floor, as if they'd bore through it like gimlets. When Jabez Stone had finished, Dan'l puffed out his cheeks and blew. Then he turned to Jabez Stone and a smile broke over his face like the sunrise over Monadnock.

"You've certainly given yourself the devil's own row to hoe, Neighbour Stone," he said, "but I'll take your case."

"You'll take it?" said Jabez Stone, hardly daring to believe.

"Yes," said Dan'l Webster. "I've got about seventy-five other things to do and the Missouri Compromise to straighten out, but I'll take your case. For if two New Hampshiremen aren't a match for the devil, we might as well give the country back to the Indians."

Then he shook Jabez Stone by the hand and said, "Did you come down here in a hurry?"

"Well, I admit I made time," said Jabez Stone.

"You'll go back faster," said Dan'l Webster, and he told 'em to hitch up Constitution and Constellation to the carriage. They were matched greys with one white forefoot, and they stepped like greased lightning.

Well, I won't describe how excited and pleased the whole Stone family was to have the great Dan'l Webster for a guest, when they finally got there. Jabez Stone had lost his hat on the way, blown off when they overtook a wind, but he didn't take much account of that. But after supper he sent the family off to bed, for he had most particular business with Mr. Webster. Mrs. Stone wanted him to sit in the front parlour, but Dan'l Webster knew front parlours and said he preferred the kitchen. So it was there they sat, waiting for the stranger, with a jug on the table between them and a bright fire on the hearth—the stranger being scheduled to show up on the stroke of midnight, according to specification.

Well, most men wouldn't have asked for better company than Dan'l Webster and a jug. But with every tick of the clock Jabez Stone got sadder and sadder. His eyes roved round, and though he sampled the jug you could see he couldn't taste it. Finally, on the stroke of 11.30 he reached over and grabbed Dan'l Webster by the arm.

"Mr. Webster, Mr. Webster!" he said, and his voice was shaking with fear and a desperate courage. "For God's sake, Mr. Webster, harness your horses and get away from this place while you can!"

"You've brought me a long way, neighbour, to tell me you don't like my company," said Dan'l Webster, quite peaceable, pulling at the jug.

"Miserable wretch that I am!" groaned Jabez Stone. "I've brought you a devilish way, and now I see my folly. Let him take me if he wills. I don't hanker after it, I must say, but I can stand it. But you're the Union's stay and New Hampshire's pride! He mustn't get you, Mr. Webster! He mustn't get you!"

Dan'l Webster looked at the distracted man, all grey and shaking in the firelight, and laid a hand on his shoulder.

"I'm obliged to you, Neighbour Stone," he said gently. "It's kindly thought of. But there's a jug on the table and a case in hand. And I never left a jug or a case half finished in my life."

And just at that moment there was a sharp rap on the door.

"Ah," said Dan'l Webster very coolly, "I thought your clock was a trifle slow, Neighbour Stone." He stepped to the door and opened it. "Come in!" he said.

The stranger came in—very dark and tall he looked in the firelight. He was carrying a box under his arm—a black japanned box with little air holes in the lid. At the sight of the box Jabez Stone gave a low cry and shrank into a corner of the room.

"Mr. Webster, I presume," said the stranger, very polite, but with his eyes glowing like a fox's deep in the woods.

"Attorney of record for Jabez Stone," said Dan'l Webster, but his eyes were glowing too. "Might I ask your name?"

"I've gone by a good many," said the stranger carelessly. "Perhaps Scratch will do for the evening. I'm often called that in these regions."

Then he sat down at the table and poured himself a drink from the jug. The liquor was cold in the jug, but it came steaming into the glass.

"And now," said the stranger, smiling and showing his teeth, "I shall call upon you, as a law-abiding citizen, to assist me in taking possession of my property."

Well, with that the argument began—and it went hot and heavy. At first Jabez Stone had a flicker of hope, but when he saw Dan'l Webster being forced back at point after point, he just sat scrunched in his corner, with his eyes on that japanned box. For there wasn't any doubt as to the deed or the signature—that was the worst of it. Dan'l Webster twisted and turned and thumped his fist on the table, but he couldn't get away from that. He offered to compromise the case; the stranger wouldn't hear of it. He pointed out the property had increased in value, and state senators ought to be worth more; the stranger stuck to the letter of the law. He was a great lawyer, Dan'l Webster, but we know who's the King of Lawyers, as the Good Book tells us, and it seemed as if for the first time, Dan'l Webster had met his match.

Finally, the stranger yawned a little. "Your spirited efforts on behalf of your client do you credit, Mr. Webster," he said, "but if you have no more arguments to adduce, I'm rather pressed for time . . ." and Jabez Stone shuddered.

Dan'l Webster's brow looked dark as a thundercloud.

"Pressed or not, you shall not have this man!" he thundered. "Mr. Stone is an American citizen, and no American citizen may be forced into the service of a foreign prince. We fought England for that in '12 and we'll fight all hell for it again!"

"Foreign?" said the stranger. "And who calls me a foreigner?"

"Well, I never yet heard of the dev—of your claiming American citizenship," said Dan'l Webster with surprise.

"And who with better right?" said the stranger with one of his terrible smiles. "When the first wrong was done to the first Indian, I was there. When the first slaver put out for the Congo, I stood on her deck. Am I not in your books and stories and beliefs, from the first settlements on? Am I not spoken of still in every church

in New England? 'Tis true the North claims me for a Southerner
and the South for a Northener, but I am neither. I am merely an
honest American like yourself—and of the best descent—for, to
tell the truth, Mr. Webster, though I don't like to boast of it, my
name is older in this country than yours."

"Aha!" said Dan'l Webster with the veins standing out in his
forehead. "Then I stand on the Constitution! I demand a trial
for my client!"

"The case is hardly one for an ordinary court," said the stranger,
his eyes flickering. "And, indeed, the lateness of the hour—"

"Let it be any court you choose, so it is an American judge and
an American jury!" said Dan'l Webster in his pride. "Let it be the
quick or the dead; I'll abide the issue!"

"You have said it," said the stranger, and pointed his finger at
the door. And with that, and all of a sudden, there was a rushing of
wind outside and a noise of footsteps. They came, clear and distinct, through the night. And yet they were not like the footsteps
of living men.

"In God's name, who comes by so late?" cried Jabez Stone in
an ague of fear.

"The jury Mr. Webster demands," said the stranger, sipping at
his boiling glass. "You must pardon the rough appearance of one or
two; they will have come a long way."

And with that the fire burned blue and the door blew open and
twelve men entered, one by one.

If Jabez Stone had been sick with terror before, he was blind
with terror now. For there was Walter Butler, the loyalist, who
spread fire and horror through the Mohawk Valley in the times
of the Revolution; and there was Simon Girty, the renegade, who
saw white men burned at the stake and whooped with the Indians
to see them burn. His eyes were green, like a catamount's, and the
stains on his hunting shirt did not come from the blood of the deer.
King Philip was there, wild and proud as he had been in life, with
the great gash in his head that gave him his death wound, and
cruel Governor Dale, who broke men on the wheel. There was Morton of Merry Mount, who so vexed the Plymouth Colony, with his
flushed, loose, handsome face and his hate of the godly. There was
Teach, the bloody pirate, with his black beard curling on his breast.
The Reverend John Smeet, with his strangler's hands and his
Geneva gown, walked as daintily as he had to the gallows. The red
print of the rope was still around his neck, but he carried a per-

fumed handkerchief in one hand. One and all, they came into the room with the fires of hell still upon them, and the stranger named their names and their deeds as they came, till the tale of twelve was told. Yet the stranger had told the truth—they had all played a part in America.

"Are you satisfied with the jury, Mr. Webster?" said the stranger mockingly, when they had taken their places.

The sweat stood upon Dan'l Webster's brow, but his voice was clear.

"Quite satisfied," he said. "Though I miss General Arnold from the company."

"Benedict Arnold is engaged upon other business," said the stranger with a glower. "Ah, you asked for a justice, I believe."

He pointed his finger once more, and a tall man, soberly clad in Puritan garb, with the burning gaze of the fanatic, stalked into the room and took his judge's place.

"Justice Hathorne is a jurist of experience," said the stranger. "He presided at certain witch trials once held in Salem. There were others who repented of the business later, but not he."

"Repent of such notable wonders and undertakings?" said the stern old justice. "Nay, hang them—hang them all!" And he muttered to himself in a way that struck ice into the soul of Jabez Stone.

Then the trial began, and, as you might expect, it didn't look anyways good for the defence. And Jabez Stone didn't make much of a witness in his own behalf. He took one look at Simon Girty and screeched, and they had to put him back in his corner in a kind of swoon.

It didn't halt the trial though; the trial went on, as trials do. Dan'l Webster had faced some hard juries and hanging judges in his time, but this was the hardest he'd ever faced, and he knew it. They sat there with a kind of glitter in their eyes, and the stranger's smooth voice went on and on. Every time he'd raise an objection, it'd be "Objection sustained", but whenever Dan'l objected, it'd be "Objection denied". Well, you couldn't expect fair play from a fellow like this Mr. Scratch.

It got to Dan'l in the end, and he began to heat, like iron in the forge. When he got up to speak he was going to flay that stranger with every trick known to the law, and the judge and jury too. He didn't care if it was contempt of court or what would happen to him for it. He didn't care any more what happened to Jabez Stone.

He just got madder and madder, thinking of what he'd say. And yet, curiously enough, the more he thought about it, the less he was able to arrange his speech in his mind.

Till, finally, it was time for him to get up on his feet, and he did so, all ready to bust out with lightnings and denunciations. But before he started he looked over the judge and jury for a moment, such being his custom. And he noticed the glitter in their eyes was twice as strong as before, and they all leaned forward. Like hounds just before they get the fox, they looked, and the blue mist of evil in the room thickened as he watched them. Then he saw what he'd been about to do, and he wiped his forehead, as a man might who's just escaped falling into a pit in the dark.

For it was him they'd come for, not only Jabez Stone. He read it in the glitter of their eyes and in the way the stranger hid his mouth with one hand. And if he fought them with their own weapons, he'd fall into their power; he knew that, though he couldn't have told you how. It was his own anger and horror that burned in their eyes; and he'd have to wipe that out or the case was lost. He stood there for a moment, his black eyes burning like anthracite. And then he began to speak.

He started off in a low voice, though you could hear every word. They say he could call on the harps of the blessed when he chose. And this was just as simple and easy as a man could talk. But he didn't start out by condemning or reviling. He was talking about the things that make a country a country and a man a man.

And he began with the simple things that everybody's known and felt—the freshness of a fine morning when you're young, and the taste of food when you're hungry, and the new day that's every day when you're a child. He took them up and he turned them in his hands. They were good things for any man. But without freedom they sickened. And when he talked of those enslaved, and the sorrows of slavery, his voice got like a big bell. He talked of the early days of America and the men who had made those days. It wasn't a spread-eagle speech, but he made you see it. He admitted all the wrong that had ever been done. But he showed how, out of the wrong and the right, the suffering and the starvations, something new had come. And everybody had played a part in it, even the traitors.

Then he turned to Jabez Stone and showed him as he was—an ordinary man who'd had hard luck and wanted to change it. And, because he'd wanted to change it, now he was going to be punished for all eternity. And yet there was good in Jabez Stone, and he showed that good. He was hard and mean, in some ways, but he was a man. There was sadness in being a man, but it was a proud thing too. And he showed what the pride of it was till you couldn't help feeling it. Yes, even in hell, if a man was a man, you'd know it. And he wasn't pleading for any one person any more, though his voice rang like an organ. He was telling the story and the failures and the endless journey of mankind. They got tricked and trapped and bamboozled, but it was a great journey. And no demon that was ever foaled could know the inwardness of it—it took a man to do that.

The fire began to die on the hearth and the wind before morning to blow. The light was getting grey in the room when Dan'l Webster finished. And his words came back at the end to New Hampshire ground, and the one spot of land that each man loves and clings to. He painted a picture of that, and to each one of that jury he spoke of things long forgotten. For his voice could search the heart, and that was his gift and his strength. And to one his voice was like the forest and its secrecy, and to another like the sea and the storms of the sea; and one heard the cry of his lost nation in it, and another saw a little harmless scene he hadn't remembered for years. But each saw something. And when Dan'l Webster finished he didn't know whether or not he'd saved Jabez Stone. But he knew he'd done a miracle. For the glitter was gone from the eyes of judge and jury, and, for the moment, they were men again, and knew they were men.

"The defence rests," said Dan'l Webster and stood there like a mountain. His ears were still ringing with his speech, and he didn't hear anything else till he heard Judge Hathorne say, "The jury will retire to consider its verdict."

Walter Butler rose in his place and his face had a dark, gay pride on it. "The jury has considered its verdict," he said and looked the stranger full in the eye. "We find for the defendant, Jabez Stone."

With that, the smile left the stranger's face, but Walter Butler did not flinch. "Perhaps 'tis not strictly in accordance with the evidence," he said, "but even the damned may salute the eloquence of Mr. Webster."

With that, the long crow of a rooster split the grey morning sky, and judge and jury were gone from the room like a puff of smoke and as if they had never been there. The stranger returned to Dan'l Webster, smiling wryly.

"Major Butler was always a bold man," he said. "I had not thought him quite so bold. Nevertheless, my congratulations, as between two gentlemen."

"I'll have that paper first, if you please," said Dan'l Webster, and he took it and tore it into four pieces. It was queerly warm to the touch. "And now," he said, "I'll have you!" and his hand came down like a bear trap on the stranger's arm. For he knew that once you bested anybody like Mr. Scratch in fair fight, his power on you was gone. And he could see that Mr. Scratch knew it too.

The stranger twisted and wriggled, but he couldn't get out of that grip. "Come, come, Mr. Webster," he said, smiling palely. "This sort of thing is ridic—ouch!—is ridiculous. If you're worried about the costs of the case, naturally, I'd be glad to pay—"

"And so you shall!" said Dan'l Webster, shaking him till his teeth rattled. "For you'll sit right down at that table and draw up a document, promising never to bother Jabez Stone nor his heirs or assigns nor any other New Hampshireman till doomsday! For any hades we want to raise in this state, we can raise ourselves, without assistance from strangers."

"Ouch!" said the stranger. "Ouch! Well, they never did run very big to the barrel, but—ouch!—I agree!"

So he sat down and drew up the document. But Dan'l Webster kept his hand on his coat collar all the time.

"And now may I go?" said the stranger, quite humble, when Dan'l'd seen the documents in proper and legal form.

"Go?" said Dan'l, giving him another shake. "I'm still trying to figure out what I'll do with you. For you've settled the costs of the case, but you haven't settled with me. I think I'll take you back to Marshfield," he said, kind of reflective. "I've got a ram there named Goliath that can butt through an iron door. I'd kind of like to turn you loose in his field and see what he'd do."

Well, with that the stranger began to beg and to plead. And he begged and he pled so humble that finally Dan'l, who was naturally kindhearted, agreed to let him go. The stranger seemed terrible grateful for that and said, just to show they were friends, he'd tell Dan'l's fortune before leaving. So Dan'l agreed to that, though he didn't take much stock in fortune-tellers ordinarily. But, naturally, the stranger was a little different.

Well, he pried and he peered at the lines in Dan'l's hands. And he told him one thing and another that was quite remarkable. But they were all in the past.

"Yes, all that's true, and it happened," said Dan'l Webster. "But what's to come in the future?"

The stranger grinned, kind of happily, and shook his head.

"The future's not as you think it," he said. "It's dark. You have a great ambition, Mr. Webster."

"I have," said Dan'll firmly, for everybody knew he wanted to be President.

"It seems almost within your grasp," said the stranger, "but you will not attain it. Lesser men will be made President and you will be passed over."

"And, if I am, I'll still be Daniel Webster," said Dan'l. "Say on."

"You have two strong sons," said the stranger, shaking his head. "You look to found a line. But each will die in war and neither reach greatness."

"Live or die, they are still my sons," said Dan'l Webster. "Say on."

"You have made great speeches," said the stranger. "You will make more."

"Ah," said Dan'l Webster.

"But the last great speech you make will turn many of your own against you," said the stranger. "They will call you Ichabod; they will call you by other names. Even in New England some will say you have turned your coat and sold your country, and their voices will be loud against you till you die."

"So it is an honest speech, it does not matter what men say," said Dan'l Webster. Then he looked at the stranger and their glances locked.

"One question," he said. "I have fought for the Union all my life. Will I see that fight won against those who would tear it apart?"

"Not while you live," said the stranger grimly, "but it will be won. And after you are dead, there are thousands who will fight for your cause, because of words that you spoke."

"Why, then, you long-barrelled, slab-sided, lantern-jawed, fortune-telling note shaver," said Dan'l Webster with a great roar of laughter, "be off with you to your own place before I put my mark on you! For, by the thirteen original colonies, I'd go to the Pit itself to save the Union!"

And with that he drew back his foot for a kick that would have stunned a horse. It was only the tip of his shoe that caught the

(Georges Méliès: 1896)

(Edison 1912)

(*Universal: 1925*)

(*Film Guild-Hodkinson: 1923*)

Osgood Perkins and the scarecrow which is brought to life in *Puritan Passions*.

The master of the horror film and the famous 'man of a thousand faces', Lon Chaney, in his classic portrayal of that tragic figure, the *Phantom of the Opera*.

(*Overleaf, top*) A rare still from one of the very first fantasy/horror films, George Méliès' *Th Devil In A Convent*.

(*Overleaf, bottom*) *The Lunatics* was based on a story by Edgar Allen Poe.

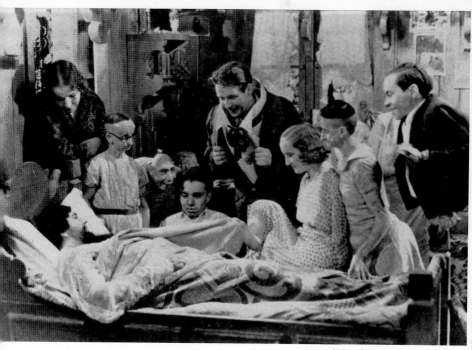

(*Metro-Goldwyn-Mayer: 1932*)

Perhaps the most horrific of all horror films, Tod Browning's *Freaks*.

The outstanding terror film of hunter and hunted, *Most Dangerous Game*, with Joel McCrea.

(*RKO Radio: 1932*)

(*Universal: 1936*)

The beautiful and sinister Gloria Holden in *Dracula's Daughter*.

Peter Lorre in a dramatic moment from *The Beast With Five Fingers*.

(*Warner Brothers: 1947*)

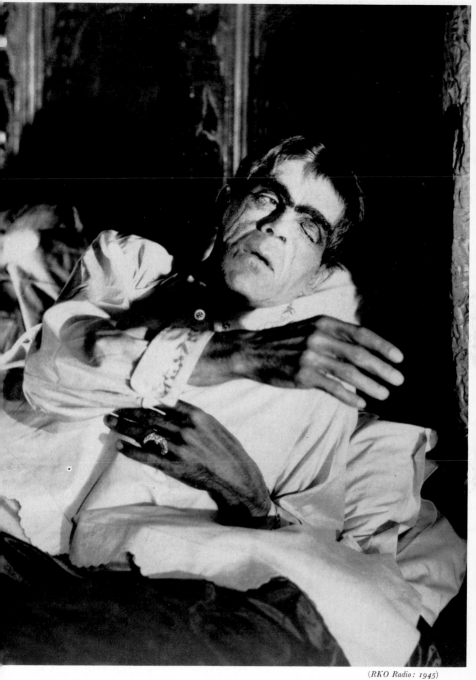

(RKO Radio: 1945)
Boris Karloff starred in *The Body Snatcher*, based on Robert Louis Stevenson's little known
story.

(Warner Brothers: 1953)

The Beast From 20,000 Fathoms on the rampage in the film version of Ray Bradbury's story.

Vincent Price and young companion confronted by *The Fly*.

(20th Century Fox: 1958)

(Galatea-Jolly Films: 1960)

Barbara Steele under torture as a witch in the Italian film *Black Sunday*.

A moment of high tension from Robert Enrico's masterpiece, *Incident at Owl Creek*.

(Robert Enrico: 1961)

(American International: 1965)

Freda Jackson decomposing in the H.P. Lovecraft tale, *Monster of Terror*.

A human skull with unearthly powers in *The Skull* by Robert Bloch.

(Paramount: 1966)

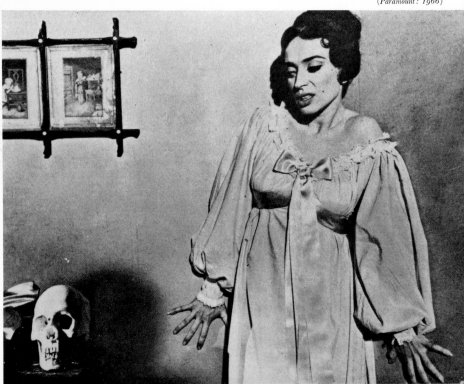

stranger, but he went flying out of the door with his collecting box
under his arm.

"And now," said Dan'l Webster, seeing Jabez Stone beginning to
rouse from his swoon, "let's see what's left in the jug, for it's dry
work talking all night. I hope there's pie for breakfast, Neighbour
Stone."

But they say that whenever the devil comes near Marshfield, even
now, he gives it a wide berth. And he hasn't been seen in the state of
New Hampshire from that day to this.

I'm not talking about Massachusetts or Vermont.

THE BODY SNATCHER

ROBERT LOUIS STEVENSON

(RKO-Radio: 1945)

Throughout the war the horror industry continued to flourish in Hollywood, and those actors not subjected to conscription found themselves haunting graveyards instead of trenches and defying monsters instead of the Axis powers.

England's great novelist, Robert Louis Stevenson (who, after Edgar Allan Poe, has contributed more material to the genre than any other writer) was again called upon in one of the lulls between remakes of the evergreen Dr. Jekyll and Mr. Hyde *—certainly the most filmed novel of all time. On this occasion it was for a nasty little story about resurrectionists in nineteenth century Edinburgh entitled* The Body Snatcher.

The film brought together those two star ghouls, Boris Karloff and Bela Lugosi, who turned in performances of outstanding malevolence and dark evil. The authentic sets and costumes in the picture owe much to the demanding and fastidious talents of the producer, Val Lewton, and his director, Robert Wise. The film remained faithful to Stevenson's tale of the old trade in disinterred corpses and scored highly with audiences both in and out of uniform. Seen again today it has lost little of its impact.

*

EVERY night in the year, four of us sat in the small parlour of the *George* at Debenham—the undertaker, and the landlord, and Fettes, and myself. Sometimes there would be more; but blow high, blow low, come rain or snow or frost, we four would be each planted in his own particular arm-chair. Fettes was an old drunken Scotsman, a man of education obviously, and a man of some property, since he lived in idleness. He had come to Debenham years ago, while still young, and by a mere continuance of living and grown to be an adopted townsman. His blue camlet cloak was a local antiquity, like the church-spire. His place in the parlour at the *George*, his absence from church, his old, crapulous, disreputable

vices, were all things of course in Debenham. He had some vague
Radical opinions and some fleeting infidelities, which he would now
and again set forth and emphasize with tottering slaps upon the
table. He drank rum—five glasses regularly every evening; and for
the greater portion of his nightly visit to the *George* sat, with his
glass in his right hand, in a state of melancholy alcoholic saturation.
We called him the Doctor, for he was supposed to have some
special knowledge of medicine and had been known, upon a pinch,
to set a fracture or reduce a dislocation; but beyond these slight
particulars, we had no knowledge of his character and antecedents.

One dark winter night—it had struck nine some time before
the landlord joined us—there was a sick man in the *George*, a great
neighbouring proprietor suddenly struck down with apoplexy on
his way to Parliament; and the great man's still greater London
doctor had been telegraphed to his bedside. It was the first time
that such a thing had happened in Debenham, for the railway was
but newly open, and we were all proportionately moved by the
occurrence.

"He's come," said the landlord, after he had filled and lighted
his pipe.

"He?" said I. "Who?—not the doctor?"

"Himself," replied our host.

"What is his name?"

"Dr. Macfarlane," said the landlord.

Fettes was far through his third tumbler, stupidly fuddled, now
nodding over, now staring mazily around him; but at the last word
he seemed to awaken and repeated the name "Macfarlane" twice,
quietly enough the first time, but with sudden emotion at the
second.

"Yes," said the landlord, "that's his name, Doctor Wolfe Macfarlane."

Fettes became instantly sober; his eyes awoke, his voice became
clear, loud and steady, his language forcible and earnest. We were
all startled by the transformation, as if a man had risen from the
dead.

"I beg your pardon," he said, "I am afraid I have not been paying much attention to your talk. Who is this Wolfe Macfarlane?"
And then, when he had heard the landlord out, "It cannot be, it
cannot be," he added; "and yet I would like well to see him face
to face."

"Do you know him, Doctor?" asked the undertaker, with a gasp.

"God forbid!" was the reply. "And yet the name is a strange one; it were too much to fancy two. Tell me, landlord, is he old?"

"Well," said the host, "he's not a young man, to be sure, and his hair is white; but he looks younger than you."

"He is older, though; years older. But," with a slap upon the table, "it's the rum you see in my face—rum and sin. This man, perhaps, may have an easy conscience and a good digestion. Conscience! Hear me speak. You would think I was some good, old, decent Christian, would you not? But no, not I; I never canted. Voltaire might have canted if he'd stood in my shoes; but the brains"—with a rattling fillip on his bald head—"the brains were clear and active and I saw and made no deductions."

"If you know this doctor," I ventured to remark, after a somewhat awful pause, "I should gather that you do not share the landlord's good opinion."

Fettes paid no regard to me.

"Yes," he said, with sudden decision, "I must see him face to face."

There was another pause and then a door was closed rather sharply on the first floor and a step was heard upon the stair.

"That's the doctor," cried the landlord. "Look sharp and you can catch him."

It was but two steps from the small parlour to the door of the old *George* inn; the wide oak staircase landed almost in the street; there was room for a Turkey rug and nothing more between the threshold and the last round of the descent; but this little space was every evening brilliantly lit up, not only by the light upon the stair and the great signal-lamp below the sign, but by the warm radiance of the bar-room window. The *George* thus brightly advertised itself to passers-by in the cold street. Fettes walked steadily to the spot and we, who were hanging behind, beheld the two men meet, as one of them had phrased it, face to face. Dr. Macfarlane was alert and vigorous. His white hair set off his pale and placid, although energetic, countenance. He was richly dressed in the finest of broadcloth and the whitest of linen, with a great gold watch-chain, and studs and spectacles of the same precious material. He wore a broad-folded tie, white and speckled with lilac, and he carried on his arm a comfortable driving-coat of fur. There was no doubt but he became his years, breathing, as he did, of wealth and consideration; and it was a surprising contrast to see our parlour sot—bald, dirty, pimpled and robed in his old camlet cloak—confront him at the bottom of the stairs.

"Macfarlane!" he said somewhat loudly, more like a herald than a friend.

The great doctor pulled up short on the fourth step, as though the familiarity of the address surprised and somewhat shocked his dignity.

"Toddy Macfarlane!" repeated Fettes.

The London man almost staggered. He stared for the swiftest of seconds at the man before him, glanced behind him with a sort of scare, and then in a startled whisper, "Fettes!" he said, "you!"

"Ay," said the other, "me! Did you think I was dead too? We are not so easy shut of our acquaintance."

"Hush, hush!" exclaimed the doctor. "Hush, hush! this meeting is so unexpected—I can see you are unmanned. I hardly knew you, I confess, at first, but I am overjoyed—overjoyed to have this opportunity. For the present it must be how-d'ye-do and goodbye in one, for my fly is waiting and I must not fail the train; but you shall—let me see—yes—you shall give me your address and you can count on early news of me. We must do something for you, Fettes. I fear you are out at elbows; but we must see to that for auld lang syne, as once we sang at suppers."

"Money!" cried Fettes; "money from you! The money that I had from you is lying where I cast it in the rain."

Dr. Macfarlane had talked himself into some measure of superiority and confidence, but the uncommon energy of this refusal cast him back into his first confusion.

A horrible, ugly look came and went across his almost venerable countenance. "My dear fellow," he said, "be it as you please; my last thought is to offend you. I would intrude on none. I will leave you my address, however—"

"I do not wish it—I do not wish to know the roof that shelters you," interrupted the other. "I heard your name; I feared it might be you; I wished to know if, after all, there were a God; I know now that there is none. Begone!"

He still stood in the middle of the rug, between the stair and the doorway; and the great London physician, in order to escape, would be forced to step to one side. It was plain that he hesitated before the thought of this humiliation. White as he was, there was a dangerous glitter in his spectacles; but while he still paused uncertain, he became aware that the driver of his fly was peering in from the street at this unusual scene and caught a glimpse at the same time of our little body from the parlour, huddled by the corner of the bar. The presence of so many witnesses decided him at once to flee. He crouched together, brushing on the wainscot, and made a dart like a serpent, striking for the door. But his tribulation was not yet entirely at an end, for even as he was passing Fettes clutched him by the arm and these words came in a whisper, and yet painfully distinct, "Have you seen it again?"

The great rich London doctor cried out aloud with a sharp, throttling cry; he dashed his questioner across the open space, and, with his hands over his head, fled out of the door like a detected thief. Before it had occurred to one of us to make a movement, the fly was already rattling towards the station. The scene was over like a dream, but the dream had left proofs and traces of its passage. Next day the servant found the fine gold spectacles broken on the threshold, and that very night we were all standing breathless by the bar-room window, and Fettes at our side, sober, pale, and resolute in look.

"God protect us, Mr. Fettes!" said the landlord, coming first into possession of his customary senses. "What in the universe is all this? These are strange things you have been saying."

Fettes turned towards us; he looked us each in succession in the face. "See if you can hold your tongues," said he. "That man Macfarlane is not safe to cross; those that have done so already have repented it too late."

And then, without so much as finishing his third glass, far less waiting for the other two, he bade us goodbye and went forth, under the lamp of the hotel, into the black night.

We three turned to our places in the parlour, with the big red fire and four clear candles; and as we recapitulated what had passed the first chill of our surprise soon changed into a glow of curiosity. We sat late; it was the latest session I have known in the old *George*. Each man, before we parted, had his theory that he was bound to prove; and none of us had any nearer business in this world than to track out the past of our condemned companion, and surprise the secret that he shared with the great London doctor. It was no great boast, but I believe I was a better hand at worming out a story than either of my fellows at the *George*; and perhaps there is now no other man alive who could narrate to you the following foul and unnatural events.

In his young days Fettes studied medicine in the schools of Edinburgh. He had talent of a kind, the talent that picks up swiftly what it hears and readily retails it for its own. He worked little at home; but he was civil, attentive, and intelligent in the presence of his masters. They soon picked him out as a lad who listened closely and remembered well; nay, strange as it seemed to me when I first heard it, he was in those days well favoured, and pleased by his exterior. There was, at that period, a certain extramural teacher of anatomy, whom I shall here designate by the letter K. His name was subsequently too well known. The man who bore it skulked through the streets of Edinburgh in disguise, while the mob that applauded at the execution of Burke called loudly for the blood of his employer. But Mr. K—— was then at the top of his vogue; he enjoyed a popularity due partly to his own talent and address, partly to the incapacity of his rival, the university professor. The students, at least, swore by his name, and Fettes believed himself, and was believed by others, to have laid the foundations of success when he had acquired the favour of this meteorically famous man. Mr. K—— was a *bon vivant* as well as an accomplished teacher; he liked a sly allusion no less than a careful preparation. In both capacities Fettes enjoyed and deserved his notice, and by the second year of his attendance he held the half-regular position of second demonstrator or sub-assistant in his class.

In this capacity, the charge of the theatre and lecture-room devolved in particular upon his shoulders. He had to answer for the cleanliness of the premises and the conduct of the other students, and it was a part of his duty to supply, receive, and divide the various subjects. It was with a view to this last—at that time very delicate—affair that he was lodged by Mr. K—— in the same wynd, and at last in the same building, with the dissecting-rooms. Here, after a night of turbulent pleasures, his hand still tottering, his sight still misty and confused, he would be called out of bed in the black hours before the winter dawn by the unclean and desperate interlopers who supplied the table. He would open the door to these men, since infamous throughout the land. He would help them with their tragic burthen, pay them their sordid price, and remain alone, when they were gone, with the unfriendly relics of humanity. From such a scene he would return to snatch another hour or two of slumber, to repair the abuses of the night, and refresh himself for the labours of the day.

Few lads could have been more insensible to the impressions of a life thus passed among the ensigns of mortality. His mind was closed against all general considerations. He was incapable of interest in the fate and fortunes of another, the slave of his own desires and low ambitions. Cold, light, and selfish in the last resort, he had that modicum of prudence, miscalled morality, which keeps a man from inconvenient drunkenness or punishable theft. He coveted, besides, a measure of consideration from his masters and his fellow-pupils, and he had no desire to fail conspicuously in the external parts of life. Thus he made it his pleasure to gain some distinction in his studies, and day after day rendered unimpeachable eye-service to his employer, Mr. K——. For his day of work he indemnified himself by nights of roaring, blackguardly enjoyment; and when that balance had been struck, the organ that he called his conscience declared itself content.

The supply of subjects was a continual trouble to him as well as to his master. In that large and busy class, the raw material of the anatomists kept perpetually running out; and the business thus rendered necessary was not only unpleasant in itself, but threatened dangerous consequences to all who were concerned. It was the policy of Mr. K—— to ask no questions in his dealings with the trade. "They bring the body, and we pay the price," he used to say, dwelling on the alliteration—"*quid pro quo*." And again, and somewhat profanely, "Ask no questions," he would tell his assistants, "for conscience' sake." There was no understanding that the subjects were provided by the crime of murder. Had that idea been broached to him in words, he would have recoiled in horror; but the lightness of his speech upon so grave a matter was, in itself, an offence against good manners, and a temptation to the men with whom he dealt. Fettes, for instance, had often remarked to himself upon the singular freshness of the bodies. He had been struck again and again by the hang-dog, abominable looks of the ruffians who came to him before the dawn; and, putting things together clearly in his private thoughts, he perhaps attributed a meaning too immoral and too categorical to the unguarded counsels of his master. He understood his duty, in short, to have three branches : to take what was brought, to pay the price, and to avert the eye from any evidence of crime.

One November morning this policy of silence was put sharply to the test. He had been awake all night with a racking toothache —pacing his room like a caged beast or throwing himself in fury on his bed—and had fallen at last into that profound, uneasy slumber that so often follows on a night of pain, when he was awakened by the third or fourth angry repetition of the concerted signal. There was a thin, bright moonshine : it was bitter cold, windy, and frosty; the town had not yet awakened, but an indefinable stir already preluded the noise and business of the day. The ghouls had come later than usual, and they seemed more than usually eager to be gone. Fettes, sick with sleep, lighted them upstairs. He heard their grumbling Irish voices through a dream; and as they stripped the sack from their sad merchandise he leaned dozing with his shoulder propped against the wall; he had to shake himself to find the men their money. As he did so his eyes lighted on the dead face. He started; he took two steps nearer, with the candle raised.

"God Almighty !" he cried. "That is Jane Galbraith !"

The men answered nothing, but they shuffled nearer the door.

"I know her, I tell you," he continued. "She was alive and hearty yesterday. It's impossible she can be dead; it's impossible you should have got this body fairly."

"Sure, sir, you're mistaken entirely," asserted one of the men.

But the other looked Fettes darkly in the eyes, and demanded the money on the spot.

It was impossible to misconceive the threat or to exaggerate the danger. The lad's heart failed him. He stammered some excuses, counted out the sum, and saw his hateful visitors depart. No sooner were they gone than he hastened to confirm his doubts. By a dozen unquestionable marks he identified the girl he had jested with the day before. He saw, with horror, marks upon her body that might well betoken violence. A panic seized him, and he took refuge in his room. There he reflected at length over the discovery that he had made; considered soberly the bearing of Mr. K——'s instructions and the danger to himself of interference in so serious a business, and at last, in sore perplexity, determined to wait for the advice of his immediate superior, the class assistant.

This was a young doctor, Wolfe Macfarlane, a high favourite among all the restless students, clever, dissipated, and unscrupulous to the last degree. He had travelled and studied abroad. His manners were agreeable and a little forward. He was an authority on the stage, skilful on the ice or the links with skate or golf-club; he dressed with nice audacity, and, to put the finishing touch upon his glory, he kept a gig and a strong trotting-horse. With Fettes he was on terms of intimacy; indeed their relative positions called for some community of life; and when subjects were scarce the pair would drive far into the country in Macfarlane's gig, visit and desecrate some lonely graveyard, and return before dawn with their booty to the door of the dissecting-room.

On that particular morning Macfarlane arrived somewhat earlier than his wont. Fettes heard him, and met him on the stairs, told him his story, and showed him the cause of his alarm. Macfarlane examined the marks on her body.

"Yes," he said with a nod, "it looks fishy."

"Well, what should I do?" asked Fettes.

"Do?" repeated the other. "Do you want to do anything? Least said soonest mended, I should say."

"Someone else might recognize her," objected Fettes. "She was as well known as the Castle Rock."

"We'll hope not," said Macfarlane, "and if anybody does—well you didn't, don't you see, and there's an end. The fact is, this has been going on too long. Stir up the mud, and you'll get K—— into the most unholy trouble; you'll be in a shocking box yourself. So will I, if you come to that. I should like to know how any one of us would look, or what the devil we should have to say for ourselves, in any Christian witness-box. For me, you know there's one thing certain—that, practically speaking, all our subjects have been murdered."

"Macfarlane!" cried Fettes.

"Come now!" sneered the other. "As if you hadn't suspected it yourself!"

"Suspecting is one thing—"

"And proof another. Yes, I know; and I'm as sorry as you are this should have come here," tapping the body with his cane. "The next best thing for me is not to recognize it; and," he added coolly, "I don't. You may, if you please. I don't dictate, but I think a man of the world would do as I do; and I may add, I fancy that is what K—— would look for at our hands. The question is, why did he choose us two for his assistants? And I answer, because he didn't want old wives."

This was the tone of all others to affect the mind of a lad like Fettes. He agreed to imitate Macfarlane. The body of the unfortunate girl was duly dissected, and no one remarked or appeared to recognize her.

One afternoon, when his day's work was over, Fettes dropped into a popular tavern and found Macfarlane sitting with a stranger. This was a small man, very pale and dark, with coal-black eyes. The cut of his features gave a promise of intellect and refinement which was but feebly realized in his manners, for he proved, upon a nearer acquaintance, coarse, vulgar, and stupid. He exercised, however, a very remarkable control over Macfarlane; issued orders like the Great Bashaw; became inflamed at the least discussion or delay, and commented rudely on the servility with which he was obeyed. This most offensive person took a fancy to Fettes on the spot, plied him with drinks, and honoured him with unusual confidences on his past career. If a tenth part of what he confessed were true, he was a very loathsome rogue; and the lad's vanity was tickled by the attention of so experienced a man.

"I'm a pretty bad fellow myself," the stranger remarked, "but Macfarlane is the boy—Toddy Macfarlane I call him. Toddy, order your friend another glass." Or it might be, "Toddy, you jump up and shut the door." "Toddy hates me," he said again. "Oh, yes, Toddy, you do!"

"Don't call me that confounded name," growled Macfarlane.

"Hear him! Did you ever see the lads play knife? He would like to do that all over my body," remarked the stranger.

"We medicals have a better way than that," said Fettes. "When we dislike a dead friend of ours, we dissect him."

Macfarlane looked up sharply, as though this jest was scarcely to his mind.

The afternoon passed. Gray, for that was the stranger's name, invited Fettes to join them at dinner, ordered a feast so sumptuous that the tavern was thrown in commotion, and when all was done commanded Macfarlane to settle the bill. It was late before they separated; the man Gray was incapably drunk. Macfarlane, sobered by his fury, chewed the cud of the money he had been forced to squander and the slights he had been obliged to swallow. Fettes, with various liquors singing in his head, returned home with devious footsteps and a mind entirely in abeyance. Next day Macfarlane was absent from the class, and Fettes smiled to himself as he imagined him still squiring the intolerable Gray from tavern to tavern. As soon as the hour of liberty had struck he posted from place to place in quest of his last night's companions. He could find them, however, nowhere; so returned early to his rooms, went early to bed, and slept the sleep of the just.

At four in the morning he was awakened by the well-known signal. Descending to the door, he was filled with astonishment to find Macfarlane with his gig, and in the gig one of those long and ghastly packages with which he was so well acquainted.

"What?" he cried. "Have you been out alone? How did you manage?"

But Macfarlane silenced him roughly, bidding him turn to business. When they had got the body upstairs and laid it on the table, Macfarlane made at first as if he were going away. Then he paused and seemed to hesitate; and then, "You had better look at the face," said he, in tones of some constraint. "You had better," he repeated, as Fettes only stared at him in wonder.

"But where, and how, and when did you come by it?" cried the other.

"Look at the face," was the only answer.

Fettes was staggered; strange doubts assailed him. He looked from the young doctor to the body, and then back again. At last, with a start, he did as he was bidden. He had almost expected the sight that met his eyes, and yet the shock was cruel. To see, fixed in the rigidity of death and naked on that coarse layer of sack-cloth, the man whom he had left well-clad and full of meat and sin upon the threshold of a tavern, awoke, even in the thoughtless Fettes, some of the terrors of the conscience. It was a *cras tibi* which re-echoed in his soul, that two whom he had known should have come to lie upon these icy tables. Yet these were only secondary thoughts. His first concern regarded Wolfe. Unprepared for a challenge so momentous, he knew not how to look his comrade in the face. He durst not meet his eye, and he had neither words nor voice at his command.

It was Macfarlane himself who made the first advance. He came up quietly behind and laid his hand gently but firmly on the other's shoulder.

"Richardson," said he, "may have the head."

Now Richardson was a student who had long been anxious for that portion of the human subject to dissect. There was no answer, and the murderer resumed : "Talking of business, you must pay me; your accounts, you see, must tally."

Fettes found a voice, the ghost of his own : "Pay you !" he cried. "Pay you for that?"

"Why, yes, of course you must. By all means and on every possible account, you must," returned the other. "I dare not give it for nothing, you dare not take it for nothing; it would compromise us both. This is another case like Jane Galbraith's. The more things are wrong the more we must act as if all were right. Where does old K—— keep his money—"

"There," answered Fettes hoarsely, pointing to a cupboard in the corner.

"Give me the key, then," said the other, calmly, holding out his hand.

There was an instant's hesitation, and the die was cast. Macfarlane could not suppress a nervous twitch, the infinitesimal mark of an immense relief, as he felt the key turn between his fingers. He opened the cupboard, brought out pen and ink and a paper-book that stood in one compartment, and separated from the funds in a drawer a sum suitable to the occasion.

"Now, look here," he said, "there is the payment made—first proof of your good faith : first step to your security. You have now to clinch it by a second. Enter the payment in your book, and then you for your part may defy the devil."

The next few seconds were for Fettes an agony of thought; but in balancing his terrors it was the most immediate that triumphed. Any future difficulty seemed almost welcome if he could avoid a present quarrel with Macfarlane. He sat down the candle which he had been carrying all the time, and with a steady hand entered the date, the nature, and the amount of the transaction.

"And now," said Macfarlane, "it's only fair that you should pocket the lucre. I've had my share already. By-the-by, when a man of the world falls into a bit of luck, has a few shillings extra in his pocket—I'm ashamed to speak of it, but there's a rule of conduct in the case. No treating, no purchase of expensive class-books, no squaring of old debts; borrow, don't lend."

"Macfarlane," began Fettes, still somewhat hoarsely. "I have put my neck in a halter to oblige you."

"To oblige me?" cried Wolfe. "Oh, come! You did, as near as I can see the matter, what you downright had to do in self defence. Suppose I got into trouble, where would you be? This second little matter flows clearly from the first. Mr. Gray is the continuation of Miss Galbraith. You can't begin and then stop. If you begin, you must keep on beginning; that's the truth. No rest for the wicked."

A horrible sense of blackness and the treachery of fate seized hold upon the soul of the unhappy student.

"My God !" he cried, "but what have I done? and when did I begin? To be made a class assistant—in the name of reason, where's

the harm in that? Service wanted the position; Service might have
got it. Would *he* have been where *I* am now?"

"My dear fellow," said Macfarlane, "what a boy you are! What
harm *has* come to you? What harm *can* come to you if you hold
your tongue? Why, man, do you know what this life is? There are
two squads of us—the lions and the lambs. If you're a lamb, you'll
come to lie upon these tables like Gray or Jane Galbraith; if you're
a lion, you'll live and drive a horse like me, like K——, like all the
world with any wit or courage. You're staggered at the first. But
look at K——! My dear fellow, you're clever, you have pluck. I
like you, and K—— likes you. You were born to lead the hunt:
and I tell you, on my honour and my experience of life, three days
from now you'll laugh at all these scarecrows like a high-school boy
at a farce."

And with that Macfarlane took his departure and drove off up
the wynd in his gig to get under cover before daylight. Fettes was
thus left alone with his regrets. He saw the miserable peril in which
he stood involved. He saw, with inexpressible dismay, that there
was no limit to his weakness, and that, from concession to concession,
he had fallen from the arbiter of Macfarlane's destiny to his paid
and helpless accomplice. He would have given the world to have
been a little braver at the time, but it did not occur to him that he
might still be brave. The secret of Jane Galbraith and the cursed
entry in the daybook closed his mouth.

Hours passed; the class began to arrive; the members of the unhappy Gray were dealt out to one and to another, and received
without remark. Richardson was made happy with the head; and
before the hour of freedom rang Fettes trembled with exultation
to perceive how far they had already gone towards safety.

For two days he continued to watch, with increasing joy, the
dreadful process of disguise.

On the third day Macfarlane made his appearance. He had
been ill, he said; but he made up for lost time by the energy with
which he directed the students. To Richardson in particular he
extended the most valuable assistance and advice, and that student,
encouraged by the praise of the demonstrator, burned high with
ambitious hopes, and saw the medal already in his grasp.

Before the week was out Macfarlane's prophecy had been fulfilled. Fettes had outlived his terrors and had forgotten his baseness.
He began to plume himself upon his courage, and had so arranged
the story in his mind that he could look back on these events with

an unhealthy pride. Of his accomplice he saw but little. They met, of course, in the business of the class; they received their orders together from Mr. K——. At times they had a word or two in private, and Macfarlane was from first to last particularly kind and jovial. But it was plain that he avoided any reference to their common secret; and even when Fettes whispered to him that he had cast in his lot with the lions and forsworn the lambs, he only signed to him smilingly to hold his peace.

At length an occasion arose which threw the pair once more into a closer union. Mr. K—— was again short of subjects; pupils were eager, and it was a part of this teacher's pretensions to be always well supplied. At the same time there came the news of a burial in the rustic graveyard of Glencorse. Time has little changed the place in question. It stood then, as now, upon the crossroad, out of call of human habitations, and buried fathom deep in the foliage of six cedar trees. The cries of the sheep upon the neighbouring hills, the streamlets upon either hand, one loudly singing among pebbles, the other dripping furtively from pond to pond, the stir of the wind in mountainous old flowering chestnuts, and once in seven days the voice of the bell and the old tunes of the precentor, were the only sounds that disturbed the silence around the rural church. The Resurrection Man—to use a by-name of the period —was not to be deterred by any of the sanctities of customary piety. It was part of his trade to despise and desecrate the scrolls and trumpets of old tombs, the paths worn by the feet of worshippers and mourners, and the offerings and the inscriptions of bereaved affection. To rustic neighbourhoods, where love is more than commonly tenacious, and where some bonds of blood or fellowship unite the entire society of a parish, the body-snatcher, far from being repelled by natural respect, was attracted by the ease and safety of the task. To bodies that had been laid in earth, in joyful expectation of a far different awakening, there came that hasty, lamp-lit, terror-haunted resurrection of the spade and mattock. The coffin was forced, the cerements torn, and the melancholy relics, clad in sack-cloth, after being rattled for hours on moonless by-ways, were at length exposed to uttermost indignities before a class of gaping boys.

Somewhat as two vultures may swoop upon a dying lamb, Fettes and Macfarlane were to be let loose upon a grave in that green and quiet resting-place. The wife of a farmer, a woman who had lived for sixty years, and been known for nothing but good butter and a godly conversation, was to be rooted from her grave at midnight and carried, dead and naked, to that far-away city that she had always honoured with her Sunday best; the place beside her family was to be empty till the crack of doom; her innocent and almost venerable members to be exposed to that last curiosity of the anatomist.

Late one afternoon the pair set forth, well wrapped in cloaks and furnished with a formidable bottle. It rained without remission—a cold, dense, lashing rain. Now and again there blew a puff of wind, but these sheets of falling water kept it down. Bottle and all, it was a sad and silent drive as far as Penicuik, where they were to spend the evening. They stopped once, to hide their implements in a thick bush not far from the churchyard, and once again at the Fisher's Tryst, to have a toast before the kitchen fire and vary their nips of whisky with a glass of ale. When they reached their journey's end the gig was housed, the horse was fed and comforted, and the two young doctors in a private room sat down to the best dinner and the best wine the house afforded. The lights, the fire, the beating rain upon the window, the cold, incongruous work that lay before them, added zest to their enjoyment of the meal. With every glass their cordiality increased. Soon Macfarlane handed a little pile of gold to his companion.

"A compliment," he said. "Between friends these little damned accommodations ought to fly like pipe-lights."

Fettes pocketed the money, and applauded the sentiment to the echo. "You are a philosopher," he cried. "I was an ass till I knew you. You and K—— between you, by the Lord Harry! but you'll make a man of me."

"Of course we shall," applauded Macfarlane. "A man? I tell you, it required a man to back me up the other morning. There are some big, brawling, forty-year-old cowards who would have turned sick at the look of the damned thing; but not you—you kept your head. I watched you."

"Well, and why not?" Fettes thus vaunted himself. "It was no affair of mine. There was nothing to gain on the one side but disturbance, and on the other I could count on your gratitude, don't you see?" And he slapped his pocket till the gold pieces rang.

Macfarlane somehow felt a certain touch of alarm at these unpleasant words. He may have regretted that he had taught his young companion so successfully, but he had no time to interfere, for the other noisily continued in this boastful strain :

"The great thing is not to be afraid. Now, between you and me, I don't want to hang—that's practical; but for all cant, Macfarlane, I was born with a contempt. Hell, God, Devil, right, wrong, sin, crime, and all the old gallery of curiosities—they may frighten boys, but men of the world, like you and me, despise them. Here's to the memory of Gray!"

It was by this time growing somewhat late. The gig, according to order, was brought round to the door with both lamps brightly shining, and the young men had to pay their bill and take the road. They announced that they were bound for Peebles, and drove in that direction till they were clear of the last houses of the town; then, extinguishing the lamps, returned upon their course, and followed a by-road towards Glencorse. There was no sound but that of their own passage, and the incessant, strident pouring of the rain. It was pitch dark; here and there a white gate or a white stone in the wall guided them for a short space across the night; but for the most part it was at a foot pace, and almost groping, that they picked their way through that resonant blackness to their solemn and isolated destination. In the sunken woods that traverse the neighbourhood of the burying-ground the last glimmer failed them, and it became necessary to kindle a match and re-illumine one of the lanterns of the gig. Thus, under the dripping trees, and environed by huge and moving shadows, they reached the scene of their unhallowed labours.

They were both experienced in such affairs, and powerful with the spade; and they had scarce been twenty minutes at their task before they were rewarded by a dull rattle on the coffin lid. At the same moment Macfarlane, having hurt his hand upon a stone, flung it carelessly above his head. The grave, in which they now stood almost to the shoulders, was close to the edge of the plateau of the graveyard; and the gig lamp had been propped, the better to illuminate their labours, against a tree, and on the immediate verge of the steep bank descending to the stream. Chance had taken a sure aim with the stone. Then came a clang of broken glass; night fell upon them; sounds alternately dull and ringing announced the bounding of the lantern down the bank, and its occasional collision with the trees. A stone or two, which it had dislodged in its descent rattled behind it into the profundities of the glen; and then silence, like night, resumed its sway; and they might bend their hearing to its utmost pitch, but naught was to be heard except the rain, now marching to the wind, now steadily falling over miles of open country.

They were so nearly at an end of their abhorred task that they judged it wisest to complete it in the dark. The coffin was exhumed and broken open; the body inserted in the dripping sack and carried between them to the gig; one mounted to keep it in its place, and the other, taking the horse by the mouth, groped along by the wall and bush until they reached the wider road by the Fisher's Tryst. Here was a faint disused radiancy, which they hailed like daylight; by that they pushed the horse to a good pace and began to rattle along merrily in the direction of the town.

They had both been wetted to the skin during their operations, and now, as the gig jumped among the deep ruts, the thing that stood propped between them fell now upon one and now upon the other. At every repetition of the horrid contact each instinctively repelled it with greater haste; and the process, natural although it was, began to tell upon the nerves of the companions. Macfarlane made some ill-favoured jest about the farmer's wife, but it came hollowly from his lips, and was allowed to drop in silence. Still their unnatural burthen bumped from side to side; and now the head would be laid, as if in confidence, upon their shoulders, and now the drenching sackcloth would flap icily about their faces. A creeping chill began to possess the soul of Fettes. He peered at the bundle, and it seemed somehow larger than at first. All over the country-side, and from every degree of distance, the farm dogs accompanied their passage with tragic ululations; and it grew and grew upon his mind that some unnatural miracle had been achieved, that some nameless change had befallen the dead body, and that it was in fear of their unholy burthen that the dogs were howling.

"For God's sake," said he, making a great effort to arrive at speech, "for God's sake, let's have a light!"

Seemingly Macfarlane was affected in the same direction; for though he made no reply, he stopped the horse, passed the reins to his companion, got down, and proceeded to kindle the remaining lamp. They had by that time got no farther than the crossroad down to Auchendinny. The rain still poured as though the deluge were returning, and it was no easy matter to make a light in such a world of wet and darkness. When at last the flickering blue flame had been transferred to the wick and began to expand and clarify, and shed a wide circle of misty brightness round the gig, it became possible for the two young men to see each other and the thing they had along with them. The rain had moulded the rough sacking to the outlines of the body underneath; the head was distinct from the trunk, the shoulders plainly modelled; something at once spectral and human riveted their eyes upon the ghastly comrade of their drive.

For some time Macfarlane stood motionless, holding up the lamp. A nameless dread was swathed, like a wet sheet, about the body, and tightened the white skin upon the face of Fettes; a fear that was meaningless, a horror of what could not be, kept mounting to his brain. Another beat of the watch, and he had spoken. But his comrade forestalled him.

"That is not a woman," said Macfarlane, in a hushed voice.

"It was a woman when we put her in," whispered Fettes.

"Hold that lamp," said the other. "I must see her face."

And as Fettes took the lamp his companion untied the fastenings of the sack and drew down the cover from the head. The light fell very clear upon the dark, well-moulded features and smooth-shaven cheeks of a too familiar countenance, often beheld in dreams of both of these young men. A wild yell rang up into the night; each leaped from his own side into the roadway; the lamp fell, broke, and was extinguished; and the horse, terrified by this unusual commotion, bounded and went off towards Edinburgh at a gallop, bearing along with it, sole occupant of the gig, the body of the dead and long-dissected Gray.

THE BEAST WITH FIVE FINGERS

W. F. HARVEY

(Warner Brothers: 1947)

In the years immediately after the Second World War the horror film went through a period of decline, indeed the only such dip in popularity it has ever experienced. The public taste had switched to comedy and music after the very real horrors of the war were brought home in newsreels and captured films, and there no longer seemed to be a place for monsters, however entertaining their activities.

In the years 1946 to 1950 less than a dozen films with a terror content were made, and of those the only true horror picture in the accepted sense of the word was The Beast With Five Fingers. *Based on a short story of the same name by the noted English macabre story writer William Fryer Harvey, it tells of a severed hand with a life—and purpose—of its own. Directed by one of the few horror specialists at work at the time, Robert Florey, the picture contains two outstanding individual performances, by Peter Lorre and by a much underestimated character actor, J. Carroll Naish.*

Due to its poor reception at the box office, the film did nothing to encourage its makers, or others in the business, to attempt a revival of the genre. That revival, as we shall see, was to come by way of Science Fiction/Fantasy.

*

THE story, I suppose, begins with Adrian Borlsover, whom I met when I was a little boy and he an old man. My father had called to appeal for a subscription, and before he left, Mr. Borlsover laid his right hand in blessing on my head. I shall never forget the awe in which I gazed up at his face and realized for the first time that eyes might be dark and beautiful and shining and yet not able to see.

For Adrian Borlsover was blind.

He was an extraordinary man, who came of an eccentric stock. Borlsover sons for some reason always seemed to marry very ordinary women; which perhaps accounted for the fact that no Borlsover had been a genius and only one Borlsover had been mad. But they were great champions of little causes, generous patrons of odd sciences, founders of querulous sects, trustworthy guides to the bypath meadows of erudition.

Adrian was an authority on the fertilization of orchids. He had held at one time the family living at Borlsover Conyers, until a congenital weakness of the lungs obliged him to seek a less rigorous climate in the sunny south-west watering-place where I had seen him. Occasionally he would relieve one or other of the local clergy. My father described him as a fine preacher, who gave long and inspiring sermons from what many men would have considered unprofitable texts. "An excellent proof," he would add, "of the truth of the doctrine of direct verbal inspiration."

Adrian Borlsover was exceedingly clever with his hands. His penmanship was exquisite. He illustrated all his scientific papers, made his own woodcuts, and carved the reredos that is at present the chief feature of interest in the church at Borlsover Conyers. He had an exceedingly clever knack in cutting silhouettes for young ladies and paper pigs and cows for little children, and made more than one complicated wind instrument of his own devising.

When he was fifty years old Adrian Borlsover lost his sight. In a wonderfully short time he adapted himself to the new conditions of life. He quickly learn to read Braille. So marvellous indeed was his sense of touch, that he was still able to maintain his interest in botany. The mere passing of his long supple fingers over a flower was sufficient means for its identification, though occasionally he would use his lips. I have found several letters of his among my father's correspondence; in no case was there anything to show that he was afflicted with blindness, and this in spite of the fact that he exercised undue economy in the spacing of lines. Towards the close of his life Adrian Borlsover was credited with powers of touch that seemed almost uncanny. It has been said that he could tell at once the colour of a ribbon placed between his fingers. My father would neither confirm nor deny the story.

Adrian Borlsover was a bachelor. His elder brother, Charles, had married late in life, leaving one son, Eustace, who lived in the gloomy Georgian mansion at Borlsover Conyers, where he could work undisturbed in collecting material for his great book on heredity.

Like his uncle, he was a remarkable man. The Borlsovers had always been born naturalists, but Eustace possessed in a special degree the power of systematizing his knowledge. He had received his university education in Germany; and then, after post-graduate work in Vienna and Naples, had travelled for four years in South America, and the East, getting together a huge store of material for a new study into the processes of variation.

He lived alone at Borlsover Conyers with Saunders, his secretary, a man who bore a somewhat dubious reputation in the district, but whose powers as a mathematician, combined with his business abilities, were invaluable to Eustace.

Uncle and nephew saw little of each other. The visits of Eustace were confined to a week in the summer or autumn—tedious weeks, that dragged almost as slowly as the bathchair in which the old man was drawn along the sunny seafront. In their way the two men were fond of each other, though their intimacy would, doubtless, have been greater had they shared the same religious views. Adrian held to the old-fashioned evangelical dogmas of his early manhood; his nephew for many years had been thinking of embracing Buddhism. Both men possessed, too, the reticence the Borlsovers had always shown, and which their enemies sometimes called hypocrisy. With Adrian it was a reticence as to the things he had left undone; but with Eustace it seemed that the curtain which he was so careful to leave undrawn hid something more than a half-empty chamber.

Two years before his death Adrian Borlsover developed, unknown to himself, the not uncommon power of automatic writing. Eustace made the discovery by accident. Adrian was sitting reading in bed, the forefinger of his left hand tracing the Braille characters, when his nephew noticed that a pencil the old man held in his right hand was moving slowly along the opposite page. He left his seat in the window and sat down beside the bed. The right had continued to move and now he could see plainly that they were letters and words which it was forming.

"Adrian Borlsover," wrote the hand, "Eustace Borlsover, Charles Borlsover, Francis Borlsover, Sigismund Borlsover, Adrian Borlsover, Eustace Borlsover, Saville Borlsover. B for Borlsover. Honesty is the Best Policy. Beautiful Belinda Borlsover."

"What curious nonsense!" said Eustace to himself.

"King George ascended the throne in 1760," wrote the hand. "Crowd, a noun of multitude; a collection of individuals. Adrian Borlsover, Eustace Borlsover."

"It seems to me," said his uncle, closing the book, "that you had much better make the most of the afternoon sunshine and take your walk now."

"I think perhaps I will," Eustace answered as he picked up the volume. "I won't go far, and when I come back I can read to you those articles in *Nature* about which we were speaking."

He went along the promenade, but stopped at the first shelter and, seating himself in the corner best protected from the wind, he examined the book at leisure. Nearly every page was scored with a meaningless jumble of pencil-marks; rows of capital letters, short words, long words, complete sentences, copy-book tags. The whole thing, in fact, had the appearance of a copy-book, and, on a more careful scrutiny, Eustace thought that there was ample evidence to show that the handwriting at the beginning of the book, good though it was, was not nearly so good as the handwriting at the end.

He left his uncle at the end of October with a promise to return early in December. It seemed to him quite clear that the old man's power of automatic writing was developing rapidly, and for the first time he looked forward to a visit that would combine duty with interest.

But on his return he was at first disappointed. His uncle, he thought, looked older. He was listless, too, preferring others to read to him and dictating nearly all his letters. Not until the day before he left had Eustace an opportunity of observing Adrian Borlsover's new-found faculty.

The old man, propped up in bed with pillows, had sunk into a light sleep. His two hands lay on the coverlet, his left hand tightly clasping his right. Eustace took an empty manuscript-book and placed a pencil within reach of the fingers of the right hand. They snatched at it eagerly, then dropped the pencil to loose the left hand from its restraining grasp.

"Perhaps to prevent interference I had better hold that hand," said Eustace to himself, as he watched the pencil. Almost immediately it began to write :

"Blundering Borlsovers, unnecessarily unnatural, extraordinarily eccentric, culpably curious."

"Who are you?" asked Eustace in a low voice.

"Never you mind," wrote the hand of Adrian.

"Is it my uncle who is writing?"

"O my prophetic soul, mine uncle!"

"Is it anyone I know?"

"Silly Eustace, you'll see me very soon."

"When shall I see you?"

"When poor old Adrian's dead."

"Where shall I see you?"

"Where shall you not?"

Instead of speaking his next question, Eustace wrote it : "What is the time?"

The fingers dropped the pencil and moved three or four times across the paper. Then, picking up the pencil, they wrote : "Ten minutes before four. Put your book away, Eustace. Adrian mustn't find us working at this sort of thing. He doesn't know what to make of it, and I won't have poor old Adrian disturbed. *Au revoir!*

Adrian Borlsover awoke with a start.

"I've been dreaming again," he said; "such queer dreams of leaguered cities and forgotten towns. You were mixed up in this one, Eustace, though I can't remember how. Eustace, I want to warn you. Don't walk in doubtful paths. Choose your friends well. Your poor grandfather . . ."

A fit of coughing put an end to what he was saying, but Eustace saw that the hand was still writing. He managed unnoticed to draw the book away. "I'll light the gas," he said, "and ring for tea." On the other side of the bed-curtain he saw the last sentences that had been written.

"It's too late, Adrian," he read. "We're friends already, aren't we, Eustace Borlsover?"

On the following day Eustace left. He thought his uncle looked ill when he said goodbye, and the old man spoke despondently of the failure his life had been.

"Nonsense, uncle," said his nephew. "You have got over your difficulties in a way not one in a hundred thousand would have done. Everyone marvels at your splendid perseverance in teaching your hands to take the place of your lost sight. To me it's been a revelation of the possibilities of education."

"Education," said his uncle dreamily, as if the word had started a new train of thought. 'Education is good so long as you know to whom and for what purpose you give it. But with the lower orders of men, the baser and more sordid spirits, I have grave doubts as to its results. Well, goodbye, Eustace; I may not see you again. You are a true Borlsover, with all the Borlsover faults. Marry, Eustace. Marry some good, sensible girl. And if by any chance I don't see you again, my will is at my solicitor's. I've not left you any legacy, because I know you're well provided for; but I thought you might

like to have my books. Oh, and there's just one other thing. You
know, before the end people often lose control over themselves and
make absurd requests. Don't pay any attention to them, Eustace.
Goodbye!" and he held out his hand. Eustace took it. It remained
in his a fraction of a second longer than he had expected and gripped him with a virility that was surprising. There was, too, in its
touch a subtle sense of intimacy.

"Why, uncle," he said, "I shall see you alive and well for many
long years to come."

Two months later Adrian Borlsover died.

Eustace Borlsover was in Naples at the time. He read the obituary
notice in the *Morning Post* on the day announced for the funeral.

"Poor old fellow!" he said. "I wonder whether I shall find room
for all his books."

The question occurred to him again with greater force when,
three days later, he found himself standing in the library at Borlsover Conyers, a huge room built for use and not for beauty in the
year of Waterloo by a Borlsover who was an ardent admirer of the
great Napoleon. It was arranged on the plan of many college lib-
raries, with tall projecting bookcases forming deep recesses of dusty
silence, fit graves for the old hates of forgotten controversy, the dead
passions of forgotten lives. At the end of the room, behind the bust
of some unknown eighteenth-century divine, an ugly iron corkscrew
stair led to a shelf-lined gallery. Nearly every shelf was full.

"I must talk to Saunders about it," said Eustace. "I suppose that
we shall have to have the billiard-room fitted up with bookcases."

The two men met for the first time after many weeks in the
dining-room that evening.

"Hallo!" said Eustace, standing before the fire with his hands in
his pockets. "How goes the world, Saunders? Why these dress togs?"
He himself was wearing an old shooting-jacket. He did not believe
in mourning, as he had told his uncle on his last visit; and, though
he usually went in for quiet-coloured ties, he wore this evening one
of an ugly red, in order to shock Morton, the butler, and to make
them thrash out the whole question of mourning for themselves in
the servants' hall. Eustace was a true Borlsover. "The world," said
Saunders, "goes the same as usual, confoundedly slow. The dress
togs are accounted for by an invitation from Captain Lockwood to
bridge."

"How are you getting there?"

"There's something the matter with the car, so I've told Jackson to drive me round in the dogcart. Any objection?"

"Oh, dear me, no! We've had all things in common for far too many years for me to raise objections at this hour of the day."

"You'll find your correspondence in the library," went on Saunders. "Most of it I've seen to. There are a few private letters I haven't opened. There's also a box with a rat or something inside it that came by the evening post. Very likely it's the six-toed beast Terry was sending us to cross with the four-toed albino. I didn't look because I didn't want to mess up my things; but I should gather from the way it's jumping about that it's pretty hungry."

"Oh, I'll see to it," said Eustace, "while you and the captain earn an honest penny."

Dinner over and Saunders gone, Eustace went into the library. Though the fire had been lit, the room was by no means cheerful.

"We'll have all the lights on, at any rate," he said, as he turned the switches. "And, Morton," he added, when the butler brought the coffee, "get me a screwdriver or something to undo this box. Whatever the animal is, he's kicking up the deuce of a row. What is it? Why are you dawdling?"

"If you please, sir, when the postman brought it, he told me that they'd bored the holes in the lid at the post office. There were no breathing holes in the lid, sir, and they didn't want the animal to die. That is all, sir."

"It's culpably careless of the man, whoever he was," said Eustace, as he removed the screws, "packing an animal like this in a wooden box with no means of getting air. Confound it all! I meant to ask Morton to bring me a cage to put it in. Now I suppose I shall have to get one myself."

He placed a heavy book on the lid from which the screws had been removed, and went into the billiard-room. As he came back into the library with an empty cage in his hand, he heard the sound of something falling, and then of something scuttling along the floor.

"Bother it! The beast's got out. How in the world am I to find it again in this library?"

To search for it did indeed seem hopeless. He tried to follow the sound of the scuttling in one of the recesses, where the animal seemed to be running behind the books in the shelves; but it was impossible to locate it. Eustace resolved to go on quietly reading.

Very likely the animal might gain confidence and show itself. Saunders seemed to have dealt in his usual methodical manner with most of the correspondence. There were still the private letters.

What was that? Two sharp clicks and the lights in the hideous candelabras that hung from the ceiling suddenly went out.

"I wonder if something has gone wrong with the fuse," said Eustace, as he went to the switches by the door. Then he stopped. There was a noise at the other end of the room, as if something was crawling up the iron corkscrew stair. "If it's gone into the gallery," he said, "well and good." He hastily turned on the lights, crossed the room, and climbed up the stair. But he could see nothing. His grandfather had placed a little gate at the top of the stair, so that children could run and romp in the gallery without fear of accident. This Eustace closed, and, having considerably narrowed the circle of his search, returned to his desk by the fire.

How gloomy the library was! There was no sense of intimacy about the room. The few busts that an eighteenth-century Borlsover had brought back from the grand tour might have been in keeping in the old library. Here they seemed out of place. They made the room feel cold in spite of the heavy red damask curtain and great gilt cornices.

With a crash two heavy books fell from the gallery to the floor; then, as Borlsover looked, another, and yet another.

"Very well. You'll starve for this, my beauty!" he said. "We'll do some little experiments on the metabolism of rats deprived of water. Go on! Chuck them down! I think I've got the upper hand." He turned once more to his correspondence. The letter was from the family solicitor. It spoke of his uncle's death, and of the valuable collection of books that had been left to him in the will.

There was one request [he read] which certainly came as a surprise to me. As you know, Mr. Adrian Borlsover had left instructions that his body was to be buried in as simple a manner as possible at Eastbourne. He expressed a desire that there should be neither wreaths nor flowers of any kind, and hoped that his friends and relatives would not consider it necessary to wear mourning. The day before his death we received a letter cancelling these instructions. He wished the body to be embalmed (he gave us the address of the man we were to employ—Pennifer, Ludgate Hill), with orders that his right hand should be sent to you stating that it was at your special request. The other arrangements about the funeral remained unaltered.

"Good Lord," said Eustace, "what in the world was the old boy driving at? And what in the name of all that's holy is that?"

Someone was in the gallery. Someone had pulled the cord attached to one of the blinds, and it had rolled up with a snap. Someone must be in the gallery, for a second blind did the same. Someone must be walking round the gallery, for one after the other the blinds sprang up, letting in the moonlight.

"I haven't got to the bottom of this yet," said Eustace, "but I will do, before the night is very much older"; and he hurried up the corkscrew stair. He had just got to the top, when the lights went out a second time, and he heard again the scuttling along the floor. Quickly he stole on tiptoe in the dim moonshine in the direction of the noise, feeling, as he went, for one of the switches. His fingers touched the metal knob at last. He turned on the electric light.

About ten yards in front of him, crawling along the floor, was a man's hand. Eustace stared at it in utter amazement. It was moving quickly in the manner of a geometer caterpillar, the fingers humped up one moment, flattened out the next; the thumb appeared to give a crablike motion to the whole. While he was looking, too surprised to stir, the hand disappeared round the corner. Eustace ran forward. He no longer saw it, but he could hear it, as it squeezed its way behind the books on one of the shelves. A heavy volume had been displaced. There was a gap in the row of books, where it had got in. In his fear lest it should escape him again, he seized the first book that came to his hand and plugged it into the hole. Then, emptying two shelves of their contents, he took the wooden boards and propped them up in front to make his barrier doubly sure.

"I wish Saunders was back," he said; "one can't tackle this sort of thing alone." It was after eleven, and there seemed little likelihood of Saunders returning before twelve. He did not dare to leave the shelf unwatched, even to run downstairs to ring the bell. Morton, the butler, often used to come round about eleven to see that the windows were fastened, but he might not come. Eustace was thoroughly unstrung. At last he heard steps down below.

"Morton!" he shouted. "Morton!"

"Sir?"

"Has Mr. Saunders got back yet?"

"Not yet, sir."

"Well, bring me some brandy, and hurry up about it. I'm up in the gallery, you duffer."

"Thanks," said Eustace, as he emptied the glass. "Don't go to bed yet, Morton. There are a lot of books that have fallen down by accident. Bring them up and put them back in their shelves."

Morton had never seen Borlsover in so talkative a mood as on that night. "Here," said Eustace, when the books had been put back and dusted, "you might hold up these boards for me, Morton. That beast in the box got out, and I've been chasing it all over the place."

"I think I can hear it clawing at the books, sir. They're not valuable, I hope? I think that's the carriage, sir; I'll go and call Mr. Saunders."

It seemed to Eustace that he was away for five minutes, but it could hardly have been more than one, when he returned with Saunders. "All right, Morton, you can go now. I'm up here, Saunders."

"What's all the row?" asked Saunders, as he lounged forward with his hands in his pockets. The luck had been with him all the evening. He was completely satisfied, both with himself and with Captain Lockwood's taste in wines. "What's the matter? You look to me to be in an absolutely blue funk."

"That old devil of an uncle of mine," began Eustace—"Oh, I can't explain it all. It's his hand that's been playing Old Harry all the evening. But I've got it cornered behind these books. You've got to help me to catch it."

"What's up with you, Eustace? What's the game?"

"It's no game, you silly idiot! If you don't believe me, take out one of those books and put your hand in and feel."

"All right," said Saunders; "but wait till I've rolled up my sleeve. The accumulated dust of centuries, eh?" He took off his coat, knelt down, and thrust his arm along the shelf.

"There's something there right enough," he said. "It's got a funny, stumpy end to it, whatever it is, and nips like a crab. Ah! no, you don't!" He pulled his hand out in a flash. "Shove in a book quickly. Now it can't get out."

"What was it?" asked Eustace.

"Something that wanted very much to get hold of me. I felt what seemed like a thumb and forefinger. Give me some brandy."

"How are we to get it out of there?"

"What about a landing-net?"

"No good. It would be too smart for us. I tell you, Saunders, it can cover the ground far faster than I can walk. But I think I see how we can manage it. The two books at the ends of the shelf are big ones, that go right back against the wall. The others are very thin. I'll take out one at a time, and you slide the rest along, until we have it squashed between the end two."

It certainly seemed to be the best plan. One by one as they took out the books, the space behind grew smaller and smaller. There was something in it that was certainly very much alive. Once they caught sight of fingers feeling for a way of escape. At last they had it pressed between the two big books.

"There's muscle there, if there isn't warm flesh and blood," said Saunders, as he held them together. "It seems to be a hand right enough, too. I suppose this is a sort of infectious hallucination. I've read about such cases before."

"Infectious fiddlesticks!" said Eustace, his face white with anger; "bring the thing downstairs. We'll get it back into the box."

It was not altogether easy, but they were successful at last. "Drive in the screws," said Eustace; "we won't run any risks. Put the box in this old desk of mine. There's nothing in it that I want. Here's the key. Thank goodness there's nothing wrong with the lock."

"Quite a lively evening," said Saunders. "Now let's hear more about your uncle."

They sat up together until early morning. Saunders had no desire for sleep. Eustace was trying to explain and to forget; to conceal from himself a fear that he had never felt before—the fear of walking alone down the long corridor to his bedroom.

"Whatever it was," said Eustace to Saunders on the following morning, "I propose that we drop the subject. There's nothing to keep us here for the next ten days. We'll motor up to the Lakes and get some climbing."

"And see nobody all day, and sit bored to death with each other every night. Not for me, thanks. Why not run up to town? Run's the exact word in this case, isn't it? We're both in such a blessed funk. Pull yourself together, Eustace, and let's have another look at the hand."

"As you like," said Eustace; "there's the key."

They went into the library and opened the desk. The box was as they had left it on the previous night.

"What are you waiting for?" asked Eustace.

"I am waiting for you to volunteer to open the lid. However, since you seem to funk it, allow me. There doesn't seem to be the likelihood of any rumpus this morning at all events." He opened the lid and picked out the hand.

"Cold?" asked Eustace.

"Tepid. A bit below blood heat by the feel. Soft and supple too. If it's the embalming, it's a sort of embalming I've never seen before. Is it your uncle's hand?"

"Oh yes, it's his all right," said Eustace. "I should know those long thin fingers anywhere. Put it back in the box, Saunders. Never mind about the screws. I'll lock the desk, so that there'll be no chance of its getting out. We'll compromise by motoring up to town for a week. If we can get off soon after lunch, we ought to be at Grantham or Stamford by night."

"Right," said Saunders, "and tomorrow—oh, well, by tomorrow we shall have forgotten all about this beastly thing."

If, when the morrow came, they had not forgotten, it was certainly true that at the end of the week they were able to tell a very vivid ghost story at the little supper Eustace gave on Hallowe'en.

"You don't want us to believe that it's true, Mr. Borlsover? How perfectly awful!"

"I'll take my oath on it, and so would Saunders here; wouldn't you, old chap?"

"Any number of oaths," said Saunders. "It was a long thin hand, you know, and it gripped me just like that."

"Don't, Mr. Saunders! Don't! How perfectly horrid! Now tell us another one, do! Only a really creepy one, please."

"Here's a pretty mess!" said Eustace on the following day, as he threw a letter across the table to Saunders. "It's your affair, though. Mrs. Merrit, if I understand it, gives a month's notice."

"Oh, that's quite absurd on Mrs. Merrit's part," replied Saunders. "She doesn't know what she's talking about. Let's see what she says."

Dear Sir [he read], This is to let you know that I must give you a month's notice as from Tuesday, the 13th. For a long time I've felt the place too big for me; but when Jane Parfit and Emma Laidlaw go off with scarcely as much as an "If you please", after frightening the wits out of the other girls, so that they can't turn out a room by themselves or walk alone down the stairs for fear of treading on half-frozen toads or hearing it run along the passages at night, all I can say is that it's no place for me. So I must ask you, Mr. Borlsover, sir, to find a new housekeeper, that has no objection to large and lonely houses, which some people do say, not that I believe them for a minute, my poor mother always having been a Wesleyan, are haunted.

Yours faithfully,
ELIZABETH MERRIT

P.S.—I should be obliged if you would give my respects to Mr. Saunders. I hope that he won't run any risks with his cold.

"Saunders," said Eustace, "you've always had a wonderful way with you in dealing with servants. You mustn't let poor old Merrit go."

"Of course she shan't go," said Saunders. "She's probably only angling for a rise in salary. I'll write to her this morning."

"No. There's nothing like a personal interview. We've had enough of town. We'll go back tomorrow, and you must work your cold for all its worth. Don't forget that it's got on to the chest, and will require weeks of feeding up and nursing."

"All right; I think I can manage Mrs. Merrit."

But Mrs. Merrit was more obstinate than he had thought. She was very sorry to hear of Mr. Saunder's cold, and how he lay awake all night in London coughing; very sorry indeed. She'd change his room for him gladly and get the south room aired, and wouldn't he have a hot basin of bread and milk last thing at night? But she was afraid that she would have to leave at the end of the month.

"Try her with an increase of salary," was the advice of Eustace.

It was no use. Mrs. Merrit was obdurate, though she knew of a Mrs. Goddard, who had been housekeeper to Lord Gargrave, who might be glad to come at the salary mentioned.

"What's the matter with the servants, Morton?" asked Eustace that evening, when he brought the coffee into the library. "What's all this about Mrs. Merrit wanting to leave?"

"If you please, sir, I was going to mention it myself. I have a confession to make, sir. When I found your note, asking me to open that desk and take out the box with the rat, I broke the lock as you told me, and was glad to do it, because I could hear the animal in the box making a great noise, and I thought it wanted food. So I took out the box, sir, and got a cage, and was going to transfer it, when the animal got away."

"What in the world are you talking about? I never wrote any such note."

"Excuse me, sir; it was the note I picked up here on the floor on the day you and Mr. Saunders left. I have it in my pocket now."

It certainly seemed to be in Eustace's handwriting. It was written in pencil, and began somewhat abruptly.

"Get a hammer, Morton," he read, "or some other tool and break open the lock in the old desk in the library. Take out the box that is inside. You need not do anything else. The lid is already open. Eustace Borlsover."

"And you opened the desk?"

"Yes, sir; and, as I was getting the cage ready, the animal hopped out."

"What animal?"

"The animal inside the box, sir."

"What did it look like?"

"Well, sir, I couldn't tell you," said Morton, nervously. "My back was turned, and it was half-way down the room when I looked up."

"What was its colour?" asked Saunders. "Black?"

"Oh no, sir; a greyish white. It crept along in a very funny way, sir. I don't think it had a tail."

"What did you do then?"

"I tried to catch it; but it was no use. So I set the rat-traps and kept the library shut. Then that girl, Emma Laidlaw, left the door open when she was cleaning, and I think it must have escaped."

"And you think it is the animal that's been frightening the maids?"

"Well, no, sir, not quite. They said it was—you'll excuse me, sir—a hand that they saw. Emma trod on it once at the bottom of the stairs. She thought then it was a half-frozen toad, only white. And then Parfit was washing up the dishes in the scullery. She wasn't thinking about anything in particular. It was close on dusk. She took her hands out of the water and was drying them absent-minded like on the roller towel, when she found she was drying someone else's hand as well, only colder than hers."

"What nonsense!" exclaimed Saunders.

"Exactly, sir; that's what I told her; but we couldn't get her to stop."

"You don't believe all this?" said Eustace, turning suddenly towards the butler.

"Me, sir? Oh no, sir! I've not seen anything."

"Nor heard anything?"

"Well, sir, if you must know, the bells do ring at odd times, and there's nobody there when we go; and when we go round to draw the blinds of a night, as often as not somebody's been there before us. But, as I says to Mrs. Merrit, a young monkey might do wonderful things, and we all know that Mr. Borlsover has had some strange animals about the place."

"Very well, Morton, that will do."

"What do you make of it?" asked Saunders, when they were alone. "I mean of the letter he said you wrote."

"Oh, that's simple enough," said Eustace. "See the paper it's written on? I stopped using that paper years ago, but there were a few odd sheets and envelopes left in the old desk. We never fastened up the lid of the box before locking it in. The hand got out, found a pencil, wrote this note, and shoved it through the crack on to the floor, where Morton found it. That's plain as daylight."

"But the hand couldn't write!"

"Couldn't it? You've not seen it do the things I've seen." And he told Saunders more of what had happened at Eastbourne.

"Well," said Saunders, "in that case we have at least an explanation of the legacy. It was the hand which wrote, unknown to your uncle, that letter to your solicitor bequeathing itself to you. Your uncle had no more to do wits that request than I. In fact, it would seem that he had some idea of his automatic writing and feared it."

"Then if it's not my uncle, what is it?"

"I suppose some people might say that a disembodied spirit had got your uncle to educate and prepare a little body for it. Now it's got into that little body and is off on its own."

"Well, what are we to do?"

"We'll keep our eyes open," said Saunders, "and try to catch it. If we can't do that, we shall have to wait till the bally clockwork runs down. After all, if it's flesh and blood, it can't live for ever."

For two days nothing happened. Then Saunders saw it sliding down the banister in the hall. He was taken unawares and lost a full second before he started in pursuit, only to find that the thing had escaped him. Three days later Eustace, writing alone in the library at night, saw it sitting on an open book at the other end of the room. The fingers crept over the page, as if it were reading; but before he had time to get up from his seat, it had taken the alarm, and was pulling itself up the curtains. Eustace watched it grimly, as it hung on to the cornice with three fingers and flicked thumb and forefinger at him in an expression of scornful derision.

"I know what I'll do," he said. "If I only get it into the open, I'll set the dogs on to it."

He spoke to Saunders of the suggestion.

"It's a jolly good idea," he said; "only we won't wait till we find it out of doors. We'll get the dogs. There are the two terriers and the under-keeper's Irish mongrel, that's on to rats like a flash. Your spaniel has not got spirit enough for this sort of game."

They brought the dogs into the house, and the keeper's Irish mongrel chewed up the slippers, and the terriers tripped up Morton, as he waited at table; but all three were welcome. Even false security is better than no security at all.

For a fortnight nothing happened. Then the hand was caught, not by the dogs, but by Mrs. Merrit's grey parrot. The bird was in the habit of periodically removing the pins that kept its seed- and water-tins in place, and of escaping through the holes in the side of the cage. When once at liberty, Peter would show no inclination to return, and would often be about the house for days. Now, after six consecutive weeks of captivity, Peter had again discovered a new way of unloosing his bolts and was at large, exploring the tapestried forests of the curtains and singing songs in praise of liberty from cornice and picture-rail.

"It's no use your trying to catch him," said Eustace to Mrs. Merrit, as she came into the study one afternoon towards dusk with a step-ladder. "You'd much better leave Peter alone. Starve him into surrender, Mrs. Merrit; and don't leave bananas and seed about for him to peck at when he fancies he's hungry. You're far too soft-hearted."

"Well, sir, I see he's right out of reach now on that picture-rail; so, if you wouldn't mind closing the door, sir, when you leave the room, I'll bring his cage in tonight and put some meat inside it. He's that fond of meat, though it does make him pull out his feathers to suck the quills. They *do* say that if you cook—"

"Never mind, Mrs. Merrit," said Eustace, who was busy writing; "that will do; I'll keep an eye on the bird."

For a short time there was silence in the room.

"Scratch poor Peter," said the bird. "Scratch poor old Peter!"

"Be quiet, you beastly bird!"

"Poor old Peter! Scratch poor Peter; do!"

"I'm more likely to wring your neck, if I get hold of you." He

looked up at the picture-rail, and there was the hand, holding on to
a hook with three fingers, and slowly scratching the head of the
parrot with the fourth. Eustace ran to the bell and pressed it hard;
then across to the window, which he closed with a bang. Frightened
by the noise, the parrot shook its wings preparatory to flight, and,
as it did so, the fingers of the hand got hold of it by the throat.
There was a shrill scream from Peter, as he fluttered across the
room, wheeling round in circles that ever descended, borne down
under the weight that clung to him. The bird dropped at last quite
suddenly, and Eustace saw fingers and feathers rolled into an in-
extricable mass on the floor. The struggle abruptly ceased, as finger
and thumb squeezed the neck; the bird's eyes rolled up to show the
whites, and there was a faint, half-choked gurgle. But, before the
fingers had time to loose their hold, Eustace had them in his own.

"Send Mr. Saunders here at once," he said to the maid who came
in answer to the bell. "Tell him I want him immediately."

Then he went with the hand to the fire. There was a ragged
gash across the back, where the bird's beak had torn it, but no
blood oozed from the wound. He noted with disgust that the nails
had grown long and discoloured.

"I'll burn the beastly thing," he said. But he could not burn it.
He tried to throw it into the flames, but his own hands, as if impelled by some old primitive feeling, would not let him. And so
Saunders found him, pale and irresolute, with the hand still clasped
tightly in his fingers.

"I've got it at last," he said, in a tone of triumph.

"Good, let's have a look at it."

"Not when it's loose. Get me some nails and a hammer and a
board of some sort."

"Can you hold it all right?"

"Yes, the thing's quite limp; tired out with throttling poor old
Peter, I should say."

"And now," said Saunders, when he returned with the things,
"what are we going to do?"

"Drive a nail through it first, so that it can't get away. Then
we can take our time over examining it."

"Do it yourself," said Saunders. "I don't mind helping you with
guinea-pigs occasionally, when there's something to be learned,
partly because I don't fear a guinea-pig's revenge. This thing's
different."

"Oh, my aunt!" he giggled hysterically, "look at it now." For the hand was writhing in agonized contortions, squirming and wriggling upon the nail like a worm upon the hook.

"Well," said Saunders, "you've done it now. I'll leave you to examine it."

"Don't go, in heaven's name! Cover it up, man; cover it up! Shove a cloth over it! Here!" and he pulled off the antimacassar from the back of a chair and wrapped the board in it. "Now get the keys from my pocket and open the safe. Chuck the other things out. Oh, Lord, it's getting itself into frightful knots! Open it quick!" He threw the thing in and banged the door.

"We'll keep it there till it dies," he said. "May I burn in hell, if I ever open the door of that safe again."

Mrs. Merrit departed at the end of the month. Her successor, Mrs. Handyside, certainly was more successful in the management of the servants. Early in her rule she declared that she would stand no nonsense, and gossip soon withered and died.

"I shouldn't be surprised if Eustace married one of these days," said Saunders. "Well, I'm in no hurry for such an event. I know him far too well for the future Mrs. Borlsover to like me. It will be the same old story again; a long friendship slowly made—marriage—and a long friendship quickly forgotten."

But Eustace did not follow the advice of his uncle and marry. Old habits crept over and covered his new experience. He was, if anything, less morose, and showed a greater inclination to take his natural part in country society.

Then came the burglary. The men, it was said, broke into the house by way of the conservatory. It was really little more than an attempt, for they only succeeded in carrying away a few pieces of plate from the pantry. The safe in the study was certainly found open and empty, but, as Mr. Borlsover informed the police inspector, he had kept nothing of value in it during the last six months.

"Then you're lucky in getting off so easily, sir," the man replied. "By the way they have gone about their business I should say they were experienced cracksmen. They must have caught the alarm when they were just beginning their evening's work."

"Yes," said Eustace, "I suppose I am lucky."

"I've no doubt," said the inspector, "that we shall be able to trace the men. I've said that they must have been old hands at the game. The way they got in and opened the safe shows that. But there's one little thing that puzzles me. One of them was careless enough not to wear gloves, and I'm bothered if I know what he was trying to do. I've traced his finger-marks on the new varnish on the window-sashes in every one of the downstairs rooms. They are very distinctive ones too."

"Right hand or left or both?" asked Eustace.

"Oh, right every time. That's the funny thing. He must have been a foolhardy fellow, and I rather think it was him that wrote that." He took out a slip of paper from his pocket. "That's what he wrote, sir : 'I've got out, Eustace Borlsover, but I'll be back before long'. Some jailbird just escaped, I suppose. It will make it all the easier for us to trace him. Do you know the writing, sir?"

"No," said Eustace. "It's not the writing of any one I know."

"I'm not going to stay here any longer," said Eustace to Saunders at luncheon. "I've got on far better during the last six months than I expected, but I'm not going to run the risk of seeing that thing again. I shall go up to town this afternoon. Get Morton to put my things together, and join me with the car at Brighton on the day after tomorrow. And bring the proofs of those two papers with you. We'll run over them together."

"How long are you going to be away?"

"I can't say for certain, but be prepared to stay for some time. We've stuck to work pretty closely through summer, and I for one need a holiday. I'll engage the rooms at Brighton. You'll find it best to break the journey at Hitchin. I'll wire to you there at the 'Crown' to tell you the Brighton address."

The house he chose at Brighton was in a terrace. He had been there before. It was kept by his old college gyp, a man of discreet silence, who was admirably partnered by an excellent cook. The rooms were on the first floor. The two bedrooms were at the back, and opened out of each other. "Mr. Saunders can have the smaller one, though it is the only one with a fireplace," he said. "I'll stick to the larger of the two, since it's got a bathroom adjoining. I wonder what time he'll arrive with the car."

Saunders came about seven, cold and cross and dirty. "We'll light the fire in the dining-room," said Eustace, "and get Prince to unpack some of the things while we are at dinner. What were the roads like?"

"Rotten. Swimming with mud, and a beastly cold wind against us all day. And this is July. Dear Old England!"

"Yes," said Eustace, "I think we might do worse than leave Old England for a few months."

They turned in soon after twelve.

"You oughtn't to feel cold, Saunders," said Eustace, "when you can afford to sport a great fur-lined coat like this. You do yourself very well, all things considered. Look at those gloves, for instance. Who could possibly feel cold when wearing them?"

"They are far too clumsy, though, for driving. Try them on and see"; and he tossed them through the door on to Eustace's bed and went on with his unpacking. A minute later he heard a shrill cry of terror. "Oh, Lord," he heard, "it's in the glove! Quick, Saunders, quick!" Then came a smacking thud. Eustace had thrown it from him. "I've chucked it into the bathroom," he gasped; "it's hit the wall and fallen into the bath. Come now, if you want to help." Saunders, with a lighted candle in his hand, looked over the edge of the bath. There it was, old and maimed, dumb and blind, with a ragged hole in the middle, crawling, staggering, trying to creep up the slippery sides, only to fall back helpless.

"Stay there," said Saunders, "I'll empty a collar-box or something, and we'll jam it in. It can't get out while I'm away."

"Yes, it can," shouted Eustace. "It's getting out now; it's climbing up the plug-chain.—No, you brute, you filthy brute, you don't!—Come back, Saunders; it's getting away from me. I can't hold it; it's all slippery. Curse its claws! Shut the window, you idiot! It's got out!" There was the sound of something dropping on to the hard flagstones below, and Eustace fell back fainting.

For a fortnight he was ill.

"I don't know what to make of it," the doctor said to Saunders. "I can only suppose that Mr. Borlsover has suffered some great emotional shock. You had better let me send someone to help you nurse him. And by all means indulge that whim of his never to be left alone in the dark. I would keep a light burning all night, if I were you. But he *must* have more fresh air. It's perfectly absurd, this hatred of open windows."

Eustace would have no one with him but Saunders. "I don't want the other man," he said. "They'd smuggle it in somehow. I know they would."

"Don't worry about it, old chap. This sort of thing can't go on indefinitely. You know I saw it this time as well as you. It wasn't half so active. It won't go on living much longer, especially after that fall. I heard it hit the flags myself. As soon as you're a bit stronger, we'll leave this place, not bag and baggage, but with only the clothes on our back, so that it won't be able to hide anywhere. We'll escape it that way. We won't give any address, and we won't have any parcels sent after us. Cheer up, Eustace! You'll be well enough to leave in a day or two. The doctor says I can take you out in a chair tomorrow."

"What have I done?" asked Eustace. "Why does it come after me? I'm no worse than other men. I'm no worse than you, Saunders; you know I'm not. It was you who was at the bottom of that dirty business in San Diego, and that was fifteen years ago."

"It's not that, of course," said Saunders. "We are in the twentieth century, and even the parsons have dropped the idea of your old sins finding you out. Before you caught the hand in the library, it was filled with pure malevolence—to you and all mankind. After you spiked it through with that nail, it naturally forgot about other people and concentrated its attention on you. It was shut up in that safe, you know, for nearly six months. That gives plenty of time for thinking of revenge."

Eustace Borlsover would not leave his room, but he thought there might be something in Saunders's suggestion of a sudden departure from Brighton. He began rapidly to regain his strength.

"We'll go on the 1st of September," he said.

The evening of August 31 was oppressively warm. Though at midday the windows had been wide open, they had been shut an hour or so before dusk. Mrs. Prince had long since ceased to wonder at the strange habits of the gentlemen on the first floor. Soon after their arrival she had been told to take down the heavy window curtains in the two bedrooms, and day by day the rooms had seemed to grow more bare. Nothing was left lying about.

"Mr. Borlsover doesn't like to have any place where dirt can collect," Saunders had said as an excuse. "He likes to see into all the corners of the room."

"Couldn't I open the window just a little?" he said to Eustace that evening. "We're simply roasting in here, you know."

"No, leave well alone. We're not a couple of boarding-school misses fresh from a course of hygiene lectures. Get the chess-board out."

They sat down and played. At ten o'clock Mrs. Prince came to the door with a note. "I am sorry I didn't bring it before," she said, "but it was left in the letter-box."

"Open it, Saunders, and see if it wants answering."

It was very brief. There was neither address nor signature.

"Will eleven o'clock tonight be suitable for our last appointment?"

"Who is it from?" asked Borlsover.

"It was meant for me," said Saunders. "There's no answer, Mrs. Prince," and he put the paper into his pocket.

"A dunning letter from a tailor; I suppose he must have got wind of our leaving."

It was a clever lie, and Eustace asked no more questions. They went on with their game.

On the landing outside Saunders could hear the grandfather's clock whispering the seconds, blurting out the quarter-hours.

"Check," said Eustace. The clock struck eleven. At the same time there was a gentle knocking on the door; it seemed to come from the bottom panel.

"Who's there?" asked Eustace.

There was no answer.

"Mrs. Prince, is that you?"

"She is up above," said Saunders; "I can hear her walking about the room."

"Then lock the door; bolt it too. Your move, Saunders."

While Saunders sat with his eyes on the chess-board, Eustace walked over to the window and examined the fastenings. He did the same in Saunders's room, and the bathroom. There were no doors between the three rooms, or he would have shut and locked them too.

"Now, Saunders," he said, "don't stay all night over your move. I've had time to smoke one cigarette already. It's bad to keep an invalid waiting. There's only one possible thing for you to do. What was that?"

"The ivy blowing against the window. There, it's your move now, Eustace."

"It wasn't the ivy, you idiot! It was someone tapping at the window"; and he pulled up the blind. On the outer side of the window, clinging to the sash, was the hand.

"What is it that it's holding?"

"It's a pocket-knife. It's going to try to open the window by pushing back the fastener with the blade."

"Well, let it try," said Eustace. "Those fasteners screw down; they can't be opened that way. Anyhow, we'll close the shutters. It's your move, Saunders. I've played."

But Saunders found it impossible to fix his attention on the game. He could not understand Eustace, who seemed all at once to have lost his fear. "What do you say to some wine?" he asked. "You seem to be taking things coolly, but I don't mind confessing that I'm in a blessed funk."

"You've no need to be. There's nothing supernatural about that hand, Saunders. I mean, it seems to be governed by the laws of time and space. It's not the sort of thing that vanishes into thin air or slides through oaken doors. And since that's so, I defy it to get in here. We'll leave the place in the morning. I for one have bottomed the depths of fear. Fill your glass, man! The windows are all shuttered; the door is locked and bolted. Pledge me my Uncle Adrian! Drink, man! What are you waiting for?"

Saunders was standing with his glass half raised. "It can get in," he said hoarsely; "it can get in! We've forgotten. There's the fire-place in my bedroom. It will come down the chimney."

"Quick!" said Eustace, as he rushed into the other room; "we haven't a minute to lose. What can we do? Light the fire, Saunders. Give me a match, quick!"

"They must be all in the other room. I'll get them."

"Hurry, man, for goodness' sake! Look in the bookcase! Look in the bathroom! Here, come and stand here; I'll look."

"Be quick!" shouted Saunders. "I can hear something!"

"Then plug a sheet from your bed up the chimney. No, here's a match!" He had found one at last, that had slipped into a crack in the floor.

"Is the fire laid? Good, but it may not burn. I know—the oil from that old reading-lamp and this cotton wool. Now the match, quick! Pull the sheet away, you fool! We don't want it now."

There was a great roar from the grate, as the flames shot up. Saunders had been a fraction of a second too late with the sheet. The oil had fallen on to it. It, too, was burning.

"The whole place will be on fire!" cried Eustace, as he tried to beat out the flames with a blanket. "It's no good! I can't manage it. You must open the door, Saunders, and get help."

Saunders ran to the door and fumbled with the bolts. The key was stiff in the lock. "Hurry," shouted Eustace, "or the heat will be too much for me." The key turned in the lock at last. For half a second Saunders stopped to look back. Afterwards he could never be quite sure as to what he had seen, but at the time he thought that something black and charred was creeping slowly, very slowly, from the mass of flames towards Eustace Borlsover. For a moment he thought of returning to his friend; but the noise and the smell of the burning sent him running down the passage, crying : "Fire ! Fire !" He rushed to the telephone to summon help, and then back to the bathroom—he should have thought of that before—for water. As he burst into the bedroom there came a scream of terror which ended suddenly, and then the sound of a heavy fall.

This is the story which I heard on successive Saturday evenings from the senior mathematical master at a second-rate suburban school. For Saunders has had to earn a living in a way which other men might reckon less congenial than his old manner of life. I had mentioned by chance the name of Adrian Borlsover, and wondered at the time why he changed the conversation with such unusual abruptness. A week later Saunders began to tell me something of his own history; sordid enough, though shielded with a reserve I could well understand, for it had to cover not only his failings, but those of a dead friend. Of the final tragedy he was at first especially loath to speak; and it was only gradually that I was able to piece together the narrative of the preceding pages. Saunders was reluctant to draw any conclusions. At one time he thought that the fingered beast had been animated by the spirit of Sigismund Borlsover, a sinister eighteenth-century ancestor, who, according to legend, built and worshipped in the ugly pagan temple that overlooked the lake. At another time Saunders believed the spirit to belong to a man whom Eustace had once employed as a laboratory assistant, "a black-haired, spiteful little brute", he said, "who died cursing his doctor, because the fellow couldn't help him to live to settle some paltry score with Borlsover".

From the point of view of direct contemporary evidence, Saunders's story is practically uncorroborated. All the letters mentioned in the narrative were destroyed, with the exception of the last note which Eustace received, or rather which he would have received, had not Saunders intercepted it. That I have seen myself. The handwriting was thin and shaky, the handwriting of an old

man. I remember the Greek "e" was used in "appointment". A
little thing that amused me at the time was that Saunders seemed
to keep the note pressed between the pages of his Bible.

I had seen Adrian Borlsover once. Saunders I learnt to know well.
It was by chance, however, and not by design, that I met a third
person of the story, Morton, the butler. Saunders and I were walking in the Zoological Gardens one Sunday afternoon, when he
called my attention to an old man who was standing before the
door of the Reptile House.

"Why, Morton," he said, clapping him on the back, "how is the
world treating you?"

"Poorly, Mr. Saunders," said the old fellow, though his face
lighted up at the greeting. "The winters drag terribly nowadays.
There don't seem no summers or springs."

"You haven't found what you were looking for, I suppose?"

"No, sir, not yet; but I shall some day. I always told them that
Mr. Borlsover kept some queer animals."

"And what is he looking for?" I asked, when we had parted from
him.

"A beast with five fingers," said Saunders. "This afternoon, since
he has been in the Reptile House, I suppose it will be a reptile
with a hand. Next week it will be a monkey with practically no
body. The poor old chap is a born materialist."

THE BEAST FROM 20,000 FATHOMS

RAY BRADBURY

(Warner Brothers: 1953)

It was Science Fiction stories which aided the re-emergence of horror films after the post-war decline. (Too often bracketed together, Science Fiction and Horror certainly do have some similarities, but while one takes our imagination into the future and away to the stars, the other is more concerned with exploiting the dark fears and superstitions in our Earth-bound minds.) With the amazing advances taking place in science and space aeronautics in the early fifties, it was hardly surprising that Science Fiction should suddenly have shot into popularity and produced a galaxy of talented writers—in months the names of Arthur C. Clarke, Robert Heinlein, Ray Bradbury and others were on the lips of all readers of modern fiction. Their speculations on the future—which had so often been quickly derided as pure fantasy—were now being proven in real life.

In true Hollywood fashion, the film producers were not slow in spotting this development and several notable films resulted. Of these, the one to play the most significant part in "reviving" our slumbering monsters was probably The Beast From 20,000 Fathoms, *based on a superb little tale* The Foghorn *by Ray Bradbury. Taking the basic idea of the story—though not its method—the picture explored the theme that the exploding of a nuclear device could awaken all kinds of giant monsters left in suspended animation from aeons past. The studios were now in a position, with their new camera techniques and special effects departments, to bring monsters of all sizes to the screen, and while the "Beast" may today have lost some of his impact, his life-like monstrosity (the work of the inventive Ray Harryhausen) was awe-inspiring at that time. As was to happen in so many films of this kind, the human actors played second fiddle to the monster and few big names are to be found in the credit lines. For Ray Bradbury, the success of the film opened up new areas of development—indeed his* Fahrenheit 451, *about a future society dedicated to destroying literature, and* The Illustrated Man *have both since been filmed. It also gave incentive to other horror story writers struggling away in the badly paid pages of a handful of macabre magazines—and the hope of better things to come for their kind of material. How much better, few could have guessed.*

*

OUT there in the cold water, far from land, we waited every night for the coming of the fog, and it came, and we oiled the brass machinery and lit the fog light up in the stone tower. Feeling like two birds in the grey sky, McDunn and I sent the light touching out, red, then white, then red again, to eye the lonely ships. And if they did not see our light, then there was always our Voice, the great deep cry of our Fog Horn shuddering through the rags of mist to startle the gulls away like decks of scattered cards and make the waves turn high and foam.

"It's a lonely life, but you're used to it now, aren't you?" asked McDunn.

"Yes," I said. "You're a good talker, thank the Lord."

"Well, it's your turn on land tomorrow," he said, smiling, "to dance the ladies and drink gin."

"What do you think McDunn, when I leave you out here alone?"

"On the mysteries of the sea." McDunn lit his pipe. It was a quarter past seven of a cold November evening, the heat on, the light switching its tail in two hundred directions, the Fog Horn bumbling in the high throat of the tower. There wasn't a town for a hundred miles down the coast, just a road, which came lonely through dead country to the sea, with few cars on it, a stretch of two miles of cold water out to our rock, and rare few ships.

"The mysteries of the sea," said McDunn thoughtfully. "You know, the ocean's the biggest damned snowflake ever? It rolls and swells a thousand shapes and colours, no two alike. Strange. One night, years ago, I was here alone, when all of the fish of the sea surfaced out there. Something made them swim in and lie in the bay, sort of trembling and staring up at the tower light going red, white, red, white across them so I could see their funny eyes. I turned cold. They were like a big peacock's tail, moving out there until midnight. Then, without so much as a sound, they slipped away, the million of them was gone. I kind of think maybe, in some sort of way, they came all those miles to worship. Strange. But think how the tower must look to them, standing seventy feet above the water, the God-light flashing out from it, and the tower declaring itself with a monster voice. They never came back, those fish, but don't you think for a while they thought they were in the Presence?"

I shivered. I looked out at the long grey lawn of the sea stretching away into nothing and nowhere.

"Oh, the sea's full." McDunn puffed his pipe nervously, blinking. He had been nervous all day and hadn't said why. "For all our engines and so-called submarines, it'll be ten thousand centuries before we set foot on the real bottom of the sunken lands, in the fairy kingdoms there, and know *real* terror. Think of it, it's still the year 300,000 Before Christ down under there. While we've paraded around with trumpets, lopping off each other's countries and heads, they have been living beneath the sea twelve miles deep and cold in a time as old as the beard of a comet."

"Yes, it's an old world."

"Come on. I got something special I been saving up to tell you."

We ascended the eighty steps, talking and taking our time. At the top, McDunn switched off the room lights so there'd be no reflection in the plate glass. The great eye of the light was humming, turning easily in its oiled socket. The Fog Horn was blowing steadily, once every fifteen seconds.

"Sounds like an animal, don't it?" McDunn nodded to himself. "A big lonely animal crying in the night. Sitting here on the edge of ten billion years calling out to the Deeps, I'm here, I'm here, I'm here. And the Deeps do answer, yes, they do. You been here now for three months, Johnny, so I better prepare you. About this time of year," he said, studying the murk and fog, "something comes to visit the lighthouse."

"The swarms of fish like you said?"

"No, this is something else. I've put off telling you because you might think I'm daft. But tonight's the latest I can put it off, for if my calendar's marked right from last year, tonight's the night it comes. I won't go into detail, you'll have to see it yourself. Just sit down there. If you want, tomorrow you can pack your duffel and take the motorboat into land and get your car parked there at the dinghy pier on the cape and drive on back to some little inland town and keep your lights burning nights. I won't question or blame you. It's happened three years now, and this is the only time anyone's been here with me to verify it. You wait and watch."

Half an hour passed with only a few whispers between us. When we grew tired waiting, McDunn began describing some of his ideas to me. He had some theories about the Fog Horn itself.

"One day many years ago a man walked along and stood in the sound of the ocean on a cold sunless shore and said, 'We need a voice to call across the water, to warn ships; I'll make one. I'll make a voice like all of time and all of the fog that ever was; I'll make a voice that is like an empty bed beside you all night long, and like an empty house when you open the door, and like trees in autumn with no leaves. A sound like the birds flying south, crying, and a sound like November wind and the sea on the hard, cold shore. I'll make a sound that's so alone that no one can miss it, that whoever hears it will weep in their souls, and hearths will seem warmer, and being inside will seem better to all who hear it in the distant towns. I'll make me a sound and an apparatus and they'll call it a Fog Horn and whoever hears it will know the sadness of eternity and the briefness of life.' "

The Fog Horn blew.

"I made up that story," said McDunn quietly, "to try to explain why this thing keeps coming back to the lighthouse every year. The Fog Horn calls, I think, it comes. . . ."

"But—" I said.

"Sssst!" said McDunn. "There!" He nodded out to the Deeps. Something was swimming towards the lighthouse tower.

It was a cold night, as I have said; the high tower was cold, the light coming and going, and the Fog Horn calling and calling through the ravelling mist. You couldn't see far and you couldn't see plain, but there was the deep sea moving on its way about the night earth, flat and quiet, the colour of grey mud, and here were the two of us alone in the high tower, and there, far out at first, was a ripple, followed by a wave, a rising, a bubble, a bit of froth. And then, from the surface of the cold sea came a head, a large head, dark-coloured, with immense eyes, and then a neck. And then—not a body—but more neck and more! The head rose a full forty feet above the water on a slender and beautiful dark neck. Only then did the body, like a little island of black coral and shells and crayfish, drip up from the subterranean. There was a flicker of tail. In all, from head to tip of tail, I estimated the monster at ninety or a hundred feet.

I don't know what I said. I said something.

"Steady, boy, steady," whispered McDunn.

"It's impossible!" I said.

"No, Johnny, *we're* impossible. *It's* like it always was ten million years ago. *It* hasn't changed. It's *us* and the land that've changed, become impossible. *Us!*"

It swam slowly and with a great dark majesty out in the icy waters, far away. The fog came and went about it, momentarily erasing its shape. One of the monster eyes caught and held and flashed back our immense light, red, white, red, white, like a disc held high and sending a message in primaeval code. It was as silent as the fog through which it swam.

"It's a dinosaur of some sort!" I crouched down, holding to the stair rail.

"Yes, one of the tribe."

"But they died out!"

"No, only hid away in the Deeps. Deep, deep down in the deepest Deeps. Isn't *that* a word now, Johnny, a real word, it says so much : the Deeps. There's all the coldness and darkness and deepness in the world in a word like that."

"What'll we do?"

"Do? We got our job, we can't leave. Besides, we're safer here than in any boat trying to get to land. That thing's as big as a destroyer and almost as swift."

"But here, why does it come *here*?"

The next moment I had my answer.

The Fog Horn blew.

And the monster answered.

A cry came across a million years of water and mist. A cry so anguished and alone that it shuddered in my head and my body. The monster cried out at the tower. The Fog Horn blew. The monster roared again. The Fog Horn blew. The monster opened its great toothed mouth and the sound that came from it was the sound of the Fog Horn itself. Lonely and vast and far away. The sound of isolation, a viewless sea, a cold night, apartness. That was the sound.

"Now," whispered McDunn, "do you know why it comes here?"

I nodded.

"All year long, Johnny, that poor monster there lying far out, a thousand miles at sea, and twenty miles deep maybe, biding its time, perhaps it's a million years old, this one creature. Think of it, waiting a million years; could *you* wait that long? Maybe it's the last of its kind. I sort of think that's true. Anyway, here come men on land and build this lighthouse, five years ago. And set up their

Fog Horn and sound it and sound it out towards the place where you bury yourself in sleep and sea memories of a world where there were thousands like yourself, but now you're alone, all alone in a world not made for you, a world where you have to hide.

"But the sound of the Fog Horn comes and goes, comes and goes, and you stir from the muddy bottom of the Deeps, and your eyes open like the lenses of two-foot cameras and you move, slow, slow, for you have the ocean sea on your shoulders, heavy. But that Fog Horn comes through a thousand miles of water, faint and familiar, and the furnace in your belly stokes up, and you begin to rise, slow, slow. You feed yourself on great slakes of cod and minnow, on rivers of jellyfish, and you rise slow through the autumn months, through September when the fogs started, through October with more fog and the horn still calling you on, and then, late in November, after pressurizing yourself day by day, a few feet higher every hour, you are near the surface and still alive. You've got to go slow; if you surfaced all at once you'd explode. So it takes you all of three months to surface, and then a number of days to swim through the cold waters to the lighthouse. And there you are, out there, in the night, Johnny, the biggest damn monster in creation. And here's the lighthouse calling to you, with a long neck like your neck sticking way up out of the water, and a body like your body, and, most important of all, a voice like your voice. Do you understand now, Johnny, do you understand?"

The Fog Horn blew.

The monster answered.

I saw it all, I knew it all—the million years of waiting alone, for someone to come back who never came back. The million years of isloation at the bottom of the sea, the insanity of time there, while the skies cleared of reptile-birds, the swamps dried on the continental lands, the sloths and sabre-tooths had their day and sank in tar pits, and men ran like white ants upon the hills.

The Fog Horn blew.

"Last year," said McDunn, "that creature swam round and round, round and round, all night. Not coming too near, puzzled, I'd say. Afraid, maybe. And a bit angry after coming all this way. But the next day, unexpectedly, the fog lifted, the sun came out fresh, the sky was as blue as a painting. And the monster swam off away from the heat and the silence and didn't come back. I suppose it's been brooding on it for a year now, thinking it over from every which way."

The monster was only a hundred yards off now, it and the Fog Horn crying at each other. As the lights hit them, the monster's eyes were fire and ice, fire and ice.

"That's life for you," said McDunn. "Someone always waiting for someone who never comes home. Always someone loving some thing more than that things loves them. And after a while you want to destroy whatever that thing is, so it can't hurt you no more."

The monster was rushing at the lighthouse.

The Fog Horn blew.

"Let's see what happens," said McDunn.

He switched the Fog Horn off.

The ensuing minute of silence was so intense that we could hear our hearts pounding in the glassed area of the tower, could hear the slow greased turn of the light.

The monster stopped and froze. Its great lantern eyes blinked. Its mouth gaped. It gave a sort of rumble, like a volcano. It twitched its head this way and that, as if to seek the sounds now dwindled off into the fog. It peered at the lighthouse. It rumbled again. Then its eyes caught fire. It reared up, threshed the water, and rushed at the tower, its eyes filled with angry torment.

"McDunn!" I cried. 'Switch on the horn!"

McDunn fumbled with the switch. But even as he flicked it on, the monster was rearing up. I had a glimpse of its gigantic paws, fishskin glittering in webs between the finger-like projections, claw-ing at the tower. The huge eye on the right side of its anguished head glittered before me like a cauldron into which I might drop, screaming. The tower shook. The Fog Horn cried; the monster cried. It seized the tower and gnashed at the glass, which shattered in upon us.

McDunn seized my arm. "Downstairs!"

The tower rocked, trembled, and started to give. The Fog Horn and the monster roared. We stumbled and half fell down the stairs. "Quick!"

We reached the bottom as the tower buckled down towards us. We ducked under the stairs into the small stone cellar. There were a thousand concussions as the rocks rained down; the Fog Horn stopped abruptly. The monster crashed upon the tower. The tower fell. We knelt together, McDunn and I, holding tight, while our world exploded.

Then it was over, and there was nothing but darkness and the wash of the sea on the raw stones.

That and the other sound.

"Listen," said McDunn quietly. "Listen."

We waited a moment. And then I began to hear it. First a great vacuumed sucking of air, and then the lament, the bewilderment, the loneliness of the great monster, folded over and upon us, above us, so that the sickening reek of its body filled the air, a stone's thickness away from our cellar. The monster gasped and cried. The tower was gone. The light was gone. The thing that had called to it across a million years was gone. And the monster was opening its mouth and sending out great sounds. The sounds of a Fog Horn, again and again. And ships far at sea, not finding the light, not seeing anything, but passing and hearing late that night, must've thought : There it is, the lonely sound, the Lonesome Bay horn. All's well. We've rounded the cape.

And so it went for the rest of that night.

The sun was hot and yellow the next afternoon when the rescuers came out to dig us from our stoned-under cellar.

"It fell apart, is all," said Mr. McDunn gravely. "We had a few bad knocks from the waves and it just crumbled." He pinched my arm.

There was nothing to see. The ocean was calm, the sky blue. The only thing was a great algaic stink from the green matter that covered the fallen tower stones and the shore rocks. Flies buzzed about. The ocean washed empty on the shore.

The next year they built a new lighthouse, but by that time I had a job in the little town and a wife and a good small warm house that glowed yellow on autumn nights, the doors locked, the chimney puffing smoke. As for McDunn, he was master of the new lighthouse, built to his own specifications, out of steel-reinforced concrete. "Just in case," he said.

The new lighthouse was ready in November. I drove down alone one evening late and parked my car and looked across the grey waters and listened to the new horn sounding, once, twice, three, four times a minute far out there, by itself.

The monster?

It never came back.

"It's gone away," said McDunn. "It's gone back to the Deeps. It's learned you can't love anything too much in this world. It's gone into the deepest Deeps to wait another million years. Ah, the poor thing ! Waiting out there, and waiting out there, while man comes and goes on this pitiful little planet. Waiting and waiting."

I sat in my car, listening. I couldn't see the lighthouse or the light standing out in Lonesome Bay. I could only hear the Horn, the Horn, the Horn. It sounded like the monster calling.

I sat there wishing there was something I could say.

THE FLY

GEORGE LANGELAAN

(20th Century-Fox: 1958)

The Fly *holds an almost unique position in the horror film genre. "It stands out from the ordinary horror movies," wrote Carlos Clarens, the biographer of the horror film, "in nearly creating an authentic science fiction monster ... it also surprised everyone including its makers by netting more than three million dollars during the first few years of its release— an unprecedented success". Contesting this opinion is Ivan Butler (*The Horror Film*), who called the picture "probably the most ludicrous, and certainly one of the most revolting, science-horror films ever perpetrated". Whichever viewpoint one subscribes to, the film undoubtedly brought the horror picture firmly back into every producer's mind as potential top box office material.*

The story concerns a scientist, experimenting with the transference of atoms, who inadvertently mixes his own up with that of a fly—causing him to be reassembled with the body of a man and the head of a fly. Based on a spine-chilling story by George Langelaan, the film is beyond question best served by Vincent Price who, as another scientist investigating the tragedy, brings to the screen for the first time the kind of sinister eloquence which has since made him the master of the genre. Price had, of course, appeared on the screen a great many times before— indeed he starred in the first 3-D terror picture, The House of Wax *in 1953—but* The Fly *is considered by most authorities to be the real moment of his emergence. As might be expected with such a commercial success, the picture bred two sequels,* The Return of the Fly *in 1959 and* The Curse of the Fly *in 1965, but neither achieved the notoriety, financial rewards or diametrically opposed critiques of the original.*

*

TELEPHONES and telephone bells have always made me uneasy. Years ago, when they were mostly wall fixtures, I disliked them, but nowadays, when they are planted in every nook and corner, they are a downright intrusion. We have a saying in France that a coalman is master in his own house; with the telephone that is no longer true, and I suspect that even the Englishman is no longer king in his own castle.

At the office, the sudden ringing of the telephone annoys me. It means that, no matter what I am doing, in spite of the switchboard operator in spite of my secretary, in spite of doors and walls, some unknown person is coming into the room and on to my desk to talk right into my very ear, confidentially—whether I like it or not. At home, the feeling is still more disagreeable, but the worst is when the telephone rings in the dead of night. If anyone could see me turn on the light and get up blinking to answer it, I suppose I would look like any other sleepy man annoyed at being disturbed. The truth in such a case, however, is that I am struggling against panic, fighting down a feeling that a stranger has broken into the house and is in my bedroom. By the time I manage to grab the receiver and say : *"Ici Monsieur Delambre. Je vous écoute,"* I am outwardly calm, but I only get back to a more normal state when I recognize the voice at the other end and when I know what is wanted of me.

This effort at dominating a purely animal reaction and fear had become so effective that when my sister-in-law called me at two in the morning, asking me to come over, but first to warn the police that she had just killed my brother, I quietly asked her how and why she had killed André.

"But, François ! ... I can't explain all that over the telephone. Please call the police and come quickly."

"Maybe I had better see you first, Hélène."

"No, you'd better call the police first; otherwise they will start asking you all sorts of awkward questions. They'll have enough trouble as it is to believe that I did it alone.... And, by the way, I suppose you ought to tell them that André ... André's body, is down at the factory. They may want to go there first."

"Did you say that André is at the factory?"

"Yes ... under the steam hammer."

"Under the what?"

"The steam hammer ! But don't ask so many questions. Please come quickly François ! Please understand that I'm afraid ... that my nerves won't stand it much longer !"

Have you ever tried to explain to a sleepy police officer that your sister-in-law has just phoned to say that she has killed your brother with a steam hammer? I tried to repeat my explanation, but he would not let me.

"*Oui, Monsieur, oui,* I hear . . . but who are you? What is your name? Where do you live? I said, where do you live!"

It was then that Commissaire Charas took over the line and the whole business. He at least seemed to understand everything. Would I wait for him? Yes, he would pick me up and take me over to my brother's house. When? In five or ten minutes.

I had just managed to pull on my trousers, wriggle into a sweater and grab a hat and coat, when a black Citroen, headlights blazing, pulled up at the door.

"I assume you have a night watchman at your factory, Monsieur Delambre. Has he called you?" asked Commissaire Charas, letting in the clutch as I sat down beside him and slammed the door of the car.

"No, he hasn't. Though of course my brother could have entered the factory through his laboratory where he often works late at night . . . all night sometimes."

"Is Professor Delambre's work connnected with your business?"

"No, my brother is, or was, doing research work for the Ministère de l'Air. As he wanted to be away from Paris and yet within reach of where skilled workmen could fix up or make gadgets big and small for his experiments, I offered him one of the old workshops of the factory and he came to live in the first house built by our grandfather on the top of the hill at the back of the factory."

"Yes, I see. Did he talk about his work? What sort of research work?"

"He rarely talked about it, you know; I suppose the Air Ministry could tell you. I only know that he was about to carry out a number of experiments he had been preparing for some months, something to do with the disintegration of matter, he told me."

Barely slowing down, the commissaire swung the car off the road, slid it through the open factory gate and pulled up sharp by a policeman apparently expecting him.

I did not need to hear the policeman's confirmation. I knew now that my brother was dead; it seemed that I had been told years ago. Shaking like a leaf, I scrambled out after the commissaire.

Another policeman stepped out of a doorway and led us towards one of the shops where all the lights had been turned on. More policemen were standing by the hammer, watching two men setting up a camera. It was tilted downwards, and I made an effort to look.

It was far less horrid than I had expected. Though I had never seen my brother drunk, he looked just as if he were sleeping off a terrific binge, flat on his stomach across the narrow line on which the white-hot slabs of metal were rolled up to the hammer. I saw at a glance that his head and arm could only be a flattened mess, but that seemed quite impossible; it looked as if he had somehow pushed his head and arm right into the metallic mass of the hammer.

Having talked to his colleagues, the commissaire turned towards me :

"How can we raise the hammer, Monsieur Delambre?"

"I'll raise it for you."

"Would you like us to get one of your men over?"

"No, I'll be all right. Look, here is the switchboard. It was originally a steam hammer, but everything is worked electrically here now. Look, Commissaire, the hammer has been set at 50 tons and its impact at zero."

"At zero . . .?"

"Yes, level with the ground if you prefer. It is also set for single strokes, which means that it has to be raised after each blow. I don't know what Hélène, my sister-in-law, will have to say about all this, but one thing I am sure of : she certainly did not know how to set and operate the hammer."

"Perhaps it was set that way last night when work stopped?"

"Certainly not. The drop is never set at zero, Monsieur le Commissaire."

"I see. Can it be raised gently?"

"No. The speed of the upstroke cannot be regulated. But in any case it is not very fast when the hammer is set for single strokes."

"Right. Will you show me what to do? It won't be very nice to watch, you know."

"No, no, Monsieur le Commissaire. I'll be all right."

"All set?" asked the commissaire of the others. "All right then, Monsieur Delambre. Whenever you like."

Watching my brother's back, I slowly but firmly pushed the upstroke button.

The unusual silence of the factory was broken by the sigh of compressed air rushing into the cylinders, a sigh that always makes me think of a giant taking a deep breath before solemnly socking another giant, and the steel mass of the hammer shuddered and then rose swiftly. I also heard the sucking sound as it left the metal base and thought I was going to panic when I saw André's body heave forward as a sickly gush of blood poured all over the ghastly mess bared by the hammer.

"No danger of it coming down again, Monsieur Delambre?"

"No, none whatever," I mumbled as I threw the safety switch and, turning around, I was violently sick in front of a young green-faced policeman.

For weeks after, Commissaire Charas worked on the case, listening, questioning, running all over the place, making out reports, telegraphing and telephoning right and left. Later, we became quite friendly and he owned up that he had for a long time considered me as suspect number one, but had finally given up that idea because, not only was there no clue of any sort, there was not even a motive.

Hélène, my sister-in-law, was so calm throughout the whole business that the doctors finally confirmed what I had long considered the only possible solution : that she was mad. That being the case, there was of course no trail.

My brother's wife never tried to defend herself in any way and even got quite annoyed when she realized that people thought her mad, and this of course was considered proof that she was indeed mad. She owned up to the murder of her husband and proved easily that she knew how to handle the hammer; but she would never say why, exactly how, or under what circumstances she had killed my brother. The great mystery was how and why had my brother so obligingly stuck his head under the hammer, the only possible explanation for his part in the drama.

The night watchman had heard the hammer all right; he had even heard it twice, he claimed. This was very strange, and the stroke counter, which was always set back to nought after a job, seemed to prove him right, since it marked the figure two. Also, the foreman in charge of the hammer confirmed that after cleaning up the day before the murder, he had as usual turned the stroke counter back to nought. In spite of this, Hélène maintained that she had only used the hammer once, and this seemed just another proof of her insanity.

Commissaire Charas who had been put in charge of the case at first wondered if the victim were really my brother. But of that there was no possible doubt, if only because of the great scar running from his knee to his thigh, the result of a shell that had landed within a few feet of him during the retreat in 1940; and there were also the fingerprints of his left hand which corresponded to those found all over his laboratory and his personal belongings up at the house.

A guard had been put on his laboratory and the next day half a dozen officials came down from the Air Ministry. They went through all his papers and took away some of his instruments, but before leaving, they told the commissaire that the most interesting documents and instruments had been destroyed.

The Lyons police laboratory, one of the most famous in the world, reported that André's head had been wrapped up in a piece of velvet when it was crushed by the hammer, and one day Commissaire Charas showed me a tattered drapery which I immediately recognized as the brown-velvet cloth I had seen on a table in my brother's laboratory, the one on which his meals were served when he could not leave his work.

After only a very few days in prison, Hélène had been transferred to a nearby asylum, one of the three in France where insane criminals are taken care of. My nephew Henri, a boy of six, the very image of his father, was entrusted to me, and eventually all legal arrangements were made for me to become his guardian and tutor.

Hélène, one of the quietest patients of the asylum, was allowed visitors and I went to see her on Sundays. Once or twice the commissaire had accompanied me and, later, I learned that he had also visited Hélène alone. But we were never able to obtain any information from my sister-in-law, who seemed to have become utterly indifferent. She rarely answered my questions and hardly ever those of the commissaire. She spent a lot of her time sewing, but her favourite pastime seemed to be catching flies which she invariably released unharmed after having examined them carefully.

Hélène only had one fit of raving—more like a nervous breakdown than a fit said the doctor who had administered morphia to quieten her—the day she saw a nurse swatting flies.

The day after Hélène's one and only fit, Commissaire Charas came to see me.

"I have a strange feeling that there lies the key to the whole business, Monsiuer Delambre," he said.

I did not ask him how it was that he already knew all about Hélène's fit.

"I do not follow you, Commissaire. Poor Madame Delambre

could have shown an exceptional interest for anything else, really. Don't you think that flies just happen to be the border-subject of her tendency to raving?"

"Do you believe she is really mad?" he asked.

"My dear Commissaire, I don't see how there can be any doubt. Do you doubt it?"

"I don't know. In spite of all the doctors say, I have the impression that Madame Delambre has a very clear brain ... even when catching flies."

"Supposing you were right, how would you explain her attitude with regard to her little boy? She never seems to consider him as her own child."

"You know, Monsieur Delambre, I have thought about that also. She may be trying to protect him. Perhaps she fears the boy or, for all we know, hates him?"

"I'm afraid I don't understand, my dear Commissaire."

"Have you noticed, for instance, that she never catches flies when the boy is there?"

"No. But come to think of it, you are quite right. Yes, that is strange ... Still, I fail to understand."

"So do I, Monsieur Delambre. And I'm very much afraid that we shall never understand, unless perhaps your sister-in-law should *get better.*"

"The doctors seem to think that there is no hope of any sort, you know."

"Yes. Do you know if your brother ever experimented with flies?"

"I really don't know, but I should think so. Have you asked the Air Ministry people? They knew all about the work."

"Yes, and they laughed at me."

"I can understand that."

"You are very fortunate to understand anything, Monsieur Delambre. I do not ... but I hope to some day."

"Tell me, Uncle, do flies live a long time?"

We were just finishing our lunch and, following an established tradition between us, I was just pouring some wine into Henri's glass for him to dip a biscuit in.

Had Henri not been staring at his glass gradually being filled to the brim, something in my look might have frightened him.

This was the first time that he had ever mentioned flies, and I shuddered at the thought that Commissaire Charas might quite easily have been present. I could imagine the glint in his eye as he would have answered my nephew's question with another question. I could almost hear him saying :

"I don't know. Henri. Why do you ask?"

"Because I have again seen the fly that *Maman* was looking for."

And it was only after drinking off Henri's own glass of wine that I realized that he had answered my spoken thought.

"I did not know that your mother was looking for a fly."

"Yes, she was. It has grown quite a lot, but I recognized it all right."

"Where did you see this fly, Henri, and . . . how did you recognize it?"

"This morning on your desk, Uncle François. Its head is white instead of black, and it has a funny sort of leg."

Feeling more and more like Commissaire Charas, but trying to look unconcerned, I went on :

"And when did you see this fly for the first time?"

"The day that Papa went away. I had caught it, but *Maman* made me let it go. And then after, she wanted me to find it again. She'd changed her mind," and shrugging his shoulders just as my brother used to, he added, "you know how women are."

"I think that fly must have died long ago, and you must be mistaken, Henri," I said, getting up and walking to the door.

But as soon as I was out of the dining room, I ran up the stairs to my study. There was no fly anywhere to be seen.

I was bothered, far more than I cared to even think about. Henri had just proved that Charas was really closer to a clue than it had seemed when he told me about his thoughts concerning Hélène's pastime.

For the first time I wondered if Charas did not really know much more than he let on. For the first time also, I wondered about Hélène. Was she really insane? A strange, horrid feeling was growing on me, and the more I thought about it, the more I felt that, somehow. Charas was right : Hélène was *getting away with it*!

What could possibly have been the reason for such a monstrous crime? What had led up to it? Just what had happened?

I thought of all the hundreds of questions that Charas had put to Hélène, sometimes gently like a nurse trying to soothe, sometimes stern and cold, sometimes barking them furiously. Hélène had answered very few, always in a calm quiet voice and never seeming to pay any attention to the way in which the question had been put. Though dazed, she had seemed perfectly sane then.

Refined, well-bred and well-read, Charas was more than just an intelligent police official. He was a keen psychologist and had an amazing way of smelling out a fib or an erroneous statement even before it was uttered. I knew that he had accepted as true the few answers she had given him. But then there had been all those questions which she had never answered : the most direct and important ones. From the very beginning, Hélène had adopted a very simple system. "I cannot answer that question," she would say in her low, quiet voice. And that was that! The repetition of the same question never seemed to annoy her. In all the hours of questioning that she underwent, Hélène did not once point out to the commissaire that he had already asked her this or that. She would simply say, "I cannot answer that question," as though it was the very first time that that particular question had been asked and the very first time she had made that answer.

This cliché had become the formidable barrier beyond which Commissaire Charas could not even get a glimpse, an idea of what Hélène might be thinking. She had very willingly answered all questions about her life with my brother—which seemed a happy and uneventful one—up to the time of his end. About his death, however, all that she would say was that she had killed him with the steam hammer, but she refused to say why, what had led up to the drama and how she got my brother to put his head under it. She never actually refused outright; she would just go blank and, with no apparent emotion, would switch over to, "I cannot answer that question."

Hélène, as I have said, had shown the commissaire that she knew how to set and operate the steam hammer.

Charas could only find one single fact which did not coincide with Hélène's declarations, the fact that the hammer had been used twice. Charas was no longer willing to attribute this to insanity. That evident flaw in Hélène's stonewall defence seemed a crack which the commissaire might possibly enlarge. But my sister-in-law finally cemented it by acknowledging :

"All right, I lied to you. I did use the hammer twice. But do not ask me why, because I cannot tell you."

"Is that your only . . . misstatement, Madame Delambre?" the commissaire had asked, trying to follow up what looked at last like an advantage.

"It is . . . and you know it, Monsieur le Commissaire."

And, annoyed, Charas had seen that Hélène could read him like an open book.

I had thought of calling on the commissaire, but the knowledge that he would inevitably start questioning Henri made me hesitate. Another reason also made me hesitate, a vague sort of fear that he would look for and find the fly Henri had talked of. And that annoyed me a good deal because I could find no satisfactory explanation for that particular fear.

André was definitely not the absent-minded sort of professor who walks about in pouring rain with a rolled umbrella under his arm. He was human, had a keen sense of humour, loved children and animals and could not bear to see anyone suffer. I had often seen him drop his work to watch a parade of the local fire brigade, or see the *Tour de France* cyclists go by, or even follow a circus parade all around the village. He liked games of logic and precision, such as billiards and tennis, bridge and chess.

How was it then possible to explain his death? What could have made him put his head under that hammer? It could hardly have been the result of some stupid bet or a test of his courage. He hated betting and had no patience with those who indulged in it. Whenever he heard a bet proposed, he would invariably remind all present that, after all, a bet was but a contract between a fool and a swindler, even if it turned out to be a toss-up as to which was which.

It seemed there were only two possible explanations for André's death. Either he had gone mad, or else he had a reason for letting his wife kill him in such a strange and terrible way. And just what could have been his wife's role in all this? They surely could not have been both insane?

Having finally decided not to tell Charas about my nephew's innocent revelations, I thought I myself would try to question Hélène.

She seemed to have been expecting my visit for she came into the parlour almost as soon as I had made myself known to the matron and been allowed inside.

"I wanted to show you my garden," explained Helen as I looked at the coat slung over her shoulders.

As one of the "reasonable" inmates, she was allowed to go into the garden during certain hours of the day. She had asked for and obtained the right to a little patch of ground where she could grow flowers, and I had sent her seeds and some rosebushes out of my garden.

She took me straight to a rustic wooden bench which had been made in the men's workshop and only just set up under a tree close to her little patch of ground.

Searching for the right way to broach the subject of André's death, I sat for a while tracing vague designs on the ground with the end of my umbrella.

"François, I want to ask you something," said Hélène after a while.

"Anything I can do for you, Hélène?"

"No, just something I want to know. Do flies live very long?"

Staring at her, I was about to say that her boy had asked the very same question a few hours earlier when I suddenly realized that here was the opening I had been searching for and perhaps even the possibility of striking a great blow, a blow perhaps powerful enough to shatter her stonewall defence, be it sane or insane.

Watching her carefully, I replied :

"I don't really know, Hélène; but the fly you were looking for was in my study this morning."

No doubt about it, I had struck a shattering blow. She swung her head round with such force that I heard the bones crack in her neck. She opened her mouth, but said not a word; only her eyes seemed to be screaming with fear.

Yes, it was evident that I had crashed through something, but what? Undoubtedly, the commissaire would have known what to do with such an advantage; I did not. All I knew was that he would never have given her time to think, to recuperate, but all I could do, and even that was a strain, was to maintain my best poker face, hoping against hope that Hélène's defences would go on crumbling.

She must have gone quite a while without breathing, because she suddenly gasped and put both her hands over her still open mouth.

"François. . . . Did you kill it?" she whispered, her eyes no longer fixed, but searching very inch of my face.

"No."

"You have it then . . . You have it on you! Give it to me!" she almost shouted, touching me with both her hands, and I knew that had she felt strong enough, she would have tried to search me.

"No, Hélène, I haven't got it."

"But you know now . . . You have guessed, haven't you?"

"No, Hélène. I only know one thing, and that is that you are not insane. But I mean to know all, Hélène and somehow I am going to find out. You can choose : either you tell me everything and I'll see what is to be done, or . . ."

"Oh what? Say Say it!"

"I was going to say it, Hélène . . . or I assure you that your friend the commissaire will have that fly first thing tomorrow morning."

She remained quite still, looking down at the palms of her hands on her lap and although it was getting chilly, her forehead and hands were moist.

Without even brushing aside a wisp of long brown hair blown across her mouth by the breeze, she murmured :

"If I tell you . . . will you promise to destroy that fly before doing anything else?"

"No, Hélène. I can make no such promise before knowing."

"But François, you must understand. I promised André that fly would be destroyed. That promise must be kept and I can say nothing until it is."

I could sense the deadlock ahead. I was not yet losing ground, but I was losing the initiative. I tried a shot in the dark :

"Hélène, of course you understand that as soon as the police examine that fly, they will know that you are not insane, and then . . ."

"François, no! For Henri's sake! Don't you see? I was expecting that fly; I was hoping it would find me here but it couldn't know what had become of me. What else could it do but go to others it loves, to Henri, to you . . . you who might know and understand what was to be done!"

Was she really mad, or was she simulating again? But mad or not, she was cornered. Wondering how to follow up and how to land the knockout blow without running the risk of seeing her slip away out of reach, I said very quietly :

"Tell me all, Hélène. I can then protect your boy."

"Protect my boy from what? Don't you understand that if I am here, it is merely so that Henri won't be the son of a woman who was guillotined for having murdered his father? Don't you understand that I would by far prefer the guillotine to the living death of this lunatic asylum?"

"I understand, Hélène, and I'll do my best for the boy whether you tell me or not. If you refuse to tell me, I'll still do the best I can to protect Henri, but you must understand that the game will be out of my hands, because Commissaire Charas will have the fly."

"But why must you know?" said, rather than asked, my sister-in-law, struggling to control her temper.

"Because I must and will know how and why my brother died, Hélène."

"All right. Take me back to the . . . house. I'll give you what your commissaire would call my 'confession'."

"Do you mean to say that you have written it!"

"Yes. It was not really meant for you, but more likely for *your friend*, the commissaire. I had foreseen that, sooner or later, he would get too close to the truth."

"You then have no objection to his reading it?"

"You will act as you think fit, François. Wait for me a minute."

Leaving me at the door of the parlour, Hélène ran upstairs to her room. In less than a minute she was back with a large brown envelope.

"Listen, François; you are not nearly as bright as was your poor brother, but you are not unintelligent. All I ask is that you read this alone. After that, you may do as you wish."

"That I promise you, Hélène," I said taking the precious envelope. "I'll read it tonight and although tomorrow is not a visiting day, I'll come down to see you."

"Just as you like," said my sister-in-law without even saying goodbye as she went back upstairs.

It was only on reaching home, as I walked from the garage to the house, that I read the inscription on the envelope :

TO WHOM IT MAY CONCERN
(Probably Commissaire Charas)

Having told the servants that I would have only a light supper to be served immediately in my study and that I was not to be disturbed after, I ran upstairs, threw Hélène's envelope on my desk and made another careful search of the room before closing the shutters and drawing the curtains. All I could find was a long-since-dead mosquito stuck to the wall near the ceiling.

Having motioned to the servant to put her tray down on a table by the fireplace, I poured myself a glass of wine and locked the door behind her. I then disconnected the telephone—I always did this now at night—and turned out all the lights but the lamp on my desk.

Slitting open Hélène's fat envelope, I extracted a thick wad of closely written pages. I read the following lines neatly centred in the middle of the top page :

This is not a confession because, although I killed my husband, I am not a murderess. I simply and very faithfully carried out his last wish by crushing his head and right arm under the steam hammer at his brother's factory.

Without even touching the glass of wine by my elbow, I turned the page and started reading.

For very nearly a year before his death (*the manuscript began*), my husband had told me of some of his experiments. He knew full well that his colleagues of the Air Ministry would have forbidden some of them as too dangerous, but he was keen on obtaining positive results before reporting his discovery.

Whereas only sound and pictures had been, so far, transmitted through space by radio and television, André claimed to have discovered a way of transmitting matter. Matter, any solid object, placed in his "transmitter" was instantly disintegrated and reintegrated in a special receiving set.

André considered his discovery as perhaps the most important since that of the wheel sawn off the end of a tree trunk. He reckoned that the transmission of matter by instantaneous "disintegration-reintegration" would completely change life as we had known it so far. It would mean the end of all means of transport, not only of goods including food, but also of human beings. André, the practical scientist who never allowed theories or daydreams to get the better of him, already foresaw the time when there would no longer be any aeroplanes, ships, trains or cars and, therefore, no longer any roads or railway lines, ports, airports or stations. All that would be replaced by matter-transmitting and receiving stations throughout the world. Travellers and goods would be placed in special cabins and, at a given signal, would simply disappear and reappear almost immediately at the chosen receiving station.

André's receiving set was only a few feet away from his transmitter, in an adjoining room of his laboratory, and he at first ran into all sorts of snags. His first successful experiment was carried out with an ashtray taken from his desk, a souvenir we had brought back from a trip to London.

That was the first time he told me about his experiments and I had no idea of what he was talking about the day he came dashing into the house and threw the ashtray in my lap.

"Hélène, look! For a fraction of a second, a bare ten-millionth of a second, that ashtray has been completely disintegrated. For one little moment it no longer existed! Gone! Nothing left, absolutely nothing! Only atoms travelling through space at the speed of light! And the moment after, the atoms were once more gathered together in the shape of an ashtray!"

"André, please . . . please! What on earth are you raving about?"

He started sketching all over a letter I had been writing. He laughed at my wry face, swept all my letters off the table and said :

"You don't understand? Right? Let's start all over again. Hélène, do you remember I once read you an article about the mysterious flying stones that seem to come from nowhere in particular, and which are said occasionally to fall in certain houses in India? They come flying in as though thrown from outside, in spite of closed doors and windows."

"Yes, I remember. I also remember that Professor Augier, your friend of the Collège de France, who had come down for a few days, remarked that if there was no trickery about it, the only possible explanation was that the stones had been disintegrated after having been thrown from outside, come through the walls, and then been reintegrated before hitting the floor or the opposite walls."

"That's right. And I added that there was, of course, one other possibility, namely the momentary and partial disintegration of the walls as the stone or stones came through."

"Yes, André. I remember all that, and I suppose you also remember that I failed to understand, and that you got quite annoyed. Well, I still do not understand why and how, even disintegrated, stones should be able to come through a wall or a closed door."

"But it is possible, Hélène, because the atoms that make up matter are not close together like the bricks of a wall. They are separated by relative immensities of space."

"Do you mean to say that you have disintegrated that ashtray, and then put it together again after pushing it through something?"

"Precisely, Hélène. I projected it through the wall that separates my transmitter from my receiving set."

"And would it be foolish to ask how humanity is to benefit from ashtrays that can go through walls?"

André seemed quite offended, but he soon saw that I was only teasing and again waxing enthusiastic, he told me of some of the possibilities of his discovery.

"Isn't it wonderful, Hélène?" he finally gasped, out of breath.

"Yes, André. But I hope you won't ever transmit me; I'd be too much afraid of coming out at the other end like your ashtray."

"What do you mean?"

"Do you remember what was written under that ashtray?"

"Yes, of course : MADE IN JAPAN. That was the great joke of our typically British souvenir."

"The words are still there André; but . . . look!"

He took the ashtray out of my hands, frowned, and walked over to the window. Then he went quite pale, and I knew that he had seen what had proved to me that he had indeed carried out a strange experiment.

The three words were still there, but reversed and reading :

uɐdɐſ uı ǝpɐW

Without a word, having completely forgotten me, André rushed off to his laboratory. I only saw him the next morning, tired and unshaven after a whole night's work.

A few days later, André had a new reverse which put him out of sorts and made him fussy and grumpy for several weeks. I stood it patiently enough for a while, but being myself bad-tempered one evening, we had a silly row over some futile thing, and I reproached him for his moroseness.

"I'm sorry, *chérie*. I've been working my way through a maze of problems and have given you all a very rough time. You see, my very first experiment with a live animal proved a complete fiasco."

"André! You tried that experiment with Dandelo, didn't you?"

"Yes. How did you know?" he answered sheepishly. 'He disintegrated perfectly, but he never reappeared in the receiving set."

"Oh, André! What became of him then?"

"Nothing . . . there is just no more Dandelo; only the dispersed atoms of a cat wandering, God knows where, in the universe."

Dandelo was a small white cat the cook had found one morning in the garden and which we had promptly adopted. Now I knew how it had disappeared and was quite angry about the whole thing, but my husband was so miserable over it all that I said nothing.

I saw little of my husband during the next few weeks. He had most of his meals sent down to the laboratory. I would often wake up in the morning and find his bed unslept in. Sometimes, if he had come in very late, I would find that storm-swept appearance which only a man can give a bedroom by getting up very early and fumbling around in the dark.

One evening he came home to dinner all smiles, and I knew that his troubles were over. His face dropped, however, when he saw I was dressed for going out.

"Oh. Were you going out, Hélène?"

"Yes, the Drillons invited me for a game of bridge, but I can easily phone them and put it off."

"No, it's all right."

"It isn't all right. Out with it, dear!"

"Well, I've at last got everything perfect and I wanted you to be the first to see the miracle."

"*Magnifique*, André! Of course I'll be delighted."

Having telephoned our neighbours to say how sorry I was and so forth, I ran down to the kitchen and told the cook that she had exactly ten minutes in which to prepare a "celebration dinner".

"An excellent idea, Hélène," said my husband when the maid appeared with the champagne after our candlelight dinner. "We'll celebrate with reintegrated champagne!" and taking the tray from the maid's hands, he led the way down to the laboratory.

"Do you think it will be as good as before its disintegration?" I asked, holding the tray while he opened the door and switched on the lights.

"Have no fear. You'll see! Just bring it here, will you," he said, opening the door of a telephone call box he had bought and which had been transformed into what he called a transmitter. "Put it down on that now," he added, putting a stool inside the box.

Having carefully closed the door, he took me to the other end of the room and handed me a pair of very dark sunglasses. He put on another pair and walked back to a switchboard by the transmitter.

"Ready, Hélène?" said my husband, turning out all the lights. "Don't remove your glasses till I give the word."

"I won't budge, André, go on," I told him, my eyes fixed on the tray which I could just see in a greenish shimmering light through the glass-panelled door of the telephone booth.

"Right," said André, throwing a switch.

The whole room was brilliantly illuminated by an orange flash. Inside the cabin I had seen a crackling ball of fire and felt its heat on my face, neck and hands. The whole thing lasted but a fraction of a second, and I found myself blinking at green-edged black holes like those one sees after having stared at the sun.

"*Et voilà!* You can take off your glasses, Hélène."

A little theatrically perhaps, my husband opened the door of the cabin. Though André had told me what to expect, I was astonished to find that the champagne, glasses, tray and stool were no longer there.

Andrew ceremoniously led me by the hand into the next room in a corner of which stood a second telephone booth. Opening the door wide, he triumphantly lifted the champagne tray off the stool.

Feeling somewhat like the good-natured kind-member-of-the-audience that has been dragged on to the music hall stage by the magician, I repressed from saying, "All done with mirrors," which I knew would have annoyed my husband.

"Sure it's not dangerous to drink?" I asked as the cork popped.

"Absolutely sure, Hélène," he said, handing me a glass. "But that was nothing. Drink this off and I'll show you something much more astounding."

We went back into the other room.

"Oh, André! Remember poor Dandelo!"

"This is only a guinea pig, Hélène. But I'm positive it will go through all right."

He set the furry little beast down on the green enamelled floor of the booth and quickly closed the door. I again put on my dark glasses and saw and felt the vivid crackling flash.

Without waiting for André to open the door, I rushed into the next room where the lights were still on and looked into the receiving booth.

"Oh, André! *Chéri!* He's there all right!" I shouted excitedly, watching the little animal trotting round and round. "It's wonderful, André. It works! You've succeeded!"

"I hope so, but I must be patient. I'll know for sure in a few weeks' time."

"What do you mean? Look! He's as full of life as when you put him in the other cabin."

"Yes, so he seems. But we'll have to see if all his organs are intact, and that will take some time. If that little beast is still full of life in a month's time, we then consider the experiment a success."

I begged André to let me take care of the guinea pig.

"All right, but don't kill it by over feeding," he agreed with a grin for my enthusiasm.

Though not allowed to take Hop-la—the name I had given the guinea pig—out of its box in the laboratory, I had tied a pink ribbon round its neck and was allowed to feed it twice a day.

Hop-la soon got used to its pink ribbon and became quite a tame little pet, but that month of waiting seemed a year.

And then one day, André put Miquette, our cocker spaniel, into his "transmitter". He had not told me beforehand, knowing full well that I would never have agreed to such an experiment with our dog. But when he did tell me, Miquette had been successfully transmitted half-a-dozen times and seemed to be enjoying the operation thoroughly; no sooner was she let out of the "reintegrator" than she dashed madly into the next room, scratching at the "transmitter" door to have "another go", as André called it.

I now expected that my husband would invite some of his colleagues and Air Ministry specialists to come down. He usually did this when he had finished a research job and, before handing them long detailed reports which he always typed himself, he would carry out an experiment or two before them. But this time, he just went on working. One morning I finally asked him when he intended throwing his usual "surprise party", as we called it.

"No, Helene; not for a long while yet. This discovery is much too important. I have an awful lot of work to do on it still. Do you realize that there are some parts of the transmission proper which I do not yet myself fully understand? It works all right, but you see, I can't just say to all these eminent professors that I do this and that and, poof, it works! I must be able to explain how and why it works. And what is even more important, I must be ready and able to refute every destructive argument they will not fail to trot out, as they usually do when faced with anything really good."

I was occasionally invited down to the laboratory to witness some new experiment, but I never went unless André invited me, and only talked about his work if he broached the subject first. Of course it never occurred to me that he would, at that stage at least, have tried an experiment with a human being; though, had I thought about it—knowing André—it would have been obvious that he would never have allowed anyone into the "transmitter" before he had been through to test it first. It was only after the accident that

I discovered he had duplicated all his switches inside the disintegration booth, so that he could try it out by himself.

The morning André tried this terrible experiment, he did not show up for lunch. I sent the maid down with a tray, but she brought it back with a note she had found pinned outside the laboratory door: "Do not disturb me, I am working."

He did occasionally pin such notes on his door and, though I noticed it, I paid no particular attention to the unusually large handwriting of his note.

It was just after that, as I was drinking my coffee, that Henri came bouncing into the room to say that he had caught a funny fly, and would I like to see it. Refusing even to look at his closed fist, I ordered him to release it immediately.

"But, *Maman*, it has such a funny white head!"

Marching the boy over to the open window, I told him to release the fly immediately, which he did. I knew that Henri had caught the fly merely because he thought it looked curious or different from other flies, but I also knew that his father would never stand for any form of cruelty to animals, and that there would be a fuss should he discover that our son had put a fly in a box or a bottle.

At dinnertime that evening, André had still not shown up and, a little worried, I ran down to the laboratory and knocked at the door.

He did not answer my knock, but I heard him moving around and a moment later he slipped a note under the door. It was typewritten:

HELENE, I AM HAVING TROUBLE. PUT THE BOY TO BED AND COME BACK IN AN HOUR'S TIME. A.

Frightened, I knocked and called, but André did not seem to pay any attention and, vaguely reassured by the familiar noise of his typewriter, I went back to the house.

Having put Henri to bed, I returned to the laboratory where I found another note slipped under the door. My hand shook as I picked it up because I knew by then that something must be radically wrong. I read:

HELENE, FIRST OF ALL I COUNT ON YOU NOT TO LOSE YOUR NERVE OR DO ANYTHING RASH BECAUSE YOU ALONE CAN HELP ME. I HAVE HAD A SERIOUS ACCIDENT. I AM NOT IN ANY PARTICULAR DANGER FOR THE TIME BEING THOUGH IT IS A MATTER OF LIFE AND DEATH. IT IS USELESS CALLING TO ME OR SAYING ANYTHING. I CANNOT ANSWER, I

CANNOT SPEAK. I WANT YOU TO DO EXACTLY AND VERY CAREFULLY
ALL THAT I ASK. AFTER HAVING KNOCKED THREE TIMES TO SHOW
THAT YOU UNDERSTAND AND AGREE, FETCH ME A BOWL OF MILK LACED
WITH RUM. I HAVE HAD NOTHING ALL DAY AND CAN DO WITH IT.

Shaking with fear, not knowing what to think and repressing a
furious desire to call André and bang away until he opened the
door, I knocked three times as requested and ran all the way home
to fetch what he wanted.

In less than five minutes I was back. Another note had been
slipped under the door :

HELENE, FOLLOW THESE INSTRUCTIONS CAREFULLY. WHEN YOU
KNOCK I'LL OPEN THE DOOR. YOU ARE TO WALK OVER TO MY DESK
AND PUT DOWN THE BOWL OF MILK. YOU WILL THEN GO INTO THE
OTHER ROOM WHERE THE RECEIVER IS. LOOK CAREFULLY AND TRY TO
FIND A FLY WHICH OUGHT TO BE THERE BUT WHICH I AM UNABLE TO
FIND. UNFORTUNATELY I CANNOT SEE SMALL THINGS VERY EASILY.

BEFORE YOU COME IN YOU MUST PROMISE TO OBEY ME IMPLICITLY.
DO NOT LOOK AT ME AND REMEMBER THAT TALKING IS QUITE USELESS.
I CANNOT ANSWER. KNOCK AGAIN THREE TIMES AND THAT WILL MEAN
I HAVE YOUR PROMISE. MY LIFE DEPENDS ENTIRELY ON THE HELP
YOU CAN GIVE ME.

I had to wait a while to pull myself together, and then I knocked
slowly three times.

I heard André shuffling behind the door, then his hand fumbling
with the lock, and the door opened.

Out of the corner of my eye, I saw that he was standing behind
the door, but without looking round, I carried the bowl of milk
to his desk. He was evidently watching me and I had to at all costs
appear calm and collected.

"*Chéri*, you can count on me," I said gently, and putting the
bowl down under his desk lamp, the only one alight, I walked into
the next room where all the lights were blazing.

My first impression was that some sort of hurricane must have
blown out of the receiving booth. Papers were scattered in every
direction, a whole row of test tubes lay smashed in a corner, chairs
and stools were upset and one of the window curtains hung half
torn from its bent rod. In a large enamel basin on the floor a heap
of burned documents was still smouldering.

I knew that I would not find the fly André wanted me to look for.

Women know things that men only suppose by reasoning and deduction; it is a form of knowledge very rarely accessible to them and which they disparingly call intuition. I already knew that the fly André wanted was the one which Henri had caught and which I had made him release.

I heard André shuffling around in the next room, and then a strange gurgling and sucking as though he had trouble in drinking his milk.

"André, there is no fly here. Can you give me any sort of indication that might help? If you can't speak, rap or something . . . you know : once for yes, twice for no."

I had tried to control my voice and speak as though perfectly calm, but I had to choke down a sob of desperation when he rapped twice for "no".

"May I come to you, André? I don't know what can have happened, but whatever it is, I'll be courageous, dear."

After a moment of silent hesitation, he tapped once on his desk.

At the door I stopped aghast at the sight of André standing with his head and shoulders covered by the brown velvet cloth he had taken from a table by his desk, the table on which he usually ate when he did not want to leave his work. Suppressing a laugh that might easily have turned to sobbing, I said :

"André, we'll search thoroughly tomorrow, by daylight. Why don't you go to bed? I'll lead you to the guest room if you like, and won't let anyone else see you."

His left hand tapped the desk twice.

"Do you need a doctor, André?"

"No," he rapped.

"Would you like to call up Professor Augier? He might be of more help . . ."

Twice he rapped "no" sharply. I did not know what to do or say. And then I told him :

"Henri caught a fly this morning which he wanted to show me, but I made him release it. Could it have been the one you are looking for? I didn't see it, but the boy said its head was white."

André emitted a strange metallic sigh, and I just had time to bite my fingers fiercely in order not to scream. He had let his right arm drop, and instead of his long-fingered muscular hand, a grey stick with little buds on it like the branch of a tree, hung out of his sleeve almost down to his knee.

"André, *mon chéri*, tell me what happened. I might be of more help to you if I knew, André . . . oh, it's terrible!" I sobbed, unable to control myself.

Having rapped once for yes, he pointed to the door with his left hand.

I stepped out and sank down crying as he locked the door behind me. He was typing again and I waited. At last he shuffled to the door and slid a sheet of paper under it.

HELENE, COME BACK IN THE MORNING. I MUST THINK AND WILL HAVE TYPED OUT AN EXPLANATION FOR YOU. TAKE ONE OF MY SLEEP-ING TABLETS AND GO STRAIGHT TO BED. I NEED YOU FRESH AND STRONG TOMORROW, MA PAUVRE CHERIE. A.

"Do you want anything for the night, André?" I shouted through the door.

He knocked twice for no, and a little later I heard the typewriter again.

The sun full on my face woke me up with a start. I had set the alarm clock for five but had not heard it, probably because of the sleeping tablets. I had indeed slept like a log, without a dream. Now I was back in my living nightmare and crying like a child I sprang out of bed. It was just on seven!

Rushing into the kitchen, without a word for the startled servants, I rapidly prepared a trayload of coffee, bread and butter with which I ran down to the laboratory.

André opened the door as soon as I knocked and closed it again as I carried the tray to his desk. His head was still covered, but I saw from his crumpled suit and his open camp bed that he must have at least tried to rest.

On his desk lay a typewritten sheet for me which I picked up. André opened the other door, and taking this to mean that he wanted to be left alone, I walked into the next room. He pushed the door to, and I heard him pouring out the coffee as I read :

DO YOU REMEMBER THE ASHTRAY EXPERIMENT? I HAVE HAD A SIMILAR ACCIDENT. I "TRANSMITTED" MYSELF SUCCESSFULLY THE NIGHT BEFORE LAST. DURING A SECOND EXPERIMENT YESTERDAY A FLY WHICH I DID NOT SEE MUST HAVE GOT INTO THE "DISINTE-GRATOR". MY ONLY HOPE IS TO FIND THAT FLY AND GO THROUGH AGAIN WITH IT. PLEASE SEARCH FOR IT CAREFULLY SINCE, IF IT IS NOT FOUND, I SHALL HAVE TO FIND A WAY OF PUTTING AN END TO ALL THIS.

If only André had been more explicit! I shuddered at the thought that he must be terribly disfigured and then cried softly as I imagined his face inside-out, or perhaps his eyes in place of his ears, or his mouth at the back of his neck, or worse!

André must be saved! For that, the fly must be found!

Pulling myself together, I said:

"André, may I come in?"

He opened the door.

"André, don't despair; I am going to find that fly. It is no longer in the laboratory, but it cannot be very far. I suppose you're disfigured, perhaps terribly so, but there can be no question of putting an end to all this, as you say in your note; that I will never stand for. If necessary, if you do not wish to be seen, I'll make you a mask or a cowl so that you can go on with your work until you get well again. If you cannot work, I'll call Professor Augier, and he and all your other friends will save you, André."

Again I heard that curious metallic sigh as he rapped violently on his desk.

"André, don't be annoyed; please be calm. I won't do anything without first consulting you, but you must rely on me, have faith in me and let me help you as best I can. Are you terribly disfigured, dear? Can't you let me see your face? I won't be afraid . . . I am your wife you know."

But my husband again rapped a decisive "no" and pointed to the door.

"All right. I am going to search for the fly now, but promise me you won't do anything foolish; promise you won't do anything rash or dangerous without first letting me know all about it!"

He extended his left hand, and I knew I had his promise.

I will never forget that ceaseless daylong hunt for a fly. Back home, I turned the house inside out and made all the servants join in the search. I told them that a fly had escaped from the Professor's laboratory and that it must be captured alive, but it was evident they already thought me crazy. They said so to the police later, and that day's hunt for a fly most probably saved me from the guillotine later.

I questioned Henri, and as he failed to understand right away what I was talking about, I shook him and slapped him and made him cry in front of the round-eyed maids. Realizing that I must not let myself go, I kissed and petted the poor boy and at last made him understand what I wanted of him. Yes, he remembered, he had found the fly just by the kitchen window; yes, he had released it immediately as told to.

Even in summertime we had very few flies because our house is on the top of a hill and the slightest breeze coming across the valley blows round it. In spite of that, I managed to catch dozens of flies that day. On all the window sills and all over the garden I had put saucers of milk, sugar, jam, meat—all the things likely to attract flies. Of all those we caught, and many others which we failed to catch but which I saw, none resembled the one Henri had caught the day before. One by one, with a magnifying glass, I examined every unusual fly, but none had anything like a white head.

At lunch time, I ran down to André with some milk and mashed potatoes. I also took some of the flies we had caught, but he gave me to understand that they could be of no possible use to him.

"If that fly has not been found by tonight, André, we'll have to see what is to be done. And this is what I propose : I'll sit in the next room. When you can't answer by the yes-no method of rapping, you'll type out whatever you want to say and then slip it under the door. Agreed?"

"Yes," rapped André.

By nightfall we had still not found the fly. At dinnertime, as I prepared André's tray, I broke down and sobbed in the kitchen in front of the silent servants. My maid thought that I had had a row with my husband, probably about the mislaid fly, but I learned later that the cook was already quite sure that I was out of my mind.

Without a word, I picked up the tray and then put it down again as I stopped by the telephone. That this was really a matter of life and death for André, I had no doubt. Neither did I doubt that he fully intended committing suicide, unless I could make him change his mind, or at least put off such a drastic decision. Would I be strong enough? He would never forgive me for not keeping a promise, but under the circumstances, did that really matter? To the devil with promises and honour! At all costs André must be saved! And having thus made up my mind, I looked up and dialled Professor Augier's number.

"The Professor is away and will not be back before the end of the week," said a polite neutral voice at the other end of the line.

That was that! I would have to fight alone and fight I would. I would save André come what may.

All my nervousness had disappeared as André let me in and, after putting the tray of food down on his desk, I went into the other room, as agreed.

"The first thing I want to know," I said as he closed the door behind me, "is what happened exactly. Can you please tell me, André?"

I waited patiently while he typed an answer which he pushed under the door a little later.

HELENE, I WOULD RATHER NOT TELL YOU. SINCE GO I MUST, I WOULD RATHER YOU REMEMBER ME AS I WAS BEFORE. I MUST DESTROY MYSELF IN SUCH A WAY THAT NONE CAN POSSIBLY KNOW WHAT HAS HAPPENED TO ME. I HAVE OF COURSE THOUGHT OF SIMPLY DISINTEGRATING MYSELF IN MY TRANSMITTER, BUT I HAD BETTER NOT BECAUSE, SOONER OR LATER, I MIGHT FIND MYSELF REINTE-GRATED. SOME DAY, SOMEWHERE, SOME SCIENTIST IS SURE TO MAKE THE SAME DISCOVERY. I HAVE THEREFORE THOUGHT OF A WAY WHICH IS NEITHER SIMPLE NOR EASY, BUT YOU CAN AND WILL HELP ME.

For several minutes I wondered if André had not simply gone stark raving mad.

"André," I said at last, "whatever you may have chosen or thought of, I cannot and will never accept such a cowardly solution. No matter how awful the result of your experiment or accident, you are alive, you are a man, a brain . . . and you have a soul. You have no right to destroy yourself. You know that!"

The answer was soon typed and pushed under the door.

I AM ALIVE ALL RIGHT, BUT I AM ALREADY NO LONGER A MAN. AS TO MY BRAIN OR INTELLIGENCE, IT MAY DISAPPEAR AT ANY MOMENT. AS IT IS, IT IS NO LONGER INTACT. AND THERE CAN BE NO SOUL WITH-OUT INTELLIGENCE . . . AND YOU KNOW THAT!

"Then you must tell the other scientists about your discovery. They will help you and save you, André!"

I staggered back frightened as he angrily thumped the door twice.

"André . . . why? Why do you refuse the aid you know they would give you with all their hearts?"

A dozen furious knocks shook the door and made me understand that my husband would never accept such a solution. I had to find other arguments.

For hours, it seemed, I talked to him about our boy, about me, about his family, about his duty to us and to the rest of humanity. He made no reply of any sort. At last I cried:

"André . . . do you hear me?"

"Yes," he knocked very gently.

'Well, listen then. I have another idea. You remember your first experiment with the ashtray? . . . Well, do you think that if you had put it through again a second time, it might possibly have come out with the letters turned back the right way?"

Before I had finished speaking, André was busily typing and a moment later I read his answer:

I HAVE ALREADY THOUGHT OF THAT, AND THAT IS WHY I NEEDED THE FLY. IT HAS GOT TO GO THROUGH WITH ME. THERE IS NO HOPE OTHERWISE.

"Try all the same, André. You never know!"

I HAVE TRIED SEVEN TIMES ALREADY, was the typewritten reply I got to that.

"André! Try again, please!"

The answer this time gave me a flutter of hope, because no woman has ever understood, or will ever understand, how a man about to die can possibly consider anything funny.

I DEEPLY ADMIRE YOUR DELICIOUS FEMININE LOGIC. WE COULD GO ON DOING THIS EXPERIMENT UNTIL DOOMSDAY. HOWEVER, JUST TO GIVE YOU THAT PLEASURE, PROBABLY THE VERY LAST I SHALL EVER BE ABLE TO GIVE YOU, I WILL TRY ONCE MORE. IF YOU CANNOT FIND THE DARK GLASSES, TURN YOUR BACK TO THE MACHINE AND PRESS YOUR HANDS OVER YOUR EYES. LET ME KNOW WHEN YOU ARE READY.

"Ready, André!" I shouted without even looking for the glasses and following his instructions.

I heard him moving around and then opening and closing the door of his "disintegrator". After what seemed a very long wait, but probably was not more than a minute or so, I heard a violent crackling noise and perceived a bright flash through my eyelids and fingers.

I turned around as the cabin door opened.

His head and shoulders still covered with the brown velvet carpet. André was gingerly stepping out of it.

"How do you feel, André? Any difference?" I asked, touching his arm.

He tried to step away from me and caught his foot in one of the stools which I had not troubled to pick up. He made a violent effort to regain his balance, and the velvet cloth slowly slid off his shoulders and head as he fell heavily backwards.

The horror was too much for me, too unexpected. As a matter of fact, I am sure that, even had I known, the horror impact could hardly have been less powerful. Trying to push both hands into my mouth to stifle my screams and although my fingers were bleeding, I screamed again and again. I could not take my eyes off him, I could not even close them, and yet I knew that if I looked at the horror much longer, I would go on screaming for the rest of my life.

Slowly, the monster, the thing that had been my husband, covered its head, got up and groped its way to the door and passed it. Though still screaming, I was able to close my eyes.

I who had ever been a true Catholic, who believed in God and another, better life hereafter, have today but one hope : that when I die, I really die, and that there may be no after-life of any sort because, if there is, then I shall never forget! Day and night, awake or asleep, I see it, and I know that I am condemned to see it forever, even perhaps into oblivion!

Until I am totally extinct, nothing can, nothing will ever make me forget that dreadful white hairy head with its low flat skull and its two pointed ears. Pink and moist, the nose was also that of a cat, a huge cat. But the eyes! Or rather, where the eyes should have been were two brown bumps the size of saucers. Instead of a mouth, animal or human, there was a long hairy vertical slit from which hung a black quivering trunk that widened at the end, trumpetlike, and from which saliva kept dripping.

I must have fainted, because I found myself flat on my stomach on the cold cement floor of the laboratory, staring at the closed door behind which I could hear the noise of André's typewriter.

Numb, numb and empty, I must have looked as people do immediately after a terrible accident, before they fully understand what has happened. I could only think of a man I had once seen on the platform of a railway station, quite conscious, and looking stupidly at his leg still on the line where the train had just passed.

My throat was aching terribly, and that made me wonder if my vocal cords had not perhaps been torn, and whether I would ever be able to speak again.

The noise of the typewriter suddenly stopped and I felt I was going to scream again as something touched the door and a sheet of paper slid from under it.

Shivering with fear and disgust, I crawled over to where I could read it without touching it :

NOW YOU UNDERSTAND. THAT LAST EXPERIMENT WAS A NEW DISASTER, MY POOR HELENE. I SUPPOSE YOU RECOGNIZED PART OF DANDELO'S HEAD. WHEN I WENT INTO THE DISINTEGRATOR JUST NOW, MY HEAD WAS ONLY THAT OF A FLY. I NOW ONLY HAVE ITS EYES AND MOUTH LEFT. THE REST HAS BEEN REPLACED BY PARTS OF THE CAT'S HEAD. POOR DANDELO WHOSE ATOMS HAD NEVER COME TO-GETHER. YOU SEE NOW THAT THERE CAN ONLY BE ONE POSSIBLE SOLUTION, DON'T YOU? I MUST DISAPPEAR. KNOCK ON THE DOOR WHEN YOU ARE READY AND I SHALL EXPLAIN WHAT YOU HAVE TO DO.

Of course he was right, and it had been wrong and cruel of me to insist on a new experiment. And I knew that there was now no possible hope, that any further experiments could only bring about worse results.

Getting up dazed, I went to the door and tried to speak, but no sound came out of my throat . . . so I knocked once !

You can of course guess the rest. He explained his plan in short typewritten notes, and I agreed, I agreed to everything !

My head on fire, but shivering with cold, like an automaton, I followed him into the silent factory. In my hand was a full page of explanations : what I had to know about the steam hammer.

Without stopping or looking back, he pointed to the switchboard that controlled the steam hammer as he passed it. I went no farther and watched him come to a halt before the terrible instrument.

He knelt down, carefully wrapped the cloth round his head, and then stretched out flat on the ground.

It was not difficult. I was not killing my husband. André, poor André, had gone long ago, years ago it seemed. I was merely carrying out his last wish . . . and mine.

Without hesitating, my eyes on the long still body, I firmly pushed the "stroke" button right in. The great metallic mass seemed to drop slowly. It was not so much the resounding clang of the hammer that made me jump as the sharp cracking which I had distinctly heard at the same time. My hus . . . the thing's body shook a second and then lay still.

It was then I noticed that he had forgotten to put his right arm, his flyleg, under the hammer. The police would never understand but the scientists would, and they must not! That had been André's last wish, also!

I had to do it and quickly, too; the night watchman must have heard the hammer and would be round any moment. I pushed the other button and the hammer slowly rose. Seeing but trying not to look, I ran up, leaned down, lifted and moved forward the right arm which seemed terribly light. Back at the switchboard, again I pushed the red button, and down came the hammer a second time. Then I ran all the way home.

You know the rest and can now do whatever you think right.

So ended Hélène's manuscript.

The following day I telephoned Commissaire Charas to invite him to dinner.

"With pleasure Monsieur Delambre. Allow me, however, to ask: is it the commissaire you are inviting, or just Monsieur Charas?"

"Have you any preference?'

"No, not at the present moment."

"Well then, make it whichever you like. Will eight o'clock suit you?"

Although it was raining, the commissaire arrived on foot that evening.

"Since you did not come tearing up to the door in your black Citroen, I take it you have opted for Monsieur Charas, off duty?"

"I left the car up a side street," mumbled the commissaire with a grin as the maid staggered under the weight of his raincoat.

"*Merci,*" he said a minute later as I handed him a glass of Pernod into which he tipped a few drops of water, watching it turn the golden amber liquid to pale blue milk.

"You heard about my poor sister-in-law?"

"Yes, shortly after you telephoned me this morning. I am sorry, but perhaps it was all for the best. Being already in charge of your brother's case, the inquiry automatically comes to me."

"I suppose it was suicide."

"Without a doubt. Cyanide the doctors say quite rightly; I found a second tablet in the unstitched hem of her dress."

"*Monsieur est servi,*" announced the maid.

"I would like to show you a very curious document afterwards, Charas."

"Ah, yes. I heard that Madame Delambre had been writing a

lot, but we could find nothing beyond the short note informing us
that she was committing suicide.'

During our tête-à-tête dinner, we talked politics, books and films,
and the local football club of which the commissaire was a keen
supporter.

After dinner, I took him up to my study where a bright fire—
a habit I had picked up in England during the war—was burning.

Without even asking him, I handed him his brandy and mixed
myself what he called "crushed-bug juice in soda water"—his
appreciation of whisky.

"I would like you to read this, Charas; first because it was partly
intended for you and, secondly, because it will interest you. If you
think Commissaire Charas has no objection, I would like to burn
it after."

Without a word, he took the wad of sheets Hélène had given me
the day before and settled down to read them.

"What do you think of it all?" I asked some 20 minutes later as
he carefully folded Hélène's manuscript, slipped it into the brown
envelope, and put it into the fire.

Charas watched the flames licking the envelope from which wisps
of grey smoke were escaping, and it was only when it burst into
flames that he said, slowly raising his eyes to mine :

"I think it proves very definitely that Madame Delambre was
quite insane."

For a long while we watched the fire eating up Hélène's "confession".

"A funny thing happened to me this morning, Charas. I went to
the cemetery, where by brother is buried. It was quite empty and
I was alone."

"Not quite, Monsieur Delambre. I was there, but I did not want
to disturb you."

"Then you saw me. . . ."

"Yes, I saw you bury a matchbox."

"Do you know what was in it?"

"A fly, I suppose."

"Yes, I had found it early this morning, caught in a spider's web
in the garden."

"Was it dead?"

"No, not quite. I . . . crushed it . . . between two stones. It's head
was . . . white . . . all white."

BLACK SUNDAY

NIKOLAI GOGOL

(Galatea-Jolly Films: 1960)

*Despite the fact that American—and to a certain extent English
—film makers have dominated the horror film genre since its
very early years, there have been some truly outstanding productions from other countries—notably European—and in
particular France and Italy. From a personal point of view I
would say that the Italian* La Maschera Del Demonio *(The
Mask of the Demon, released in America as* Black Sunday)
and La Rivière Du Hibou *(Incident at Owl Creek) from
France, are my candidates for the select company of the all-
time best horror films from any source.*

*In order to preserve a chronological sequence we shall first
deal with* Black Sunday *and then turn to the French production. Carlos Clarens calls the film a "relentless nightmare"
containing "the best black and white photography to enhance
a horror movie in the past two decades" (the work of camera-
man Ubaldo Terzano).*

*The story concerns a sensual vampire woman, burned at the
stake during the seventeenth century, who returns two hundred
years later to wreak her vengeance on the descendants of those
who persecuted her. Set in Middle Europe, the picture owed
its inspiration to a superb folk tale by the great Russian writer,
Nikolai Gogol, entitled* The Viy.

*The vampire was played by Barbara Steele, a talented and
very beautiful actress then as now almost completely unknown
outside the horror film genre. Although the film was released
with considerable success in America and Europe, a ban was
placed on it in Britain until 1968 when it finally appeared
under the title* Revenge of the Vampire.

*

AS soon as the rather musical seminary bell which hung at the gate
of the Bratsky Monastery rang out every morning in Kiev, school-
boys and students hurried thither in crowds from all parts of the
town. Students of grammar, rhetoric, philosophy and theology,

trudged to their classrooms with exercise books under their arms. The grammarians were quite small boys : they shoved each other as they went along and quarrelled in a shrill alto; they almost all wore muddy or tattered clothes, and their pockets were full of all manner of rubbish, such as knucklebones, whistles made of feathers, or a half-eaten pie, sometimes even little sparrows, one of whom suddenly chirruping at an exceptionally quiet moment in the classroom would cost its owner some sound whacks on both hands and sometimes a thrashing. The rhetoricians walked with more dignity; their clothes were often quite free from holes; on the other hand, their countenances almost all bore some decoration, after the style of a figure of rhetoric; either one eye had sunk right under the forehead, or there was a monstrous swelling in place of a lip, or some other disfigurement. They talked and swore among themselves in tenor voices. The philosophers conversed an octave lower in the scale; they had nothing in their pockets but strong, cheap tobacco. They laid in no stores of any sort, but ate on the spot anything they came across; they smelt of pipes and vodka to such a distance that a passing workman would sometimes stop a long way off and sniff the air like a setter dog.

As a rule the market was just beginning to stir at that hour, and the women with bread-rings, rolls, melon seeds and poppy cakes would tug at the skirts of those whose coats were of fine cloth or some cotton material.

"This way, young gentlemen, this way!" they kept saying from all sides. "Here are bread-rings, poppy cakes, twists, good white rolls; they are really good! Made with honey! I baked them myself."

Another woman lifting up a sort of long twist made of dough would cry: "Here's a bread-stick! Buy my bread-stick, young gentlemen!"

"Don't buy anything off her; see what a horrid woman she is, her nose is nasty and her hands are dirty...."

But the women were afraid to worry the philosophers and the theologians, for the latter were fond of taking things to taste and always a good handful.

On reaching the seminary, the crowd dispersed to their various classes, which were held in low-pitched but fairly large rooms, with little windows, wide doorways and dirty benches. The classroom was at once filled with all sorts of buzzing sounds : the "auditors" heard their pupils repeat their lessons; the shrill alto of a grammarian rang out, and the window-pane responded with almost the same note; in a corner a rhetorician, whose mouth and thick lips should have belonged at least to a student of philosophy, was droning something in a bass voice, and all that could be heard at a distance was "Boo, boo, boo. . . ." The "auditors", as they heard the lesson, kept glancing with one eye under the bench, where a roll or a cheese-cake or some pumpkin seeds were peeping out of a scholar's pocket.

When this learned crowd managed to arrive a little too early, or when they knew that the professors would be later than usual, then by general consent they got up a fight, and everyone had to take part in it, even the monitors whose duty it was to maintain discipline and look after the morals of all the students. Two theologians usually settled the arrangements for the battle : whether each class was to defend itself individually, or whether all were to be divided into two parties, the bursars and the seminarists. In any case the grammarians first began the attack, and as soon as the rhetoricians entered the fray, they ran away and stood at points of vantage to watch the contest. Then the devotees of philosophy, with long black moustaches, joined in, and finally those of theology, very thick in the neck and attired in shocking trousers, took part. It commonly ended in theology beating all the rest, and the philosophers, rubbing their ribs, were forced into the classroom and sat down on the benches to rest. The professor, who had himself at one time taken part in such battles, could, on entering the class, see in a minute from the flushed faces of his audience that the battle had been a good one, and while he was caning a rhetorician on the fingers, in another classroom another professor would be smacking philosophy's hands with a wooden bat. The theologians were dealt with in quite a different way : they received, to use the expression of a professor of theology, "a peck of peas apiece", in other words, a liberal drubbing with short leather thongs.

On holidays and ceremonial occasions the bursars and the seminarists went from house to house as mummers. Sometimes they acted a play, and then the most distinguished figure was always some theologian, almost as tall as the belfry of Kiev, who took the part of Herodias or Pohiphar's wife. They received in payment a piece of linen, or a sack of millet or half a boiled goose, or something of the sort. All this crowd of students—the seminarists as well as the bursars, with whom they maintain an hereditary feud—were exceedingly badly off for means of subsistence, and at the same time had extraordinary appetites, so that to reckon how many dumplings each of them tucked away at supper would be utterly impossible, and therefore the voluntary offerings of prosperous citizens could not be sufficient for them. Then the "senate" of the philosophers and theologians dispatched the grammarians and rhetoricians, under the supervision of a philosopher (who sometimes took part in the raid himself), with sacks on their shoulders to plunder the kitchen gardens—and pumpkin porridge was made in the bursars' quarters. The members of the "senate" ate such masses of melons that next day their "auditors" heard two lessons from them instead of one, one coming from their lips, another muttering in their stomachs. Both the bursars and the seminars wore long garments resembling frock-coats, "prolonged to the utmost limit", a technical expression signifying below their heels.

The most important event for the seminarists was the coming of the vacation : it began in June, when they usually dispersed to their homes. Then the whole high road was dotted with philosophers, grammarians and theologians. Those who had nowhere to go went to stay with some comrade. The philosophers and theologians took a situation, that is, undertook the tuition of the children in some prosperous family, and received in payment a pair of new boots or sometimes even a coat. The whole crowd trailed along together like a gipsy encampment, boiled their porridge, and slept in the fields. Everyone hauled a long sack in which he had a shirt and a pair of leg-wrappers. The theologians were particularly careful and precise : to avoid wearing out their boots, they took them off, hung them on sticks and carried them on their shoulders, particularly if it was muddy; then, tucking their trousers up above their knees, they splashed fearlessly through the puddles. When they saw a village they turned off the high road and, going up to any house which seemed a little better looking than the rest, stood in a row before the windows and began singing a chant at the top of their voices. The master of the house, some old Cossack villager, would listen to them for a long time, his head propped on his hands, then he would sob bitterly and say, turning to his wife : "Wife! What the scholars are singing must be very deep; bring them fat bacon and anything else that we have." And a whole bowl of dumplings was emptied into the sack, a good sized piece of bacon, several flat loaves, and sometimes a trussed hen would go into it too. Fortified with such stores, the grammarians, rhetoricians, philosophers and theologians went on their way again. Their numbers lessened, however, the farther they went. Almost all wandered off towards their homes, and only those were left whose parental abodes were farther away.

Once, at the time of such a migration, three students turned off the high road in order to replenish their store of provisions at the first homestead they could find, for their sacks had long been empty. They were the theologian Halyava; the philosopher Homa Brut; and the rhetorician Tibery Gorobets.

The theologian was a well-grown, broad-shouldered fellow; he had an extremely odd habit—anything that lay within his reach he invariably stole. In other circumstances, he was of an excessively gloomy temper, and when he was drunk he used to hide in the rank grass, and the seminarists had a lot of trouble to find him there.

The philosopher, Homa Brut, was of a cheerful temper, he was very fond of lying on his back, smoking a pipe; when he was drinking he always engaged musicians and danced the trepak. He often had a taste of the "peck of peas", but took it with perfect philosophical indifference, saying that there is no escaping what has to be. The rhetorician, Tibery Gorobets, had not yet the right to wear a moustache, to drink vodka, and to smoke a pipe. He only wore a curl round his ear, and so his character was as yet hardly formed; but, judging from the big bumps on the forehead, with which he often appeared in class, it might be presumed that he would make a good fighter. The theologian, Halyava, and the philosopher, Homa, often pulled him by the forelock as a sign of their favour, and employed him as their messenger.

It was evening when they turned off the high road; the sun had only just set and the warmth of the day still lingered in the air. The theologian and the philosopher walked along in silence smoking their pipes; the rhetorician, Tibery Gorobets, kept knocking off the heads of the wayside thistles with his stick. The road ran between scattered groups of oak and nut trees standing here and there in the meadows. Sloping uplands and little hills, green and round as cupolas, were interspersed here and there about the plain. The cornfields of ripening wheat, which came into view in two places, showed that some village must soon be seen. It was more than an hour, however, since they had passed the cornfields, yet they had come upon no dwelling. The sky was now completely wrapped in darkness, and only in the west there was a pale streak left of the glow of sunset.

"What the devil does it mean?" said the philosopher, Homa Brut. "It looked as though there must be a village in a minute."

The theologian did not speak, he gazed at the surrounding country, then put his pipe back in his mouth, and they continued on their way.

"Upon my soul!" the philosopher said, stopping again, "not a devil's fist to be seen."

"Maybe some village will turn up farther on," said the theologian, not removing his pipe.

But meantime night had come on, and a rather dark night. Small storm-clouds increased the gloom, and by every token they could expect neither stars nor moon. The students noticed that they had lost their way and for a long time had been walking off the road.

The philosopher, after feeling about with his feet in all directions, said at last, abruptly: "I say, where's the road?"

The theologian did not speak for a while, then after pondering, he brought out: "Yes, it is a dark night."

The rhetorician walked off to one side and tried on his hands and knees to feel for the road, but his hands came upon nothing but foxes' holes. On all sides of them there was the steppe, which, it seemed, no one had ever crossed.

The travellers made another effort to press on a little, but there was the same wilderness in all directions. The philosopher tried shouting, but his voice seemed completely lost on the steppe, and met with no reply. All they heard was, a little afterwards, a faint moaning like the howl of a wolf.

"I say, what's to be done?" said the philosopher.

"Why, halt and sleep in the open!" said the theologian, and he felt in his pocket for flint and tinder to light his pipe again. But the philosopher could not agree to this: it was always his habit at night to put away a quartern loaf of bread and four pounds of fat bacon, and he was conscious on this occasion of an insufferable sense of loneliness in his stomach. Besides, in spite of his cheerful temper, the philosopher was rather afraid of wolves.

"No, Halyava, we can't," he said. "What, stretch out and lie down like a dog, without a bite or a sup of anything? Let's make another try for it; maybe we shall stumble on some dwelling-place and get at least a drink of vodka for supper."

At the word "vodka" the theologian spat to one side, and brought out: "Well, of course, it's no use staying in the open."

The students walked on, and to their intense delight caught the sound of barking in the distance. Listening which way it came from, they walked on more boldly and a little later saw a light.

"A village! It really is a village!" said the philosopher.

He was not mistaken in his supposition; in a little while they actually saw a little homestead consisting of only two cottages looking into the same farmyard. There was a light in the windows; a dozen plum trees stood up by the fence. Looking through the cracks in the paling-gate the students saw a yard filled with carriers' wagons. Stars peeped out here and there in the sky at the moment.

"Look, mates, don't let's be put off! We must get a night's lodging somehow!"

The three learned gentlemen banged on the gate with one accord and shouted, "Open!"

The door of one of the cottages creaked, and a minute later they saw before them an old woman in sheepskin.

"Who is there?" she cried, with a hollow cough.

"Give us a night's lodging, granny; we have lost our way; a night in the open is as bad as a hungry belly."

"What manner of folks may you be?"

"Oh, harmless folks: Halyava, a theologian; Brut, a philosopher; and Gorobets, a rhetorician."

"I can't," grumbled the old woman. "The yard is crowded with folk and every corner in the cottage is full. Where am I to put you? And such great hulking fellows, too! Why, it would knock my cottage to pieces if I put such fellows in it. I know these philosophers and theologians; if one began taking in these drunken fellows, there'd soon be no home left. Be off, be off! There's no place for you here!"

"Have pity on us, granny! How can you let Christian souls perish for no rhyme or reason? Put us where you please; and if we do aught amiss or anything else, may our arms be withered, and God only knows what befall us—so there!"

The old woman seemed somewhat softened.

"Very well," she said, as though reconsidering, "I'll let you in, but I'll put you all in different places; for my mind won't be at rest if you are all together."

"That's as you please; we'll make no objection," answered the students.

The gate creaked and they went into the yard.

"Well, granny," said the philosopher, following the old woman, "how would it be, as they say ... upon my soul I feel as though somebody were driving a cart in my stomach : not a morsel has passed my lips all day."

"What next will he want!" said the old woman. "No, I've nothing to give you, and the oven's not been heated today."

"But we'd pay for it all," the philosopher went on, "tomorrow morning, in hard cash. Yes!" he added in an undertone, "the devil a bit you'll get!"

"Go in, go in! and you must be satisfied with what you're given. Fine young gentlemen the devil has brought us!"

Homa the philosopher was thrown into utter dejection by these words; but his nose was suddenly aware of the odour of dried fish; he glanced towards the trousers of the theologian who was walking at his side, and saw a huge fish tail sticking out of his pocket. The theologian had already succeeded in filching a whole carp from a wagon. And as he had done this from no interested motive but simply from habit, and, quite forgetting his carp, was already looking about for anything else he could carry off, having no mind to miss even a broken wheel, the philosopher slipped his hand into his friend's pocket, as though it were his own, and pulled out the carp.

The old woman put the students in their several places : the rhetorician she kept in the cottage, the theologian she locked in an empty closet, the philosopher she assigned a sheep's pen, also empty.

The latter, on finding himself alone, instantly devoured the carp, examined the hurdle-walls of the pen, kicked an inquisitive pig that woke up and thrust its snout in from the next pen, and turned over on his right side to fall into a sound sleep. All at once the low door opened, and the old woman bending down stepped into the pen.

"What is it, granny, what do you want?" said the philosopher.

But the old woman came towards him with oustretched arms.

"Aha, ha!" thought the philosopher. "No, my dear, you are too old!"

He turned a little away, but the old woman unceremoniously approached him again.

"Listen, granny!" said the philosopher. "It's a fast time now; and I am a man who wouldn't sin in a fast for a thousand golden pieces."

But the old woman opened her arms and tried to catch him without saying a word.

The philosopher was frightened, especially when he noticed a strange glitter in her eyes. "Granny, what is it? Go—go away—God bless you!" he cried.

The old woman said not a word, but tried to clutch him in her arms.

He leapt on to his feet, intending to escape; but the old woman stood in the doorway, fixed her glittering eyes on him and again began approaching him.

The philosopher tried to push her back with his hands, but to his surprise found that his arms would not rise, his legs would not move, and he perceived with horror that even his voice would not obey him; words hovered on his lips without a sound. He heard nothing but the beating of his heart. He saw the old woman approach him. She folded his arms, bent his head down, leapt with the swiftness of a cat upon his back, and struck him with a broom on the side; and he, prancing like a horse, carried her on his shoulders. All this happened so quickly that the philisopher scarcely knew what he was doing. He clutched his knees in both hands, trying to stop his legs from moving, but to his extreme amazement they were lifted against his will and executed capers more swiftly than a Circassian racer. Only when they had left the farm, and the wide plain lay stretched before them with a forest black as coal on one side, he said to himself: "Aha! she's a witch!"

The waning crescent of the moon was shining in the sky. The timid radiance of midnight lay mistily over the earth, light as a transparent veil. The forests, the meadows, the sky, the dales, all seemed as though slumbering with open eyes; not a breeze fluttered anywhere; there was a damp warmth in the freshness of the night; the shadows of the trees and bushes fell on the sloping plain in pointed wedge shapes like comets. Such was the night when Homa Brut, the philosopher, set off galloping with a mysterious rider on his back. He was aware of an exhausting, unpleasant, and at the same time, voluptuous sensation assailing his heart. He bent his head and saw that the grass which had been almost under his feet seemed growing at a depth far away, and that above it there lay water, transparent as a mountain stream, and the grass seemed to be at the bottom of a clear sea, limpid to its very depths; anyway, he saw clearly in it his own reflection with the old woman sitting on his back. He saw shining there a sun instead of the moon; he heard the bluebells ringing as they bent their little heads; he saw a water-nymph float out from behind the reeds, there was the gleam of her leg and back, rounded and supple, all brightness and shimmering. She turned towards him and now her face came nearer, with eyes clear, sparkling, keen, with singing that pierced to the heart; now it was on the surface, and shaking with sparkling laughter it moved away; and now she turned on her back, and her cloud-like breasts, dead white like unglazed china, gleamed in the sun at the edges of their white, soft and supple roundness. Little bubbles of water like beads bedewed them. She was all quivering and laughing in the water. . . .

Did he see this or did he not? Was he awake or dreaming? But what was that? The wind or music? It is ringing and ringing and eddying and coming closer and piercing to his heart with an insufferable thrill. . . .

"What does it mean?" the philosopher wondered, looking down as he flew along, full speed. The sweat was streaming from him. He was aware of a fiendishly voluptuous feeling, he felt a stabbing, exhaustingly terrible delight. It often seemed to him as though his heart had melted away, and with terror he clutched at it. Worn out, desperate, he began trying to recall all the prayers he knew. He went through all the exorcisms against evil spirits, and all at once felt somewhat refreshed; he felt that his step was growing slower, the witch's hold upon his back seemed feebler, thick grass touched him, and now he saw nothing extraordinary in it. The clear, crescent moon was shining in the sky.

"Good!" the philosopher Homa thought to himself, and he began repeating the exorcisms almost aloud. At last, quick as lightning, he sprang from under the old woman and in his turn leapt on her back. The old woman, with a tiny tripping step, ran so fast that her rider could scarcely breathe. The earth flashed by under him; everything was clear in the moonlight, though the moon was not full; the ground was smooth, but everything flashed by so rapidly that it was confused and indistinct. He snatched up a piece of wood that lay on the road and began whacking the old woman with all his might. She uttered wild howls; at first they were angry and menacing, then they grew fainter, sweeter, clearer, then rang out gently like delicate silver bells that stabbed him to the heart; and the thought flashed through his mind : was it really an old woman?

"Oh, I can do no more!" she murmured, and sank exhausted on the ground.

He stood up and looked into her face (there was the glow of sunrise, and the golden domes of the Kiev churches were gleaming in the distance) : before him lay a lovely creature with luxuriant tresses all in disorder and eyelashes as long as arrows. Senseless she tossed her bare white arms and moaned, looking upwards with eyes full of tears.

Homa trembled like a leaf on a tree; he was overcome by pity and a strange emotion and timidity, feelings he could not himself explain. He set off running, full speed. His heart throbbed uneasily as he went, and he could not account for the strange new feeling that had taken possession of it. He did not want to go back to the farm; he hastened to Kiev, pondering all the way on this incomprehensive adventure.

There was scarcely a student left in the town. All had dispersed about the countryside, either to situations, or simply without them; because in the villages of Little Russia they could get dumplings, cheese, sour cream, and puddings as big as a hat without paying a kopeck for them. The big rambling house in which the students were lodged was absolutely empty, and although the philosopher rummaged in every corner, and even felt in all the holes and cracks in the roof, he could not find a bit of bacon or even a stale roll such as were commonly hidden there by the students.

The philosopher, however, soon found means to improve his lot : he walked whistling three times through the market, finally winked at a young widow in a yellow bonnet who was selling ribbons, shot and wheels—and was that very day regaled with wheat dumplings, a chicken . . . in short, there is no telling what was on the table laid for him in a little mud house in the middle of a cherry orchard.

That same evening the philosopher was seen in a tavern : he was lying on the bench, smoking a pipe as his habit was, and in the sight of all he flung the Jew who kept the house a gold coin. A mug stood before him. He looked at all that came in and went out with eyes full of cool satisfaction, and thought no more of his extraordinary adventure.

Meanwhile rumours were circulating everywhere that the daughter of one of the richest Cossack *sotniks** who lived nearly forty miles from Kiev, had returned one day from a walk, terribly injured, hardly able to crawl home to her father's house, was lying at the point of death, and had expressed a wish that one of the Kiev seminarists, Homa Brut, should read the prayers over her and the psalms for three days after her death. The philosopher heard of this from the rector himself, who summoned him to his room and informed him that he was to set off on the journey without any

* An officer in command of a company of Cossacks.

delay, that the noble *sotnik* had sent servants and a carriage to fetch him.

The philosopher shuddered from an unaccountable feeling which he could not have explained to himself. A dark presentiment told him that something evil was awaiting him. Without knowing why, he bluntly declared that he would not go.

"Listen, Domine Homa!" said the rector. (On some occasions he expressed himself very courteously with those under his authority.) "Who the devil is asking you whether you want to go or not? All I have to tell you is that if you go on jibbing and making difficulties, I'll order you such a whacking with a young birch tree, on your back and the rest of you, that there will be no need for you to go to the bath after."

The philosopher, scratching behind his ear, went out without uttering a word, proposing at the first suitable opportunity to put his trust in his heels. Plunged in thought he went down the steep staircase that led into a yard shut in by poplars, and stood still for a minute, hearing quite distinctly the voice of the rector giving orders to his butler and someone else—probably one of the servants sent to fetch him by the *sotnik*.

"Thank his honour for the grain and the eggs," the rector was saying: "and tell him that as soon as the books about which he writes are ready I will send them at once. I have already given them to a scribe to be copied, and don't forget, my good man, to mention to his honour that I know there are excellent fish at his place, especially sturgeon, and he might on occasion send some; here in the market it's bad and dear. And you, Yavtuh, give the young fellows a cup of vodka each, and bind the philosopher or he'll be off directly."

"There, the devil's son!" the philosopher thought to himself. "He scented it out, the wily long-legs!" He went down and saw a covered chaise, which he almost took at first for a baker's oven on wheels. It was, indeed, as deep as the oven in which bricks are baked. It was only the ordinary Cracow carriage in which Jews travel fifty together with their wares to all the towns where they smell out a fair. Six healthy and stalwart Cossacks, no longer young, were waiting for him. Their tunics of fine cloth, with tassels, showed that they belonged to a rather important and wealthy master; some small scars proved that they had at some time been in battle, not ingloriously.

"What's to be done? What is to be must be!" the philosopher

thought to himself, and turning to the Cossacks, he said aloud :
"Good day to you, comrades!"

"Good health to you, master philosopher," some of the Cossacks
replied.

"So I am to get in with you? It's a goodly chaise!" he went on,
as he clambered in, "we need only hire some musicians and we
might dance here."

"Yes, it's a carriage of ample proportions," said one of the Cossacks, seating himself on the box beside the coachman, who had
tied a rag over his head to replace the cap which he had managed
to leave behind at a pot-house. The other five and the philosopher
crawled into the recesses of the chaise and settled themselves on
sacks filled with various purchases they had made in the town. "It
would be interesting to know," said the philosopher, "if this chaise
were loaded up with goods of some sort, salt for instance, or iron
wedges, how many horses would be needed then?"

"Yes," the Cossack, sitting on the box, said after a pause, "it
would need a sufficient number of horses."

After this satisfactory reply the Cossack thought himself entitled
to hold his tongue for the remainder of the journey.

The philosopher was extremely desirous of learning more in
detail, who this *sotnik* was, what he was like, what had been heard
about his daughter who in such a strange way returned home and
was found on the point of death, and whose story was now connected with his own, what was being done in the house, and how
things were there. He addressed the Cossacks with inquiries, but no
doubt they too were philosophers, for by way of a reply they remained silent, smoking their pipes and lying on their backs. Only
one of them turned to the driver on the box with a brief order.
"Mind, Overko, you old booby, when you are near the tavern on
the Tchuhraylovo road, don't forget to stop and wake me and the
other chaps, if any should chance to drop asleep."

After this he fell asleep rather audibly. These instructions were,
however, quite unnecessary, for as soon as the gigantic chaise drew
near the pot-house, all the Cossacks with one voice shouted :
"Stop!" Moreover, Overko's horses were already trained to stop of
themselves at every pot-house.

In spite of the hot July day, they all got out of the chaise and
went into the low-pitched dirty room, where the Jew who kept the
house hastened to receive his old friends with every sign of delight.
The Jew brought from under the skirt of his coat some ham saus-

ages, and, putting them on the table, turned his back at once on this food forbidden by the Talmud. All the Cossacks sat down round the table; earthenware mugs were set for each of the guests. Homa had to take part in the general festivity, and, as Little Russians infallibly begin kissing each other or weeping when they are drunk, soon the whole room resounded with smacks. "I say, Spirid, a kiss." "Come here, Dorosh, I want to embrace you!"

One Cossack with grey moustaches, a little older than the rest, propped his cheek on his hand and began sobbing bitterly at the thought that he had no father nor mother and was all alone in the world. Another one, much given to moralizing, persisted in consoling him, saying: "Don't cry; upon my soul, don't cry! What is there in it...? The Lord knows best, you know."

The one whose name was Dorosh became extremely inquisitive, and turning to the philosopher Homa, kept asking him: "I should like to know what they teach you in the college. Is it the same as what the deacon reads in church, or something different?"

"Don't ask!" the sermonizing Cossack said emphatically: "let it be as it is, God knows what is wanted, God knows everything."

"No, I want to know," said Dorosh, "what is written there in those books? Maybe it is quite different from what the deacon reads."

"Oh my goodness, my goodness!" said the sermonizing worthy, "and why say such a thing, it's as the Lord wills. There is no changing what the Lord has willed!"

"I want to know all that's written. I'll go to college, upon my word, I will. Do you suppose I can't learn, I'll learn it all, all!"

"Oh my goodness...!" said the sermonizing Cossack, and he dropped his head on the table, because he was utterly incapable of supporting it any longer on his shoulders. The other Cossacks were discussing their masters and the question why the moon shone in the sky. The philosopher, seeing the state of their minds, resolved to seize his opportunity and make his escape. To begin with he turned to the grey-headed Cossack who was grieving for his father and mother.

"Why are you blubbering, uncle?" he said, "I am an orphan myself! Let me go in freedom, lads! What do you want with me?"

"Let him go!" several responded, "why, he is an orphan, let him go where he likes."

"Oh my goodness, my goodness!" the moralizing Cossack articulated, lifting his head. "Let him go!"

"Let him go where he likes!"

And the Cossacks meant to lead him out into the open air themselves, but the one who had displayed his curiosity stopped them,
saying : "Don't touch him. I want to talk to him about college : I
am going to college myself. . . ."

It is doubtful, however, whether the escape could have taken
place, for when the philosopher tried to get up from the table his
legs seemed to have become wooden, and he began to perceive such
a number of doors in the room that he could hardly discover the
real one.

It was evening before the Cossacks bethought themselves that
they had farther to go. Clambering into the chaise, they trailed
along the road, urging on the horses and singing a song of which
nobody could have made out the words or the sense. After trundling
on for the greater part of the night, continually straying off the
road, though they knew every inch of the way, they drove at last
down a steep hill into a valley, and the philosopher noticed a paling
or hurdle that ran alongside, low trees and roofs peeping out behind
it. This was a big village belonging to the *sotnik*. By now it was
long past midnight; the sky was dark, but there were little stars
twinkling here and there. No light was to be seen in a single cottage. To the accompaniment of the barking of dogs, they drove
into the courtyard. Thatched barns and little houses came into sight
on both sides; one of the latter, which stood exactly in the middle
opposite the gates, was larger than the others, and was apparently
the *sotnik's* residence. The chaise drew up before a little shed that
did duty for a barn, and our travellers went off to bed. The
philosopher, however, wanted to inspect the outside of the *sotnik's*
house; but though he stared his hardest, nothing could be seen
distinctly; the house looked to him like a bear; the chimney turned
into the rector. The philosopher gave it up and went to sleep.

When he woke up, the whole house was in commotion : the
sotnik's daughter had died in the night. Servants were running
hurriedly to and fro; some old women were crying; an inquisitive
crowd was looking through the fence at the house, as though something might be seen there. The philosopher began examining at his
leisure the objects he could not make out in the night. The *sotnik's*
house was a little, low-pitched building, such as was usual in Little
Russia in old days; its roof was of thatch; a small, high, pointed
gable with a little window that looked like an eye turned upwards,
was painted in blue and yellow flowers and red crescents; it was

supported on oak posts rounded above and hexagonal below, with carving at the top. Under this gable was a little porch with seats on each side. There were verandahs round the house resting on similar posts, some of them carved in spirals. A tall pyramid pear tree, with trembling leaves, made a patch of green in front of the house. Two rows of barns for storing grain in the middle of the yard, formed a sort of wide street leading to the house. Beyond the barns, close to the gate, stood facing each other two three-cornered storehouses, also thatched. Each triangular wall was painted in various designs and had a little door in it. On one of them was depicted a Cossack sitting on a barrel, holding a mug above his head with the inscription : "I'll drink it all !" On the other, there was a bottle, flagons, and at the sides, by way of ornament, a horse upside down, a pipe, a tambourine, and the inscription : "Wine is the Cossack's comfort !" A drum and brass trumpets could be seen through the huge window in the loft of one of the barns. At the gates stood two cannons. Everything showed that the master of the house was fond of merry-making, and that the yard often resounded with the shouts of revellers. There were two windmills outside the gate. Behind the house stretched gardens, and through the tree-tops the dark caps of chimneys were all that could be seen of cottages smothered in green bushes. The whole village lay on the broad sloping side of a hill. The steep side, at the very foot of which lay the courtyard, made a screen from the north. Looked at from below, it seemed even steeper, and here and there on its tall top uneven stalks of rough grass stood up black against the clear sky; its bare aspect was somehow depressing; its clay soil was hollowed out by the fall and trickle of rain. Two cottages stood at some distance from each other on its steep slope; one of them was overshadowed by the branches of a spreading apple tree, banked up with soil and supported by short stakes near the root. The apples knocked down by the wind, were falling right into the master's courtyard. The road, coiling about the hill from the very top, ran down beside the courtyard to the village. When the philosopher scanned its terrific steepness and recalled their journey down it the previous night, he came to the conclusion that either the *sotnik* had very clever horses or that the Cossacks had very strong heads to have managed, even when drunk, to escape flying head over heels with the immense chaise and baggage. The philosopher was standing on the very highest point in the yard. When he turned and looked in the opposite direction he saw quite a different view. The village sloped away into a plain.

Meadows stretched as far as the eye could see; their brilliant verdure was deeper in the distance, and whole rows of villages looked
like dark patches in it, though they must have been more than
fifteen miles away. On the right of the meadowlands was a line of
hills, and a hardly perceptible streak of flashing light and darkness
showed where the Dnieper ran.

"Ah, a splendid spot!" said the philosopher, "this would be the
place to live, fishing in the Dnieper and the ponds, bird-catching
with nets, or shooting king-snipe and little bustard. Though I do
believe there would be a few great bustards too in those meadows!
One could dry lots of fruit, too, and sell it in the town, or, better
still, make vodka of it, and there's no drink to compare with fruit-
vodka. But it would be just as well to consider how to slip away
from here."

He noticed outside the fence a little path completely overgrown
with weeds; he was mechanically setting his foot on it with the idea
of simply going first out for a walk, and then stealthily passing
between the cottages and dashing out into the open country, when
he suddenly felt a rather strong hand on his shoulder.

Behind him stood the old Cossack who had on the previous
evening so bitterly bewailed the death of his father and mother
and his own solitary state.

"It's no good you thinking of making off, Mr. Philosopher!" he
said: "this isn't the sort of establishment you can run away from;
and the roads are bad, too, for anyone on foot; you had better
come to the master: he's been expecting you this long time in the
parlour."

"Let us go! To be sure ... I'm delighted," said the philosopher,
and he followed the Cossack.

The *sotnik,* an elderly man with grey moustaches and an expression of gloomy sadness, was sitting at a table in the parlour, his
head propped on his hands. He was about fifty; but the deep
despondency on his face and its wan pallor showed that his soul
had been crushed and shattered at one blow, and all his old gaiety
and noisy merrymaking had gone for ever. When Homa went in
with the old Cossack, he removed one hand from his face and gave
a slight nod in response to their low bows.

Homa and the Cossack stood respectfully at the door.

"Who are you, where do you come from, and what is your calling, good man?" said the *sotnik,* in a voice neither friendly nor
ill-humoured.

"A bursar, student in philosophy, Homa Brut. . . ."

"Who was your father?"

"I don't know, honoured sir."

"Your mother?"

"I don't know my mother either. It is reasonable to suppose, of course, that I had a mother; but who she was and where she came from, and when she lived—upon my soul, good sir, I don't know."

The old man paused and seemed to sink into a reverie for a minute.

"How did you come to know my daughter?"

"I didn't know her, honoured sir, upon my word, I didn't. I have never had anything to do with young ladies, never in my life. Bless them, saving your presence!"

"Why did she fix on you and no other to read the psalms over her?"

The philosopher shrugged his shoulders. "God knows how to make that out. It's a well-known thing, the gentry are for ever taking fancies that the most learned man couldn't explain, and the proverb says: 'The devil himself must dance at the master's bidding'."

"Are you telling the truth, philosopher?"

"May I be struck down by thunder on the spot if I'm not."

"If you had but lived one brief moment longer," the *sotnik* said to himself mournfully, "I should have learned all about it. 'Let no one else read over me, but send, father, at once to Kiev Seminary and fetch the bursar, Homa Brut; let him pray three nights for my sinful soul. He knows . . . !' But what he knows, I did not hear; she, poor darling, could say no more before she died. You, good man, are no doubt well known for your holy life and pious works, and she, maybe, heard tell of you."

"Who? I?" said the philosopher, stepping back in amazement. "I —holy life!" he articulated, looking straight in the *sotnik's* face. "God be with you, sir? What are you talking about! Why—though it's not a seemly thing to speak of—I paid the baker's wife a visit on Maundy Thursday."

"Well . . . I suppose there must be some reason for fixing on you. You must begin your duties this very day."

"As to that, I would tell your honour . . . Of course, any man versed in holy scriptures may, as far as in him lies . . . but a deacon or a sacristan would be better fitted for it. They are men of understanding, and know how it is all done; while I . . . Besides I haven't the right voice for it, and I myself am good for nothing. I'm not the figure for it."

"Well, say what you like. I shall carry out all my darling's wishes, I will spare nothing. And if for three nights from today you duly recite the prayers over her, I will reward you, if not . . . I don't advise the devil himself to anger me."

The last words were uttered by the *sotnik* so vigorously that the philosopher fully grasped their significance.

"Follow me!" said the *sotnik*.

They went out into the hall. The *sotnik* opened the door into another room, opposite the first. The philosopher paused a minute in the hall to blow his nose and crossed the threshold with unaccountable apprehension.

The whole floor was covered with red cotton stuff. On a high table in the corner under the holy images lay the body of the dead girl on a coverlet of dark blue velvet adorned with gold fringe and tassels. Tall wax candles, entwined with sprigs of guelder rose, stood at her feet and head, shedding a dim light that was lost in the brightness of daylight. The dead girl's face was hidden from him by the inconsolable father, who sat down facing her with his back to the door. The philosopher was impressed by the words he heard :

"I am grieving, my dearly beloved daughter, not that in the flower of your age you have left the earth, to my sorrow and mourning, without living your allotted span; I grieve, my darling, that I know not him, my bitter foe, who was the cause of your death. And if I knew the man who could but dream of hurting you, or even saying anything unkind of you, I swear to God he should not see his children again, if he be as old as I, nor his father and mother, if he be of that time of life, and his body should be cast out to be devoured by the birds and beasts of the steppe ! But my grief it is, my wild marigold, my birdie, light of my eyes, that I must live out my days without comfort, wiping with the skirt of my coat the trickling tears that flow from my old eyes, while my enemy will be making merry and secretly mocking at the feeble old man. . . ."

He came to a standstill, due to an outburst of sorrow, which found vent in a flood of tears.

The philosopher was touched by such inconsolable sadness; he coughed, uttering a hollow sound in the effort to clear his throat. The *sotnik* turned round and pointed him to a place at the dead girl's head, before a small lectern with books on it.

"I shall get through three nights somehow," thought the philosopher : "and the old man will stuff my pockets with gold pieces for it."

He drew near, and, clearing his throat once more, began reading, paying no attention to anything else and not venturing to glance at the face of the dead girl. A profound stillness reigned in the apartment. He noticed that the *sotnik* had withdrawn. Slowly he turned his head to look at the dead, and . . .

A shudder ran through his veins : before him lay a beauty whose like had surely never been on earth before. Never, it seemed, could features have been formed in such striking yet harmonious beauty. She lay as though living : the lovely forehead, fair as snow, as silver, looked deep in thought; the even brows—dark as night in the midst of sunshine—rose proudly above the closed eyes; the eyelashes, that fell like arrows on the cheeks, glowed with the warmth of secret desires; the lips were rubies, ready to break into the laugh of bliss, the flood of joy. . . . But in them, in those very features, he saw something terrible and poignant. He felt a sickening ache stirring in his heart, as though, in the midst of a whirl of gaiety and dancing crowds, someone had begun singing a funeral dirge. The rubies of her lips looked like blood surging up from her heart. All at once he was aware of something dreadfully familiar in her face. "The witch!" he cried in a voice not his own, as, turning pale, he looked away and fell to repeating his prayers. It was the witch that he had killed!

When the sun was setting, they carried the corpse to the church. The philosopher supported the coffin swathed in black on his shoulder, and felt something cold as ice on it. The *sotnik* walked in front, with his hand on the right side of the dead girl's narrow resting home. The wooden church, blackened by age and overgrown with green lichen, stood disconsolately, with its three cone-shaped domes, at the very end of the village. It was evident that no service had been performed in it for a long time. Candles had been lighted before almost every image. The coffin was set down in the centre opposite the altar. The old *sotnik* kissed the dead girl once more, bowed to the ground, and went out together with the coffin-bearers, giving orders that the philosopher should have a good supper and then be taken to the church. On reaching the kitchen all the men who had carried the coffin began putting their hands on the stove, as the custom is with Little Russians, after seeing a dead body.

The hunger, of which the philosopher began at that moment to be conscious, made him for some minutes entirely oblivious of the dead girl. Soon all the servants began gradually assembling in the kitchen, which in the *sotnik's* house was something like a club, where all the inhabitants of the yard gathered together, including even the dogs, who, wagging their tails, came to the door for bones and slops. Wherever anybody might be sent, and with whatever duty he might be charged, he always went first to the kitchen to rest for at least a minute on the bench and smoke a pipe. All the unmarried men in their smart Cossack tunics lay there almost all day long, on the bench, under the bench, or on the stove—anywhere, in fact, where a comfortable place could be found to lie on. Then everybody invariably left behind in the kitchen either his can or a whip to keep stray dogs off or some such thing. But the biggest crowd always gathered at supper-time, when the drover who had brought the cows in to be milked, and all the others who were not to be seen during the day, came in. At supper, even the moist taciturn tongues were moved to loquacity. It was then that all the news was talked over : who had got himself new breeches, and what was hidden in the bowels of the earth, and who had seen a wolf. There were witty talkers among them; indeed, there is no lack of them anywhere among the Little Russians.

The philosopher sat down with the rest in a big circle in the open air before the kitchen door. Soon a peasant woman in a red bonnet popped out, holding in both hands a steaming bowl of dumplings, which she set down in their midst. Each pulled out a wooden spoon from his pocket, or for lack of a spoon, a wooden stick. As soon as their jaws began moving more slowly, and the wolfish hunger of the whole party was somewhat assuaged, many of them began talking. The conversation naturally turned on the dead maiden.

"Is it true," said a young shepherd who had put so many buttons and copper discs on the leather strap on which his pipe hung that he looked like a small haberdasher's shop, "is it true that the young lady, saving your presence, was on friendly terms with the Evil one?"

"Who? The young mistress?" said Dorosh, a man our philosopher already knew, "why, she was a regular witch ! I'll take my oath she was a witch !"

"Hush, hush, Dorosh," said another man, who had shown a great disposition to soothe the others on the journey, "that's no business of ours, God bless it ! It's no good talking about it."

But Dorosh was not at all inclined to hold his tongue; he had just been to the cellar on some job with the butler, and, having applied his lips to two or three barrels, he had come out extremely merry and talked away without ceasing.

"What do you want? Me to be quiet?" he said, "why, I've been ridden by her myself! Upon my soul, I have!"

"Tell us, uncle," said the young shepherd with the buttons, "are there signs by which you can tell a witch?"

"No, you can't," answered Dorosh, "there's no way of telling : you might read through all the psalm-books and you couldn't tell."

"Yes, you can, Dorosh, you can; don't say that," the former comforter objected; "it's with good purpose God has given every creature its peculiar habit; folks that have studied say that a witch has a little tail."

"When a woman's old, she's a witch," the grey-haired Cossack said coolly.

"Oh! you're a nice set!" retorted the peasant woman, who was at that instant pouring a fresh lot of dumplings into the empty pot; "regular fat hogs!"

The old Cossack, whose name was Yavtuh and nickname Kovtun, gave a smile of satisfaction seeing that his words had cut the old woman to the quick; while the herdsman gave vent to a guffaw, like the bellowing of two bulls as they stand facing each other.

The beginning of the conversation had aroused the philosopher's curiosity and made him intensely anxious to learn more details about the *sotnik's* daughter, and so, wishing to bring the talk back to that subject, he turned to his neighbour with the words : "I should like to ask why all the folk sitting at supper here look upon the young mistress as a witch? Did she do a mischief to anybody or bring anybody to harm?"

"There were all sorts of doings," answered one of the company, a man with a flat face strikingly resembling a spade. "Everybody remembers the dog-boy Mikita and the..."

"What about the dog-boy Mikita?" said Dorosh.

"I'll tell about him," said the drover, "for he was a great crony of mine."

"I'll tell about Mikita," said Spirid.

"Let him, let Spirid tell it!" shouted the company.

Spirid began : "You don't know Mikita, Mr. Philosopher Homa. Ah, he was a man! He knew every dog as well as he knew his own father. The dog-boy we've got now, Mikola, who's sitting next but one from me, isn't worth the sole of his shoe. Though he knows his job, too, but beside the other he's trash, slops."

"You tell the story well, very well!" said Dorosh, nodding his head approvingly.

Spirid went on: "He'd see a hare quicker than you'd wipe the snuff from your nose. He'd whistle: 'Here, Breaker! here, Swift-foot!' and he in full gallop on his horse; and there was no saying which would outrace the other, he the dog, or the dog him. He'd toss off a mug of vodka without winking. He was a fine dog-boy! Only a little time back he began to be always staring at the young mistress. Whether he had fallen in love with her, or whether she had simply bewitched him, anyway the man was done for, he went fairly silly; the devil only knows what he turned into... pfoo! No decent word for it....'

"That's good," said Dorosh.

"As soon as the young mistress looks at him, he drops the bridle out of his hand, calls Breaker Bushybrow, is all of a fluster and doesn't know what he's doing. One day the young mistress comes into the stable where he is rubbing down a horse.

" 'I say, Mikita,' says she, 'let me put my foot on you.' And he, silly fellow, is pleased at that. 'Not your foot only,' says he, 'you may sit on me altogether.' The young mistress lifted her foot, and as he saw her bare, plump, white leg, he went fairly crazy, so he said. He bent his back, silly fellow, and clasping her bare leg in his hands, ran galloping like a horse all over the countryside. And he couldn't say where he was driven, but he came back more dead than alive, and from that time he withered up like a chip of wood; and one day when they went into the stable, instead of him they found a heap of ashes lying there and an empty pail; he had burnt up entirely, burnt up of himself. And he was a dog-boy such as you couldn't find another all the world over."

When Spirid had finished his story, reflections upon the rare qualities of the deceased dog-boy followed from all sides.

"And haven't you heard tell of Sheptun's wife?" said Dorosh, addressing Homa.

"No."

"Well, well! You are not taught with too much sense, it seems, in the seminary. Listen, then. There's a Cossack called Sheptun in our village—a good Cossack! He is given to stealing at times, and telling lies when there's no occasion, but... he's a good Cossack. His cottage is not so far from here. Just about the very hour that we sat down this evening to table, Sheptun and his wife finished their supper and lay down to sleep, and as it was fine weather, his wife lay down in the yard, and Sheptun in the cottage on the bench; or no ... it was the wife lay indoors on the bench and Sheptun in the yard...."

"Not on the bench, she was lying on the floor," put in a peasant woman, who stood in the doorway with her cheek propped in her hand.

Dorosh looked at her, then looked down, then looked at her again, and after a brief pause, said: "When I strip off your petticoat before everybody, you won't be pleased."

This warning had its effect; the old woman held her tongue and did not interrupt the story again.

Dorosh went on: "And in the cradle hanging in the middle of the cottage lay a baby a year old—whether of the male or female sex I can't say. Sheptun's wife was lying there when she heard a dog scratching at the door and howling fit to make you run out of the cottage. She was scared, for women are such foolish creatures that, if towards evening you put your tongue out at one from behind a door, her heart's in her mouth. However, she thought: 'Well, I'll go and give that damned dog a whack on its nose, and maybe it will stop howling,' and taking the oven-fork she went to open the door. She had hardly opened it when a dog dashed in between her legs and straight to the baby's cradle. She saw that it was no longer a dog but the young mistress, and if it had been the young lady in her own shape as she knew her, it would not have been so bad. But the peculiar thing is that she was all blue and her eyes glowing like coals. She snatched up the child, bit its throat, and began sucking its blood. Sheptun's wife could only scream: 'Oh, horror!' and rushed towards the door. But she sees the door's locked in the passage; she flies up to the loft and there she sits all of a shake, silly woman; and then she sees the young mistress coming up to her in the loft; she pounced on her, and began biting the silly woman. When Sheptun pulled his wife down from the loft in the morning she was bitten all over and had turned black and blue; and next day the silly woman died. So you see what uncanny and wicked doings happen in the world! Though it is of the gentry's breed, a witch is a witch."

After telling this story, Dorosh looked about him complacently and thrust his finger into his pipe, preparing to fill it with tobacco. The subject of the witch seemed inexhaustible. Each in turn hast-

ened to tell some tale of her. One had seen the witch in the form
of a haystack come right up to the door of his cottage; another had
had his cap or his pipe stolen by her; many of the girls in the
village had had their hair cut off by her; others had lost several
quarts of blood sucked by her.

At last the company pulled themselves together and saw that
they had been chattering too long, for it was quite dark in the yard.
They all began wandering off to their several sleeping places, which
were either in the kitchen, or the barns, or in the middle of the
courtyard.

"Well, Mr. Homa! Now it's time for us to go to the deceased
lady," said the grey-haired Cossack, addressing the philosopher;
and together with Spirid and Dorosh they set off to the church,
lashing with their whips at the dogs, of which there were a great
number in the road, and which gnawed at their sticks angrily.

Though the philosopher had managed to fortify himself with a
good mugful of vodka, he felt a fearfulness creeping stealthily over
him as they approached the lighted church. The stories and strange
tales he had heard helped to work upon his imagination. The darkness under the fence and trees grew less thick as they came into the
more open place. At last they went into the church enclosure and
found a little yard, beyond which there was not a tree to be seen,
nothing but open country and meadows swallowed up in the darkness of night. The three Cossacks and Homa mounted the steep
steps to the porch and went into the church. Here they left the
philosopher with the best wishes that he might carry out his duties
satisfactorily, and locked the door after them, as their master had
bidden them.

The philosopher was left alone. First he yawned, then he
stretched, then he blew into both hands, and at last he looked about
him. In the middle of the church stood the black coffin; candles
were gleaming under the dark images; the light from them only lit
up the ikon-stand and shed a faint glimmer in the middle of the
church; the distant corners were wrapped in darkness. The tall
old-fashioned ikon-stand showed traces of great antiquity; its carved
fretwork, once gilt, only glistened here and there with splashes of
gold; the gilt had peeled off in one place, and was completely
tarnished in another; the faces of the saints, blackened by age, had
a gloomy look. The philosopher looked round him again. "Well,"
he said, "what is there to be afraid of here? No living man can
come in here, and to guard me from the dead and ghosts from the

other world I have prayers that I have but to read aloud to keep them from laying a finger on me. It's all right!" he repeated with a wave of his hand, "let's read." Going up to the lectern he saw some bundles of candles. "That's good," thought the philosopher; "I must light up the whole church so that it may be as bright as by daylight. Oh, it is a pity that one must not smoke a pipe in the temple of God!"

And he proceeded to stick up wax candles at all the cornices, lecterns and images, not stinting them at all, and soon the whole church was flooded with light. Only overhead the darkness seemed somehow more profound, and the gloomy ikons looked even more sullenly out of their antique carved frames, which glistened here and there with specks of gilt. He went up to the coffin, looked timidly at the face of the dead—and could not help closing his eyelids with a faint shudder: such terrible, brilliant beauty!

He turned and tried to move away; but with the strange curiosity, the self-contradictory feeling, which dogs a man especially in times of terror, he could not, as he withdrew, resist taking another look. And then, after the same shudder, he looked again. The striking beauty of the dead maiden certainly seemed terrible. Possibly, indeed, she would have overwhelmed him with such panic fear if she had been a little less lovely. But there was in her features nothing faded, tarnished, dead; her face was living, and it seemed to the philosopher that she was looking at him with closed eyes. He even fancied that a tear was oozing from under her right eyelid, and when it rested on her cheek, he saw distinctly that it was a drop of blood.

He walked hastily away to the lectern, opened the book, and to give himself more confidence began reading in a very loud voice. His voice smote upon the wooden church walls, which had so long been deaf and silent; it rang out, forlorn, unechoed, in a deep bass in the absolutely dead stillness, and seemed somehow uncanny even to the reader himself. "What is there to be afraid of?" he was saying meanwhile to himself. "She won't rise up out of her coffin, for she will fear the word of God. Let her lie there! And a fine Cossack I am, if I should be scared. Well, I've drunk a drop too much— that's why it seems dreadful. I'll have a pinch of snuff. Ah, the good snuff! Fine snuff! good snuff!" However, as he turned over the pages, he kept taking sidelong glances at the coffin, and an involuntary feeling seemed whispering to him: "Look, look, she is going to get up! See, she'll sit up, she'll look out from the coffin!"

But the silence was deathlike; the coffin stood motionless; the candles shed a perfect flood of light. A church lighted up at night with a dead body in it and no living soul near is full of terror!

Raising his voice, he began singing in various keys, trying to drown the fears that still lurked in him, but every minute he turned his eyes to the coffin, as though asking, in spite of himself: "What if she does sit up, if she gets up?"

But the coffin did not stir. If there had but been some sound! some living creature! There was not so much as a cricket churring in the corner! There was nothing but the faint splutter of a faraway candle, the light tap of a drop of wax falling on the floor.

"What if she were to get up . . . ?"

She was raising her head. . . .

He looked at her wildly and rubbed eyes. She was, indeed, not lying down now, but sitting up in the coffin. He looked away, and again turned his eyes with horror on the coffin. She stood up . . . she was walking about the church with her eyes shut, moving her arms to and fro as though trying to catch someone.

She was coming straight towards him. In terror he drew a circle round him; with an effort he began reading the prayers and pronouncing the exorcisms which had been taught him by a monk who had all his life seen witches and evil spirits.

She stood almost on the very line; but it was clear that she had not the power to cross it, and she turned livid all over like one who has been dead for several days. Homa had not the courage to look at her; she was terrifying. She ground her teeth and opened her dead eyes; but, seeing nothing, turned with fury—that was apparent in her quivering face—in another direction, and flinging her arms, clutched in them each column and corner, trying to catch Homa. At last she stood still, holding up a menacing finger, and lay down again in her coffin.

The philosopher could not recover his self-possession, but kept gazing at the narrow dwelling-place of the witch. At last the coffin suddenly sprang up from its place and with a hissing sound began flying all over the church, zigzagging through the air in all directions.

The philosopher saw it almost over his head, but at the same time he saw that it could not cross the circle he had drawn, and he redoubled his exorcisms. The coffin dropped down in the middle of the church and stayed there without moving. The corpse got up out of it, livid and greenish. But at that instant the crow of the cock was heard in the distance; the corpse sank back in the coffin and closed the lid.

The philosopher's heart was throbbing and the sweat was streaming down him, but emboldened by the cock's crowing, he read on more rapidly the pages he ought to have read through before. At the first streak of dawn the sacristant came to relieve him, together with old Yavtuh, who was at that time performing the duties of a beadle.

On reaching his distant sleeping-place, the philosopher could not for a long time get to sleep; but weariness gained the upper hand at last and he slept on till dinner-time. When he woke up, all the events of the night seemed to him to have happened in a dream. To keep up his strength he was given at dinner a mug of vodka.

Over dinner he soon grew lively, made a remark or two, and devoured a rather large sucking pig almost unaided; but some feeling he could not have explained made him unable to bring himself to speak of his adventures in the church, and to the inquiries of the inquisitive he replied : "Yes, all sorts of strange things happened." The philosopher was one of those people who, if they are well fed, are moved to extraordinary benevolence. Lying down with his pipe in his teeth he watched them all with a honeyed look in his eyes and kept spitting to one side.

After dinner the philosopher was in excellent spirits. He went round the whole village and made friends with almost everybody; he was kicked out of two cottages, indeed; one good-looking young woman caught him a good smack on the back with a spade when he took it into his head to try her shift and skirt, and inquire what stuff they were made of. But as evening approached the philosopher grew more pensive. An hour before supper almost all the servants gathered together to play *kragli*—a sort of skittles in which long sticks are used instead of balls, and the winner has the right to ride on the loser's back. This game became very entertaining for the spectators; often the drover, a man as broad as a pancake, was mounted on the swineherd, a feeble little man, who was nothing but wrinkles. Another time it was the drover who had to bow his back, and Dorosh, leaping on it, always said : "What a fine bull !" The more dignified of the company sat in the kitchen doorway. They looked on very gravely, smoking their pipes, even when the young people roared with laughter at some witty remark from the drover or Spirid. Homa tried in vain to give himself up to this game; some gloomy thought stuck in his head like a nail. At supper, in spite of his efforts to be merry, terror grew within him as the darkness spread over the sky.

"Come, it's time to set off, Mr. Seminarist!" said his friend, the grey-headed Cossack, getting up from the table, together with Dorosh; "let us go to our task."

Homa was taken to the church again in the same way; again he was left there alone and the door was locked upon him. As soon as he was alone, fear began to take possession of him again. Again he saw the dark ikons, the gleaming frames, and the familiar black coffin standing in menacing stillness and immobility in the middle of the church.

"Well," he said to himself, "now there's nothing marvellous to me in this marvel. It was only alarming the first time. Yes, it was only rather alarming the first time, and even then it wasn't so alarming; now it's not alarming at all."

He made haste to take his stand at the lectern, drew a circle round him, pronounced some exorcisms, and began reading aloud, resolving not to raise his eyes from the book and not to pay attention to anything. He had been reading for about an hour and was beginning to cough and feel rather tired; he took his horn out of his pocket and, before putting the snuff to his nose, stole a timid look at the coffin. His heart turned cold; the corpse was already standing before him on the very edge of the circle, and her dead, greenish eyes were fixed upon him. The philosopher shuddered, and a cold chill ran through his veins. Dropping his eyes to the book, he began reading the prayers and exorcisms more loudly, and heard the corpse again grinding her teeth and waving her arms trying to catch him. But with a sidelong glance out of one eye, he saw that the corpse was feeling for him where he was not standing, and that she evidently could not see him. He heard a hollow mutter, and she began pronouncing terrible words with her dead lips; they gurgled hoarsely like the bubbling of boiling pitch. He could not have said what they meant; but there was something fearful in them. The philosopher understood with horror that she was making an incantation.

A wind blew through the church at her words, and there was a sound as of multitudes of flying wings. He heard the beating of wings on the panes of the church windows and on the iron window-frames, the dull scratching of claws upon the iron, and an immense troop thundering on the doors and trying to break in. His heart was throbbing violently all this time; closing his eyes, he kept reading prayers and exorcisms. At last there was a sudden shrill sound in the distance; it was a distant cock crowing. The philosopher, utterly spent, stopped and took breath.

When they came in to fetch him, they found him more dead than alive; he was leaning with his back against the wall, while with his eyes almost staring out of his head, he stared at the Cossacks as they came in. They could scarcely get him along and had to support him all the way back. On reaching the courtyard, he pulled himself together and bade them give him a mug of vodka. When he had drunk it, he stroked down the hair on his head and said : "There are lots of foul things of all sorts in the world! And the panics they give one, there...." With that the philosopher waved his hand in despair.

The company sitting round him bowed their heads, hearing such sayings. Even a small boy, whom everybody in the servants' quarters felt himself entitled to depute in his place when it was a question of cleaning the stables or fetching water, even this poor youngster stared open-mouthed at the philosopher.

At that moment the old cook's assistant, a peasant woman, not yet past middle age, a terrible coquette, who always found something to pin to her cap—a bit of ribbon, a pink, or even a scrap of coloured paper, if she had nothing better—passed by, in a tightly girt apron, which displayed her round, sturdy figure.

"Good day, Homa!" she said, seeing the philosopher. "Aie, aie, aie! what's the matter with you?" she shrieked, clasping her hands.

"Why, what is it, silly woman?"

"Oh, my goodness! Why, you've gone quite grey!"

"Aha! why, she's right!" Spirid pronounced, looking attentively at the philosopher. "Why, you have really gone as grey as our old Yavtuh."

The philosopher, hearing this, ran headlong to the kitchen, where he had noticed on the wall a fly-blown triangular bit of looking-glass before which were stuck forget-me-nots, periwinkles and even wreaths of marigolds, testifying to its importance for the toilet of the finery-loving coquette. With horror he saw the truth of their words : half of his hair had in fact turned white.

Homa Brut hung his head and abandoned himself to reflection. "I will go to the master" he said at last. "I'll tell him all about it and explain that I cannot go on reading. Let him send me back to Kiev straight away."

With these thoughts in his mind he bent his steps towards the porch of the house.

The *sotnik* was sitting almost motionless in his parlour. The same hopeless grief which the philosopher had seen in his face before was still apparent. Only his cheks were more sunken. It was evident that he had taken very little food, or perhaps had not eaten at all. The extraordinary pallor of his face gave it a look of stony immobility.

"Good day," he pronounced on seeing Homa, who stood, cap in hand, at the door. "Well, how goes it with you? All satisfactory?"

"It's satisfactory, all right; such devilish doing, that one can but pick up one's cap and take to one's heels."

"How's that?"

"Why, your daughter, your honour . . . Looking at it reasonably, she is, to be sure, of noble birth, nobody is going to gainsay it; only, saving your presence, God rest her soul. . . ."

"What of my daughter?"

"She had dealings with Satan. She gives one such horrors that there's no reading scripture at all."

"Read away! read away! She did well to send for you; she took much care, poor darling, about her soul and tried to drive away all evil thoughts with prayers."

"That's as you like to say, your honour; upon my soul, I cannot go on with it!"

"Read away!" the *sotnik* persisted in the same persuasive voice, "you have only one night left; you will do a Christian deed and I will reward you."

"But whatever rewards . . . Do as you please, your honour, but I will not read!" Homa declared resolutely.

"Listen, philosopher!" said the *sotnik,* and his voice grew firm and menacing. "I don't like these pranks. You can behave like that in your seminary; but with me it is different. When I flog, it's not the same as your rector's flogging. Do you know what good leather whips are like?"

"I should think I do!" said the philosopher, dropping his voice; "everybody knows what leather whips are like : in a large dose, it's quite unendurable."

"Yes, but you don't know yet how my lads can lay them on!" said the *sotnik,* menacingly, rising to his feet, and his face assumed an imperious and ferocious expression that betrayed the unbridled violence of his character, only subdued for the time by sorrow.

"Here they first give a sound flogging, then sprinkle with vodka, and begin over again. Go along, go along, finish your task! If you don't—you'll never get up again. If you do—a thousand gold pieces!"

"Oho, ho! he's a stiff one!" thought the philosopher as he went out: "he's not to be trifled with. Wait a bit, friend; I'll cut and run, so that you and your hounds will never catch me."

And Homa made up his mind to run away. He only waited for the hour after dinner when all the servants were accustomed to lie about in the hay barns and to give vent to such snores and wheezing that the backyard sounded like a factory.

The time came at last. Even Yavtuh closed his eyes as he lay stretched out in the sun. With fear and trembling, the philosopher stealthily made his way into the pleasure garden, from which he fancied he could more easily escape into the open country without being observed. As is usual with such gardens, it was dreadfully neglected and overgrown, and so made an extremely suitable setting for any secret enterprise. Except for one little path, trodden by the servants on their tasks, it was entirely hidden in a dense thicket of cherry trees, elders and burdock, which thrust up their tall stems covered with clinging pinkish burs. A network of wild hop was flung over this medley of trees and bushes of varied hues, forming a roof over them, clinging to the fence and falling mingled with wild bell-flowers, from it in coiling snakes. Beyond the fence, which formed the boundary of the garden, there came a perfect forest of rank grass and weeds, which looked as though no one cared to peep enviously into it, and as though any scythe would be broken to bits trying to mow down the stout stubbly stalks.

When the philosopher tried to get over the fence, his teeth chattered and his heart beat so violently that he was frightened at it. The skirts of his long coat seemed to stick to the ground as though someone had nailed them down. As he climbed over, he fancied he heard a voice shout in his ears with a deafening hiss: "Where are you off to?" The philosopher dived into the long grass and fell to running, frequently stumbling over old roots and trampling upon moles. He saw that when he came out of the rank weeds he would have to cross a field, and that beyond it lay a dark thicket of blackthorn, in which he thought he would be safe. He expected after making his way through to find the road leading straight to Kiev. He ran across the field at once and found himself in the thicket.

He crawled through the prickly bushes, paying a toll of rags from his coat on every thorn, and came out into a little hollow. A willow with spreading branches went down almost to the earth. A little brook sparkled pure as silver. The first thing the philosopher did was to lie down and drink, for he was insufferably thirsty. "Good water!" he said, wiping his lips; I might rest here!"

"No, we had better go straight ahead; they'll be coming to look for you!"

These words rang out above his ears. He looked round—before him was standing Yavtuh. "Curse Yavtuh!" the philosopher thought in his wrath; "I could take you and fling you ... And I could batter in your ugly face and all of you with an oak post."

"You needn't have gone such a long way round," Yavtuh went on, "you'd have done better to keep to the road I have come by, straight by the stable. And it's a pity about your coat. It's good cloth. What did you pay a yard for it? But we've walked far enough; it's time to go home."

The philosopher trudged after Yavtuh, scratching himself. "Now the cursed witch will give it to me!" he thought. "Though, after all, what am I thinking about? What am I afraid of? Am I not a Cossack? Why, I've been through two nights, God will succour me the third also. The cursed witch committed a fine lot of sins, it seems, since the Evil One makes such a fight for her."

Such were the reflections that absorbed him as he walked into the courtyard. Keeping up his spirits with these thoughts, he asked Dorosh, who through the patronage of the butler sometimes had access to the cellars, to pull out a keg of vodka; and the two friends, sitting in the barn, put away not much less than half a pailful, so that the philosopher, getting on to his feet, shouted: "Musicians! I must have musicians!" and without waiting for the latter fell to dancing a jig in a clear space in the middle of the yard. He danced till it was time for the afternoon snack, and the servants who stood round him in a circle, as is the custom on such occasions, at last spat on the ground and walked away, saying: "Good gracious, what a time the fellow keeps it up!" At last the philosopher lay down to sleep on the spot, and a good sousing of cold water was needed to wake him up for supper. At supper he talked of what it meant to be a Cossack, and how he should not be afraid of anything in the world.

"Time is up," said Yavtuh, "let us go."

"A splinter through your tongue, you damned hog!" thought the philosopher, and getting to his feet he said: "Come along."

On the way the philosopher kept glancing from side to side and made faint attempts at conversation with his companions. But Yuvtuh said nothing; and even Dorosh was disinclined to talk. It was a hellish night. A whole pack of wolves was howling in the distance, and even the barking of the dogs had a dreadful sound.

"I fancy something else is howling; that's not a wolf," said Dorosh. Yavtuh was silent. The philosopher could find nothing to say.

They drew near the church and stepped under the decaying wooden domes that showed how little the owner of the place thought about God and his own soul. Yavtuh and Dorosh withdrew as before, and the philosopher was left alone.

Everything was the same, everything wore the same sinister familiar aspect. He stood still for a minute. The horrible witch's coffin was still standing motionless in the middle of the church.

"I won't be afraid; by God, I will not!" he said, and, drawing a circle around himself as before, he began recalling all his spells and exorcisms. There was an awful stillness; the candles spluttered and flooded the whole church with light. The philosopher turned one page, then turned another and noticed that he was not reading what was written in the book. With horror he crossed himself and began chanting. This gave him a little more courage; the reading made progress, and the pages turned rapidly one after the other.

All of a sudden . . . in the midst of the stillness . . . the iron lid of the coffin burst with a crash and the corpse rose up. It was more terrible than the first time. Its teeth clacked horribly against each other, its lips twitched convulsively, and incantations came from them in wild shrieks. A whirlwind swept through the church, the ikons fell to the ground, broken glass came flying down from the windows. The doors were burst from their hinges and a countless multitude of monstrous beings trooped into the church of God. A terrible noise of wings and scratching claws filled the church. All flew and raced about looking for the philosopher.

All trace of drink had disappeared, and Homa's head was quite clear now. He kept crossing himself and repeating prayers at random. And all the while he heard the unclean horde whirring around him, almost touching him with their loathsome tails and the tips of their wings. He had not the courage to look at them; he only saw a huge monster, the whole width of the wall, standing in the shade of its matted locks as of a forest; through the tangle of hair two eyes glared horribly with eyebrows slightly lifted. Above it something was hanging in the air like an immense bubble with a thou-

sand claws and scorpion-stings stretching from the centre; black
earth hung in clods on them. They were all looking at him, seeking
him, but could not see him, surrounded by his mysterious circle.
"Bring Viy! Fetch Viy!" he heard the corpse cry.

And suddenly a stillness fell upon the church; the wolves' howling was heard in the distance, and soon there was the thud of heavy
footsteps resounding through the church. With a sidelong glance he
saw they were bringing a squat, thick-set bandy-legged figure. He
was covered all over with black earth. His arms and legs grew out
like strong sinewy roots. He trod heavily, stumbling at every step.
His long eyelids hung down to the very ground. Homa saw with
horror that his face was of iron. He was supported under the arms
and led straight to the spot where Homa was standing.

"Lift up my eyelids. I do not see!" said Viy in a voice that
seemed to come from underground—and all the company flew to
raise his eyelids.

"Do not look!" an inner voice whispered to the philosopher. He
could not restrain himself, and he looked.

"There he is!" shouted Viy, and thrust an iron finger at him.
And all pounced upon the philosopher together. He fell expiring
to the ground, and his soul fled from his body in terror.

There was the sound of a cock crowing. It was the second cock-
crow; the first had been missed by the gnomes. In panic they
rushed pell-mell to the doors and windows to fly out in utmost
haste; but they could not; and so they remained there, stuck in the
doors and windows.

When the priest went in, he stopped short at the sight of this
defamation of God's holy place, and dared not serve the requiem
on such a spot. And so the church was left for ever, with monsters
stuck in the doors and windows; it was overgrown with forest trees,
roots, rough grass and wild thorns, and no one can now find the
way to it.

When the rumours of this reached Kiev, and the theologian,
Halyava, heard at last the fate of the philosopher Homa, he spent a
whole hour plunged in thought. Great changes had befallen him
during that time. Fortune had smiled on him; on the conclusion of
his course of study, he was made bellringer of the very highest belfry,
and he was almost always to be seen with a damaged nose, as the
wooden staircase to the belfry had been extremely carelessly made.

"Have you heard what has happened to Homa?" Tibery Gorobets, who by now was a philosopher and had a newly-grown moustache, asked, coming up to him.

"Such was the lot God sent him," said Halyava the bellringer. "Let us go to the pot-house and drink to his memory!"

The young philosopher, who was beginning to enjoy his privileges with the ardour of an enthusiast, so that his full trousers and his coat and even his cap reeked of spirits and coarse tobacco, instantly signified his readiness.

"He was a fine fellow, Homa!" said the bellringer, as the lame innkeeper set the third mug before him. "He was a fine man! And he came to grief for nothing."

"I know why he came to grief : it was because he was afraid; if he had not been afraid the witch could not have done anything to him. You have only to cross yourself and spit just on her tail, and nothing will happen. I know all about it. Why, all the old women who sit in our market in Kiev are all witches."

To this the bellringer bowed his head in token of agreement. But, observing that his tongue was incapable of uttering a single word, he cautiously got up from the table, and, lurching to right and to left, went to hide in a remote spot in the rough grass; from the force of habit, however, he did not forget to carry off the sole of an old boot that was lying about on the bench.

INCIDENT AT OWL CREEK

AMBROSE BIERCE

(Robert Enrico: 1961)

*As I intimated in the previous introduction the French film
Incident at Owl Creek is in my opinion one of the finest of all
horror pictures. It is a film which capitalizes on a feeling, introduced almost at the start, that "something is not quite right",
and progresses through slow realization of impending danger to
a final, shattering climax.*

*Taken from a story every bit its equal in horror by the mysteri-
ous American writer, Ambrose Bierce (who disappeared inexplicably in Mexico in 1914), the picture has won accolades from
everyone who has seen it. Produced on a minimal budget by the
avant-garde French director Robert Enrico, it records the apparent escape of a civilian about to be hanged during the American
Civil War. The audience follows his progress as he travels home
to his wife, where a strange inertia at first becomes evident in
him and then in the actual movement of the film. Almost as
if weighted down by some unearthly force, man and film stumble
forward towards a woman waiting in the distance—a woman
who never seems to get any closer. Then in one vivid, terrible
moment we realize the awful truth about what has happened
... just as you will on reading this remarkable story.*

*

A MAN stood upon a railroad bridge in northern Alabama, looking
down into the swift water twenty feet below. The man's hands were
behind his back, the wrists bound with cord. A rope closely encircled
his neck. It was attached to a stout cross-timber above his head and
the slack fell to the level of his knees. Some loose boards laid upon the
sleepers supporting the metals of the railway supplied a footing for
him and his executioners—two private soldiers of the Federal Army,
directed by a sergeant who in civil life may have been a deputy
sheriff. At a short remove upon the same temporary platform was an
officer in the uniform of his rank, armed. He was a captain. A sentinel
at each end of the bridge stood with the rifle in the position known
as "support", that is to say, vertical in front of the left shoulder, the

hammer resting on the forearm thrown straight across the chest—a formal and unnatural position, enforcing an erect carriage of the body. It did not appear to be the duty of these two men to know what was occurring at the centre of the bridge; they merely blockaded the two ends of the foot planking that traversed it.

Beyond one of the sentinels nobody was in sight; the railroad ran straight away into a forest for a hundred yards, then, curving, was lost to view. Doubtless there was an outpost farther along. The other bank of the stream was open ground—a gentle acclivity topped with a stockade of vertical tree trunks, loop-holed for rifles, with a single embrasure through which protruded the muzzle of a brass cannon commanding the bridge. Midway of the slope between bridge and fort were the spectators—a single company of infantry in line, at "parade rest", the butts of the rifles on the ground, the barrels inclining slightly backward against the right shoulder, the hands crossed upon the stock. A lieutenant stood at the right of the line, the point of his sword upon the ground, his left hand resting upon his right. Excepting the group of four at the centre of the bridge, not a man moved. The company faced the bridge, staring stonily, motionless. The sentinels, facing the banks of the stream, might have been statues to adorn the bridge. The captain stood with folded arms, silent, observing the work of his subordinates, but making no sign. Death is a dignitary who, when he comes announced, is to be received with formal manifestations of respect, even by those most familiar with him. In the code of military etiquette silence and fixity are forms of deference.

The man who was engaged in being hanged was apparently about thirty-five years of age. He was a civilian, if one might judge from his habit, which was that of a planter. His features were good—a straight nose, firm mouth, broad forehead, from which his long dark hair was combed straight back, falling behind his ears to the collar of his well-fitting frock coat. He wore a moustache and pointed beard, but no whiskers; his eyes were large and dark grey, and had a kindly expression which one would hardly have expected in one whose neck was in the hemp. Evidently this was no vulgar assassin. The liberal military code makes provision for hanging many kinds of persons, and gentlemen are not excluded.

The preparations being complete, the two private soldiers stepped aside and each drew away the plank upon which he had been standing. The sergeant turned to the captain, saluted and placed himself immediately behind that officer, who in turn moved apart one pace.

These movements left the condemned man and the sergeant standing on the two ends of the same plank, which spanned three of the cross-ties of the bridge. The end upon which the civilian stood almost, but not quite, reached a fourth. This plank had been held in place by the weight of the captain; it was now held by that of the sergeant. At a signal from the former the latter would step aside, the plank would tilt and the condemned man go down between two ties. The arrangement commended itself to his judgment as simple and effective. His face had not been covered nor his eyes bandaged. He looked a moment at his "unsteadfast footing", then let his gaze wander to the swirling water of the stream racing madly beneath his feet. A piece of dancing driftwood caught his attention and his eyes followed it down the current. How slowly it appeared to move! What a sluggish stream!

He closed his eyes in order to fix his last thoughts upon his wife and children. The water, touched to gold by the early sun, the brooding mists under the banks at some distance down the stream, the fort, the soldiers, the piece of drift—all had distracted him. And now he became conscious of a new disturbance. Striking through the thought of his dear ones was a sound which he could neither ignore nor understand, a sharp, distinct, metallic percussion like the stroke of a blacksmith's hammer upon the anvil; it had the same ringing quality. He wondered what it was, and whether immeasurably distant or near by—it seemed both. Its recurrence was regular, but as slow as the tolling of a death knell. He awaited each stroke with impatience and—he knew not why—apprehension. The intervals of silence grew progressively longer; the delays became maddening. With their greater infrequency the sounds increased in strength and sharpness. They hurt his ear like the thrust of a knife; he feared he would shriek. What he heard was the ticking of his watch.

He unclosed his eyes and saw again the water below him. "If I could free my hands," he thought, "I might throw off the noose and spring into the stream. By diving I could evade the bullets and, swimming vigorously, reach the bank, take to the woods and get away home. My home, thank God, is as yet outside their lines; my wife and little ones are still beyond the invader's farthest advance."

As these thoughts, which have here to be set down in words, were flashed into the doomed man's brain rather than evolved from it, the captain nodded to the sergeant. The sergeant stepped aside.

Peyton Farquhar was a well-to-do planter, of an old and highly respected Alabama family. Being a slave-owner and, like other slave-owners, a politician, he was naturally an original secessionist and ardently devoted to the Southern cause. Circumstances of an imperious nature, which it is unnecessary to relate here, had prevented him from taking service with the gallant army that had fought the disastrous campaigns ending with the fall of Corinth, and he chafed under the inglorious restraint, longing for the release of his energies, the larger life of the soldier, the opportunity for distinction. That opportunity he felt, would come, as it comes to all in war-time. Meanwhile he did what he could. No service was too humble for him to perform in aid of the South, no adventure too perilous for him to undertake if consistent with the character of a civilian who was at heart a soldier, and who in good faith and without too much qualification assented to at least a part of the frankly villainous dictum that all is fair in love and war.

One evening while Farquhar and his wife were sitting on a rustic bench near the entrance to his grounds, a grey-clad soldier rode up to the gate and asked for a drink of water. Mrs. Farquhar was only too happy to serve him with her own white hands. While she was fetching the water her husband approached the dusty horseman and inquired eagerly for news from the front.

"The Yanks are repairing the railroads," said the man, "and are getting ready for another advance. They have reached the Owl Creek bridge, put it in order and built a stockade on the north bank. The commandant has issued an order, which is posted everywhere, declaring that any civilian caught interfering with the railroad, its bridges, tunnels, or trains will be summarily hanged. I saw the order."

"How far is it to Owl Creek bridge?" Farquhar asked.

"About thirty miles."

"Is there no force on this side of the creek?"

"Only a picket post half a mile out, on the railroad, and a single sentinel at this end of the bridge."

"Suppose a man—a civilian and student of hanging—should elude the picket post and perhaps get the better of the sentinel," said Farquhar, smiling, "what could he accomplish?"

The soldier reflected. "I was there a month ago," he said. "I observed that the flood of last winter had lodged a great quantity of driftwood against the wooden pier at this end of the bridge. It is now dry and would burn like tow."

The lady had now brought the water, which the soldier drank. He thanked her ceremoniously, bowed to her husband and rode away.

An hour later, after nightfall, he repassed the plantation, going north-ward in the direction from which he had come. He was a Federal scout.

As Peyton Farquhar fell straight downward through the bridge he lost consciousness and was as one already dead. From this state he was awakened—ages later, it seemed to him—by the pain of a sharp pressure upon his throat, followed by a sense of suffocation. Keen, poignant agonies seemed to shoot from his neck downward through every fibre of his body and limbs. These pains appeared to flash along well-defined lines of ramification and to beat with inconceivably rapid periodicity. They seemed like streams of pulsating fire heating him to an intolerable temperature. As to his head, he was conscious of nothing but a feeling of fullness—of congestion. These sensations were unaccompanied by thought. The intellectual part of his nature was already effaced; he had power only to feel, and feeling was tor-ment. He was conscious of motion. Encompassed in a luminous cloud, of which he was now merely the fiery heart, without material substance, he swung through unthinkable arcs of oscillation, like a vast pendulum. Then all at once, with terrible suddenness, the light about him shot upward with the noise of a loud plash; a frightful roaring was in his ears, and all was cold and dark. The power of thought was restored; he knew that the rope had broken and he had fallen into the stream. There was no additional strangulation; his noose about his neck was already suffocating him and kept the water from his lungs. To die of hanging at the bottom of a river! the idea seemed to him ludicrous. He opened his eyes in the darkness and saw above him a gleam of light, but how distant, how inaccessible! He was still sinking, for the light became fainter and fainter until it was a mere glimmer. Then it began to grow and brighten, and he knew that he was rising towards the surface—knew it with reluctance, for he was now very comfortable. "To be hanged and drowned," he thought, "that is not so bad; but I do not wish to be shot. No; I will not be shot; that is not fair."

He was not conscious of an effort, but a sharp pain in his wrist apprised him that he was trying to free his hands. He gave the struggle his attention, as an idler might observe the feat of a juggler, without interest in the outcome. What splendid effort! What magnificent, what superhuman strength! Ah, that was a fine endeavour! Bravo! The cord fell away; his arms parted and floated upward, the hands

dimly seen on each side in the growing light. He watched them with
a new interest as first one and then the other pounced upon the
noose at his neck. They tore it away and thrust it fiercely aside, its
undulations resembling those of a water-snake. "Put it back, put it
back!" He thought he shouted these words to his hands, for the
undoing of the noose had been succeeded by the direst pang that he
had yet experienced. His neck ached horribly; his brain was on fire;
his heart, which had been fluttering faintly, gave a great leap, trying
to force itself out at his mouth. His whole body was racked and
wrenched with an insupportable anguish! But his disobedient hands
gave no heed to the command. They beat the water vigorously with
quick, downward strokes, forcing him to the surface. He felt his head
emerge; his eyes were blinded by the sunlight; his chest expanded
convulsively, and with a supreme and crowning agony his lungs engulfed a great draught of air, which instantly he expelled in a shriek!

He was now in full possession of his physical senses. They were
indeed, preternaturally keen and alert. Something in the awful disturbance of his organic system had so exalted and refined them that
they made record of things never before perceived. He felt the ripples
upon his face and heard their separate sounds as they struck. He
looked at the forest on the bank of the stream, saw the individual
trees, the leaves, and the veining of each leaf—saw the very insects
upon them; the locusts, the brilliant-bodied flies, the grey spiders
stretching their webs from twig to twig. He noted the prismatic
colours in all the gnats that danced above the eddies of the stream,
the beating of the dragon-flies' wings, the strokes of the water-spiders'
legs, like oars which had lifted their boat—all these made audible
music. A fish slid along beneath his eyes and he heard the rush of its
body parting the water.

He had come to the surface facing down the stream; in a moment
the visible world seemed to wheel slowly round, himself the pivotal
point, and he saw the bridge, the fort, the soldiers upon the bridge,
the captain, the sergeant, the two privates, his executioners. They
were in silhouette against the blue sky. They shouted and gesticula-
ted, pointing at him. The captain had drawn his pistol, but did not
fire; the others were unarmed. Their movements were grotesque and
horrible, their forms gigantic.

Suddenly he heard a sharp report and something struck the water
smartly within a few inches of his head; spattering his face with spray.
He heard a second report, and saw one of the sentinels with his rifle
at his shoulder, a light cloud of blue smoke rising from the muzzle.

The man in the water saw the eye of the man on the bridge gazing into his own through the sights of the rifle. He observed that it was a grey eye and remembered having read that grey eyes were keenest, and that all famous marksmen had them. Nevertheless, this one had missed.

A counter-swirl had caught Farquhar and turned him half round; he was again looking into the forest on the bank opposite the fort. The sound of a clear, high voice in a monotonous singsong now rang out behind him, and came across the water with a distinctness that pierced and subdued all other sounds, even the beating of the ripples in his ears. Although no soldier, he had frequented camps enough to know the dread significance of that deliberate, drawling, aspirated chant; the lieutenant on shore was taking a part in the morning's work. How coldly and pitilessly—with what an even, calm intonation, presaging and enforcing tranquillity in the men—with what accurately measured intervals fell those cruel words :

"Attention, company ! . . . Shoulder arm ! . . . Ready ! . . . Aim ! . . . Fire ! "

Farquhar dived—dived as deeply as he could. The water roared in his ears like the voice of Niagara, yet he heard the dulled thunder of the volley and, rising again towards the surface, met shining bits of metal, singularly flattened, oscillating slowly downwards. Some of them touched him on the face and hands, then fell away, continuing their descent. One lodged between his collar and neck; it was uncomfortably warm and he snatched it out.

As he rose to the surface, gasping for breath, he saw that he had been a long time under water, he was perceptibly farther downstream—nearer to safety. The soldiers had almost finished reloading; the metal ramrods flashed all at once in the sunshine as they were drawn from the barrels, turned in the air, and thrust into their sockets. The two sentinels fired again, independently and ineffectually.

The hunted man saw all this over his shoulder; he was now swimming vigorously with the current. His brain was as energetic as his arms and legs; he thought with the rapidity of lightning.

"The officer," he reasoned, "will not make that martinet's error a second time. It is as easy to dodge a volley as a single shot. He has probably already given the command to fire at will. God help me, I cannot dodge them all ! "

An appalling splash within two yards of him was followed by a loud, rushing sound, *diminuendo*, which seemed to travel back through the air to the fort and died in an explosion which stirred the very river to its deeps! A rising sheet of water curved over him, fell down upon him, blinded him, strangled him! The cannon had taken a hand in the game. As he shook his head free from the commotion of the smitten water he heard the deflected shot humming through the air ahead, and in an instant it was cracking and smashing the branches in the forest beyond.

"They will not do that again," he thought, "the next time they will use a charge of grape. I must keep my eye upon the gun; the smoke will apprise me—the report arrives too late; it lags behind the missile. That is a good gun."

Suddenly he felt himself whirled round and round—spinning like a top. The water, the banks, the forests, the now distant bridge, fort, and men—all were commingled and blurred. Objects were represented by their colours only; circular horizontal streaks of colour—that was all he saw. He had been caught in the vortex and was being whirled on with a velocity of advance and gyration that made him giddy and sick. In a few moments he was flung upon the gravel at the foot of the left bank of the stream—the southern bank—and behind a projecting point which concealed him from his enemies. The sudden arrest of his motion, the abrasion of one of his hands on the gravel, restored him, and he wept with delight. He dug his fingers into the sand, threw it over himself in handfuls and audibly blessed it. It looked like diamonds, rubies, emeralds; he could think of nothing beautiful which it did not resemble. The trees upon the bank were giant garden plants; he noted a definite order in their arrangement, inhaled the fragrance of their blooms. A strange, roseate light shone through the spaces among their trunks and the wind made in their branches the music of aeolian harps. He had no wish to perfect his escape—was content to remain in that enchanting spot until retaken.

A whiz and rattle of grapeshot among the branches high above his head roused him from his dream. The baffled cannoneer had fired him a random farewell. He sprang to his feet, rushed up the sloping bank, and plunged into the forest.

All that day he travelled, laying his course by the rounding sun. The forest seemed interminable; nowhere did he discover a break in it, not even a woodman's road. He had not known that he lived in so wild a region. There was something uncanny in the revelation.

By nightfall he was fatigued, footsore, famishing. The thought of his wife and children urged him on. At last he found a road which led him in what he knew to be the right direction. It was as wide and straight as a city street, yet it seemed untravelled. No fields bordered it, no dwelling anywhere. Not so much as the barking of a dog suggested human habitation. The black bodies of the trees formed a straight wall on both sides, terminating on the horizon in a point, like a diagram in a lesson in perspective. Overhead, as he looked up through this rift in the wood, shone great golden stars looking unfamiliar and grouped in strange constellations. He was sure they were arranged in some order which had a secret and malign significance. The wood on either side was full of singular noises, among which—once, twice, and again—he distinctly heard whispers in an unknown tongue.

His neck was in pain and lifting his hand to it he found it horribly swollen. He knew it had a circle of black where the rope had bruised it. His eyes felt congested; he could no longer close them. His tongue was swollen with thirst; he relieved its fever by thrusting it forward from between his teeth into the cold air. How softly the turf had carpeted the untravelled avenue—he could no longer feel the roadway beneath his feet!

Doubtless, despite his suffering, he had fallen asleep while walking, for now he sees another scene—perhaps he has merely recovered from a delirium. He stands at the gate of his own home. All is as he left it, and all bright and beautiful in the morning sunshine. He must have travelled the entire night. As he pushes open the gate and passes up the wide white walk, he sees a flutter of female garments : his wife, looking fresh and cool and sweet, steps down from the veranda to meet him. At the bottom of the steps she stands waiting, with a smile of ineffable joy, an attitude of matchless grace and dignity. Ah, how beautiful she is! He springs forward with extended arms. As he is about to clasp her he feels a stunning blow upon the back of the neck; a blinding white light blazes all about him with a sound like the shock of a cannon—then all is darkness and silence!

Peyton Farquhar was dead; his body, with a broken neck swung gently from side to side beneath the timbers of the Owl Creek bridge.

MONSTER OF TERROR

H. P. LOVECRAFT

(American-International: 1965)

By the middle nineteen-sixties no one could doubt that the great days of monsters and evil scientists were back again. In England a once small company named Hammer Films had grown into a giant horror film business serving the world (so much so that in 1968 they earned the Queen's Award to Industry for "outstanding contributions to export"). Across the Atlantic, American-International was dominating the market, many of their productions having come from the prolific "cult-figure" director Roger Corman.

The two companies were alike in many ways and had stars of equal stature to wage unholy war in the cinemas of the world. But while Hammer tended to concentrate on original screenplays (albeit based on traditional characters such as Dracula and Frankenstein), American-International plumped for the work of Edgar Allan Poe—even if, in all fairness to the master of horror, often only the title remained true to the original story once the film was finished!

American-International also brought to the screen for the first time the work of H. P. Lovecraft, a fantasy writer who had lived as a recluse and died in 1937 and whose stories had not really come to public attention for almost a decade. Monster of Terror (or Die, Monster, Die *as it was called in America) was based on a story by Lovecraft entitled* The Colour Out Of Space, *and although not directed by Corman, was entrusted to one of his protégés, Daniel Haller. The picture contains one of the last really fine performance by Boris Karloff as a man affected by radiation from space who slowly turns into a monster.*

*

WEST of Arkham the hills rise wild, and there are valleys with deep woods that no axe has ever cut. There are dark narrow glens where the trees slope fantastically, and where thin brooklets trickle without ever having caught the glint of sunlight. On the gentler slopes there are farms, ancient and rocky, with squat, moss-coated

cottages brooding eternally over old New England secrets in the lee
of great ledges; but these are all vacant now; the wide chimneys
crumbling and the shingled sides bulging perilously beneath low
gambrel roofs.

The old folk have gone away, and foreigners do not like to live
there. French-Canadians have tried it, Italians have tried it, and
the Poles have come and departed. It is not because of anything
that can be seen or heard or handled, but because of something that
is imagined. The place is not good for imagination, and does not
bring restful dreams at night. It must be this which keeps the
foreigners away, for old Ammi Pierce has never told them of anything he recalls from the strange days. Ammi, whose head has been
a little queer for years, is the only one who still remains, or who
ever talks of the strange days; and he dares to do this because his
house is so near the open fields and the travelled roads around
Arkham.

There was once a road over the hills and through the valleys,
that ran straight where the blasted heath is now; but people ceased
to use it and a new road was laid curving far towards the south.
Traces of the old one can still be found amidst the weeds of a
returning wilderness, and some of them will doubtless linger even
when half the hollows are flooded for the new reservoir. Then the
dark woods will be cut down and the blasted heath will slumber far
below blue waters whose surface will mirror the sky and ripple in
the sun. And the secrets of the strange days will be one with the deep's
secrets; one with the hidden lore of old ocean, and all the mystery
of primal earth.

When I went into the hills and vales to survey for the new
reservoir they told me the place was evil. They told me this in
Arkham, and because that is a very old town full of witch legends I
thought the evil must be something which grandmas had whispered
to children through centuries. The name "blasted heath" seemed to
me very odd and theatrical, and I wondered how it had come into the
folklore of a Puritan people. Then I saw that dark westward tangle
of glens and slopes for myself, and ceased to wonder at anything
beside its own elder mystery. It was morning when I saw it, but
shadow lurked always there. The trees grew too thickly, and their
trunks were too big for any healthy New England wood. There was
too much silence in the dim alleys between them, and the floor was
too soft with the dank moss and mattings of infinite years of decay.

In the open spaces, mostly along the line of the old road, there were little hillside farms; sometimes with all the buildings standing, sometimes with only one or two, and sometimes with only a lone chimney or fast-filling cellar. Weeds and briars reigned, and furtive wild things rustled in the undergrowth. Upon everything was a haze of restlessness and oppression; a touch of the unreal and the grotesque, as if some vital element of perspective or chiaroscuro were awry. I did not wonder that the foreigners would not stay, for this was no region to sleep in. It was too much like a landscape of Salvator Rosa; too much like some forbidden woodcut in a tale of terror.

But even all this was not so bad as the blasted heath. I knew it the moment I came upon it at the bottom of a spacious valley; for no other name could fit such a thing, or any other thing fit such a name. It was as if the poet had coined the phrase from having seen this one particular region. It must, I thought as I viewed it, be the outcome of a fire; but why had nothing new ever grown over those five acres of grey desolation that sprawled open to the sky like a great spot eaten by acid in the woods and fields? It lay largely to the north of the ancient road line, but encroached a little on the other side. I felt an odd reluctance about approaching, and did so at last only because my business took me through and past it. There was no vegetation of any kind on that broad expanse, but only a fine grey dust or ash which no wind seemed ever to blow about. The trees near it were sickly and stunted, and many dead trunks stood or lay rotting at the rim. As I walked hurriedly by I saw the tumbled bricks and stones of an old chimney and cellar on my right, and the yawning black maw of an abandoned well whose stagnant vapours played strange tricks with the hues of the sunlight. Even the long, dark woodland climb beyond seemed welcome in contrast, and I marvelled no more at the frightened whispers of Arkham people. There had been no house or ruin near; even in the old days the place must have been lonely and remote. And at twilight, dreading to repass that ominous spot, I walked circuitously back to the town by the curving road on the south. I vaguely wished some clouds would gather, for an odd timidity about the deep skyey voids above had crept into my soul.

In the evening I asked old people in Arkham about the blasted heath, and what was meant by that phrase "strange days" which so many evasively muttered. I could not, however, get any good answers, except that all the mystery was much more recent than I had dreamed. It was not a matter of old legendry at all, but something within the lifetime of those who spoke. It had happened in the 'eighties, and a family had disappeared or was killed. Speakers would not be exact; and because they all told me to pay no attention to old Ammi Pierce's crazy tales, I sought him out the next morning, having heard that he lived alone in the ancient tottering cottage where the trees first begin to get very thick. It was a fearsomely ancient place, and had begun to exude the faint miasmal odour which clings about houses that have stood too long. Only with persistent knocking could I rouse the aged man, and when he shuffled timidly to the door I could tell he was not glad to see me. He was not so feeble as I had expected; but his eyes dropped in a curious way, and his unkempt clothing and white beard made him seem very worn and dismal.

Not knowing just how he could best be launched on his tales, I feigned a matter of business; told him of my surveying, and asked vague questions about the district. He was far brighter and more educated than I had been led to think, and before I knew it had grasped quite as much of the subject as any man I had talked with in Arkham. He was not like other rustics I had known in the sections where reservoirs were to be. From him there were no protests at the miles of old wood and farmland to be blotted out, though perhaps there would have been had not his home lain outside the bounds of the future lake. Relief was all that he showed; relief at the doom of the dark ancient valleys through which he had roamed all his life. They were better under water now—better under water since the strange days. And with this opening his husky voice sank low, while his body leaned forward and his right forefinger began to point shakily and impressively.

It was then that I heard the story, and as the rambling voice scraped and whispered on I shivered again and again despite the summer day. Often I had to recall the speaker from ramblings, piece out scientific points which he knew only by a fading parrot memory of professors' talk, or bridge over gaps where his sense of logic and continuity broke down. When he was done I did not wonder that his mind had snapped a trifle, or that the folk of Arkham would not speak much of the blasted heath. I hurried back before sunset to my hotel, unwilling to have the stars come out above me in the open; and the next day returned to Boston to give up my position. I could not go into that dim chaos of old forest and slope again, or face another time that grey blasted heath where the black well yawned deep beside the tumbled bricks and stones. The reservoir will soon be built now, and all those elder secrets will be safe forever under watery fathoms. But even then I do not believe I would like to visit that country by night—at least not when the sinister stars are out; and nothing could bribe me to drink the new city water of Arkham.

It all began, old Ammi said, with the meteorite. Before that time there had been no wild legends at all since the witch trials, and even then these western woods were not feared half so much as the small island in the Miskatonic where the devil held court beside a curious stone altar older than the Indians. These were not haunted woods, and their fantastic dusk was never terrible till the strange days. Then there had come that white noontide cloud, that string of explosions in the air, and that pillar of smoke from the valley far in the wood. And by night all Arkham had heard of the great rock that fell out of the sky and bedded itself in the ground beside the well at the Nahum Gardner place. That was the house which had stood where the blasted heath was to come—the trim white Nahum Gardner house amidst its fertile gardens and orchards.

Nahum had come to town to tell people about the stone, and dropped in at Ammi Pierce's on the way. Ammi was forty then, and all the queer things were fixed very strongly in his mind. He and his wife had gone with the three professors from Miskatonic University who hastened out the next morning to see the weird visitor from unknown stellar space, and had wondered why Nahum had called it so large the day before. It had shrunk, Nahum said, as he pointed out the big brownish mound above the ripped earth and charred grass near the archaic well-sweep in his front yard; but the wise men answered that stones do not shrink. Its heat lingered persistently, and Nahum declared that it had glowed faintly in the night. The professors tried it with a geologist's hammer and found it was oddly soft. It was, in truth, so soft as to be almost plastic; and they gouged rather than chipped a specimen to take back to the college for testing. They took it in an old pail borrowed from Nathum's kitchen, for even the small piece refused to grow cool. On the trip back they stopped at Ammi's to rest, and seemed thoughtful when Mrs. Pierce remarked that the fragment was growing smaller and burning the bottom of the pail. Truly, it was not large, but perhaps they had taken less than they thought.

The day after that—all this was in June of '82—the professors had trooped out again in a great excitement. As they
passed Ammi's they told him what queer things the specimen
had done, and how it had faded wholly away when they put it
in a glass beaker. The beaker had gone, too, and the wise men
talked of the strange stone's affinity for silicon. It had acted
quite unbelievably in that well-ordered laboratory; doing nothing at all and showing no occluded gases when heated on
charcoal, being wholly negative in the borax bead, and soon
proving itself absolutely non-volatile at any producible temperature, including that of the oxy-hydrogen blowpipe. On an anvil
it appeared highly malleable, and in the dark its luminosity was
very marked. Stubbornly refusing to grow cool, it soon had the
college in a state of real excitement; and when upon heating
before the spectroscope it displayed shining bands unlike any
known colours of the normal spectrum there was much breathless talk of new elements, bizarre optical properties, and other
things which puzzled men of science are wont to say when faced
by the unknown.

Hot as it was, they tested it in a crucible with all the proper
reagents. Water did nothing. Hydrochloric acid was the same.
Nitric acid and even aqua regia merely hissed and spattered
against its torrid invulnerability. Ammi had difficulty in recalling all these things, but recognized some solvents as I mentioned
them in the usual order of use. There were ammonia and caustic
soda, alcohol and ether, nauseous carbon disulphide and a dozen
others; but although the weight grew steadily less as time passed,
and the fragment seemed to be slightly cooling, there was no
change in the solvents to show that they had attacked the substance at all. It was a metal, though, beyond a doubt. It was
magnetic, for one thing; and after its immersion in the acid
solvents there seemed to be faint traces of the Widmänstätten
figures found on meteoric iron. When the cooling had grown
very considerable, the testing was carried on in glass; and it was
in a glass beaker that they left all the chips made of the original
fragment during the work. The next morning both chips and
beaker were gone without trace, and only a charred spot marked
the place on the wooden shelf where they had been.

All this the professors told Ammi as they paused at his door,
and once more he went with them to see the stony messenger
from the stars, though this time his wife did not accompany

him. It had now most certainly shrunk, and even the sober professors could not doubt the truth of what they saw. All around the dwindling brown lump near the well was a vacant space, except where the earth had caved in; and whereas it had been a good seven feet across the day before, it was now scarcely five. It was still hot, and the sages studied its surface curiously as they detached another and larger piece with hammer and chisel. They gouged deeply this time, and as they pried away the smaller mass they saw that the core of the thing was not quite homogeneous.

They had uncovered what seemed to be the side of a large coloured globule embedded in the substance. The colour, which resembled some of the bands in the meteor's strange spectrum, was almost impossible to describe; and it was only by analogy that they called it colour at all. Its texture was glossy, and upon tapping it appeared to promise both brittleness and hollowness. One of the professors gave it a sharp blow with a hammer, and it burst with a nervous little plop. Nothing was emitted, and all trace of the thing vanished with the puncturing. It left behind a hollow spherical space about three inches across, and all thought it probable that others would be discovered as the enclosing substance wasted away.

Conjecture was vain; so after a futile attempt to find additional globules by drilling, the seekers left again with their new specimen—which proved, however, as baffling in the laboratory as its predecessor. Aside from being almost plastic, having heat, magnetism, and slight luminosity, cooling slightly in powerful acids, possessing an unknown spectrum, wasting away in air, and attacking silicon compounds with mutual destruction as a result, it presented no identifying features whatsoever; and at the end of the tests the college scientists were forced to own that they could not place it. It was nothing of this earth, but a piece of the great outside; and as such dowered with outside properties and obedient to outside laws.

That night there was a thunderstorm, and when the professors went out to Nahum's the next day they met with a bitter disappointment. The stone, magnetic as it had been, must have had some peculiar electrical property; for it had "drawn the lightning," as Nahum said, with a singular persistence. Six times within an hour the farmer saw the lightning strike the furrow in the front yard, and when the storm was over nothing re-

mained but a ragged pit by the ancient well-sweep, half-choked
with a caved-in earth. Digging had borne no fruit, and the
scientists verified the fact of the utter vanishment. The failure
was total; so that nothing was left to do but go back to the
laboratory and test again the disappearing fragment left carefully cased in lead. That fragment lasted a week, at the end of
which nothing of value had been learned of it. When it had gone,
no residue was left behind, and in time the professors felt
scarcely sure they had indeed seen with waking eyes that cryptic
vestige of the fathomless gulfs outside; that lone, weird message from other universes and other realms of matter, force, and
entity.

As was natural, the Arkham papers made much of the
incident with its collegiate sponsoring, and sent reporters to talk
with Nahum Gardner and his family. At least one Boston daily
also sent a scribe, and Nahum quickly became a kind of local
celebrity. He was a lean, genial person of about fifty, living with
his wife and three sons on the pleasant farmstead in the valley.
He and Ammi exchanged visits frequently, as did their wives;
and Ammi had nothing but praise for him after all these years.
He seemed slightly proud of the notice his place had attracted,
and talked often of the meteorite in the succeeding weeks. That
July and August were hot; and Nahum worked hard at his haying in the ten-acre pasture across Chapman's Brook; his rattling
wain wearing deep ruts in the shadowy lanes between. The labour
tired him more than it had in other years, and he felt that age
was beginning to tell on him.

Then fell the time of fruit and harvest. The pears and apples
slowly ripened, and Nahum vowed that his orchards were pros-
pering as never before. The fruit was growing to phenomenal
size and unwonted gloss, and in such abundance that extra
barrels were ordered to handle the future crop. But with the
ripening came sore disappointment, for of all that gorgeous
array of specious lusciousness not one single jot was fit to eat.
Into the finer flavour of the pears and apples had crept a stealthy
bitterness and sickishness, so that even the smallest bites
induced a lasting disgust. It was the same with the melons and
tomatoes, and Nahum sadly saw that his entire crop was lost.
Quick to connect events, he declared that the meteorite had
poisoned the soil, and thanked Heaven that most of the other
crops were in the upland lot along the road.

Winter came early, and was very cold. Ammi saw Nahum less often than usual, and observed that he had begun to look worried. The rest of his family too, seemed to have grown taciturn; and were far from steady in their church-going or their attendance at the various social events of the countryside. For this reserve or melancholy no cause could be found, though all the household confessed now and then to poorer health and a feeling of vague disquiet. Nahum himself gave the most definite statement of anyone when he said he was disturbed about certain footprints in the snow. They were the usual winter prints of red squirrels, white rabbits, and foxes, but the brooding farmer professed to see something not quite right about their nature and arrangement. He was never specific, but appeared to think that they were not as characteristic of the anatomy and habits of squirrels and rabbits and foxes as they ought to be. Ammi listened without interest to this talk until one night when he drove past Nahum's house in his sleigh on the way back from Clark's Corners. There had been a moon, and a rabbit had run across the road, and the leaps of that rabbit were longer than either Ammi or his horse liked. The latter, indeed, had almost run away until brought up by a firm rein. Thereafter Ammi gave Nahum's tales more respect, and wondered why the Gardner dogs seemed so cowed and quivering every morning. They had, it developed, nearly lost the spirit to bark.

In February the McGregor boys from Meadow Hill were out shooting woodchucks, and not far from the Gardner place bagged a very peculiar specimen. The proportions of its body seemed slightly altered in a queer way impossible to describe, while its face had taken on an expression which no one ever saw in a woodchuck before. The boys were genuinely frightened, and threw the thing away at once, so that only their grotesque tales of it ever reached the people of the countryside. But the shying of horses near Nahum's house had now become an acknowledged thing, and all the basis for a cycle of whispered legend was fast taking form.

People vowed that the snow melted faster around Nahum's than it did anywhere else, and early in March there was an awed discussion in Potter's general store in Clark's Corners. Stephen Rice had driven past Gardner's in the morning, and had noticed the skunk-cabbages coming up through the mud by the woods across the road. Never were things of such size seen before, and they held strange colours that could not be put into any words. Their shapes were monstrous, and the horse had snorted at an odour which struck Stephen as wholly unprecedented. That afternoon several persons drove past to see the abnormal growth, and all agreed that plants of that kind ought never to sprout in a healthy world. The bad fruit of the fall before was freely mentioned, and it went from mouth to mouth that there was poison in Nahum's ground. Of course it was the meteorite; and remembering how strange the men from the college had found that stone to be, several farmers spoke about the matter to them.

One day they paid Nahum a visit; but having no love of wild tales and folklore were very conservative in what they inferred. The plants were certainly odd, but all skunk-cabbages are more or less odd in shape and hue. Perhaps some mineral element from the stone had entered the soil, but it would soon be washed away. And as for the footprints and frightened horses—of course this was mere country talk which such a phenomenon as the aerolite would be certain to start. There was really nothing for serious men to do in cases of wild gossip, for superstitious rustics will say and believe anything. And so all through the strange days the professors stayed away in contempt. Only one of them, when given two phials of dust for analysis in a police job over a year and a half later, recalled that the queer colour of that skunk-cabbage had been very like one of the anomalous bands of light shown by the meteor fragment in the college spectroscope, and like the brittle globule found imbedded in the stone from the abyss. The samples in this analysis case gave the same odd bands at first, though later they lost the property.

The trees budded prematurely around Nahum's, and at night they swayed ominously in the wind. Nahum's second son Thaddeus, a lad of fifteen, swore that they swayed also when there was no wind; but even the gossips would not credit this. Certainly, however, restlessness was in the air. The entire Gardner family developed the habit of stealthy listening, though not for any sound which they could consciously name. The listening was, indeed, rather a product of moments when consciousness seemed half to slip away. Unfortunately such moments increased week by week, till it became common speech that "something was wrong with all Nahum's folks". When the early saxifrage came out it had another strange colour; not quite

that of the skunk-cabbage, but plainly related and equally unknown to anyone who saw it. Nahum took some blossoms to
Arkham and showed them to the editor of the *Gazette*, but that
dignitary did no more than write a humorous article about them,
in which the dark fears of rustics were held up to polite ridicule.
It was a mistake of Nahum's to tell a stolid city man about the
way the great, overgrown mourning-cloak butterflies behaved in
connection with these saxifrages.

April brought a kind of madness to the country folk, and
began that disuse of the road past Nahum's which led to its
ultimate abandonment. It was the vegetation. All the orchard
trees blossomed forth in strange colours, and through the stony
soil of the yard and adjacent pasturage there sprang up a bizarre
growth which only a botanist could connect with the proper
flora of the region. No sane wholesome colours were anywhere
to be seen except in the green grass and leafage; but everywhere
were those hectic and prismatic variants of some diseased, under-
lying primary tone without a place among the known tints of
earth. The "Dutchman's breeches" became a thing of sinister
menace, and the bloodroots grew insolent in their chromatic
perversion. Ammi and the Gardners thought that most of the
colours had a sort of haunting familiarity, and decided that they
reminded one of the britle globule in the meteor. Nahum
ploughed and sowed the ten-acre pasture and the upland lot, but
did nothing with the land around the house. He knew it would
be of no use, and hoped that the summer's strange growths
would draw all the poison from the soil. He was prepared for
almost anything now, and had grown used to the sense of something near him waiting to be heard. The shunning of his house
by neighbours told on him, of course; but it told on his wife
more. The boys were better off, being at school each day; but
they could not help being frightened by the gossip. Thaddeus,
an especially sensitive youth, suffered the most.

In May the insects came, and Nahum's place became a nightmare of buzzing and crawling. Most of the creatures seemed not
quite usual in their aspects and motions, and their nocturnal
habits contradicted all former experience. The Gardners took
to watching at night—watching in all directions at random for
something—they could not tell what. It was then that they all
owned that Thaddeus had been right about the trees. Mrs.
Gardner was the next to see it from the window as she watched

the swollen boughs of a maple against a moonlit sky. The boughs surely moved, and there was no wind. It must be the sap. Strangeness had come into everything growing now. Yet it was none of Nahum's family at all who made the next discovery. Familiarity had dulled them, and what they could not see was glimpsed by a timid windmill salesman from Bolton who drove by one night in ignorance of the country legends. What he told in Arkham was given a short paragraph in the *Gazette*; and it was there that all the farmers, Nahum included, saw it first. The night had been dark and the buggy-lamps faint, but around a farm in the valley which everyone knew from the account must be Nahum's, the darkness had been less thick. A dim though distinct luminosity seemed to inhere in all the vegetation, grass, leaves, and blossoms alike, while at one moment a detached piece of the phosphorescence appeared to stir furtively in the yard near the barn.

The grass had so far seemed untouched, and the cows were freely pastured in the lot near the house, but towards the end of May the milk began to be bad. Then Nahum had the cows driven to the uplands, after which this trouble ceased. Not long after this the change in grass and leaves became apparent to the eye. All the verdure was going grey, and was developing a highly singular quality of brittleness. Ammi was now the only person who ever visited the place, and his visits were becoming fewer and fewer. When school closed the Gardners were virtually cut off from the world, and sometimes let Ammi do their errands in town. They were failing curiously both physically and mentally, and no one was surprised when the news of Mrs. Gardner's madness stole around.

It happened in June, about the anniversary of the meteor's fall, and the poor woman screamed about things in the air which she could not describe. In her raving there was not a single specific noun, but only verbs and pronouns. Things moved and changed and fluttered, and ears tingled to impulses which were not wholly sounds. Something was taken away—she was being drained of something—something was fastening itself on her that ought not to be—someone must make it keep off—nothing was ever still in the night—the walls and windows shifted. Nathum did not send her to the county asylum, but let her wander about the house as long as she was harmless to herself and others. Even when her expression changed he did nothing.

But when the boys grew afraid of her, and Thaddeus nearly fainted at the way she made faces at him, he decided to keep her locked in the attic. By July she had ceased to speak and crawled on all fours, and before that month was over Nahum got the mad notion that she was slightly luminous in the dark, as he now clearly saw was the case with the nearby vegetation.

It was a little before this that the horses had stampeded. Something had aroused them in the night, and their neighing and kicking in their stalls had been terrible. There seemed virtually nothing to do to calm them, and when Nahum opened the stable door they all bolted out like frightened woodland deer. It took a week to track all four, and when found they were seen to be quite useless and unmanageable. Something had snapped in their brains, and each one had to be shot for its own good. Nahum borrowed a horse from Ammi for his haying, but found it would not approach the barn. It shied, baulked, and whinnied, and in the end he could do nothing but drive it into the yard while the men used their own strength to get the heavy wagon near enough the hayloft for convenient pitching. And all the while the vegetation was turning grey and brittle. Even the flowers whose hues had been so strange were greying now, and the fruit was coming out grey and dwarfed and tasteless. The asters and golden-rod bloomed grey and distorted, and the roses and zinnias and hollyhocks in the front yard were such blasphe-mous-looking things that Nahum's oldest boy Zenas cut them down. The strangely puffed insects died about that time, even the bees that had left their hives and taken to the woods.

By September all the vegetation was fast crumbling to a grey-ish powder, and Nahum feared that the trees would die before the poison was out of the soil. His wife now had spells of terrific screaming, and he and the boys were in a constant state of nervous tension. They shunned people now, and when school opened the boys did not go. But it was Ammi, on one of his rare visits, who first realized that the well water was no longer good. It had an evil taste that was not exactly foetid nor exactly salty, and Ammi advised his friend to dig another well on higher ground to use till the soil was good again. Nahum, how-ever, ignored the warning, for he had by that time become cal-loused to strange and unpleasant things. He and the boys continued to use the tainted supply, drinking it as listlessly and mechanically as they ate their meagre and ill-cooked meals and did their thankless and monotonous chores through the aimless days. There was something of stolid resignation about them all, as if they walked half in another world between lines of nameless guards to a certain and familiar doom.

Thaddeus went mad in September after a visit to the well. He had gone with a pail and had come back empty-handed, shrieking and waving his arms, and sometimes lapsing into an inane titter or a whisper about "the moving colours down there". Two in one family was pretty bad, but Nahum was very brave about it. He let the boy run about for a week until he began stumbling and hurting himself, and then he shut him in an attic room across the hall from his mother's. The way they screamed at each other from behind their locked doors was very terrible, especially to little Merwin, who fancied they talked in some terrible language that was not of earth. Merwin was getting frightfully imaginative, and his restlessness was worse after the shutting away of the brother who had been his greatest playmate.

Almost at the same time the mortality among the livestock commenced. Poultry turned greyish and died very quickly, their meat being found dry and noisome upon cutting. Hogs grew inordinately fat, then suddenly began to undergo loathsome changes which no one could explain. Their meat was of course useless, and Nahum was at his wits' end. No rural veterinary would approach his place, and the city veterinary from Arkham was openly baffled. The swine began growing grey and brittle and falling to pieces before they died, and their eyes and muzzles developed singular alterations. It was very inexplicable, for they had never been fed from the tainted vegetation. Then something struck the cows. Certain areas or sometimes the whole body would be uncannily shrivelled or compressed, and atrocious collapses or disintegrations were common. In the last stages— and death was always the result—there would be a greying and turning brittle like that which beset the hogs. There could be no question of poison, for all the cases occurred in a locked and undisturbed barn. No bites of prowling things could have brought the virus, for what live beast of earth can pass through solid obstacles? It must be only natural disease—yet what disease could wreak such results was beyond any mind's guessing. When the harvest came there was not an animal surviving on the place, for the stock and poultry were dead and the dogs

had run away. These dogs, three in number, had all vanished
one night and were never heard of again. The five cats had left
some time before, but their going was scarcely noticed since there
now seemed to be no mice, and only Mrs. Gardner had made
pets of the graceful felines.

On the nineteenth of October Nahum staggered into Ammi's
house with hideous news. The death had come to poor Thaddeus
in his attic room, and it had come in a way which could not be
told. Nahum had dug a grave in the railed family plot behind
the farm, and had put therein what he found. There could have
been nothing from outside, for the small barred window and
locked door were intact; but it was much as it had been in the
barn. Ammi and his wife consoled the stricken man as best as
they could, but shuddered as they did so. Stark terror seemed
to cling round the Gardners and all they touched, and the very
presence of one in the house was a breath from regions un-
named and unnameable. Ammi accompanied Nahum home with
the greatest reluctance, and did what he might to calm the
hysterical sobbing of little Merwin. Zenas needed no calming.
He had come of late to do nothing but stare into space and obey
what his father told him; and Ammi thought that his fate was
very merciful. Now and then Merwin's screams were answered
faintly from the attic, and in response to an inquiring look
Nahum said that his wife was getting very feeble. When night
approached, Ammi managed to get away; for not even friendship could make him stay in that spot when the faint glow of the
vegetation began and the trees may or may not have swayed without wind. It was really lucky for Ammi that he was not more
imaginative. Even as things were, his mind was bent ever so
slightly; but had he been able to connect and reflect upon all the
portents around him he must inevitably have turned a total
maniac. In the twilight he hastened home, the screams of the
mad woman and the nervous child ringing horribly in his ears.

Three days later Nahum burst into Ammi's kitchen in the
early morning, and in the absence of his host stammered out a
desperate tale once more, while Mrs. Pierce listened in a clutching fright. It was little Merwin this time. He was gone. He had
gone out late at night with a lantern and pail of water, and had
never come back. He'd been going to pieces for days, and hardly
knew what he was about. Screamed at everything. There had
been a frantic shriek from the yard then, but before the father

could get to the door the boy was gone. There was no glow from the lantern he had taken, and of the child himself no trace. At the time Nahum thought the lantern and pail were gone too; but when dawn came, and the man had plodded back from his all-night search of the woods and fields, he had found some very curious things near the well. There was a crushed and apparently somewhat melted mass of iron which had certainly been the lantern; while a bent handle and twisted iron hoops beside it, both half-fused, seemed to hint at the remains of the pail. That was all. Nahum was past imagining, Mrs. Pierce was blank, and Ammi, when he had reached home and heard the tale, could give no guess. Merwin was gone, and there would be no use in telling the people around, who shunned all Gardners now. No use, either, in telling the city people at Arkham who laughed at everything. Thad was gone, and now Merwin was gone. Something was creeping and creeping and waiting to be seen and heard. Nahum would go soon, and he wanted Ammi to look after his wife and Zenas if they survived him. It must all be a judgment of some sort; though he could not fancy what for, since he had always walked uprightly in the Lord's ways so far as he knew.

For over two weeks Ammi saw nothing of Nahum; and then, worried about what might have happened, he overcame his fears and paid the Gardner place a visit. There was no smoke from the great chimney, and for a moment the visitor was apprehensive of the worst. The aspect of the whole farm was shocking—greyish withered grass and leaves on the ground, vines falling in brittle wreckage from archaic walls and gables, and great bare trees clawing up at the grey November sky with a studied malevolence which Ammi could not but feel had come from some subtle change in the tilt of the branches. But Nahum was alive, after all. He was weak, and lying on a couch in the low-ceiled kitchen, but perfectly conscious and able to give simple orders to Zenas. The room was deadly cold; and as Ammi visibly shivered, the host shouted huskily to Zenas for more wood. Wood, indeed, was sorely needed; since the cavernous fireplace was unlit and empty, with a cloud of soot blowing about in the chill wind that came down the chimney. Presently Nahum asked him if the extra wood had made him any more comfortable, and then Ammi saw what had happened. The stoutest cord had broken at last, and the hapless farmer's mind was proof against more sorrow.

Questioning tactfully, Ammi could get no clear data at all about the missing Zenas. 'In the well—he lives in the well—' was all that the clouded father would say. Then there flashed across the visitor's mind a sudden thought of the mad wife, and he changed his line of enquiry. "Nabby? Why, here she is!" was the surprised response of poor Nahum, and Ammi soon saw that he must search for himself. Leaving the harmless babbler on the couch, he took the keys from their nail beside the door and climbed the creaking stairs to the attic. It was very close and noisome up there, and no sound direction. Of the four doors in sight only one was locked, and on this he tried various keys of the ring he had taken. The third key proved the right one, and after some fumbling Ammi threw open the low white door.

It was quite dark inside, for the window was small and half-obscured by the crude wooden bars; and Ammi could see nothing at all on the wide-planked floor. The stench was beyond enduring, and before proceeding further he had to retreat to another room and return with his lungs filled with breathable air. When he did enter he saw something dark in the corner, and upon seeing it more clearly he screamed outright. While he screamed he thought a momentary cloud eclipsed the window, and a second later he felt himself brushed as if by some hateful current of vapour. Strange colours danced before his eyes; and had not a present horror numbed him he would have thought of the globule in the meteor that the geologist's hammer had shattered, and of the morbid vegetation that had sprouted in the spring. As it was he thought only of the blasphemous monstrosity which confronted him, and which all too clearly had shared the nameless fate of young Thaddeus and the livestock. But the terrible thing about the horror was that it very slowly and perceptibly moved as it continued to crumble.

Ammi would give me no added particulars of this scene, but the shape in the corner does not reappear in his tale as a moving object. There are things which cannot be mentioned, and what is done in common humanity is sometimes cruelly judged by the law. I gathered that no moving thing was left in that attic room, and that to leave anything capable of motion there would have been a deed so monstrous as to damn any accountable being to eternal torment. Anyone but a stolid farmer would have fainted or gone mad, but Ammi walked conscious through that low

doorway and locked the accursed secret behind him. There would
be Nahum to deal with now; he must be fed and tended, and
removed to some place where he could be cared for.

Commencing his descent of the dark stairs, Ammi heard a
thud below him. He even thought a scream had been suddenly
choked off, and recalled nervously the clammy vapour which
had brushed by him in that frightful room above. What presence
had his cry and entry started up? Halted by some vague fear, he
heard still further sounds below. Indubitably there was a sort of
heavy dragging, and a most detestably sticky noise as of some
fiendish and unclean species of suction. With an associative sense
goaded to feverish heights, he thought unaccountably of what
he had seen upstairs. Good God! What eldritch dream-world
was this into which he had blundered? He dared move neither
backward nor forward, but stood there trembling at the black
curve of the boxed-in staircase. Every trifle of the scene burned
itself into his brain. The sounds, the sense of dread expectancy,
the darkness, the steepness of the narrow steps—and merciful
Heaven!—the faint but unmistakable luminosity of all the
woodwork in sight; steps, sides, exposed laths, and beams alike.

Then there burst forth a frantic whinny from Ammi's horse
outside, followed at once by a clatter which told of a frenzied
runaway. In another moment horse and buggy had gone beyond
earshot, leaving the frightened man on the dark stairs to guess
what had sent them. But that was not all. There had been another
sound out there. A sort of liquid splash—water—it must have
been the well. He had left Hero untied near it, and a buggy-
wheel must have brushed the coping and knocked in a stone.
And still the pale phosphorescence glowed in that detestably
ancient woodwork. God! how old the house was! Most of it
built before 1670, and the gambrel roof no later than 1730.

A feeble scratching on the floor downstairs now sounded
distinctly, and Ammi's grip tightened on a heavy stick he had
picked up in the attic for some purpose. Slowly nerving himself,
he finished his descent and walked boldly towards the kitchen.
But he did not complete the walk, because what he sought was
no longer there. It had come to meet him, and it was still alive
after a fashion. Whether it had crawled or whether it had been
dragged by any external forces, Ammi could not say; but the
death had been at it. Everything had happened in the last half-
hour, but collapse, greying, and disintegration were already far

advanced. There was a horrible brittleness, and dry fragments were scaling off. Ammi could not touch it, but looked horrifiedly into the distorted parody that had been a face. "What was it, Nahum—what was it?" he whispered, and the cleft, bulging lips were just able to crack out a final answer.

"Nothin' . . . nothin' . . . the colour . . . it burns . . . cold an' wet, but it burns . . . it lived in the well. . . . I seen it . . . a kind of smoke . . . jest like the flowers last spring . . . the well shone at night . . . Thad an' Merwin an' Zenas . . . everything alive . . . suckin' the life out of everything . . . in that stone . . . it must a' come in that stone . . . pizened the whole place . . . dun't know what it wants . . . that round thing them men from the college dug outen the stone . . . they smashed it . . . it was that same colour . . . jest the same, like the flowers an' plants . . . must a' ben more of 'em . . . seeds . . . seeds . . . they growed . . . I seen it the fust time this week . . . must a' got strong on Zenas . . . he was a big boy, full o' life . . . it beats down your mind an' then gets ye . . . burns ye up . . . in the well water . . . you was right about that . . . evil water . . . Zenas never come back from the well . . . can't git away . . . draws ye . . . ye know summ'at's comin' but tain't no use . . . I seen it time an' agin sence Zenas was took . . . whar's Nabby, Ammi? . . . my head's no good . . . dun't know how long sence I fed her . . . it'll git her ef we ain't keerful . . . jest a colour . . . her face is gittin' to hev that colour sometimes towards night . . . an' it burns an' sucks . . . it come from some place whar things ain't as they is here . . . one o' them professors said so . . . he was right . . . look out, Ammi, it'll do suthin' more . . . sucks the life out . . ."

But that was all. That which spoke could speak no more because it had completely caved in. Ammi laid a red checked tablecloth over what was left and reeled out the back door into the fields. He climbed the slope to the ten-acre pasture and stumbled home by the north road and the woods. He could not pass that well from which his horse had run away. He had looked at it through the window, and had seen that no stone was missing from the rim. Then the lurching buggy had not dislodged anything after all—the splash had been something else—something which went into the well after it had done with poor Nahum. . . .

When Ammi reached his house the horse and buggy had arrived before him and thrown his wife into fits of anxiety.

Reassuring her without explanations, he set out at once for Arkham and notified the authorities that the Gardner family was no
more. He indulged in no details, but merely told of the deaths
of Nahum and Nabby, that of Thaddeus being already known,
and mentioned that the cause seemed to be the same strange ail-
ment which had killed the livestock. He also stated that Merwin
and Zenas had disappeared. There was considerable questioning
at the police station, and in the end Ammi was compelled to take
three officers to the Gardner farm, together with the coroner,
the medical examiner, and the veterinary who had treated the
diseased animals. He went much against his will, for the afternoon was advancing and he feared the fall of night over that
accursed place, but it was some comfort to have so many people
with him.

The six men drove out in a democrat-wagon, following
Ammi's buggy, and arrived at the pest-ridden farmhouse about
four o'clock. Used as the officers were to gruesome experiences,
not one remained unmoved at what was found in the attic and
under the red checked tablecloth on the floor below. The whole
aspect of the farm with its grey desolation was terrible enough,
but those two crumbling objects were beyond all bounds. No one
could look long at them, and even the medical examiner admitted
that there was very little to examine. Specimens could be
analysed, of course, so he busied himself in obtaining them—
and here it develops that a very puzzling aftermath occurred at
the college laboratory where the two phials of dust were finally
taken. Under the spectroscope both samples gave off an unknown spectrum, in which many of the baffling bands were
precisely like those which the strange meteor had yielded in the
previous year. The property of emitting this spectrum vanished
in a month, the dust therafter consisting mainly of alkaline
phosphates and carbonates.

Ammi would not have told the men about the well if he had
thought they meant to do anything then and there. It was getting
towards sunset, and he was anxious to be away. But he could not
help glancing nervously at the stony kerb by the great sweep,
and when a detective questioned him he admitted that Nahum
had feared something down there—so much so that he had
never even thought of searching it for Merwin or Zenas. After
that nothing would do but that they empty and explore the well
immediately, so Ammi had to wait trembling while pail after

pail of rank water was hauled up and splashed on the soaking
ground outside. The men sniffed in disgust at the fluid, and
towards the last held their noses against the foetor they were un-
covering. It was not so long a job as they had feared it would be,
since the water was phenomenally low. There is no need to speak
too exactly of what they found. Merwin and Zenas were both
there, in part, though the vestiges were mainly skeletal. There
were also a small deer and a large dog in about the same state,
and a number of bones of small animals. The ooze and slime
at the bottom seemed enexplicably porous and bubbling, and a
man who descended on hand-holds with a long pole found that
he could sink the wooden shaft to any depth in the mud of the
floor without meeting any solid obstruction.

Twilight had now fallen, and lanterns were brought from the
house. Then, when it was seen that nothing further could be
gained from the well, everyone went indoors and conferred in
the ancient sitting-room while the intermittent light of a spectral
half-moon played wanly on the grey desolation outside. The
men were frankly nonplussed by the entire case, and could find
no convincing common element to link the strange vegetable conditions, the unknown disease of livestock and humans, and the
unaccountable deaths of Merwin and Zenas in the tainted well.
They had heard the common country talk, it is true; but could
not believe that anything contrary to natural law had occurred.
No doubt the meteor had poisoned the soil, but the illness of
persons and animals who had eaten nothing grown in that soil
was another matter. Was it the well water? Very possibly. It
might be a good idea to analyse it. But what peculiar madness
could have made both boys jump into the well? Their deeds were
so similar—and the fragments showed that they had both
suffered from the grey brittle death. Why was everything so grey
and brittle?

It was the coroner, seated near a window overlooking the yard,
who first noticed the glow about the well. Night had fully set in,
and all the abhorrent grounds seemed faintly luminous with
more than the fitful moonbeams; but this new glow was something definite and distinct, and appeared to shoot up from the black
pit like a softened ray from a searchlight, giving dull reflections in
the little ground pools where the water had been emptied. It had
a very queer colour, and as all the men clustered round the window
Ammi gave a violent start. For this strange beam of ghastly miasma

was to him of no unfamiliar hue. He had seen that colour before, and feared to think what it might mean. He had seen it in the nasty brittle globule in that aerolite two summers ago, had seen it in the crazy vegetation of the springtime, and had thought he had seen it for an instant that very morning against the small barred window of that terrible attic room where nameless things had happened. It had flashed there a second, and a clammy and hateful current of vapour had brushed past him—and then poor Nahum had been taken by something of that colour. He had said so at the last—said it was like the globule and the plants. After that had come the runaway in the yard and the splash in the well—and now that well was belching forth to the night a pale insidious beam of the same demoniac tint.

It does credit to the alertness of Ammi's mind that he puzzled even at that tense moment over a point which was essentially scientific. He could not but wonder at his gleaning of the same impression from a vapour glimpsed in the daytime, against a window opening on the morning sky, and from a nocturnal exhalation seen as a phosphorescent mist against the black and blasted landscape. It wasn't right—it was against Nature—and he thought of those terrible last words of his stricken friend, "It come from some place what things ain't as they is here . . . one o' them professors said so. . . ."

All three horses outside, tied to a pair of shrivelled saplings by the road, were now neighing and pawing frantically. The wagon driver started for the door to do something, but Ammi laid a shaky hand on his shoulder. "Duon't go out thar," he whispered. "They's more to this nor what we know. Nahum said somethin' lived in the well that sucks your life out. He said it must be some'at growed from a round ball like one we all seen in the meteor stone that fell a year ago June. Sucks an' burns, he said, an' is jest a cloud of colour like that light out thar now, that ye can hardly see an' can't tell what it is. Nahum thought it feeds on everything livin' an' gits stronger all the time. He said he seen it this last week. It must be somethin' from away off in the sky like the men from the college last year says the meteor stone was. The way it's made an' the way it works ain't like no way o' God's world. It's summ'at from beyond."

So the men paused indecisively as the light from the well grew stronger and the hitched horses pawed and whinnied in increasing frenzy. It was truly an awful moment; with terror in that ancient and accursed house itself, four monstrous sets of fragments—two from the house and two from the well—in the woodshed behind, and that shaft of unknown and unholy iridescence from the slimy depths in front. Ammi had restrained the driver on impulse, forgetting how uninjured he himself was after the clammy brushing of that coloured vapour in the attic room, but perhaps it is just as well that he acted as he did. No one will ever know what was abroad that night; and though the blasphemy from beyond had not so far hurt any human of unweakened mind, there is no telling what it might not have done at that last moment, with its seemingly increased strength and the special signs of purpose it was soon to display beneath the half-clouded moonlit sky.

All at once one of the detectives at the window gave a short, sharp gasp. The others looked at him, and then quickly followed his own gaze upward to the point at which its idle straying had been suddenly arrested. There was no need for words. What had been disputed in country gossip was disputable no longer, and it is because of the thing which every man of that party agreed in whispering later on, that the strange days are never talked about in Arkham. It is necessary to premise that there was no wind at that hour of the evening. One did arise not long afterward, but there was absolutely none then. Even the dry tips of the lingering hedge-mustard, grey and blighted, and the fringe on the roof of the standing democrat-wagon were unstirred. And yet amid that tense, godless calm the high bare boughs of all the trees in the yard were moving. They were twitching morbidly and spasmodically, clawing in convulsive and epileptic madness at the moonlit clouds; scratching impotently in the noxious air as if jerked by some allied and bodiless line of linkage with subterrene horrors writhing and struggling below the black roots.

Not a man breathed for several seconds. Then a cloud of darker depth passed over the moon, and the silhouette of clutching branches faded out momentarily. At this there was a general cry; muffled with awe, but husky and almost identical from every throat. For the terror had not faded with the silhouette, and in a fearsome instant of deeper darkness the watchers saw wriggling at that tree-top height a thousand tiny points of faint and unhallowed radiance, tipping each bough like the fire of St. Elmo or the flames that come down on the apostles' heads of Pentecost. It was a monstrous constellation of unnatural light, like a glutted swarm of corpse-fed fireflies dancing hellish sarabands over an accursed marsh; and its colour was that same nameless intrusion which Ammi had come to recognize and dread. All the while the shaft of phosphorescence from the well was getting brighter and brighter, bringing, to the minds of the huddled men, a sense of doom and abnormality. It was no longer *shining* out; it was *pouring* out; and as the shapeless stream of unplaceable colour left the well it seemed to flow directly into the sky.

The veterinary shivered, and walked to the front door to drop the heavy extra bar across it. Ammi shook no less, and had to tug and point for lack of controllable voice when he wished to draw notice to the growing luminosity of the trees. The neighing and stamping of the horses had become utterly frightful, but not a soul of that group in the old house would have ventured forth for any earthly reward. With the moments the shining of the trees increased, while their restless branches seemed to strain more and more towards verticality. The wood of the well-sweep was shining now, and presently a policeman dumbly pointed to some wooden sheds and beehives near the stone wall on the west. They were commencing to shine, too, though the tethered vehicles of the visitors seemed so far unaffected. Then there was a wild commotion and clopping in the road, and as Ammi quenched the lamp for better seeing they realized that the span of frantic greys had broken their sapling and run off with the democrat-wagon.

The shock served to loosen several tongues, and embarrassed whispers were exchanged. "It spreads on everything organic that's been around here," muttered the medical examiner. No one replied, but the man who had been in the well gave a hint that his long pole must have stirred up something intangible. "It was awful," he added. "There was no bottom at all, just ooze and bubbles and the feeling of something lurking under there." Ammi's horse still pawed and screamed deafeningly in the road outside, and nearly drowned its owner's faint quaver as he mumbled his formless reflections. "It come from that stone—it growed down thar—it got everything livin'—it fed itself on 'em, mind and body—Thad an' Merwin, Zenas an' Nabby—Nahum was the last—they all drunk the water—it got strong on 'em—it come from beyond, what things ain't like they be here—now it's goin' home—"

At this point, as the column of unknown colour flared suddenly stronger and began to weave itself into fantastic suggestions of shape which each spectator later described differently, there came from poor tethered Hero such a sound as no man before or since ever heard from a horse. Every person in that low-pitched sitting-room stopped his ears, and Ammi turned away from the window in

horror and nausea. Words could not convey it—when Ammi looked
out again the hapless beast lay huddled inert on the moonlit ground
between the splintered shafts of the buggy. That was the last of
Hero till they buried him next day. But the present was no time
to mourn, for almost at this instant a detective silently called attention to something terrible in the very room with them. In the
absence of the lamplight it was clear that a faint phosphorescence
had begun to pervade the entire apartment. It glowed on the broad-
planked floor and the fragment of rag carpet, and shimmered over
the sashes of the small-paned windows. It ran up and down the
exposed corner-posts, coruscated about the shelf and mantel, and
infected the very doors and furniture. Each minute saw it strengthen,
and at last it was very plain that healthy living things must leave
that house.

Ammi showed them the back door and the path up through the
fields to the ten-acre pasture. They walked and stumbled as in a
dream, and did not dare look back till they were far away on the
high ground. They were glad of the path, for they could not have
gone the front way, by that well. It was bad enough passing the
glowing barn and sheds, and those shining orchard trees with their
gnarled, fiendish contours; but thank Heaven the branches did
their worst twisting high up. The moon went under some very
black clouds as they crossed the rustic bridge over Chapman's
Brook, and it was blind groping from there to the open meadows.

When they looked back towards the valley and the distant Gardner place at the bottom they saw a fearsome sight. All the farm was
shining with the hideous unknown blend of colour : trees, buildings,
and even such grass and herbage as had not been wholly changed
to lethal grey brittleness. The boughs were all straining skyward,
tipped with tongues of foul flame, and lambent tricklings of the
same monstrous fire were creeping about the ridgepoles of the house,
barn and sheds. It was a scene from a vision of Fuseli, and over
all the rest reigned that riot of luminous amorphousness, that alien
and undimensioned rainbow of cryptic poison from the well—
seething, feeling, lapping, reaching, scintillating, straining, and
malignly bubbling in its cosmic and unrecognizable chromaticism.

Then without warning the hideous thing shot vertically up towards the sky like a rocket or meteor, leaving behind no trail and
disappearing through a round and curiously regular hole in the
clouds before any man could gasp or cry out. No watcher can ever
forget that sight, and Ammi stared blankly at the stars of Cygnus,

Deneb twinkling above the others, where the unknown colour had melted into the Milky Way. But his gaze was the next moment called swiftly to earth by the crackling in the valley. It was just that. Only a wooden ripping and crackling, and not an explosion, as so many others of the party vowed. Yet the outcome was the same, for in one feverish kaleidoscopic instant there burst up from that doomed and accursed farm a gleamingly eruptive cataclysm of unnatural sparks and substance; blurring the glance of the few who saw it, and sending forth to the zenith a bombarding cloudburst of such coloured and fantastic fragments as our universe must needs disown. Through quickly re-closing vapours they followed the great morbidity that had vanished, and in another second they had vanished too. Behind and below was only a darkness to which the men dared not return, and all about was a mounting wind which seemed to sweep down in black, frore gusts from interstellar space. It shrieked and howled, and lashed the fields and distorted woods in a mad cosmic frenzy, till soon the trembling party realized it would be no use waiting for the moon to show what was left down there at Nahum's.

Too awed even to hint theories, the seven shaking men trudged back towards Arkham by the north road. Ammi was worse than his fellows, and begged them to see him inside his own kitchen, instead of keeping straight on to town. He did not wish to cross the blighted wind-whipped woods alone to his home on the main road. For he had had an added shock that the others were spared, and was crushed forever with a brooding fear he dared not even mention for many years to come. As the rest of the watchers on that tempestuous hill had stolidly set their faces towards the road, Ammi had looked back an instant at the shadowed valley of desolation so lately sheltering his ill-starred friend. And from that stricken, faraway spot he had seen something feebly rise, only to sink down again upon the place from which the great shapeless horror had shot into the sky. It was just a colour—but not any colour of our earth or heavens. And because Ammi recognized that colour, and knew that this last faint remnant must still lurk down there in the well, he has never been quite right since.

Ammi would never go near the place again. It is forty-four years now since the horror happened, but he has never been there, and will be glad when the new reservoir blots it out. I shall be glad, too, for I do not like the way the sunlight changed colour around the mouth of that abandoned well I passed. I hope the water will always be very deep—but even so, I shall never drink it. I do not think I shall visit the Arkham country hereafter. Three of the men who had been with Ammi returned the next morning to see the ruins by daylight, but there were not any real ruins. Only the bricks of the chimney, the stones of the cellar, some mineral and metallic litter here and there, and the rim of that nefandous well. Save for Ammi's dead horse, which they towed away and buried, and the buggy which they shortly returned to him, everything that had ever been living had gone. Five eldritch acres of dusty grey desert remained, nor has anything ever grown there since. To this day it sprawls open to the sky like a great spot eaten by acid in the woods and fields, and the few who have ever dared glimpse it in spite of the rural tales have named it "the blasted heath".

The rural tales are queer. They might be even queerer if city men and college chemists could be interested enough to analyse the water from that disused well, or the grey dust that no wind seems to disperse. Botanists, too, ought to study the stunted flora on the borders of that spot, for they might shed light on the country notion that the blight is spreading—little by little, perhaps an inch a year. People say the colour of the neighbouring herbage is not quite right in the spring, and that wild things leave queer prints in the light winter snow. Snow never seems quite so heavy on the blasted heath as it is elsewhere. Horses—the few that are left in this motor age— grow skittish in the silent valley; and hunters cannot depend on their dogs too near the splotch of greyish dust.

They say the mental influences are very bad, too; numbers went queer in the years after Nahum's taking, and always they lacked the power to get away. Then the stronger-minded folk all left the region, and only the foreigners tried to live in the crumbling old homesteads. They could not stay, though; and one sometimes wonders what insight beyond ours their wild, weird stories of whispered magic have given them. Their dreams at night, they protest, are very horrible in that grotesque country; and surely the very look of the dark realm is enough to stir a morbid fancy. No traveller has ever escaped a sense of strangeness in those deep ravines, and artists shiver as they paint thick woods whose mystery is as much of the spirit as of the eye. I myself am curious about the sensation I derived from my one lone walk before Ammi told me his tale. When twilight came I had vaguely wished some clouds would gather, for an odd timidity about the deep skyey voids above had crept into my soul.

Do not ask me for my opinion. I do not know—that is all. There was no one but Ammi to question; for Arkham people will not talk about the strange days, and all three professors who saw the aerolite and its coloured globule are dead. There were other globules—depend upon that. One must have fed itself and escaped, and probably there was another which was too late. No doubt it is still down the well—I know there was something wrong with the sunlight I saw above the miasmal brink. The rustics say the blight creeps an inch a year, so perhaps there is a kind of growth or nourishment even now. But whatever daemon hatching is there, it must be tethered to something or else it would quickly spread. Is it fastened to the roots of those trees that claw the air? One of the current Arkham tales is about fat oaks that shine and move as they ought not to do at night.

What it is, only God knows. In terms of matter I suppose the things Ammi described would be called a gas, but this gas obeyed the laws that are not of our cosmos. This was no fruit of such worlds and suns as shine on the telescopes and photographic plates of our observatories. This was no breath from the skies whose motions and dimensions our astronomers measure or deem too vast to measure. It was just a colour out of space—a frightful messenger from unformed realms of infinity beyond all Nature as we know it; from realms whose mere existence stuns the brain and numbs us with the black extra-cosmic gulfs it throws open before our frenzied eyes.

I doubt very much if Ammi consciously lied to me, and I do not think his tale was all a freak of madness as the townsfolk had forewarned. Something terrible came to the hills and valleys on that meteor, and something terrible—though I know not in what proportion—still remains. I shall be glad to see the water come. Meanwhile I hope nothing will happen to Ammi. He saw so much of the thing—and its influence was so insidious. Why has he never been able to move away? How clearly he recalled those dying words of Nahum's—"can't git away—draws ye—ye know summ'at's comin' but tain't no use—" Ammi is such a good old man—when the reservoir gang gets to work I must write the chief engineer to keep a sharp watch on him. I would hate to think of him as the grey, twisted, brittle monstrosity which persists more and more in troubling my sleep.

THE SKULL

ROBERT BLOCH

(Paramount: 1966)

Eager to cash in on the success of Hammer and American-International, new film companies blossomed on either side of the Atlantic. The quality of their productions varied enormously. In England a pace-making team headed by Max Rosenberg and Milton Subotsky concentrated on real talent, using writers like Robert Bloch (who, strangely, had had little screen work since the enormous success of Psycho*) and stars such as Peter Cushing and Christopher Lee.*

An early and highly successful combination of this triumverate was The Skull, *based on a short story,* The Skull of the Marquis de Sade, *by Bloch himself. The tale concerned a skull, reputedly that of the infamous French nobleman and apparently still imbued with his evil power. It presented Cushing at his controlled and sardonic best and Lee demonstrating that he could be very much at home in horror without the use of his Frankenstein make-up or Dracula teeth.*

The film was also a success for Robert Bloch and happily brought him back to work in the genre to which he had given one of the most terrifying of all pictures. Space alone prevents me from including more of his superb stories, which have since provided the basis for excellent horror films.

*

CHRISTOPHER MAITLAND sat back in his chair before the fireplace and fondled the binding of an old book. His thin face, modelled by the flickering firelight, bore a characteristic expression of scholarly preoccupation.

Maitland's intellectual curiosity was focused on the volume in his hands. Briefly, he was wondering if the human skin binding this book came from a man, a woman or a child.

He had been assured by the bookseller that this tome was bound in a portion of the skin of a woman, but Maitland, much as he desired to believe this, was by nature sceptical. Booksellers who deal in such *curiosa* are not overly reputable, as a rule, and Christopher Maitland's years of dealing with such people had done much to destroy his faith in their veracity.

Still, he hoped the story was true. It was nice to have a book bound in a woman's skin. It was nice to have a *crux ansata* fashioned from a thighbone; a collection of Dyack heads; a shrivelled Hand of Glory stolen from a graveyard in Mainz. Maitland owned all of these items, and many more. For he was a collector of the unusual.

Maitland held the book up to the light and sought to distinguish pore-formation beneath the tanned surface of the binding. Women had finer pores than men, didn't they?

"Beg pardon, sir."

Maitland turned as Hume entered. "What is it?" he asked.

"That person is here again."

"Person?"

"Mr. Marco."

"Oh?" Maitland rose, ignoring the butler's almost grotesque expression of distaste. He suppressed a chuckle. Poor Hume didn't like Marco, or any of the raffish gentry who supplied Maitland with items for his collection. Hume didn't care for the collection itself, either—Maitland vividly remembered the old servant's squeamish trembling as he dusted off the case containing the mummy of the priest of Horus decapitated for sorcery.

"Marco, eh? Wonder what's up?" Maitland mused. "Well— better show him in."

Hume turned and left with a noticeable lack of enthusiasm. As for Maitland, his eagerness mounted. He ran his hand along the reticulated back of a jadeite *tao-tieh* and licked his lips with very much the same expression as adorned the face of the Chinese image of gluttony.

Old Marco was here. That meant something pretty special in the way of acquisitions. Perhaps Marco wasn't exactly the kind of chap one invited to the Club—but he had his uses. Where he laid hands on some of the things he offered for sale Maitland didn't know; he didn't much care. That was Marco's affair. The rarity of his offerings was what interested Christopher Maitland. If one wanted a book bound in human skin, old Marco was just the chap to get hold of it—if he had to do a bit of flaying and binding himself. Great character, old Marco!

"Mr. Marco, sir."

Hume withdrew, a sedate shadow, and Maitland waved his visitor forward.

Mr. Marco oozed into the room. The little man was fat, greasily so; his flesh lumped like the tallow coagulating about the guttering stump of a candle. His waxen pallor accentuated the simile. All that seemed needed was a wick to sprout from the bald ball of fat that served as Mr. Marco's head.

The fat man stared up at Maitland's lean face with what was meant to be an ingratiating smile. The smile oozed, too, and contributed to the aura of uncleanliness which seemed to surround Marco.

But Maitland was not conscious of these matters. His attention was focused on the curious bundle Marco carried under one arm—the large package, wrapped in prosaic butcher's paper which somehow contributed to its fascination for him.

Marco shifted the package gingerly as he removed his shoddy grey ulster. He did not ask permission to divest himself of the coat, nor did he wait for an invitation to be seated.

The fat little man merely made himself comfortable in one of the chairs before the fire, reached for Maitland's open cigar case, helped himself to a stogie, and lit it. The large round package bobbed up and down on his lap as his rotund stomach heaved convulsively.

Maitland stared at the package. Marco stared at Maitland. Maitland broke first.

"Well?" he asked.

The greasy smile expanded. Marco inhaled rapidly, then opened his mouth to emit a puff of smoke and a reply.

"I am sorry to come unannounced, Mr. Maitland. I hope I'm not intruding?"

"Never mind that," Maitland snapped. "What's in the package, Marco?"

Marco's smile expanded. "Something choice," he whispered. "Something tasty."

Maitland bent over the chair, his head out-thrust to throw a vulpine shadow on the wall.

"What's in the package?" he repeated.

"You're my favourite client, Mr. Maitland. You know I never come to you unless I have something really rare. Well, I have that, sir. I have that. You'd be surprised what this butcher's paper hides, although it's rather appropriate. Yes, appropriate it is!"

"Stop that infernal gabbling, man! What is in the package?"

Marco lifted the bundle from his lap. He turned it over gingerly, yet deliberately.

"Doesn't seem to be much," he purred. "Round. Heavy enough. Might be a medicine ball, eh? Or a beehive. I say, it could even be a head of cabbage. Yes, one might mistake it for a head of common cabbage. But it isn't. Oh no, it isn't. Intriguing problem, eh?"

If it was the little man's intention to goad Maitland into a fit of apoplexy, he almost succeeded.

"Open it up, damn you!" he shouted.

Marco shrugged, smiled, and scrabbled at the taped edges of the paper. Christopher Maitland was no longer the perfect gentleman, the perfect host. He was a collector, stripped of all pretences—quivering eagerness incarnate. He hovered over Marco's shoulder as the butcher's paper came away in the fat man's pudgy fingers.

"Now!" Maitland breathed.

The paper fell to the floor. Resting in Marco's lap was a large, glittering silver ball of—tinfoil.

Marco began to strip the tinfoil away, unravelling it in silvery strands. Maitland gasped as he saw what emerged from the wrappings.

It was a human skull.

Maitland saw the horrid hemisphere gleaming ivory-white in the firelight—then, as Marco shifted it, he saw the empty eye sockets and the gaping nasal aperture that would never know human breath. Maitland noted the even structure of the teeth, adherent to a well-formed jaw. Despite his instinctive repulsion, he was surprisingly observant.

It appeared to him that the skull was unusually small and delicate, remarkably well preserved despite a yellow tinge hinting of age. But Christopher Maitland was most impressed by one undeniable peculiarity. The skull was *different*, indeed.

This skull did not grin!

Through some peculiar formation or malformation of cheekbone in juxtaposition of jaws, the death's-head did not simulate a smile. The classic mockery of mirth attributed to all skulls was absent here.

The skull had a sober, serious look about it.

Maitland blinked and uttered a self-conscious cough. What was he doing, entertaining these idiotic fancies about a skull? It was ordinary enough. What was old Marco's game in bringing him such a silly object with so much solemn preamble?

Yes, what *was* Marco's game?

The little fat man held the skull up before the firelight, turning it from time to time with an impressive display of pride.

His smirk of self-satisfaction contrasted oddly with the sobriety set indelibly upon the skull's bony visage.

Maitland's puzzlement found expression at last. "What are you so smug about?" he demanded. "You bring me the skull of a woman or an adolescent youth—"

Marco's chuckle cut across his remark. "Exactly what the phrenologists said!" he wheezed.

"Damn the phrenologists, man! Tell me about this skull, if there's anything to tell."

Marco ignored him. He turned the skull over in his fat hands, with a gloating expression which repelled Maitland.

"It may be small, but it's a beauty, isn't it?" the little man mused. "So delicately formed, and look—there's almost the illusion of a patina upon the surface."

"I'm not a paleontologist," Maitland snapped. "Nor a grave robber, either. You'd think we were Burke and Hare! Be reasonable, Marco—why should I want an ordinary skull?"

"Please, Mr. Maitland! What do you take me for? Do you think I would presume to insult your intelligence by bringing you an ordinary skull? Do you imagine I would ask a thousand pounds for the skull of a nobody?"

Maitland stepped back.

"A thousand pounds?" he shouted. "A thousand pounds for *that?*"

"And cheap at the price," Marco assured him. "You'll pay it gladly when you know the story."

"I wouldn't pay such a price for the skull of Napoleon," Maitland assured him. "Or Shakespeare, for that matter."

"You'll find that the owner of this skull tickles your fancy a bit more," Marco assured him.

"Enough of this. Let's have it, man!"

Marco faced him, one pudgy forefinger tapping the osseous brow of the death's-head.

"You see before you," he murmured, "the skull of Donatien Alphonce François, the Marquis de Sade."

Giles de Retz was a monster. Torquemada's inquisitors exercised the diabolic ingenuity of the fiends they professed to exorcise. But it remained for the Marquis de Sade to epitomize the living lust for pain. His name symbolizes cruelty incarnate—the savagery men call "sadism".

Maitland knew de Sade's weird history, and mentally reviewed it.

The Count, or Marquis, de Sade was born in 1740, of distinguished Provençal lineage. He was a handsome youth when he joined his cavalry regiment in the Seven Years' War—a pale, delicate, blue-eyed man, whose foppish diffidence cloaked an evil perversity.

At the age of twenty-three he was imprisoned for a year as the result of a barbaric crime. Indeed, twenty-seven years of his subsequent life he spent in incarceration for his deeds—deeds which even today are only hinted at. His flagellations, his administration of outer drugs and his tortures of women have served to make his name infamous.

But de Sade was no common libertine with a primitive urge towards the infliction of suffering. He was, rather, the "philosopher of pain"—a keen scholar, a man of exquisite taste and breeding. He was wonderfully well-read, a disciplined thinker, a remarkable psychologist—and a sadist.

How the mighty Marquis would have squirmed had he envisioned the petty perversions which today bear his name! The tormenting of animals by ignorant peasants, the beating of children by hysteric attendants in institutions, the infliction of senseless cruelties by maniacs upon others or by others upon maniacs—all these matters are classified as "sadistic" today. And yet none of them are manifestation of de Sade's unnatural philosophy.

De Sade's concept of cruelty had in it nothing of concealment or deceit. He practised his beliefs openly and wrote explicity of such matters during his years in prison. For he was the Apostle of Pain, and his gospel was made known to all men in *Justine, Juliette, Aline et Valcour*, the curious *La Philosophie dans le Boudoir* and the utterly abominable *Les 120 Journées*.

And de Sade practised what he preached. He was a lover of many women—a jealous lover, willing to share the embraces of his mistresses with but one rival. That rival was Death, and it is said that all women who knew de Sade's caresses came to prefer those of his rival, in the end.

Perhaps the tortures of the French Revolution were indirectly inspired by the philosophy of the Marquis—a philosophy that gained circulation throughout France following the publication of his notorious tomes.

When the guillotine arose in the public squares of the cities, de Sade emerged from his long series of imprisonments and walked abroad among men maddened at the sight of blood and suffering.

He was a grey, gentle little ghost—short, bald, mild-mannered and soft-spoken. He raised his voice only to save his aristocratic relatives from the knife. His public life was exemplary during these latter years.

But men still whispered of his private life. His interest in sorcery was rumoured. It is said that to de Sade the shedding of blood was a sacrifice. And sacrifices made to certain beings bring black boons. The screams of pain-maddened women are as prayer to the creatures of the Pit. . . .

The Marquis was cunning. Years of confinement for his "offences against society" had made him wary. He moved quite cautiously and took full advantage of the troubled times to conduct quiet and unostentatious burial services whenever he terminated an amour.

Caution did not suffice, in the end. An ill-chosen diatribe directed against Napoleon served as an excuse for the authorities. There were no civil charges; no farcical trial was perpetrated.

De Sade was simply shut up in Charenton as a common lunatic. The men who knew his crimes were too shocked to publicize them —and yet there was a satanic grandeur about the Marquis which somehow precluded destroying him outright. One does not think of assassinating Satan. But Satan chained—

Satan, chained, languished. A sick, half-blind old man who tore the petals from roses in a last gesture of demoniac destructiveness, the Marquis spent his declining days forgotten by all men. They preferred to forget, preferred to think him mad.

In 1814, he died. His books were banned, his memory desecrated, his deeds denied. But his name lived on—lives on as an eternal symbol of innate evil. . . .

Such was de Sade, as Christopher Maitland knew him. And as a collector of *curiosa,* the thought of possessing the veritable skull of the fabulous Marquis intrigued him.

He glanced up from revery, glanced at the unsmiling skull and the grinning Marco.

"A thousand pounds, you said?"

"Exactly," Marco nodded. "A most reasonable price, under the circumstances."

"Under what circumstances?" Maitland objected. "You bring me a skull. But what proofs can you furnish me as to its authenticity? How did you come by this rather unusual *memento mori?*"

'Come, come, Mr. Maitland—please? You know me better than to question my source of supply. That is what I choose to call a trade secret, eh?"

"Very well. But I can't just take your word, Marco. To the best of my recollection, de Sade was buried when he died at Charenton, in 1814."

Marco's oozing grin expanded.

"Well, I can set you right about that point," he conceded "Do you happen to have a copy of Ellis's *Studies* about? In the section entitled *Love and Pain* there is an item which may interest you."

Maitland secured the volume, and Marco rifled through the pages.

"Here!" he exclaimed triumphantly. "According to Ellis, the skull of the Marquis de Sade was exhumed and examined by a phrenologist. Phrenology was a popular pseudo-science in those days, eh? The chap wanted to see if the cranial formation indicated the Marquis was truly insane.

"It says he found the skull to be small and well formed, like a woman's. Exactly your remark, as you may recall!

"But the real point is this. The skull wasn't reinterred.

"It fell into the hands of a Dr. Londe, but around 1850 it was stolen by another physician, who took it to England. That is all Ellis knows of the matter. The rest I could tell—but it's better not to speak. Here is the skull of the Marquis de Sade, Mr. Maitland.

"Will you meet my offer?"

"A thousand pounds," Maitland sighed. "It's too much for a shoddy skull and a flimsy story."

"Well—let us say eight hundred, perhaps. A quick deal and no hard feelings?"

Maitland stared at Marco. Marco stared at Maitland. The skull stared at them both.

"Five hundred, then," Marco ventured. "Right now."

"You must be faking," Maitland said. "Otherwise you wouldn't be so anxious for a sale."

Marco's smile oozed off again. "On the contrary, sir. If I were trying to do you, I certainly wouldn't budge on my price. But I want to dispose of this skull quickly."

"Why?"

For the first time during the interview, fat little Marco hesitated. He twisted the skull between his hands and set it down on the table. I seemed to Maitland as if he avoided looking at it as he answered.

"I don't exactly know. It's just that I don't fancy owning such an item, really. Works on my imagination. Rot, isn't it?"

"Works on your imagination?"

"I get ideas that I'm being followed. Of course it's all nonsense, but—"

"You get ideas that you're followed by the police, no doubt," Maitland accused. "Because you stole the skull. Didn't you, Marco?"

Marco averted his gaze. "No," he mumbled. "It isn't that. But I don't like skulls—not my idea of ornaments, I assure you. Squeamish I am, a bit.

"Besides, you live in this big house here. You're safe. I live in Wapping now. Down on my luck at the moment and all that. I sell you the skull. You tuck it away here in your collection, look at it when you please—and the rest of the time it's out of sight, not bothering you. I'll be free of it knocking around in my humble diggings. Matter of fact, when I sell it, I'll vacate the premises and move to decent lodgings. That's why I want to be rid of it, really. For five hundred, cash in hand."

Maitland hesitated. "I must think it over," he declared. "Give me your address. Should I decide to purchase it, I'll be down tomorrow with the money. Fair enough?"

"Very well." Marco sighed. He produced a greasy stub of pencil and tore a bit of paper from the discarded wrappings on the floor.

"Here's the address," he said.

Maitland pocketed the slip as Marco commenced to enclose the skull in tinfoil once more. He worked quickly, as though eager to obscure the shining teeth and the yawning emptiness of the eye-sockets. He twisted the butcher's paper over the tinfoil, grasped his overcoat in one hand, and balanced the round bundle in the other.

"I'll be expecting you tomorrow," he said. "And by the way—be careful when you open the door. I've a police dog now, a savage brute. He'll tear you to pieces—or anyone else who tries to take the skull of the Marquis de Sade."

It seemed to Maitland that they had bound him too tightly. He knew that the masked men were about to whip him, but he could not understand why they had fastened his wrists with chains of steel.

Only when they held the metal scourges over the fire did he comprehend the reason—only when they raised the white-hot rods high above their heads did he realize why he was held so securely.

For at the fiery kiss of the lash Maitland did not flinch—he convulsed. His body, seared by the hideous blow, described an arc. Bound by thongs, his hands would tear themselves free under the stimulus of the unbearable torment. But the steel chains held, and Maitland gritted his teeth as the two black-robed men flogged him with living fire.

The outlines of the dungeon blurred, and Maitland's pain blurred too. He sank down into a darkness broken only by the consciousness of rhythm—the rhythm of the savage, sizzling steel flails that descended upon his naked back.

When awareness returned, Maitland knew that the flogging was over. The silent, black-robed men in masks were bending over him, unfastening the shackles. They lifted him tenderly and led him gently across the dungeon floor to the great steel casket.

Casket? This was no casket. Caskets do not stand open and upended. Caskets do not bear upon their lids the raised, moulded features of a woman's face.

Caskets are not spiked, inside.

Recognition was simultaneous with horror.

This was the Iron Maiden!

The masked men were strong. They dragged him forward, thrust him into the depths of the great metal matrix of torment. They fastened wrists and ankles with clamps. Maitland knew what was coming.

They would close the lid upon him. Then, by turning a crank, they would move the lid down—move it down as spikes drove in at his body. For the interior of the Iron Maiden was studden with cruel barbs, sharpened and lengthened with the cunning of the damned.

The longest spikes would pierce him first as the lid descended. These spikes were set so as to enter his wrists and ankles. He would hang there, crucified, as the lid continued its inexorable descent. Shorter spikes would next enter his thighs, shoulders and arms. Then, as he struggled, impaled in agony, the lid would press closer until the smallest spikes came close enough to penetrate his eyes, his throat, and—mercifully—his heart and brain.

Maitland screamed, but the sound served only to shatter his ear-drums as they closed the lid. The rusty metal grated, and then came the harsher grating of the machinery. They were turning the crank, bringing the banks of spikes closer to his cringing body. . . .

Maitland waited, tensed in the darkness, for the first sharp kiss of the Iron Maiden.

Then, and then only, he realized that he was not *alone* here in the blackness.

There were no spikes set in the lid! Instead, a figure was pressed against the opposite iron surface. As the lid descended, it merely brought the figure closer to Maitland's body.

The figure did not move, or even breathe. It rested against the lid, and as the lid came forward Maitland felt the pressure of cold and alien flesh against his own. The arms and legs met his in un-responsive embrace, but still the lid pressed down, squeezing the lifeless form closer and closer. It was dark, but now Maitland could see the face that loomed scarcely an inch from his eyes. The face was white, phosphorescent. The face was—*not a face!*

And then, as the body gripped his body in blackness, as the head touched his head, as Maitland's lips pressed against the place where lips *should* be, he knew the ultimate horror.

The face that was *not* a face was the skull of the Marquis de Sade!

And the weight of charnel corruption stifled Maitland, and he went down into darkness again with the obscene memory pursuing him to oblivion.

Even oblivion has an end, and once more Maitland woke. The masked men had released and were reviving him. He lay on a pallet and glanced towards the open doors of the Iron Maiden. He was oddly grateful to see that the interior was empty. No figure rested against the inside of the lid. Perhaps there had been no figure.

The torture played strange tricks on a man's mind. But it was needed now. He could tell that the solicitude of the masked ones was not assumed. They had subjected him to this ordeal for strange reasons, and he had come through unscathed.

They anointed his back, lifted him to his feet, led him from the dungeon. In the great corridor beyond, Maitland saw a mirror. They guided him up to it.

Had the torture changed him? For a moment Maitland feared to gaze into the glass.

But they held him before the mirror, and Maitland stared at his reflection—stared at his quivering body, on which was set the grim, unsmiling death's-head of the Marquis de Sade!

Maitland told no one of his dream, but he lost no time in discussing Marco's visit and offer.

His confidant was an old friend and fellow-collector, Sir Fitzhugh Kissroy. Seated in Sir Fitzhugh's comfortable study the following afternoon, he quickly unburdened himself of all pertinent details.

Genial, red-bearded Kissroy heard him out in silence.

"Naturally, I want that skull," Maitland concluded. "But I can't understand why Marco is so anxious to dispose of it at once. And I'm considerably worried about its authenticity. So I was wondering—you're quite an expert, Fitzhugh. Would you be willing to visit Marco with me and examine the skull?"

Sir Fitzhugh chuckled and shook his head.

"There's no need to examine it," he declared. "I'm quite sure the skull, as you describe it, is that of the Marquis de Sade. It's genuine enough."

Maitland gaped at him.

"How can you be so positive?" he asked.

Sir Fitzhugh beamed. "Because, my dear fellow—that skull was stolen from me!"

"What?"

"Quite so. About ten days ago, a prowler got into the library through the French windows facing the garden. None of the servants were aroused, and he made off with the skull in the night."

Maitland rose. "Incredible," he murmured. "But of course you'll come with me, now. We'll identify your property, confront old Marco with the facts, and recover the skull at once."

"Nothing of the sort," Sir Fitzhugh replied. "I'm just as glad the skull was stolen. And I advise you to leave it alone.

"I didn't report the theft to the police, and I have no intention of doing so. Because that skull is—unlucky."

"Unlucky?" Maitland peered at his host. "You, with your collection of cursed Egyptian mummies, tell me that? You've never taken any stock in such superstitious rubbish."

"Exactly. Therefore, when I tell you that I sincerely believe that skull is dangerous, you must have faith in my words."

Maitland pondered. He wondered if Sir Fitzhugh had experienced the same dreams that tormented his own sleep upon seeing the skull. Was there an associative aura about the relic? If so, it only added to the peculiar fascination exerted by the unsmiling skull of the Marquis de Sade.

"I don't understand you at all," he declared. "I should think you couldn't wait to lay hands on that skull."

"Perhaps I'm not the only one who can't wait," Sir Fitzhugh muttered.

"What are you getting at?"

"You know de Sade's history. You know the power of morbid fascination such evil geniuses exert upon the imagination of men. You feel that fascination yourself; that's why you want the skull.

"But you're a normal man, Maitland. You want to *buy* the skull and keep it in your collection of *curiosa*. An abnormal man might not think of buying. He might think of stealing it—or even killing the owner to possess it. Particularly if he wanted to do more than merely own it; if, for example, he wanted to *worship* it."

Sir Fitzhugh's voice sank to a whisper as he continued, "I'm not trying to frighten you, my friend. But I know the history of that skull. During the last hundred years it has passed through the hands of many men. Some of them were collectors, and sane. Others were perverted members of secret cults—worshippers of pain, devotees of Black Magic. Men have died to gain that grisly relic, and other men have been—sacrificed to it.

"It came to me quite by chance, six months ago. A man like your friend Marco offered it to me. Not for a thousand pounds, or five hundred. He gave it to me as a gift, because he was afraid of it.

"Of course I laughed at his notions, just as you are probably laughing at mine now. But during the six months that the skull remained in my hands, I've suffered.

"I've had queer dreams. Just staring at the unnatural, unsmiling grimace is enough to provoke nightmares. Didn't you sense an emanation from the thing? They said de Sade wasn't mad—and I believe them. He was far worse—he was *possessed*. There's something *unhuman* about that skull. Something that attracts others, living men whose skulls hide a bestial quality that is also unhuman or inhuman.

"And I've had more than my dreams to deal with. Phone calls came, and mysterious letters. Some of the servants have reported lurkers on the grounds at dusk."

"Probably ordinary thieves, like Marco, after a valuable object," Maitland commented.

"No," Sir Fitzhugh sighed. "Those unknown seekers did more than attempt to steal the skull. *They came into my house at night and adored it!*

"Oh, I'm quite positive about the matter, I assure you! I kept the skull in a glass case in the library. Often, when I came to see it in the mornings, I found that it had been moved during the night.

"Yes, moved. Sometimes the case was smashed and the skull placed on the table. Once it was on the floor.

"Of course I checked up on the servants. Their alibis were perfect. It was the work of outsiders—outsiders who probably feared to possess the skull completely, yet needed access to it from time to time in order to practice some abominable and perverted rite.

"They came into my house, I tell you, and worshipped that filthy skull! And when it was stolen, I was glad—very glad.

"All I can say to you is, keep away from the whole business! Don't see this man Marco, and don't have anything to do with that accursed graveyard relic!"

Maitland nodded. "Very well," he said. "I am grateful to you for your warning."

He left Sir Fitzhugh shortly thereafter.

Half an hour later, he was climbing the stairs to Marco's dingy attic room.

He climbed the stairs to Marco's room; climbed the creaking steps in the shabby Soho tenement and listened to the curiously muffled thumping of his own heartbeat.

But not for long. A sudden howl resounded from the landing above, and Maitland scrambled up the last few stairs in frantic haste.

The door of Marco's room was locked, but the sounds that issued from within stirred Maitland to desperate measures.

Sir Fitzhugh's warnings had prompted him to carry his service revolver on this errand; now he drew it and shattered the lock with a shot.

Maitland flung the door back against the wall as the howling reached the ultimate frenzied crescendo. He started into the room, then checked himself.

Something hurtled towards him from the floor beyond; something launched itself at his throat.

Maitland raised his revolver blindly and fired.

For a moment sound and vision blurred. When he recovered, he was half-kneeling on the floor before the threshold. A great shaggy form rested at his feet. Maitland recognized the carcass of a gigantic police dog.

Suddenly he remembered Marco's reference to the beast. So that explained it! The dog howled and attacked. But—why?

Maitland rose and entered the sordid bedroom. Smoke still curled upward from the shots. He gazed again at the prone animal, noting the gleaming yellow fangs grimacing even in death. Then he stared around at the shoddy furniture, the disordered bureau, the rumpled bed—

The rumpled bed on which Mr. Marco lay, his throat torn in a red rosary of death.

Maitland stared at the body of the little fat man and shuddered.

Then he saw the skull. It rested on the pillow near Marco's head, a grisly bedfellow that seemed to peer curiously at the corpse in ghastly *camaraderie*. Blood had spattered the hollow cheekbones, but even beneath this sanguinary stain Maitland could see the peculiar solemnity of the death's-head.

For the first time he fully sensed the aura of evil which clung to the skull of de Sade. It was palpable in this ravaged room, palpable as the presence of death itself. The skull seemed to glow with actual charnel phosphorescence.

Maitland knew now that his friend had spoken the truth. There *was* a dreadful magnetism inherent in this bony horror, a veritable Elixir of Death that worked and preyed upon the minds of men— and beasts.

It must have been that way. The dog, maddened by the urge to kill, had finally attacked Marco as he slept and destroyed him. Then it had sought to attack Maitland when he entered. And through it all the skull watched, watched and gloated just as de Sade would gloat had his pale blue eyes flickered in the shadowed sockets.

Somewhere within the cranium, perhaps, the shrivelled remnants of his cruel brain were still attuned to terror. The magnetic force it focused had a compelling enchantment even in the face of what Maitland knew.

That is why Maitland, driven by a compulsion he could not

wholly explain or seek to justify, stooped down and lifted the skull. He held it for a long moment in the classic pose of Hamlet.

Then he left the room, forever, carrying the death's-head in his arms.

Fear rode Maitland's shoulders as he hurried through the twilit streets. Fear whispered strangely in his ear, warning him to hurry, lest the body of Marco be discovered and the police pursue him. Fear prompted him to enter his own house by a side door and go directly to his rooms so that none would see the skull he concealed beneath his coat.

Fear was Maitland's companion all that evening. He sat there, staring at the skull on the table, and shivered with repulsion.

Sir Fitzhugh was right, he knew it. There *was* a damnable influence issuing from the skull and the black brain within. It had caused Maitland to disregard the sensible warnings of his friend; it had caused Maitland to steal the skull itself from a dead man; it had caused him now to conceal himself in this lonely room.

He should call the authorities; he knew that. Better still, he should dispose of the skull. Give it away, throw it away, rid the earth of it forever. There was something puzzling about the cursed thing—something he didn't quite understand.

For, knowing these truth, he still desired to possess the skull of the Marquis de Sade. There was an evil enchantment here; the dormant baseness in every man's soul was aroused and responded to the loathsome lust which poured from the death's-head in waves.

He stared at the skull, shivered—yet knew he would not give it up; could not. Nor had he the strength to destroy it. Perhaps possession would lead him to madness in the end. The skull would incite others to unspeakable excesses.

Maitland pondered and brooded, seeking a solution in the impassive object that confronted him with the stolidity of death.

It grew late. Maitland drank wine and paced the floor. He was weary. Perhaps in the morning he could think matters through and reach a logical, sane, conclusion.

Yes, he was upset. Sir Fitzhugh's outlandish hints had disturbed him; the gruesome events of the late afternoon preyed on his nerves.

No sense in giving way to foolish fancies about the skull of the mad Marquis ... better to rest.

Maitland flung himself on the bed. He reached out for the switch and extinguished the light. The moon's rays slithered through the window and sought out the skull on the table, bathing it in eerie luminescence. Maitland stared once more at the jaws that should grin and did not.

Then he closed his eyes and willed himself to sleep. In the morning he'd call Sir Fitzhugh, make a clean breast of things, and give the skull over to the authorities.

Its evil career—real or imaginary—would come to an end. So be it.

Maitland sank into slumber. Before he dozed off he tried to focus his attention on something . . . something puzzling . . . an impression he'd received upon gazing at the body of the police dog in Marco's room. The way its fangs gleamed.

Yes. That was it. There had been no blood on the muzzle of the police dog. Strange. For the police dog had bitten Marco's throat. No blood—how could that be?

Well, that problem was best left for morning too. . . .

It seemed to Maitland that as he slept, he dreamed. In his dream he opened his eyes and blinked in the bright moonlight. He stared at the table top and saw that the skull was no longer resting on its surface.

That was curious, too. No one had come into the room, or he would have been aroused.

If he had not been sure that he was dreaming, Maitland would have started up in terror when he saw the stream of moonlight on the floor—the stream of moonlight through which the skull was rolling.

It turned over and over again, its bony visage impassive as ever, and each revolution brought it closer to the bed.

Maitland's sleeping ears could almost hear the thump as the skull landed on the bare floor at the foot of the bed. Then began the grotesque progress so typical of night fantasies. The skull climbed the side of the bed!

Its teeth gripped the dangling corner of a bedsheet, and the death's-head literally whirled the sheet out and up, swinging it in an arc which landed the skull on the bed at Maitland's feet.

The illusion was so vivid he could feel the thud of its impact against the mattress. Tactile sensation continued, and Maitland felt the skull rolling along up the covers. It came up to his waist, then approached his chest.

Maitland saw the bony features in the moonlight, scarcely six inches away from his neck. He felt a cold weight resting on his throat. The skull was moving now.

Then he realized the grip of utter nightmare and struggled to awake before the dream continued.

A scream rose in his throat—but never issued from it. For Maitland's throat was seized by champing teeth—teeth that bit into his neck with all the power of a moving human jawbone.

The skull tore at Maitland's jugular in cruel haste. There was a gasp, a gurgle and then no sound at all.

After a time, the skull righted itself on Maitland's chest. Maitland's chest no longer heaved with breathing, and the skull rested there with a curious simulation of satisfied repose.

The moonlight shone on the death's-head to reveal one very curious circumstance. It was a trivial thing, yet somehow fitting under the circumstances.

Reposing on the chest of the man it had killed, the skull of the Marquis de Sade was no longer impassive. Instead, its bony features bore a definite, unmistakably *sadistic* grin.

THE OBLONG BOX

EDGAR ALLAN POE

(American-International: 1970)

For our final story we turn almost full circle and return to the author who throughout the life history of the horror film genre has provided more material—and exerted a stronger influence —than anyone else: Edgar Allan Poe. Indeed as we have briefly traced the history of the genre through this book, the presence of this extraordinary genius has hardly been missing from a single page. His methods of evoking horror have inspired many stories and films, while his tales retain their originality and inventiveness even today. Small wonder, then, that he should still head the list of contributors.

Even as I write these words in the spring of 1970 plans are already under way to bring no less than three more of his stories to the screen, not including The Oblong Box, *which was only recently completed. It would be foolhardy to predict any falling off in the popularity of Poe-on-film. And as long as actors as talented as Vincent Price and Christopher Lee (who star together in* The Oblong Box) *are available to tackle the acting, there would also seem to be no danger that the horror film itself will in the future lose its appeal for the millions of fans around the world.*

*

SOME years ago I engaged a passage from Charleston, S.C., to the city of New York, in the fine packet-ship *Independence,* Captain Hardy. We were to sail on the fifteenth of the month (June), weather permitting, and on the fourteenth I went on board to arrange some matters in my state-room.

I found that we were to have a great many passengers, including a more than usual number of ladies. On the list were several of my acquaintances, and among other names I was rejoiced to see that of Mr. Cornelius Wyatt, a young artist for whom I entertained feelings of warm friendship. He had been with me a fellow-student at C— University, where we were very much together. He had the ordinary temperament of genius and was a compound of mis-

anthropy, sensibility and enthusiasm. To these qualities he united
the warmest and truest heart which ever beat in a human bosom.

I observed that his name was carded upon *three* state-rooms; and
upon again referring to the list of passengers, I found that he had
engaged passage for himself, wife and two sisters—his own. The
state-rooms were sufficiently roomy and each had two berths, one
above the other. These berths, to be sure, were so exceedingly narrow as to be insufficient for more than one person; still I could not
comprehend why there were *three* state-rooms for these four persons. I was just at that epoch, in one of those moody frames of
mind which make a man abnormally inquisitive about trifles, and
I confess with shame that I busied myself in a variety of ill-bred
and preposterous conjectures about this matter of the supernumer-
ary state-room. It was no business of mine, to be sure; but with
none the less pertinacity did I occupy myself in attempts to resolve
the enigma. At last I reached a conclusion which wrought in me
great wonder why I had not arrived at it before. "It is a servant,
of course," I said, "what a fool I am not sooner to have thought of
so obvious a solution!" And then I again repaired to the list—but
here I saw distinctly that *no* servant was to come with the party;
although, in fact, it had been the original design to bring one—for
the words "and servant" had been first written and then overscored.
"Oh, extra baggage to be sure," I now said to myself—"something
he wishes not to be put in the hold—something to be kept under his
own eye—ah, I have it—a painting or so—and this is what he has
been bargaining about with Nicolino, the Italian Jew." This idea
satisfied me and I dismissed my curiosity for the nonce.

Wyatt's two sisters I knew very well, and most amiable and
clever girls they were. His wife he had newly married and I had
never yet seen her. He had often talked about her in my presence,
however, and in his usual style of enthusiasm. He described her as of
surpassing beauty, wit and accomplishment. I was therefore quite
anxious to make her acquaintance.

On the day in which I visited the ship (the fourteenth) Wyatt
and party were also to visit it—so the captain informed me—and I
waited on board an hour longer than I had designed, in hope of
being presented to the bride; but then an apology came. "Mrs. W.
was a little indisposed and would decline coming on board until
tomorrow, at the hour of sailing."

The morrow having arrived, I was going from my hotel to the
wharf when Captain Hardy met me and said that, "owing to cir-

cumstances" (a stupid but convenient phrase) "he rather thought the *Independence* would not sail for a day or two and that when all was ready he would send up and let me know". This I thought strange, for there was a stiff southerly breeze : but as "the circumstances" were not forthcoming, although I pumped for them with much perseverance, I had nothing to do but to return home and digest my impatience at leisure.

I did not receive the expected message from the captain for nearly a week. It came at length, however, and I immediately went on board; the ship was crowded with passengers and everything was in the bustle attendant upon making sail. Wyatt's party arrived in about ten minutes after myself. There were the two sisters, the bride and the artist—the later in one of his cusomary fits of moody misanthropy. I was too well used to these, however, to pay them any special attention. He did not even introduce me to his wife—this courtesy devolving, perforce, upon his sister Marian—a very sweet and intelligent girl who, in a few hurried words, made us acquainted.

Mrs. Wyatt had been closely veiled, and when she raised her veil, in acknowledging my bow, I confess that I was very profoundly astonished. I should have been much more so, however, had not long experience advised me not to trust, with too implicit a reliance, the enthusiastic descriptions of my friend the artist when indulging in comments upon the loveliness of woman. When beauty was the theme, I well knew with what facility he soared into the regions of the purely ideal.

The truth is, I could not help regarding Mrs. Wyatt as a decidedly plain-looking woman. If not positively ugly, she was not, I think, very far from it. She was dressed, however, in exquisite taste —and then I had no doubt that she had captivated my friend's heart by the more enduring graces of the intellect and soul. She said very few words and passed at once into her state-room with Mr. W.

My old inquisitiveness now returned. There was *no* servant—that was a settled point. I looked, therefore, for the extra baggage. After some delay, a cart arrived at the wharf with an oblong pine box, which was everything that seemed to be expected. Immediately upon its arrival we made sail and in a short time were safely over the bar and standing out to sea.

The box in question was, as I say, oblong. It was about six feet in length by two and a half in breadth; I observed it attentively and like to be precise. Now this shape was *peculiar*; and no sooner had I seen it than I took credit to myself for the accuracy of my guessing. I had reached the conclusion, it will be remembered, that the extra baggage of my friend the artist would prove to be pictures, or at least a picture, for I knew he had been for several weeks in conference with Nicolino; and now here was a box which, from its shape, *could* possibly contain nothing in the world but a copy of Leonardo's "Last Supper"; and a copy of this very "Last Supper", done by Rubini the younger, at Florence, I had known for some time to be in the possession of Nicolino. This point therefore I considered as sufficiently settled. I chuckled excessively when I thought of my acumen. It was the first time I had ever known Wyatt to keep from me any of his artistical secrets, but here he evidently intended to steal a march upon me and smuggle a fine picture to New York under my very nose, expecting me to know nothing of the matter. I resolved to quiz him *well*, now and hereafter.

One thing, however, annoyed me not a little. The box did *not* go into the extra state-room. It was deposited in Wyatt's own, and there, too, it remained, occupying very nearly the whole of the floor—no doubt to the exceeding discomfort of the artist and his wife—this the more especially as the tar or paint with which it was lettered in sprawling capitals emitted a strong, disagreeable and, to *my* fancy, a peculiarly disgusting odour. On the lid were painted the words—*"Mrs. Adelaide Curtis, Albany, New York. Charge of Cornelius Wyatt, Esq. This side up. To be handled with care"*.

Now, I was aware that Mrs. Adelaide Curtis, of Albany, was the artist's wife's mother, but then I looked upon the whole address as a mystification, intended especially for myself. I made up my mind of course that the box and contents would never get farther north than the studio of my misanthropic friend in Chambers Street, New York.

For the first three or four days we had fine weather, although the wind was dead ahead, having chopped round to the northward immediately upon our losing sight of the coast. The passengers were consequently in high spirits and disposed to be social. I *must* except, however, Wyatt and his sisters, who behaved stiffly, and I could not help thinking uncourteously to the rest of the party. *Wyatt's* conduct I did not so much regard. He was gloomy, even beyond his usual habit—in fact he was *morose*—but in him I was prepared for eccentricity. For the sisters, however, I could make no excuse. They secluded themselves in their state-rooms during the greater part of the passage and absolutely refused, although I repeatedly urged them, to hold communication with any person on board.

Mrs. Wyatt herself was far more agreeable. That is to say, she was *chatty*; and to be chatty is no slight recommendation at sea. She became *excessively* intimate with most of the ladies and, to my profound astonishment, evinced no equivocal disposition to coquet with the men. She amused us all very much. I say *"amused"* —and scarcely know how to explain myself. The truth is, I soon found that Mrs. W. was far oftener laughed *at* than *with*. The gentlemen said little about her, but the ladies, in a little while, pronounced her "a good-hearted thing, rather indifferent-looking, totally uneducated and decidedly vulgar". The great wonder was how Wyatt had been entrapped into such a match. Wealth was the general solution—but this I knew to be no solution at all, for Wyatt had told me that she neither brought him a dollar, nor had any expectations from any source whatever. "He had married," he said, "for love, and for love only; and his bride was far more than worthy of his love." When I thought of these expressions on the part of my friend, I confess that I felt indescribably puzzled. Could it be possible that he was taking leave of his senses? What else could I think? *He*, so refined, so intellectual, so fastidious, with so exquisite a perception of the faulty, and so keen an appreciation of the beautiful! To be sure, the lady seemed especially fond of *him*—particularly so in his absence—when she made herself ridiculous by frequent quotations of what had been said by her "beloved husband, Mr. Wyatt". The word "husband" seemed for ever—to use one of her own delicate expressions—for ever "on the tip of her tongue". In the meantime, it was observed by all on board, that he avoided *her* in the most pointed manner and for the most part shut himself up alone in his state-room, where, in fact, he might have been said to live altogether, leaving his wife at full liberty to amuse herself as she thought best in the public society of the main-cabin.

My conclusion, from what I saw and heard, was that the artist, by some unaccountable freak of fate, or perhaps in some fit of enthusiastic and fanciful passion, had been induced to unite himself with a person altogether beneath him, and that the natural result, entire and speedy disgust, had ensued. I pitied him from the bottom of my heart—but could not, for that reason, quite forgive his incommunicativeness in the matter of the "Last Supper". For this I resolved to have my revenge.

One day he came upon deck and, taking his arm as had been my wont, I sauntered with him backwards and forwards. His gloom, however (which I considered quite natural under the circumstances), seemed entirely unabated. He said little, and that moodily and with evident effort. I ventured a jest or two and he made a sickening attempt at a smile. Poor fellow!—as I thought of *his wife,* I wondered that he could have heart to put on even the semblance of mirth. At last I ventured a home thrust. I determined to commence a series of covert insinuations or innuendoes about the oblong box —just to let him perceive gradually that I was *not* altogether the butt or victim of his little bit of pleasant mystification. My first observation was by way of opening a masked battery. I said something about the "peculiar shape of *that* box" and, as I spoke the words, I smiled knowingly, winked and touched him gently with my fore-finger in the ribs.

The manner in which Wyatt received this harmless pleasantry convinced me at once that he was mad. At first he stared at me as if he found it impossible to comprehend the witticism of my remark, but as its point seemed slowly to make its way into his brain his eyes in the same proportion seemed protruding from their sockets. Then he grew very red—then hideously pale—then, as if highly amused with what I had insinuated, he began a loud and boisterous laugh, which, to my astonishment, he kept up with gradually increasing vigour for ten minutes or more. In conclusion he fell flat and heavily upon the dock. When I ran to uplift him, to all appearance he was *dead.*

I called assistance and with much difficulty we brought him to himself. Upon reviving he spoke incoherently for some time. At length we bled him and put him to bed. The next morning he was quite recovered, so far as regarded his mere bodily health. Of his mind I say nothing, of course. I avoided him during the rest of the passage by advice of the captain, who seemed to coincide with me altogether in my views of his insanity, but cautioned me to say nothing on this head to any person on board.

Several circumstances occurred immediately after this fit of Wyatt's which contributed to heighten the curiosity with which I was already possessed. Among other things, this : I had been nervous —drank too much strong green tea and slept ill at night—in fact, for two nights I could not be properly said to sleep at all. Now, my state-room opened into the main-cabin, or dining-room, as did those of all the single men on board. Wyatt's three rooms were in the after-cabin, which was separated from the main one by a slight sliding-door, never locked even at night. As we were almost constantly on a wind, and the breeze was not a little stiff, the ship heeled to leeward very considerably; and whenever her starboard was to leeward, the sliding-door between the cabins slid open, and so remained, nobody taking the trouble to get up and shut it. But my berth was in such a position that when my own state-room door was open, as well as the sliding-door in question (and my own door was *always* open on account of the heat) I could see into the after-cabin quite distinctly, and just at that portion of it, too, where were situated the state-rooms of Mr. Wyatt. Well, during two nights (*not* consecutive) while I lay awake, I clearly saw Mrs. W., about eleven o'clock upon each night, steal cautiously from the state-room of Mr. W. and enter the extra room, where she remained until daybreak, when she was called by her husband and went back. That they were virtually separated was clear. They had separate apartments—no doubt in contemplation of a more permanent divorce; and here, after all, I thought, was the mystery of the extra state-room.

There was another circumstance, too, which interested me much. During the two wakeful nights in question, and immediately after the disappearance of Mrs. Wyatt into the extra state-room, I was attracted by certain singular, cautious, subdued noises in that of her husband's. After listening to them for some time with thoughtful attention, I at length succeeded perfectly in translating their import. They were sounds occasioned by the artist in prying open the oblong box by means of a chisel and mallet, the latter being apparently muffled or deadened by some soft woollen or cotton substance in which its head was enveloped.

In this manner I fancied I could distinguish the precise moment when he fairly disengaged the lid—also, that I could determine when he removed it altogether, and when he deposited it upon the lower berth in his room; this latter point I knew, for example, by certain slight taps which the lid made in striking against the wooden edges of the berth as he endeavoured to lay it down *very* gently, there being no room for it on the floor. After this there was a dead stillness and I heard nothing more upon either occasion until nearly daybreak; unless, perhaps, I may mention a low sobbing or murmuring sound, so very much suppressed as to be nearly inaudible, if indeed the whole of this latter noise were not rather produced by my imagination. I say it seemed to *resemble* sobbing or sighing, but of course it would not have been either. I rather think it was a ringing in my own ears. Mr. Wyatt, no doubt, according to custom, was merely giving the rein to one of his hobbies—indulging in one of his fits of artistic enthusiasm. He had opened his oblong box in order to feast his eyes on the pictorial treasure within. There was nothing in this, however, to make him *sob*. I repeat therefore that it must have been simply a freak of my own fancy, distempered by good Captain Hardy's green tea. Just before dawn, on each of the two nights of which I speak, I distinctly heard Mr. Wyatt replace the lid upon the oblong box and force the nails into their old places by means of the muffled mallet. Having done this, he issued from his state-room, fully dressed, and proceeded to call Mrs. W. from hers.

We had been at sea seven days and were now off Cape Hatteras, when there came a tremendously heavy blow from the south-west. We were in a measure prepared for it, however, as the weather had been holding out threats for some time. Everything was made snug, alow and aloft, and as the wind steadily freshened we lay-to at length under spanker and foretopsail, both double-reefed.

In this trim we rode safely enough for forty-eight hours—the ship proving herself an excellent sea-boat in many respects and shipping no water of any consequence. At the end of this period, however, the gale had freshened into a hurricane and our after-sail split into ribbons, bringing us so much in the trough of the water that we shipped several prodigious seas, one immediately after the other. By this accident we lost three men overboard with the caboose and nearly the whole of the larboard bulwarks. Scarcely had we recovered our senses before the foretopsail went into shreds, when we got up a storm stay-sail, and with this did pretty well for some hours, the ship heading the sea much more steadily than before.

The gale still held on, however, and we saw no signs of its abating. The rigging was found to be ill-fitted and greatly strained; and on the third day of the blow, about five in the afternoon, our mizzen-mast, in a heavy lurch to windward, went by the board. For an hour or more we tried in vain to get rid of it, on account of the prodigious rolling of the ship, and before we had succeeded the carpenter came aft and announced four feet of water in the hold. To add to our dilemma, we found the pumps choked and nearly useless.

All was now confusion and despair—but an effort was made to lighten the ship by throwing overboard as much of her cargo as could be reached and by cutting away the two masts that remained. This we at last accomplished—but we were still unable to do anything at the pumps, and in the meantime the leak gained on us very fast.

At sundown the gale had sensibly diminished in violence, and as the sea went down with it, we still entertained faint hopes of saving ourselves in the boats. At eight p.m. the clouds broke away to the windward and we had the advantage of a full moon—a piece of good fortune which served wonderfully to cheer our drooping spirits.

After incredible labour we succeeded at length in getting the long-boat over the side without material accident, and into this we crowded the whole of the crew and most of the passengers. This party made off immediately and after undergoing much suffering finally arrived in safety at Ocracoke Inlet on the third day after the wreck.

Fourteen passengers, with the captain, remained on board, resolving to trust their fortunes to the jolly-boat at the stern. We lowered it without difficulty, although it was only by a miracle that we prevented it from swamping as it touched the water. It contained, when afloat, the captain and his wife, Mr. Wyatt and party, a Mexican officer, wife, four children, and myself, with a Negro valet.

We had no room, of course, for anything except a few positively necessary instruments, some provisions and the clothes upon our backs. No one had thought of even attempting to save anything more. What must have been the astonishment of all then, when, having proceeded a few fathoms from the ship, Mr. Wyatt stood up in the stern-sheets and coolly demanded of Captain Hardy that the boat should be put back for the purpose of taking in his oblong box!

"Sit down, Mr. Wyatt," replied the captain, somewhat sternly; "you will capsize us if you do not sit quite still. Our gunwale is almost in the water now."

"The box!" vociferated Mr. Wyatt, still standing—"the box, I say! Captain Hardy, you cannot, you *will* not refuse me. Its weight will be but a trifle—it is nothing—mere nothing. By the mother who bore you—for the love of Heaven—by your hope of salvation, I *implore* you to put back for the box!"

The captain, for a moment, seemed touched by the earnest appeal of the artist, but he regained his stern composure and merely said :

"Mr. Wyatt, you are *mad*. I cannot listen to you. Sit down, I say, or you will swamp the boat. Stay—hold him—seize him!—he is about to spring overboard! There—I knew it—he is over!"

As the captain said this, Mr. Wyatt, in fact, sprang from the boat, and as we were yet in the lee of the wreck, succeeded by almost superhuman exertion in getting hold of a rope which hung from the fore-chains. In another moment he was on board and rushing frantically down into the cabin.

In the meantime we had been swept astern of the ship and, being quite out of her lee, were at the mercy of the tremendous sea which was still running. We made a determined effort to put back, but our little boat was like a feather in the breath of the tempest. We saw at a glance that the doom of the unfortunate artist was sealed.

As our distance from the wreck rapidly increased, the madman (for as such only could we regard him) was seen to emerge from the companion-way, up which, by dint of a strength that appeared gigantic, he dragged bodily the oblong box. While we gazed in the extremity of astonishment, he passed rapidly several turns of a three-inch rope, first around the box and then around his body. In another instant both body and box were in the sea—disappearing suddenly, at once and for ever.

We lingered a while sadly upon our oars, with our eyes riveted upon the spot. At length we pulled away. The silence remained unbroken for an hour. Finally, I hazarded a remark.

"Did you observe, captain, how suddenly they sank? Was not that an exceedingly singular thing? I confess that I entertained some feeble hope of his final deliverance, when I saw him lash himself to the box and commit himself to the sea."

"They sank as a matter of course," replied the captain, "and that like a shot. They will soon rise again, however, *but not till the salt melts.*"

"The salt!" I ejaculated.

"Hush!" said the captain, pointing to the wife and sisters of the deceased. "We must talk of these things at some more appropriate time."

We suffered much and made a narrow escape, but fortune befriended us as well as our mates in the long-boat. We landed, in fine weather, more dead than alive, after four days of intense distress, upon the beach opposite Roanoke Island. We remained here a week, were not ill-treated by the wreckers and at length obtained a passage to New York.

About a month after the loss of the *Independence,* I happened to meet Captain Hardy in Broadway. Our conversation turned, naturally, upon the disaster, and especially upon the sad fate of poor Wyatt. I thus learned the following particulars.

The artist had engaged passage for himself, wife, two sisters and a servant. His wife was, indeed, as she had been represented, a most lovely and most accomplished woman. On the morning of the fourteenth of June (the day in which I first visited the ship), the lady suddenly sickened and died. The young husband was frantic with grief—but circumstances imperatively forbade deferring his voyage to New York. It was necessary to take to her mother the corpse of his adored wife, and on the other hand, the universal prejudice which would prevent his doing so openly was well known. Nine-tenths of the passengers would have abandoned the ship rather than take passage with a dead body.

In this dilemma, Captain Hardy arranged that the corpse, being first partially embalmed, and packed with a large quantity of salt in a box of suitable dimensions, should be conveyed on board as merchandise. Nothing was to be said of the lady's decease, and as it was well understood that Mr. Wyatt had engaged passage for his wife, it became necessary that some person should impersonate her during the voyage. This the deceased's lady's maid was easily prevailed on to do. The extra state-room, originally engaged for this girl during her mistress's life, was now merely retained. In this state-room the pseudo wife slept of course every night. In the day-time she performed, to the best of her ability, the part of her mistress— whose person, it had been carefully ascertained, was not known to any of the passengers on board. My own mistakes arose, naturally enough, through too careless, too inquisitive and too impulsive a temperament. But of late, it is a rare thing that I sleep soundly at night. There is a countenance which haunts me, turn as I will. There is an hysterical laugh which will for ever ring within my ears.

AFTERWORD

by CHRISTOPHER LEE

IF someone were to take a survey of cinema audiences and the kind of pictures they like, I have a feeling the horror film would come out as number one in popularity. There can be little disputing the fact that people go to see these films, not out of an excessive taste for morbidity, or to be frightened out of their wits, but simply to *enjoy* them. For we all like to escape the daily routine occasionally and blow off some emotional steam, and horror films provide as good a release as any.

It is a strange thought, you know, but there is a kind of illusion-reality about horror. It's a contradiction in terms : it can't happen—but there are people up on the screen *making* it happen. This is true of writers of macabre stories, too. They make you *believe* their stories as you sit reading, and if they are very good indeed you'll look under the bed or behind the door afterwards to convince yourself there's really nothing there after all!

I am, of course, speaking from personal experience on the subject of horror pictures; and I know from meeting people around the world that audiences react in different ways to the different kinds of terror we know can be engendered. The French and Germans, for instance, like to be frightened in quite different ways, the French dwelling on the terrors of cynicism and the Germans—who gave horror to the cinema with *The Cabinet of Dr. Caligari*—on the terrors of the mind. In the Far East, where the standards of literacy are lower and the powers of superstition stronger, you find audiences enjoy a totally different kind of terror. Generally speaking, though, everyone enjoys the ghoulish pleasures of the "graveyard horror tales" which it has been my pleasure and that of my distinguished co-contributor to this volume, Vincent Price, to make.

Over the years that I have been making these films, I have met many writers of horror stories, which gives me a particular interest in a collection such as this—for we in the film business rely on tales like the ones you have just read for our raw material. I have, for instance, been an admirer of Ray Russell, the author of numerous horror film scripts, for years. And Ray Bradbury, who wrote *The Beast From 20,000 Fathoms*, has become a close personal friend of mine, along with the remarkable Robert Bloch, creator of *Psycho* and *The Skull*, which is included here. My connections with Bram

Stoker and his story *Dracula* are, of course, too well known to need more than a mention, but it was my good fortune to meet his granddaughter and great-grandson recently when I was making a record of *Dracula's Daughter*. Incidentally, this story was originaly part of *Dracula,* but Mrs. Stoker talked Bram out of putting it in because the book was already too long for the publisher.

But I am digressing somewhat. My real purpose in being here is to comment on the actors who have played ghouls and give my estimation of them. Let me say right away that I consider Lon Chaney the greatest of them all, a genius in fact, with Boris Karloff running a close second.

Lon Chaney was a most remarkable man. He was born the son of deaf mutes, and although there was a great sadness and introspection about him, he still managed to overcome all his handicaps before the cameras. He was a master of make-up, too, and was widely known as "The Man of a Thousand Faces". He underwent the most excruciating pains to deform himself for his parts, and nothing was ever too much trouble to achieve realism and conviction in his acting. I find it hardly surprising that he died in his early forties looking exhausted and a great deal older than his years.

Boris Karloff, with whom I had the pleasure of working on several occasions (including one of his last films, *Curse of the Crimson Altar*), was also a brilliant actor and greatly underrated. His *Frankenstein* is the most famous of all horror films and his performance probably the finest piece of individual acting we have ever seen on the screen. I think we shall not see his like again.

Although these two are head and shoulders above all others, the terror film genre has been served by so many great actors that I must also accord mention to several others : Basil Rathbone, Bela Lugosi, Peter Lorre, and my contemporaries, Vincent Price and Peter Cushing. Their ability has brought credit and distinction—not to mention popularity—to a branch of film-making too often unfairly derided for containing excesses of torture and violence, blood and gore.

I could say more, but actors prefer to let their acting speak for them and most readers will have their own very definite ideas and preferences where horror films are concerned. Just let me say in conclusion, then, that I believe "The Ghouls" have their own special place in the cinema—and I am more than proud to be one of their number. London, 1970.

THE GHOULS

Cast and Credits

THE DEVIL IN A CONVENT
(Georges Méliès: 1896)
From a story, *The Devil In A Nunnery,* by Francis Oscar Mann.
Director : Georges Méliès.
Starring : Georges Méliès.

THE LUNATICS
(Edison: 1912)
From a story, *The System of Doctor Tarr and Professor Fether,*
by Edgar Allan Poe.
Director : Thomas Edison.
Stars unknown. One later version.

PURITAN PASSIONS
(Film Guild-Hodkinson: 1923)
Originally based on a story, *Feathertop,* by Nathaniel Hawthorne.
Director : Frank Tuttle.
Starring : Glen Hunter, Mary Astor and Osgood Perkins.

PHANTOM OF THE OPERA
(Universal: 1925)
Based on a novella of the same name by Gaston Leroux.
Director : Rupert Julian.
Starring : Lon Chaney and Mary Philbin. Two later versions.

THE MAGICIAN
(Metro-Goldwyn-Mayer: 1926)
From a story by W. Somerset Maugham.
Director : Rex Ingram.
Starring : Paul Wegener and Alice Terry. Now lost.

FREAKS
(Metro-Goldwyn-Mayer: 1932)
From a story, *Spurs,* by Tod Robbins.
Director : Tod Browning.
Starring : Wallace Ford, Leila Hyams, Olga Baclanova and Roscoe
Ates.

MOST DANGEROUS GAME

(RKO Radio: 1932)

From a story, *The Most Dangerous Game,* by Richard Connell.

Director : Irving Pichel and Ernest B. Schoedsack.

Starring : Joel McCrea, Fay Wray and Leslie Banks. Two later versions.

DRACULA'S DAUGHTER

(Universal: 1936)

From a story, *Dracula's Guest,* by Bram Stoker.

Director : Lambert Hillyer.

Starring : Gloria Holden and Otto Kruger.

ALL THAT MONEY CAN BUY

(RKO Radio: 1941)

From a story, *The Devil and Daniel Webster,* by Stephen Vincent Benét.

Director : William Dieterle.

Starring : Edward Arnold, Walter Huston and Simone Simon.

THE BODY SNATCHER

(RKO Radio: 1945)

From a story of the same name by Robert Louis Stevenson.

Director : Val Lewton.

Starring : Boris Karloff, Bela Lugosi and Henry Daniell.

THE BEAST WITH FIVE FINGERS

(Warner Brothers: 1947)

From a story of the same name by William Fryer Harvey.

Director : Robert Florey.

Starring : Robert Alda, Peter Lorre, J. Carroll Naish and Barbara Brown.

BEAST FROM 20,000 FATHOMS

(Warner Brothers: 1953)

From a story, *The Foghorn,* by Ray Bradbury.

Director : Eugene Lourie.

Starring : Paul Christian and Paula Raymond.

THE FLY

(20th Century-Fox: 1958)
From a story by George Langelaan.
Director : Kurt Neumann.
Starring : Vincent Price, Al Hedison, Patricia Owens and Herbert Marshall. Two "sequels".

BLACK SUNDAY

(Galatea-Jolly Films: 1960)
From a story, *The Viy,* by Nikolai Gogol.
Director : Mario Bava.
Starring : Barbara Steele, John Richardson and Ivo Garrani. (Also known as *Revenge of the Vampire.*)

INCIDENT AT OWL CREEK

(Robert Enrico: 1961)
From a story, *An Occurrence at Owl Creek Bridge,* by Ambrose Bierce.
Director : Robert Enrico.

MONSTER OF TERROR

(American-International: 1965)
From a story, *The Colour Out Of Space,* by H. P. Lovecraft.
Director : Daniel Haller.
Starring : Boris Karloff, Nick Adams and Freda Jackson. (Also known as *Die, Monster, Die.*)

THE SKULL

(Paramount: 1966)
From a story, *The Skull of the Marquis de Sade,* by Robert Bloch.
Director : Freddie Francis.
Starring : Peter Cushing, Christopher Lee and Patrick Wymark.

THE OBLONG BOX

(American-International: 1970)
From a story of the same name by Edgar Allan Poe.
Director : Gordon Hesler.
Starring : Vincent Price, Christopher Lee and Hilary Dwyer.